# AWAKEN

A BRIGHTEST KIND OF DARKNESS NOVEL

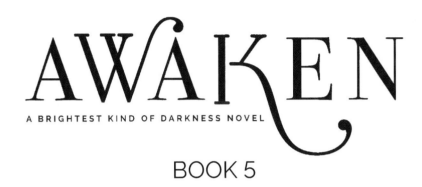

# AWAKEN

A BRIGHTEST KIND OF DARKNESS NOVEL

## BOOK 5

*NEW YORK TIMES* AND *USA TODAY* BESTSELLING AUTHOR

# P.T. MICHELLE

To stay informed when the next **P.T. Michelle** book will be released, join P.T. Michelle's free newsletter http://bit.ly/11tqAQN

Interior design and formatting by E.M. Tippetts Book Designs
www.emtippettsbookdesigns.com

*The epic conclusion to the*
*BRIGHTEST KIND OF DARKNESS series...*

With her family life in emotional turmoil, Nara turns her focus to the one thing she knows is most important for everyone: convincing the raven spirit inside Ethan that he *is* the Master Corvus. Of course, Ethan trying to protect her by keeping his distance makes that goal near impossible to accomplish.

But once the archangel, Michael, warns her that Lucifer is almost upon them and she›s running out of time for the Master Corvus to accept who he is, Nara receives help bringing Ethan back to her from the most unlikely source.

Searching for answers leads Ethan and Nara to London, where allies and enemies converge. There, the couple must fight pure evil in the biggest battle of their lives and ultimately discover who they really are and what they stand for when faced with the hardest decision of all.

*Save the world or the one you love...*

**NOTE: AWAKEN is the last book in the BRIGHTEST KIND OF DARKNESS series. It is not a standalone novel. You must read the previous books in the following order before reading AWAKEN: BRIGHTEST KIND OF DARKNESS, LUCID, DESTINY and DESIRE. There is also a novella prequel, ETHAN, that can be read at any point, but is best read before LUCID.**

# Glossary of Terms

**Celestial realm** – Heaven

**Mortal realm** – Earth

**Under realm** - Hell

**Veil** - a safety zone around the Mortal realm where angels constantly fight demons to keep them from breaking through the veil and entering the Mortal realm

**Inferi** - a demon who followed Lucifer when he was cast from the Celestial realm, ie a Lucifer demon

**Inferni** - plural of Inferi

**Furia** - a lower demon created if a Corvus kills a human who is fully possessed (corrupted) by an Inferi.

**Furiae** - plural of Furia

**Corvus** - a human who has been chosen to host a piece of the Master Corvus ' spirit. The Corvus' sole purpose is to maintain balance between good and evil in the Mortal realm by fighting demons who possess humans. The Corvus expels the demon from the human, sending it back to Under (if it's a Inferi demon) or killing it for good (if it's a Furia demon).

**Master Corvus** - a powerful spirit who creates all Corvus.

**Order** - A secret organization that oversees finding newly formed Corvus and assigning a Paladin to help the human adjust to the physical and mental changes he/she will experience as a Corvus.

**Paladin** - a human, with his/her own special ability, who has dedicated his/her life to the Order to help the Corvus. A Paladin gives the Corvus moral support by offering a human connection who understands the Corvus' purpose. The Paladin's goal is to help the Corvus stay grounded to the human world so that the Corvus won't go dark from the demonic evil he/she has to fight on a constant basis.

**Archangel** – The highest-ranking angel

# Chapter One

*Nara*

"I wish you were here. I could use your guidance right now." Brisk wind whips against me as I bend down and slowly brush the wet, dead leaves from the gravestone. The melted snow has left them damp and musky. The need to claw away at the underbrush is strong, but I force myself to move slowly. Once the leaves are cleared, I exhale a sob and touch the etched letters on the stone.

Ravens make constant *gronk, gronk* sounds in the trees all around me. And somewhere among them, I hear Patch. I don't have to see the raven staring at me with that white circle of feathers around his eye to know he's there. He's been my constant companion this past week, following no matter where I go. While I'm driving, he flies overhead, and once I'm home, he hammers his beak incessantly on my window until I let him in. Patch's guttural sounds are deeper and more intense than the other ravens and they seem to be responding to his mood.

"Ethan hasn't called or texted—" My voice cracks when I say my boyfriend's name as I stare at the gravestone. "Dad told me he asked Ethan to give me the space I need right now, but how can Ethan not know that with my family in crisis mode what I need more than anything is *him*? I miss him so much. I'm just glad school starts back tomorrow. At least then I'll see him and make him tell me why he's being so distant." I stop speaking and absorb the ache in my heart with a deep breath before I let out a grunt of frustrated annoyance. "Michael refuses to answer my plea for advice. You would think the fate of the Mortal world hanging in the balance with Lucifer's imminent return and my boyfriend going AWOL would at least warrant a response from the archangel." Glancing down at the recently disturbed dirt, I take a deep breath. "I'm so sorry that I failed to protect—"

My phone rings, cutting me off. Blinking back the moisture in my eyes, I retrieve it from my winter coat. "Hey, Dad."

"Your mom and I are pulling up to Jefferson now. Apparently Corda has been giving the staff a fit during her last therapy session this morning."

I sniff back my tears, the heaviness in my heart lifting. Only Gran could get her point across without uttering a word. "We knew she was ready to leave. I hoped I could go with you and Mom today, but Westminster called and asked me to stop by. The whole retirement community pitched in for a going away basket for Gran. I'll head over there now and pick it up. If Gran's checkout paperwork takes a while, maybe I can still make it in time. "

"We've got it covered, Nari. Corda's a tough woman. She'll be all right. I think being with family full time will make all the difference in her progress back to the quick-with-a-quip, cantankerous woman we know and love."

"I hope so. See you soon." Hanging up, I exhale a sigh of relief that Gran's hospital antics means that she's on the mend, but when I realize the birds' sounds have grown louder, their croaks resonating full alert, my breath catches and I quickly glance around. *Is Ethan here? Do the ravens sense him?*

Excitement fills my chest as I scan the cemetery, then my anticipation quickly plummets. No one is here. Only the creak of tree limbs moving in the biting wind joins the birds' raucous din. The cacophony elevates as dozens of birds glide down from the trees, landing with soft thumps on the hard ground near me. Unfurling their wings, they hop into place and form a circle around the gravesite, their neck feathers fluffed in defensive postures. At the same moment a shiver of concern crawls along my back, Patch lets out a loud squawk and lands on my right shoulder, curling one of his wings over my head. I freeze because he's never acted so protective. Not like this. Black beak swiveling back and forth, he clacks it loudly as his black eyes dart between several mausoleums with focused intent.

*Is a demon around?* I twist the ring on my finger, swiping my thumb over the protective symbols until I reach the yin-yang ravens engraved along the silver. The Corvus symbol will protect me from demon possession, but it can't prevent an attack, so I anxiously scan the area, wishing dogs were allowed in the cemetery. Houdini would alert me well before a demon got close enough to surprise me. I grab my backpack, preparing to stand when a gentle softness brushes across the left side of my face.

Patch ceases his aggressive clacking and folds his unfurled wing to his side. As the birds stop making alarm noises, I shift my gaze back to Freddie's tombstone. "You're here with me now, aren't you?" The sudden silence in Oak Lawn Cemetery is so peaceful my tense muscles loosen. After a couple minutes, I glance up at the raven next to me. "All clear?"

In answer, Patch soars back up to the trees and the other ravens quickly follow his lead.

Rolling my shoulders, I pull a trowel from my backpack and push the disturbed dirt back into the hole the demon had left behind when he dug Freddie's book up. "I'm sorry I did such a terrible job protecting your book," I finish my thought from earlier as I pat the dirt down, then scatter fresh underbrush over the disturbed area. "A demon possessed Gran to force me to tell him where I hid it. When I resisted, he broke her wrist and threatened far worse. I tried to get Ethan to move the book to another location, but he came straight to Gran's to protect us instead.

"The book might still hold undiscovered Corvus' secrets, but you can rest easy knowing the demon who took it won't ever see the scroll that was hidden in its spine." I touch the triskele charm dangling around my neck. "My grandmother's necklace released the scroll from the book's spine, so you were right, Freddie. I *was* meant to have the book. Just like I'm apparently meant to help the Master Corvus remember who he is. Well, at least according to—" I pause and look up at the sky, grumbling, "Michael-the-Absent-Angel."

My gaze returns to Freddie's tombstone, and I grimace at the memory of the small scroll turning to dust the moment I unrolled it. "The demons are convinced the book contains the key to destroying the Master Corvus. They'll do whatever it takes to keep the Master Corvus from sending Lucifer back to Under."

I rub my forehead to try to ward off the headache of guilt and worry. "I just wish I could remember what I briefly glimpsed on that scroll. For all I know, there was something on it or in the *Ravens* book itself that could help the Master Corvus residing inside Ethan to regain his lost memory. What will happen if Lucifer confronts Ethan before his Corvus can remember *he's* the Master Corvus? With a volatile spirit's uncontrolled power surging through him, Ethan needs my help to stay grounded, but how am I supposed to do that when he's not talking to me?"

I slam the side of the trowel against the hard ground, knocking the dirt off the tool before I return it to my backpack. "Sorry to lay all this on you, but now that Gran's starting to recover, all the worries I'd shoved to the back of my mind feel like they're crushing me. My family has no clue about any of this Corvus stuff, so talking things out with you and a temperamental raven are my only alternatives."

That technically isn't true…there is one other person who knows Corvus exist, but I've avoided calling Drystan, since he just went with his uncle to live in the sanctuary in London. He hasn't technically joined the Order lead by his uncle—a group of people with special abilities known as Paladins that support the humans who've been infused with a demon-fighting Corvus spirit—but I know Drystan will worry. He needs to get on with his new life and not get pulled into my troubles here in Virginia. Once I'm feeling more in control of my emotions, I'll contact him.

The quiet stillness in the cemetery no longer feels comforting. It's heavy with loneliness even with Freddie's calming presence. I won't feel better until I can talk to Ethan. As if they understand my angst, the birds begin to caw loudly. They take flight just as the ground starts to rumble underneath my knees. Gasping, I drop the trowel and flatten my hands on the damp earth, steadying myself. The rumbling suddenly stops and all I can hear is my own pulse racing in my ears. *Was that an aftershock from the small earthquake that rocked Richmond yesterday?*

I'd felt the earthquake while sitting beside Gran in her hospital room last night. Was a small earthquake enough to create yet another tear in the veil, allowing even more demons to sneak into our world from Under? I sent Ethan a text asking if he'd felt it. I'd been so wrapped up in worrying about Gran, it was only the second time I'd reached out to him since the night she was attacked. The first text was to ask if he'd moved the book. He never answered it, but then rounds of hospital visits took over my life, overshadowing Christmas and the New Year.

When he didn't respond last night though, his prolonged silence worried me. Had he been able to convince his Corvus that he's the Master? Are Ethan and the spirit inside him getting along without me around to keep the human part of Ethan grounded? This latest rumbling in the cemetery knots my stomach with a sudden new worry...*God, instead of getting along...what if the Corvus has completely taken over Ethan?* The Master Corvus was definitely growing stronger. Is that why Ethan has gone radio silent?

My heartbeat stutters as the story Drystan's uncle, Mr. Wicklow, told me about the Master Corvus destroying the sanctuary thirty years ago comes back to me. If the spirit was powerful enough to take down an entire building with focused intent back then, could an amnesiac Master Corvus', unaware of the extent of his power, cause natural-disaster-level damage while on a demon hunting rampage? Like say...an earthquake?

I unzip my backpack and grab my phone, sending Ethan a text.

*Gran is coming home with us from the hospital today. I'm fine. I don't need space. We need to talk.*

When he doesn't respond, I quickly send another message.

*What happened to TTTWFO?*

Three dots instantly pop up on my screen, letting me know he's typing something. My heart jerks as I wait for him to finally break his silence. Then the dots disappear.

When I don't receive a text back, my heart sinks while another part of me gets angry. I send one last text.

*School starts back tomorrow. We* will *talk.*

Tucking my phone into my backpack, I slide it onto my shoulder and stand.

Tomorrow can't get here soon enough.

I rush outside as my dad parks his car along the curb. With an encouraging smile, I wave to Gran who's sitting in the front seat. A slight smirk tilts her lips, but her green eyes are what really get to me. They're alight with excitement as she stares at the house. It's the first time I've seen anything close to genuine happiness since she woke up with a cast on her arm in the hospital, grunted repeatedly, then began to wail her frustration.

That's when we first learned the stroke hadn't just weakened Gran, but it also took away her ability to speak. She's been going to therapists all week to get control of her limbs, build strength back into her legs, and to retrain her brain to convert her thoughts into spoken words. It would be a lot for someone half her age. Until today, Gran had taken most of it in stride, but when I tug her door open and she pulls her ear buds out, bright eyes dancing to the pop music, I know that bringing her to live with us was the right call. She's happy to be here.

While Dad retrieves Gran's wheelchair out of the trunk and mom collects Gran's stuff from the back of the car, I smile and hold my hand out for my grand aunt. In a week she'll refuse to use the wheelchair, which will mean she'll be that much closer to her old self again. I'm just so relieved she doesn't remember what happened during her demon possession. I carry enough guilt for both of us that I couldn't get to her apartment sooner to save her friend from the demon that possessed Gran. I know Gran would never forgive herself if she knew the demon had used her body to smother her best friend, Clara. Thankfully the police who came with the paramedics didn't look too deeply. Instead they determined that Clara died of natural causes while taking a nap on Gran's couch. Considering Clara was close to eighty and the paramedics were frantically working to restart Gran's heart, no one questioned it.

Just as I help my mom settle Gran in the wheelchair, a deep voice says from behind me, "I'm glad she's going to be okay, Nara."

My heart leaps. Turning, I drink in the sight of Ethan standing there in a black leather jacket, a heather gray RUSH T-shirt, and jeans. The tiredness in his deep blue eyes worries me only until the pair of candy apple red headphones draped around his neck steals my attention. A bright shade like that isn't Ethan. When my questioning gaze snaps to his, the yearning I catch in his stare before he shutters it away melts me down to my toes, obliterating all thoughts of teasing him. I'm relieved to see his eyes are their normal gorgeous shade of deep blue, without a bit of Corvus black in them. My heart feels both light and heavy at once; I miss him…

*us...so much. Why has he been so quiet?* Before I can say anything, my father's brisk comment cuts the tension arcing between us.

"What are you doing here, Ethan?"

"Dad!"

"Don't be rude, Jonathan," Mom cuts in as she lays Gran's speech therapy tablet on her lap, then grips the wheelchair's handles.

Stepping to the side of Gran's wheelchair, my father answers my mom while directing a stony gaze on Ethan. "This is important family time."

Just as I open my mouth to speak, Gran's arm starts flailing, her cast catching my father right in the crotch. As he bends over with a loud groan of pain, Mom shoots him a worried glance and deftly captures Gran's arm just as Gran calls out, "Respect!" then begins to spell out each letter to the tune of Aretha Franklin's famous song.

Tucking Gran's arm gently between her leg and the wheelchair arm, Mom continues, "I guess the weight of the cast isn't helping to control her limb spasms like we thought it would. Let's get you inside, Corda. It's freezing out here." My mom completely misses Gran's satisfied smirk as she turns to address me, "We'll see you inside in a few minutes, Inara. That should give your father time to regain his sense of humor along with his ability to breathe. Take a few breaths, Jonathan. I need you to help me get the wheelchair up the steps."

"I can assist you with the wheelchair," Ethan offers, but Mom just waves him off.

"We've got it covered."

Before she can push the wheelchair forward, Ethan says, "One second, Mrs. Collins." Stepping in front of Gran, he lifts the pair of headphones from around his neck and crouches down to drape them around Gran's. "I heard a rumor that you don't like in-ear headphones much. I found the most comfortable pair I could."

As far as I know, Ethan hasn't been by the hospital or was even aware of the details of Gran's condition, yet here he is giving her a gift that'll help with the music therapy she just started. A few days ago, when Gran repeated a lyric she'd heard from my phone's ring tone, her words sharp and coherent, we discovered that her brain allowed her to sing song lyrics, even though she still wasn't able to form coherent speech.

Of course, with Gran's knack for creative metaphors, we'd

heard her say all kinds of crazy things once she started listening to songs to help her communicate. Deciphering what she's trying to get across is like a game of *Charades* and *Name That Tune* rolled into one, but every once in a while, like just now with my father, her meaning is crystal clear.

While I stare, surprised by Ethan's knowledge about Gran's condition, my grand aunt lifts her free hand from her lap. She pats him on the jaw, and her eyes glisten with tears as she sings, "Leader of the Pack". My heart jerks. What does she mean by that? She can't possibly know about Ethan's "Master Corvus" status.

Clearing his throat, Ethan stands and smiles at Gran. "I understand getting lost in the music. Keep those with you so you'll never be without a word."

Ethan and I silently watch Mom and Dad wheel Gran into the house. Once they close the door, he says, "I'm glad your Gran's coming to live with you."

"How did you know about her condition?" I ask, trying not to let it bother me that he kept up with Gran's medical progress, yet he didn't reply to any of my texts.

He turns to face me. "Samson is dating a nurse at the hospital. Emily let me know how your Gran was doing."

"I didn't know your brother had met someone—" I pause when the brisk wind whips his dark hair and a two-inch long wound appears along his hairline. My heart constricting, I lift my hand to his brow. "What happened?"

When the tips of my fingers brush against his skin, Ethan closes his eyes for a second, then takes a step back and jams his hands in his jean pockets. "I'm fine, Nara."

I curl my fingers against my palm and lower my hand to my side, my tone flat. "The book is gone."

"I know." Ethan glances away and shrugs. "Now there's no reason for that demon to come after you. You're safe."

"Did you let the demon steal the book on purpose?" When he doesn't respond, I throw my hands out in frustration. "That book might tell them how to defeat the Master Corvus!"

"One demon," he scoffs, unruffled.

"Ethan—

He shakes his head and stares at my house. "I don't believe the demon has told any others about the book or me yet. Otherwise I would've been overrun by demons this past week."

"They could be coming after you armed with the knowledge how to defeat the Master Corvus at any point!"

"Let them try." He jerks dark eyes my way, his voice deadly.

Sheer arrogance stares back at me. Corvus arrogance. It's hard not to gasp at the sudden change in his eye color. The blue is so dark, I can't see his pupils, but I don't let my worry show and instead focus on the issue I wanted to talk to him about. "Were you in Richmond last night?"

"Richmond?" His brow furrows. "Why?"

"The earthquake."

"You think I had something to do with that?" His dark eyebrows hike and he snorts out a laugh. "My Corvus might be the Master, but he's not *that* powerful."

"Do you know that for sure, Ethan? Does he? You haven't shared anything with me. You disappeared from my life for a week."

"Which is where I'll stay," he says, his tone curt, final.

"How can you say that?" My heart sinks and I do my best to ignore the nausea churning in my belly. "What about us?"

A brief flicker of pain reflects in his eyes, but he shutters it away. "There can't be any more 'us,' Nara. I have a duty to fulfill, and no matter how much I want to strangle the egotistical spirit living inside me, I will honor my duty to protect our world. The stubborn bird might still be denying that he's the Master Corvus, but this isn't your burden or fight any more. You did your part; you convinced me that the spirit is the Master Corvus. It's *my* job to show him the truth. At least now that the demon got what he wanted, you're safe. And that's how you'll stay. I won't let you put yourself in danger anymore."

"Do you love me, Ethan? Do you still want us?" My heart feels like it's jammed in my throat as I wait for his response.

He sets his jaw. "This isn't about what I want."

When he turns and walks away, fury whips inside me. I can't believe he's willing to set us aside after everything we've been through. He freaking knows we're better together; *he's* better with me. All the worry I've felt this last week for Gran's recovery and guilt about the death of her friend, layered on top of my angst over the status of our relationship bubbles to the surface. "You're not the only one; I have a duty to fulfill too."

He stops mid-stride and glances over his shoulder. "Your part is over. Stay far away from anything Corvus related, Nara. *All* of it."

Ethan might be hiding behind this "he's protecting me BS," but his tone is unemotional and there's a dogged coldness in his eyes I've never seen. It feels as if I'm speaking to his Corvus, whose sole focus is on sending demons back to Under, whether they're Lucifer's Inferni demons or the damned Furiae. The last thing the spirit inside Ethan cares about is catering to a human girl's relationship with her boyfriend.

I might be projecting a calm expression, but I'm shaking with worry on the inside. *Has* the Corvus fully taken over Ethan? Ethan's eyes are blue, not the black I've seen the few times Rave—the name I gave his Corvus—has fluffed his battle feathers whenever a demon has been near. Despite the physical proof that Ethan is still in control, something definitely feels off. I lift my chin, refusing to back down no matter whom I'm speaking to right now. "I make my own decisions, not you, not Rave, not Fate, not Michael, or my father. *None* of you get a vote."

I start up my driveway and Ethan calls after me, "Then do it for your Gran, Nara."

*He went straight for the jugular.* My shoulders instantly hunch with remorse, but I force them to straighten and keep walking as I shove away the painful thought that I might have already lost the boy who stole my heart.

Ethan's sudden curse makes me pause. I glance back to see Patch swooping up from dive-bombing him before he flies over our rooftop. I know the raven's heading straight for my windowsill to impatiently wait for me.

As Ethan glares after the one animal he's never been able to mentally connect with, I smirk and open our front door. Patch is my constant; the keeper of my worries. The raven assures that Ethan and I stay connected even when it feels like we're far apart. In his own ornery way, he bonds us.

I can't imagine my life without Ethan in it. Actually, I refuse to, but for now I'll focus on helping his Corvus. I won't be pushed away, no matter who's talking to me.

As soon as I walk inside, my father looks up from putting away groceries Mom had bought to get ready for Gran's arrival. It's weird to see him in the kitchen as if he belongs here. Nothing has changed between them. Mom hasn't invited him to live with us, so he's staying with his sister, Aunt Sage. But while Gran was in recovery mode, our family issues took a back seat. I still haven't shown Mom the video Dad made for me years ago explaining that he left to protect us from Fate's vengeful wrath over my father using his ability to see his next day to help the government prevent disasters. For now, we seem to be existing on autopilot, our focus on helping get Gran settled.

Holding a box of crackers, my dad cuts his gaze to the stairway where Mom and Gran are upstairs, then says in a low tone, "After everything your Gran has been through this past week and the worry and stress this has put on your mother, it's best if you stay away from Ethan and the danger that surrounds him. If I hadn't heard that strange call you received from Corda and then called the police, the ambulance might not have gotten to her in time." He ignores that I press my lips together and continues on, "I won't apologize for cloning your phone. I trusted my instincts about Ethan. Whatever these Inferi are you referred to in that phone call to him, I know they had something to do with what happened to your Gran. At this point, I don't want to know the details. I just want *you* away from it."

That's the most my father has said about Ethan since that awful night at Gran's. I'm thankful that his fast response saved Gran, but I don't want my every move monitored. Mom would be pissed if she found out he did that, but then I don't want her learning why he felt the need. She might agree with him. "You don't have to worry. Ethan just dumped me, so you can stop tracking me."

When his harsh expression quickly shifts to a sympathetic one, I raise my hand, relieved to hear Mom helping Gran back down the stairs. "I don't want to talk about it. Let's just get Gran moved in."

After Mom settles Gran into her wheelchair in the living room, Dad clears his throat to get our attention. "I have an announcement to make."

When we all look his way, his green eyes shine with excitement. "I've just taken a job teaching Intro to Business Economics at Blue Ridge High. I start tomorrow when the break is over. Isn't that fantastic, Nari?"

I should be glad that my father recently let Fate take away his ability to see his next day in order to protect our family. That way he no longer feels obligated to stay in that secret government job, but instead my stomach feels like Mom's face looks, a bit green. I know what she's thinking; that up until my father walked back into our lives over a week ago, she'd been dating my Spanish teacher, Mr. Dixon, and the last thing she wants is the two men working together. Granted, Mom doesn't know that while under the influence of a demon, Mr. Dixon attacked me in our home right before Christmas. The poor man doesn't remember any of it, but he was definitely freaked out when he blinked back to consciousness. So yeah, even though I know why he's been dodging Mom's calls, I'm feeling a bit ill for Mom and for myself.

The thought of my father at school every day watching my every move, on top of the fact he hates my boyfriend who happens to go to the same school, doesn't make me feel all warm and fuzzy about his new job.

Gran's guffaw draws Mom and me out of our stunned silence.

Apparently the stroke didn't hinder her ability to express delighted amusement at the awkward moment. When she starts belting out a lyric to Katy Perry's "Firework" song, I mutter, "Congrats on the new job, Dad."

# Chapter Two

### *Ethan*

"Don't walk away from her!" the Corvus booms so loudly in my head that my brain feels like it's liquefying.

I grit my teeth and put one foot in front of the other. It takes all my strength to keep moving forward, but the more he fights me and tries to force my body to his will, the harder I work to continue moving away from Nara. I feel his fury, his outrage over my defiance, but Nara truly is safer with both of us out of her life. I might not be keeping my distance from Nara for the reason her father believes, but the spirit currently raging inside me brought the point home harder than her father ever could. I experienced his euphoria as I stood next to her as well as his volcanic fury when I walked away.

He covets time with Nara and resents the fact that I'm preventing him from seeing her. But keeping demons from her door isn't my only worry. The Master Corvus' power has grown and I'm terrified that this spirit inside me, with his whiplash anger and swift reflexes, could inadvertently hurt Nara. He still hasn't acknowledged the extent of his own strength or that it's beyond any other Corvus.

All this past week, I felt him growing angrier while he battled with demons. I didn't realize how much my thoughts of Nara or the anticipation of seeing her calms him. Without Nara around, he'd been snarky and quick tempered, his sarcastic monologue in my head demanding that I take a nap and give him unfettered access to my body for as long as he wants. *I could obliterate dozens more demons if you'd just let go. Let me give them my own special brand of punishment.*

*You want this body for even a little bit, then you'll follow my rules,* I mentally grate as I head away from Nara's house. My whole body aches, every muscle twitching from fighting the Corvus so hard until Nara disappeared inside.

As I walk down the sidewalk, a car drives up beside me, and a dark-haired man in a black business suit says, "Are you Ethan Harris?"

He rolls to a stop and I pause, while mentally gauging how far it is to the end of the road that'll lead to the woods connecting our neighborhoods. "You've got the wrong guy."

His dark brown eyes hold mine, then he glances down at a piece of paper in his hand. "I was told I might find you here."

*Step up to the car and set your hands on his door; demand to know why he's following you. If he doesn't comply, pull the door off.* The command in the spirit's voice makes me want to punch something.

The fact that my Corvus—Rave as Nara calls him—wants me to face this guy head on and scare the crap out of him so he'll state his business, rankles. The dude isn't a demon and the spirit knows that. But I'm instantly on guard that he followed me here. "I don't know what you're talking about," I grumble, then take off toward the woods.

# Chapter Three

### *Nara*

No one gets to stick his tongue down my throat and then pretend that I don't exist. That's not how I roll. I glance away from staring at the redhead standing super close to Ethan near the locker hallway entrance. She's gesturing to a workbook in her hand, a wide smile on her face. Annoyed, I close my locker door hard enough to draw people's attention. Well, except Ethan's. So far he has completely ignored me all day. With Ethan keeping to himself, I avoided any disapproving scowls from my father who'd passed me three times in the hall so far today. But I'd rather deal with that, than Ethan's utter silence. I've had enough. I start to walk over and blast him when a slurred voice echoes in my head. *"S'jus a brilliant plaze to chill. Forget aboot wat I've done, forget evrathin.'"*

*Drystan?* I know my friend can't hear my mental response, even though I hear his Welsh accent as clearly as if he's standing in front of me. In my mind's eye, I picture his green gaze holding mine, a slight smirk on his lips while he runs a hand through his light brown spiked hair. Our across-the-world connection is sharp, almost strident. Maybe it's because he sounds drunk…or high.

I've seen Drystan enjoy a drink or two while out with friends, but I've never heard him like this. My chest instantly tightens with concern and I pull out my phone to dial his London number. I don't care that it's an international call. I need to know that he's okay.

My call goes straight to voicemail, so I hang up and send him a note asking him to video chat with me later, then walk over to my best friend unlocking her locker. At least Lainey's locker is closer to the hallway entrance. Maybe I'll catch what Ethan and that girl are chatting about.

"Hey, Lainey, has Matt talked to Drystan since he left for London?"

My best friend heaves a sigh and brushes her long auburn hair over her shoulder, then leans down to shove books into her backpack. "I wish! Maybe then Matt would chill out. He's been so on edge lately, Nara." She briefly glances up from straightening a folder inside her backpack. "When the snow rave I hosted didn't do the trick, I thought finally getting that tattoo he wanted would settle him. Nope. Instead my boyfriend's reaching Ethan-level intensity. I told him to call Drystan. He really misses him." She dives back into her locker, rambling, "He's left voicemails for Drystan, but the guy seems to have dropped us completely after he left for London. He hasn't returned a single message. How's that for gratitude to Matt's family for hosting him as an exchange student?"

I'm half-listening to Lainey as I try to filter out noisy students mingling in the hall and I focus on the redhead girl. Suddenly her excited, high-pitched voice comes through as she playfully touches Ethan's arm. "I heard you sometimes play for the band Weylaid over at McCormicks. Maybe I'll come listen to you. When do you play next?"

Ethan shrugs and her hand falls away. "I'm not sure. My schedule's pretty busy lately." Pointing to the notebook in her hand, he continues, "Mr. Helms said we need to get that back to him on Wednesday, so when will you be done with your part?"

I strain to hear past the general buzz of students at their lockers. The girl flashes a wide smile. "I'll be happy to drop it off at your house later on tonight. We can go over my part so you can make sure yours flows well. Where do you live?"

She's interested in homework, my ass! I curl my hand tight around my backpack strap. Setting my jaw, I turn to face Lainey so Ethan doesn't see me listening to them.

"—think you can ask Drystan to call him?" Lainey's voice briefly overrides their conversation.

"As soon as *I* get in touch with him," I say in a dry tone.

Lainey sighs. "You too?"

"Just be sure to drop it off before nine," Ethan says. "I have a thing I don't want to miss."

If it's not a gig, what *thing* does he have? I wonder even as I answer Lainey. "Don't worry. I'll find a way to get through and when I do, I'll remind him to connect with Matt."

"Uh oh, right behind you...Devon is getting all close quarters with your man," Lainey warns, her auburn eyebrows pulling down into a deep frown as she stares at Ethan and the girl over my shoulder. When I don't react, her attention slides back to me. "Why are you still standing here? Go stake your claim."

Lainey has no clue about any of the Corvus stuff, so I just say, "Ethan and I are...on a break. I'm just too busy helping out with Gran to focus on a relationship right now."

Her brown eyes widen and she blinks a couple of times. "While I'm glad your Gran came home from the hospital, I can't believe Ethan bought that load of crap? What's really going on, Nara?" she continues, her tone turning serious.

"We've both just got a lot going on." When she purses her lips, I sigh. "That's the truth." Well, as close as I can get to telling her anyway.

Lainey folds her arms and scowls. "So you're going to take a chance on losing him to someone else while on this fictitious break? What is *wrong* with you two?"

She said that last sentence loud enough for Ethan to hear while staring right at him to make her point. I grit my teeth and grab her arm, pulling her down the hall.

"Please just let it go, Lainey." My insides are wound so tight I feel like I might throw up. "I really don't want to talk about it."

"Did he dump you, Nara?" she asks in a shocked hush. Glaring in Ethan's direction, she continues in a low, lethal tone, "I'm going to rip his balls off."

"Whoa, take it down a few," I say, a bit shocked by her vehemence. "What's going on with you?"

Cutting her focus back to me, she narrows her gaze, then exhales, the fight in her tone melting away. "If you and Ethan can't work through whatever is going on, then Matt and I don't have a prayer."

I grasp onto the desperation in her comment. "Are you two having problems?"

"I feel like I don't know who he is lately, you know?" Lainey shrugs and fiddles with the zipper on her purse. "Matt should be focused on basketball and making good grades so he can get into the college he wants. Instead he's obsessing about the future beyond college and talking about how he feels like he has a bigger purpose. Ever since he told me about his raven dreams, this is the kind of stuff he talks about. He's really freaking me out. You know I don't get into this New Agey, enlightened stuff. I'm black and white and practical to the core."

*Hence the reason I've never told you about my abilities, Ethan's, or even Drystan's. I knew you couldn't handle it.* Poor Lainey, she's surrounded by people who live in the gray. I clasp her hand and turn my shoulder as a pack of students crowd into the locker hall. "When was the last time you went for a good long run?"

"Hey Nara," Kenny says while passing by.

I smile as he spins the combination to open his locker, remembering the last time I spoke to him. He was on crutches and our teacher asked me to carry his textbooks at the end of the day. "How's the ankle?"

"It's a little stiff, especially when it rains." He lifts his foot and turns it left and right, his auburn eyebrows shooting up. "It'll be fine by time soccer starts back up."

"The last time I went running was around Christmas, why?" Lainey asks drawing my attention back to her.

"Because you're coming with me after dinner. Coach will make us do laps if we don't stay in shape. Not to mention, it'll be a great way to blow off some steam." Hooking my arm with hers, I turn her away from the locker hall and call over my shoulder to Kenny, "Spring season is just around the corner, so keep working that ankle."

Tugging Lainey along, I walk right past Ethan. I can't help the small smirk of satisfaction tilting my lips when his gaze shifts in Kenny's direction and instantly darkens.

# Chapter Four

### *Nara*

"Thanks for suggesting a run." Lainey had stopped running completely and put her hands on her knees, panting hard. "It really has helped to settle my thoughts."

I glance at the tendrils of hair falling from her ponytail and sticking to her damp face and smile in the darkness. "Technically I suggested we slow down."

Lainey squints up at me from her bent position and snorts. "Like you didn't need a break."

When I don't react right away, she follows my line of sight as I stare at Devon talking to Ethan in the pool of light on his front porch. "So we just happened to need to stop at this exact location. On a break, huh?"

"I never suggested that we stop." I purse my lips and furrow my brow at her eye roll. "It's hard to explain, Lainey. Ethan and I aren't done, but we both really do have stuff going on that's making it hard, you know?"

"Why do I get the feeling this is more Ethan than you?" Lainey asks, her eyes thinning in Ethan's direction.

Of course she goes there. "He's just being…" I sigh, unable to get the word "protective" out. It would just make my friend ask even more questions that I can't answer. "Intense."

Lainey straightens and touches my ponytail. "Is he going to shut you out every time he's got something going on? What an *ass*! At least Matt isn't pushing me away. If anything, I'm the one running. Ha, literally." When I don't laugh at her joke, because I'm too busy watching Devon get in her car and drive off, Lainey nudges my shoulder. "Ethan sees us. I think he's coming over here. Don't let him off easy."

Ethan had already walked off his porch and my heart jerks with each step he takes. But then he quickly reaches for his car door and climbs into his Mustang. As the vehicle rumbles to life, Lainey grimaces. "Oh, guess I was wrong."

"He...he's got that thing tonight," I say, like I totally know where he's going, even though I don't have a clue.

Lainey nods. "Try to get him talking tomorrow. He can't resist you, Nara. Make him grovel a bit. It's weird-ing me out seeing you two not speaking at all."

He *can* resist me quite well apparently. I force a confident smile I don't feel. "Don't worry. I'll talk to him."

"What are you doing, Gran?" I ask as soon as I walk in from my run.

Gran is in the process of sliding the orchid planter back onto the table from her lap.

"Puppies grumble bee."

When I squeeze my right eye and give her a "that's not quite right" look, she sighs and reaches for the therapy tablet in the pouch hanging from her wheelchair. Slowly typing a note with her one good hand, she glances up at me as a robotic voice says: "Putting ice cubes in the plant Clara gave me. It takes three cubes a week."

I glance over at the plant, but don't have the heart to tell her that it's plastic. Instead I place a saucer underneath it to catch the water and smile when she slowly types another sentence. "Clara said, 'No more gummy worms in your plants, Corda. This one you can't kill.'" Her green eyes mist and she hits another button on her tablet to say the sentence she'd typed out. "She laughed every time I put ice in it like it was the biggest joke in the world."

My heart cinches a little bit when Gran moves a piece of ice closer to the plant's stem.

Just as the thought runs through my mind that Clara was a bit of a stinker for giving her "friend" a plant and laughing her butt off that Gran kept watering it, Gran gives me a toothy smile. "Plastic."

We both laugh that Gran had pulled one over on Clara, but then it hits us at the same time…she'd said the *right* word. Our laughter turns to giggles of delight as I rush over and hug her.

When I pull back, tears of happiness in my eyes, Gran taps the headphones around her neck. "Ethan."

"Music," I gently correct her. I worked with her at the hospital and some earlier today before I went running. I sing songs and she pipes here and there, then I hold up flash cards that I also tie to music to help her pick out the right words associated with the pictures on the cards. Music has really started to unlock the puzzle for her brain. Gran shakes her head and turns her headphones so I can see the Corvus symbol etched on the inside of the headband. "Ethan?"

My heart tugs that Ethan made sure to replace the pin she lost during that demon attack by incorporating the protective symbol on the headphones. I nod, knowing she's asking where Ethan is. She wants to know why he hasn't come by. I pat her soft gray hair and squat next to her wheelchair. "He's super busy with school right now."

Gran's lips press together in frustration. I can tell she wants to say so much more, but she stays quiet, probably because she knows the words won't come out the way she wants them to. Switching to the screen of images meant to help her speak her mind faster, she hits the heart image.

I nod when the robotic voice says, "Love," and then she taps the exclamation point and the robotic voice continues, "Important. Pay attention."

I stand so I don't burst into tears. "I know, Gran. Love is important." Taking a breath, I glance away to gather my emotions, then smile down at her. "It's kind of late. I need to get a shower and do my homework. Do you want me to help you upstairs now?"

Later while I'm working on homework, I quickly check my email and see I have one from TheWelshArse. Apparently Drystan had sent it while I was out running. I'm a bit disappointed that he didn't try to video with me, but for now I'm just relieved to be hearing from him.

> *Hey Nara,*
> *I'm kind of going through some stuff. I'm fine, no worries.*
> *Just knackered. I'll video you when I get my head sorted.*
> *Your favorite Welsh Arse*

I start to type out that I heard him earlier today and that I'm worried about him, but instead I delete that note and keep it simple.

> *Hey Dryst,*
> *Remember when I said I would kick your ass if you didn't keep in touch? Just a friendly reminder. :)*
> *Your favorite sparring partner*

I'm surprised when I get an email back from him right away. It has to be two in the morning his time.

> *Since you're in the mood for a visual, here's a couple pictures of the cool place I told you about…you know the one I said you'd call "grunge punk". I'm finally crashing. I'll video you soon. I miss your smile too much.*
> *Dryst*

I stare at the pictures he sent. The graffiti is very good, but the area seems as if it's not on the best side of town, considering the number of bottles lined up along the wall. Maybe it was a heavy party night? I keep optimistic thoughts in my head as I reply back.

> *Interesting place. Is this where you've been spending your time?*

Knowing he's in bed, I save the images to my phone so I can pull them up faster when he video calls me later. At least he's replying. I'll get him talking once he calls me.

After I'm done with homework, Houdini joins me on the bed. Turning off the lights, I pull up the covers and my dog rests his big head on the crook of my arm, his big brown eyes glancing up at me in the darkness. I rub the top of his head and think about Ethan. "I know, buddy. I promise I'll take you running with me tomorrow. Got any ideas on how to deal with a stubborn boyfriend who thinks he knows best for me?"

My dog just closes his eyes and sighs, completely happy to bask in my attention.

As I lay here listening to Houdini make contented sounds, I wish it was this easy to snag Ethan's attention. I want to know what's going on with him and his Corvus, but more than anything…I miss him. How do I get *us* back? Why doesn't he want that too? Are we really over? Doubt begins to cloud my thoughts and my heart grows heavy.

I glance at the window where Patch has chosen to perch. He refuses to stay inside at night, but he won't leave either. The moment I close the window for the evening, he returns as my night sentinel, his head swiveling left and right. Always on alert, always looking out into the darkness.

Watching the raven do this night after night makes me feel both guilty and safe, but tonight an idea forms. Maybe Patch can help.

# Chapter Five

*Nara*

"I think this belongs to you."

Stomach fluttering, I turn from pulling a pen from my backpack at the wonderful sound of Ethan's voice. He's standing beside my desk and the smell of his leather jacket combined with Ethan's own masculine scent instantly makes my pulse race. I miss his smell so much. My heart sinks when I glance up and lock gazes with his annoyed expression as he sets a quarter on my desk.

"Keep that bird away from me, Nara. He about took my eye out after dropping this on my head."

I gape at the light red claw marks standing out against his temple and stammer. "I—I'm sorry, Ethan. I had no idea Patch would do that."

"Didn't you?" he challenges, scowling down at me.

"Hey, Nara," Kenny calls from a couple rows over as he sets his books down and slides into his seat.

My plan to snag Ethan's attention backfired in the most spectacular way. That'll teach me to trust an unpredictable raven with my love life. I glance Kenny's way, so Ethan doesn't see the hurt in my eyes. "What's up?"

He leans forward, an expectant look on his face. "I heard you talking to Lainey about running. Want to run together some time? You're right. I need to get my ankle back in shape."

Unsure what to say, I nod. "Um, sure."

Kenny smiles and flips his pencil around his finger a couple times. "Great. Does this Thursday work for you? We can set up a meet time and place later if you want."

I nod and turn back to speak to Ethan, but he's already moved on to his seat in the back of the classroom.

I stare at him, hoping he'll look up, but he just opens a notebook and pulls out a pencil.

When he doesn't start drawing right away, but just holds the pencil over the paper, I want to scream at him, "Look up. I know you're avoiding my gaze. Talk to me!"

Sighing, I turn back to my desk to see a text from Ethan on my phone.

*Ethan: Trust no one. Drystan should've taught you that.*

The fact that Ethan is breaking his text silence only to remind me that I was almost killed by a demon who'd taken over Drystan's body makes me see red. My Welsh friend is obviously still dealing with the guilt he feels over hurting me. I'm the only one who knows he remembers being possessed. I don't know everything he did while under the demon's control, but whatever it was, he can't shake it off. Yeah, I'm worried about him. I'm so angry, I send Ethan a text back.

*Me: Thanks for the tip. You're now blocked.*

Just as he jerks his head up, I turn off my phone and tuck it into my backpack. I refuse to look his way the rest of class. If his goal was to royally piss me off, he certainly accomplished it.

To avoid Lainey, who's still focused on trying to fix Ethan and my issues, I spend my entire lunch helping one of my teachers with a project. At the end of the day, I quickly grab my books from my locker and slip out a side door.

I'm surprised to find my father cooking at the stove when I walk in close to eight. As the spicy, sweet aroma of cooked meat, vegetables, teriyaki and ginger assail my senses, several thoughts rush through my mind: *Why is he here? When did he learn to cook...all I remember was him barbequing, and why is he cooking so late?* "Hey, Dad. That smells good..." I trail of at his fierce stare.

"Where have you been? You had us worried, Nari."

I glance at Gran, who's in the process of slowly moving her wheelchair from the living room to the kitchen. She meets my gaze and shrugs, her expression saying, "I wasn't worried."

I'm still upset with Ethan, so my dad giving me a hard time annoys me more than it should. Moving behind Gran's wheelchair, I answer him as I push her until she's on the edge of the kitchen next to the island. "What's wrong? Did your inability to track my every move today drive you nuts?"

"Inara Collins!" my father barks his authority at the same time Gran waves her good arm.

"Break your neck, Jonathan! Rebels are freedom."

Grunting her frustration, Gran rips out her tablet and pokes at her machine. Finally a robotic voice says, "Give Inara space. Don't smother her."

As my father and Gran stare each other down, I feel bad for creating a tense environment, so I slip off my backpack and sigh. "I was at the library working on a project. I had to turn off my phone while I was there. Where's Mom?"

My father holds my gaze for a second as if he's trying to decide if he believes me, then turns back to the vegetables and chicken he's stir-frying, swirling them around in the pan with the flair of an experienced chef. "She's running late, but at least she'll be surprised with a nice home-cooked meal when she gets here."

Turning off the burner, he sets the food aside and covers it with a lid. "While we're waiting for your mom, I'd like to take some measurements. Can you go grab the measuring tape from my briefcase, Nari?"

"Measurements for what?" I ask while moving toward his briefcase he'd left by the stairs.

"A project. It's in the side pocket," Dad calls around the corner.

"What kind of project?" I mumble as I dig into his briefcase. I realize it's the wrong side and pull my hand out, but paperwork comes with it. I start to slide the paper back inside, then my gaze locks on the name at the top of the page: Ethan Harris.

Glancing over my shoulder to make sure my father can't see me, I pull the paper out. My hands shake as I slowly read over it.

"Did you find it?" he asks as I round the corner into the kitchen, my heart racing and cheeks flushed with anger.

"You took out a *restraining* order on Ethan?"

He raises a calming hand. "Now, Nari—"

"Is this why Ethan has stopped speaking to me?" I raise my voice and jab my finger into the paper. "How could you do that to me? What kind of father does that to the child he claims to love?"

"One who wants to keep you safe!" my father bellows over me. "You know darkness surrounds that boy, yet you blindly run straight for him, without a thought about anyone else, such as how it might impact the rest of your family. If you took the time to look at the paper, you'd see that I haven't signed it or sent it in."

"Don't you dare do that to Ethan!"

"Do you plan to put your mom at risk just to be with him? What about Aunt Sage?" He gestures to Gran. "And Corda? At least Ethan acknowledges the danger. Why do you refuse to see it?"

"*Stop* in the name of love," Gran sings at the top of her lungs like a fierce warrior. Pointing to my father, she belts out, "Stop being a—" to the same tune, then furrows her brow. Punching a couple of buttons on her tablet, a robotic voice finishes her thought. "Horse's ass!"

I'm stunned silent. I've never seen Gran so angry and upset. The last thing I want to do is cause her to have another heart attack. I gather my backpack and set the paper on the island. "I've already eaten and my homework isn't going to get done on it's own." Leaning over, I kiss her cheek and whisper in her ear. "Thank you for sticking up for me. See you in the morning."

Gran lifts her bony fingers to my face. Her eyes misty, she cups my cheek in a firm grip. "Here…fourteen…you."

I can tell she's aggravated that the words aren't coming, but her eyes fill in the blanks for me. *She's here only because of me.* I know it's not her intention, but the knowledge slaps a heavy layer of mortar over the crap-ton of bricks my father just laid at my door.

While sitting at my desk in my room, I try to concentrate on my upcoming Spanish quiz, but I'm too upset. With my father. With Ethan. How much of everything Ethan has said and done was because of my father? Did he threaten Ethan with that stupid restraining order?

When I hear Mom standing in the kitchen talking to Dad, I quietly make my way down the hall. I pause when I catch Gran's eye as I pass her doorway. She chuckles at my full on tiptoe mode, then blows a kiss my way before putting her headphones on. I leave by the back door, not planning to be gone long. Heaven forbid that I'm not in my room if my father comes up to try to talk to me. At least now that Mom's home, he'll serve her dinner and wine, which means I've got at least an hour to myself.

I want to bring Houdini with me, but I know he'll be missed and it's too last minute to call and see if Kenny would like to join me, so I tug my thermal sleeves down over my thumbs and make sure my phone is secure in my fitted jacket's zip-up arm pocket. After adjusting the ties on my shoes, I take off, because at this moment running from my problems is the only thing keeping me sane.

Once I've run until I can barely walk, I find myself in the darkness across the street from Ethan's house. Even though I'm still angry with him about what he said earlier today, a part of me wants to hammer on his door and demand to know if my father influenced his decision to end our relationship, or if that is all him (or his Corvus) talking? I have so many doubts whirling in my head, I wouldn't even know where to start.

While I stand there in indecision, Ethan walks out of his house, gets in his car and drives away. I glance down at my watch. It's almost nine. Another appointment? Where is he going?

The sense of dejection hits me hard and instead of running home through the woods that connect our neighborhoods, I decide to walk back via the roads. It'll take me longer, but maybe that will clear my head. I just reach the top of Ethan's street when an approaching car slows. Samson rolls down his passenger window and waves to me.

"Hey, Samson," I say, leaning on the open window.

"Hey, stranger. It's great to see you. I've missed seeing your sunny smile around the place. Ethan's been a pain lately. I'm sure he'll be in a better mood now."

Has Ethan not told his brother that we're no longer seeing each other? "Um, thanks Samson. It's good to see you too. I need to head home now."

He frowns. "Do you want me to drop you off? You live close by, right?"

I wave him off. "No, thanks, I'm good. I need to walk and slow my pulse."

His handsome face crinkles with concern, making him look older than his twenty-three years. "I really don't mind taking you, Nara. You shouldn't be running around by yourself, especially at night."

I know he's right. Smiling at his big-brotherly concern, I open the door and sit down. "Thanks for the ride."

He waits for me to buckle up and then turns his car around in a neighbor's driveway. We ride along quietly for a bit, but I feel uncomfortable with the silence so I start rambling. "Ethan says you're dating a nurse now."

A wide grin spreads across Samson's face. "Yeah, Emily is great. She's currently at a conference in California for a couple of weeks. I had no idea how much I would miss her but I really do."

Once we turn into my neighborhood, I ask him to let me out at the top of my street. The last thing I want is my father seeing some older guy dropping me off. I could do without the third degree. Samson rolls the window down as I shut the passenger door. "Get inside where it's warm."

Leaning over, I smile. "I will. Thanks for the ride."

"You're welcome," he says, nodding. "I hope you'll come over for dinner soon, Nara. Ethan's always happiest when you're around."

Unsure what to say to that, I just kind of bob my head and mumble, "Um hmm."

When I start to move away, Samson calls out, "Hey, before you go—" He gestures toward me. "Do you mind telling me where you bought your necklace? I want to surprise Emily with a gift when she gets back. Your charm necklace looks like something she would like. With her Irish heritage, she's into all that Celtic stuff."

I clasp the triskele pendant between my fingers and give an apologetic smile. "Sorry, I can't give you any leads. It was a gift from my grandmother a long time ago."

He nods his understanding. "No problem. You've definitely given me some gift ideas though. Have a good night."

"You too," I say and wave goodbye as he drives off.

My conversation with Samson makes me even more anxious about Ethan. Why hasn't he told his brother that we're no longer seeing each other? Is *not sharing* a guy thing? Or is Ethan questioning his decision? I'd like to think it's the latter, but I pull my phone from the zip pocket to ask someone who might have some insight into male sibling behavior.

"Hey Inara, I've missed hearing from you," Aunt Sage says. Her tone is breezy and I can tell she's working once I hear music playing in the background. It's more soothing than the usual music she plays when she's creating. She's probably putting orders together from her on-line jewelry store.

"Apparently, I heard your inner thoughts," I tease and start walking toward my house down the street. "But it sounds like you're busy."

"I'm actually getting ready to start on a project that'll take all my focus. Can I call you back?"

"We can talk later this week. I just had a quick question if you don't mind."

"Fire away, sweetie."

"Since you grew up with a brother, you probably know the answer. Did he hold back a lot? Is that a male thing…not sharing?"

"Hmm, in what way do you mean?"

I run my hand through my sweat-dampened hair and sigh. "I mean as in not sharing changes in their life with their family. For instance, I know Dad told you why he was leaving our family all those years ago, but when he was younger, was he pretty tight-lipped with you about stuff?"

"I guess he was sometimes. It really depended."

"So 'yes' and 'no' then?" I say, shaking my head. So much for that answer helping me understand guys.

Aunt Sage chuckles softly. "That about sums it up. Is this about your dad?"

"No, but thanks for the feedback. Good luck with your project."

"I'll need it. I'm vested in this one. I really want it to turn out well. When do you plan to come see me again? We can discuss guys' weirdness in depth. I'll make your favorite…"

Thoughts of her amazing cooking makes my mouth water. My aunt lives thirty minutes away in Barboursville, but with Gran's issues it has been a while since I drove out to see her. Glancing up, my gaze lands on my father's car still in our driveway. While that may be a good sign that Mom and Dad are getting along, it just means I won't be entering through the front door.

I miss my aunt. She's so easy going and always makes me smile. "I'll come see you and the boys soon."

"Expect them to give you extra puppy kisses. I'm happy to hear it. Goodnight, Inara."

"Night, Aunt Sage."

Ethan's on my mind as I quietly make my way up the stairs while Mom and Dad are doing dishes together. I need to know what's going on in Ethan's head about us. I pause in the doorway and frown at the new spot of dirt on my carpet. "Houdini!" I fuss quietly under my breath and step over to the area. Shutting my door to keep the dog out, I grab the cleaners I've been storing on my desk and get down on my knees to clean the carpet. This is the third time in as many days that I've had to clean random dirt spots showing up in my room. The frustrating part is I can't even complain this time, because Mom had to have let the dog out for me. I just don't understand why my dog has started leaving dirt now, but it has to be him. The spots have been too big to be from Patch.

*Where is Ethan going? What appointment does he have?*

*What has he been doing that he got that cut the other day?*

*Is his Corvus taking over? Is that why he's pushing me away? Or is it because of my father? Is he really trying to protect me or is that just a smokescreen?*

"What are you doing?"

Michael's deep voice yanks me out of my swirling thoughts and my gaze zeros in on the cleaning products I'd just subconsciously lined up on the carpet in descending size from big to little bottles. Of course, the dirt spot is still untouched.

Frustrated that my stress OCD has apparently kicked in, I rest my butt on my heels and slide an annoyed gaze from the archangel's blond head, over his business suit, and then frown at his leather dress shoes. "Have you been in my room this week leaving messes behind instead of much-needed advice?" When his only answer is to stare at me with intense golden eyes, I cross my arms and continue, "For someone who professes to want to save the mortal world, you're sure doing a lousy job."

"Enough!" Michael booms so loud I cover my ears while the whole house shakes.

When my eyes widen with worry that my parents will come bursting through my door, Michael is suddenly standing next to me, his voice in my head. *Uncover your ears, Inara. No one experienced that but you.*

I lower my hands and look up at him, awe rolling through me. I never saw him move. Taking my hand, he helps me rise to my feet, but I don't remember moving a single muscle. He'd borne all my weight as if I was a speck of dust. And in his mind, that's probably exactly what he thinks of me.

Feeling so insignificant in his presence makes me nervous, so I quickly pull my hand away and grumble, "I suppose dirt wouldn't poof in here with you."

An amused smile flashes on his handsome face. "Certainly not, but I am here for a reason."

"Wait? You're not here because I called you?"

"I'm here about Ethan," he simply says.

My shoulders sag in relief and I exhale. "Thank Go—" but cut myself off at his reprimanding look. "Um, I mean…that's good."

"Your Mortal world is running out of time, Inara. You must convince Ethan's Corvus that he's the Master. Lucifer is almost here."

I snort and pace away, folding my arms. "Ethan's not even talking to me. I can't help you."

"He needs you."

His assured statement pulls at my heart. *I wish.* I turn to face him once more. "No, he doesn't. Ethan says he's got it covered and that I've done my part."

"You are *wrong.*" Michael's imperial tone floats across the room in sonic waves, vibrating all the way to my bones. My eyes must widen in fear, because he sighs and steps forward to gently rest his hands on my shoulders, tempering his tone. "The spirit can't do this alone."

Despite the hum of powerful energy emanating from the angel's touch, my confidence in the rock-solidness of my relationship with Ethan has taken a huge hit the last couple of days. "*He's* the Master Corvus—"

"Who hasn't accepted who he is," the archangel interrupts, blond brows pulling together. "Fate is right about one thing…the Master Corvus without an identity *is* dangerous, but a Master Corvus without an accord with his mortal host is a nuclear explosion on the verge of detonation. Inara, *you* balance them both. The Corvus must embrace his true identity and all that entails. If he doesn't, when he faces off with Lucifer, my brother will sense his hesitancy and take full advantage. He'll use the Corvus' lack of knowledge of his own powers and their previous battles against him."

"Ethan's going out of his way to avoid me." I throw my hands up, dislodging his hold. "*You* tell him. Maybe he'll listen to you."

"You know I can't. He can't see me."

"Why can't he see you?" I ask, scrunching my nose. "He can see demons."

Michael sighs. "He can't see the demon's spirit either. He can only see them inside a human, and that's only because demons are no longer of the Celestial realm."

"But you're solid, not spirit." I put my hand on his arm. "See, I can touch you."

He pats my hand, then uncurls my fingers. "I can briefly take solid form, but we don't take over humans to battle. That's not our role."

"What is your role, then?" I challenge, letting my frustration show.

Michael shakes his head. "I'm not even supposed to be here, Inara, but when I saw you as a child and witnessed what you were capable of— he pauses and smiles. "You can help the Corvus see. Trust your instincts."

"See what?"

"You'll find a way to reconnect with Ethan," he says, his expression shuttering. "Don't give him a choice. Force him to acknowledge you."

"Nari?" my father's voice precedes a soft knock. "Can we talk?"

I cast a worried look toward the door, then turn back, but Michael's gone.

Blowing out a shaky breath of relief, I drop to my knees and pick up a sponge and a bottle of cleaner. "Come in," I say, hitting the stain with the spray.

My father walks in and sets the restraining order on the floor next to me. Just as I glance at it and see that he's torn it in half, he steps in front of me, his expression serious. "I'm trusting you'll do the right thing for your family."

When he walks out and shuts the door quietly behind him, I mutter, "Good talk," then attack the stain as if a whole slew of demons could bubble up through it from Under at any moment.

# Chapter Six

*Ethan*

"Once dinner is served, the door will be shut on this private dining room. That way…" Gerald Harris pins his sharp gaze on me. "no one can run out of here just because he feels like it."

As the wait staff brings out our food and the spicy sauces and appetizing smells make my stomach grumble, the Corvus roars for me to rip into my father and tell him that saving Nara will always come first over his need to control every situation. I curl my hands into fists on my knees under the table and clamp my jaw closed, ignoring the spirit's ruffled rant. My father is trying. And Samson wants to reconcile. I see it in his face every time he's driven us to meet our parents. Since I was the one who cut our dinner short the last time when I ran off to save Nara's Gran from demon possession, I need to see this meal through. My relationship with my father may never be salvageable, but Samson wants to build bridges, so I stay quiet for my brother.

While my father rattles off the things he doesn't like about the house he and my mom are renting and what they would change if they owned the property, I check my phone for the fiftieth time to see if Nara has sent me another text after her last one telling me she'd blocked me.

Nothing.

Nara and my brother are the only two contacts I have on my

phone. I don't use it otherwise. When she sent me that text yesterday saying she'd blocked me, true panic expelled the air from my lungs. I might be keeping my distance, but she just yanked away my security of knowing we could still communicate in an emergency. Staying away from her has been hard enough. Even though I know she's safer without me in her life, I can't let her cut me off completely. I need to know she's continuing to *stay* safe. What if my instinct to sense when she's in danger fails? What if the Corvus blocks it somehow while he's in battle mode with demons?

I watch my brother talking to my parents but I don't hear a word. *I need redundancy and fail safes in place for Nara.*

*What you* need *is a backbone! Walk right up to her father tomorrow at school and tell him what he can do with his restraining-order threat. Better yet, tell him what* you'll *do with it if he tries to file one on you. Then go find Nara and grovel. That part shouldn't be hard for you, since you've been walking around like a jellyfish since that day he challenged you.*

*Shut up!* I bark at the spirit, furious that he'd heard my last thought. *Get the hell out of my head, you damn bird. I'm letting you battle with demons and do what you do best. Don't make me regret it.*

A low, arrogant chuckle rumbles in my head. Its bass is so powerful, I feel it all the way through my body. *As if you have any say-so.*

I close my eyes for a second, concentrating on shoving him out. And just like that, he's gone. Exhaling deeply, I roll my head from one shoulder to the other to relieve the tension his unwelcome thoughts caused, then refocus my attention on what's being said around me.

"I can't believe how long it took to get back together with you two. If your work is keeping you that busy, you need a raise, son," our father says to Samson, a bit of pride lacing his comment.

I snort that our dad has the nerve to say anything about working crazy hours. That's all I remember him doing throughout our childhood. I notice Samson's jaw starting to tense, so I change the subject. Punching my brother in the arm, I grin. "Nah, he's just been spending all his time with Emily."

"Emily?" our mother says, her blonde eyebrows raised in interest. "When are we going to get to meet this young woman who's snagging all your time?"

Samson cuts me an annoyed look, then hedges, "She's busy

with her career, Mom."

"But surely she has time to meet your family. Maybe she can come to the next family dinner?" Mom pushes as she cuts her steak.

"Let it go, Sherri," our dad says as he lifts his Scotch to his lips. "If they're still together in six months, we'll have her over for dinner."

Clearly irritated by our father's dismissive comment, Samson gestures to me. "Why don't we invite Nara to the next meal? How do you think that'll go over?"

I slit my gaze on my brother. He knows my parents didn't like Nara confronting them over their ignorance how my life had improved since I came to live with him. What point is he trying to make? That my parents will never accept Nara because she dared to stand up to them while I was in a coma? Granted, I haven't told any of my family that Nara and I aren't dating any longer, but why is he pulling her into this at all? I was only trying to lighten the mood by mentioning a part of his life our parents would approve of. When I slide my attention to my parents and they're both suddenly busy with their food, neither of them jumping on Samson's suggestion they get to know Nara under more normal circumstances…that sets me off.

I throw my napkin down and stand. "It's good to know your acceptance only extends to one son."

"Sit down, Ethan," my father commands.

"And here we go," Samson mutters with a sigh.

*I just gave up the most important thing in my life—the only person who truly believes in me and made me a better version of myself—and the fact that you're showing no interest in getting to know her infuriates me!* I want to shout my thoughts as my parents stare at me like I've lost my mind. Instead I ignore my father and shift my focus to my brother. "I tried, Samson, but I can't do this…"

"Nara and Emily will come with us next time, Ethan," Samson says, gesturing to my seat. "Now sit."

Clamping my mouth shut, I take my seat and dig into my food so I don't have to think about the fact that I just painted myself into a corner. My father will never let it go if Nara doesn't come to our next dinner, but I know I won't be inviting her.

*This is so fucked up it's not even funny.*

*Actually, it's quite hilarious*, Rave laughs heartily in my ear.

*Shut your beak or I'll find a way to pound it closed permanently!*

*You will* not *address me with such disrespect,* the spirit snaps, his amusement swiftly gone.

I almost choke on my steak as a surge of power flashes from my skull to my feet so quickly I'm sure my organs have singe marks. Swallowing down the lump of meat, I lock my jaw and grit though the force humming through me. *I can't believe you're choosing now to acknowledge that you're the Master Corvus. During a battle with demons would've made more sense.*

"*Your family dinners* are *a battlefield,*" Rave blasts, sarcasm ripe in his tone. "*I'm not the Master Corvus. I'm just showing you your own insignificance in the presence of a far superior being. Go on, sit there and pretend like your whole body isn't vibrating, your skin isn't stretching, your bones cracking. I want you to feel every molecule threaten to dissolve as you try to* contain *me!*

While my family shifts to benign conversation, the spirit amps the pressure. I don't get a chance to mentally retaliate. It takes all my concentration to stay seated. Shaking with tension on the inside, I grip my fork and knife tighter and chew vigorously as sweat beads along my scalp and trickles down my spine.

When the floor underneath my feet begins to rumble, shaking the whole room, and my father grabs the table's edge, saying, "Is that an earthquake?" I'm finally able to express my fury at the spirit.

*If you kill me, you may as well hand the demons this world. You know I'm different. You hate that you can't break my mind, that you haven't been able to fully absorb me.* I let out a mental roar as I jerk upright to my feet.

"It's okay, Ethan. The rumbling has stopped," Mom says, concern in her eyes. Holding her hand to her chest, she glances between Sampson and me. "I had no idea Virginia could get earthquakes."

"It's fine," my father says, gesturing for me to sit. "On the news they said they had one in Richmond too."

This is why I *must* stay away from Nara. Until this moment, I thought she was worrying too much when she asked me if I'd been in Richmond recently. I'm still gripping the knife and fork, so I set them down and exhale my relief to be free of the Corvus' influence. "Got to go to the restroom."

In the bathroom I splash cold water on my face and stare back at my reflection in the mirror. Beads of water are standing out on my flushed skin and my eyes are no longer blue. They're obsidian black and have a knowing shine to them that's eerie as hell. I'm so thankful for the restaurant's dim lighting, or my family would definitely have questioned the change. *How can you not believe you're the Master Corvus when you can cause the ground to rumble?*

The spirit snorts hard in my ear. Pffft, *I can walk through walls. What makes you think a Corvus can't cause the ground to shake?*

*Because you're doing it outside of the environment, not as you're passing through it,* I mentally snap.

A couple beats pass. *At least you're starting to understand how insignificant you are.*

It's hard to ignore his droll response when I watch my lips quirk and my eyes flash with arrogance. The fact he paused before answering makes me think he's starting to question himself. Part of me is terrified about what will happen when he accepts who he really is, while the other part is gearing up, reinforcing my mind with varied layers for when that day happens. If today was just a taste, what kind of power will emanate through me when he's at full capacity? Will I be able to think my own thoughts? Or will I exist purely on the instinct of hunting demons and sending them back to Under?

I grip the edge of the sink, my chest constricting. This is the first time I've seen him manipulating my facial muscles to control my expression. Worried, I lash out. *I'm not insignificant, you puffed-up, self-important asshole! What's the longest any of your hosts have held you off? Five seconds? A day? You need me. My strong mind fascinates you. I'm the fastest and my fighting skills are exceptional. You don't even have to do much other than boost my speed, because my body fights automatically when threatened, so back-the-fuck-off and stop trying to control my every move!*

*I never said any of that,* he snaps, sounding defensive.

I smile coldly at my reflection. *You're not the only one who catches glimpses of random thoughts,* Corvus.

*My name is Rave. Use it.*

*Save it for someone who likes you.*

She *is what makes you special,* the Corvus grates, obviously irritated, his tone less combative but full of haughty superiority. The sensation of warm breath moving from one ear to the other, as if he's standing behind me, makes my back muscles tense. *That, we agree on.*

Even though he's speaking the truth, I close my eyes and shake my head to shove him completely out and take back control of myself.

When I glance at the mirror once more, a man is standing a few feet behind me. It's the same guy who tried to get my attention yesterday. I whirl and grab his lapels, hauling him against the stall door. My tone is harsh. "Why are you following me?"

"I need to talk to you." Panic filling his expression, he grips my hands and tries to dislodge them.

A crumple of paper in one of his hands draws my attention. "What's that?"

"If you'll let me go, I'll show you. I'm just trying to deliver a message." The guy's voice is shaking and I smell his nervous sweat. He's no threat to me.

Releasing him, I step back and scowl. "What message?"

"My name is Grant Rockford and I'm officially informing you that you're the sole beneficiary of the Gaston estate and all it's holdings." He straightens his suit jacket and tie, his confident demeanor slowly returning. Clearing his throat, he hands the paper to me. "I've been assigned to act as your legal advisor in all matters."

I frown and shake my head. "I don't know any Gastons. You've got the wrong person."

"You're Ethan Harris and that is your address," the man says, pointing to the paper. "Danielle's instructions were clear. She said you'd be difficult to contact and convince, so I *definitely* have the right person. In light of her sudden disappearance, and with no leads as to if she'll return, you've become heir to the estate and all she owned. She gave specific instructions not to let the estate go without your leadership in her absence, so I await your instructions on what you'd like to do."

I stare at him in disbelief. His mention of Danielle brings it all back. Her training me as a Corvus, her fixated, territorial attachment that I blindly believed was just one Corvus helping another...until she joined forces with a demon.

*I'm her beneficiary?* Between the properties and investments, Danielle told me she was worth billions. I didn't question why the Corvus who'd mentored her and had left her everything upon his death had died so young. After all, Corvus live dangerous lives and dying young is probably more the norm than the exception.

Danielle was more than territorial…she was devious. She made a deal with a demon and taught him how to be undetectable by a Corvus while inside a human. But her worst violation, beyond putting all Corvus at risk, was using a demon to try to kill Nara. That was her downfall. If the demon hadn't double-crossed Danielle and taken her out, I would have.

Her action violated the very essence of what it means to be Corvus. We're sworn to protect mortals from demons; we don't use them to plot mortal deaths. Curling my lip in disgust, I crumple the paper in my hand. "I want nothing to do with this *inheritance*," I say and walk out of the bathroom.

# Chapter Seven

*Nara*

"Hey, Nara," Kenny says, running to catch up to my stride after school. "Thanks for running with me. I think it's really helping loosen up my ankle."

"You're welcome." I smile as I grasp a strap on my backpack, thankful that Lainey had to stay after for an art project. She would see Kenny as competition for Ethan and that's so not what he is. The last thing I need is for her to try to intervene on my behalf by speaking to Ethan. Reaching my car, I lower my backpack to the ground and unlock the door. "We'll both be in good shape by the time practice rolls around." I try to ignore Patch making annoyed *tok,tok,tok* sounds in a tree above us. I can only hope he doesn't dive bomb Kenny in broad daylight. I had to give the raven a stern talking to last night after he scared the crap out of the poor guy, ripping at his hair the moment we started running. Kenny thought for sure a bat had attacked him.

Glancing ahead of us, I notice Ethan walking at a much slower pace than usual toward his car. One ear bud is in and one is out. I can't remember him ever not having both in at the same time. When he zones, he prefers his music in surround-sound.

Kenny shoves his hands in his jean pockets, his expression hopeful. "Would you like to go running again this afternoon?

Patch starts snapping his beak over and over, the clacking sound showing his irritation. I quickly unlock my car door. "Can we do it next Monday? I have a project I need to work on this week."

Kenny runs his fingers through his thick auburn hair and smiles. "Sure, that sounds good. I'll try to keep running on my own until then, but it's always more fun to have someone there who won't let me slack off."

"No trying, only doing!" I tease, wagging a finger at him.

Laughing, he grabs my finger. "See, that's what I mean. *This, right here, is what I need.*"

The second Patch lets out a loud squawk, tension tightens my shoulders and I suddenly feel the prickly sensation of being watched. Sliding my finger free of Kenny's grasp, I snicker at him. "You'd better get going on that running then. I need to head home."

Once Kenny walks away, I open my car door while glancing around for the source—like a magnetic pull in the air.

When my gaze locks with Ethan's penetrating one across the parking lot, warmth shoots up my cheeks and a jolt of awareness rocks through me. The memory of earlier in the hall coming back to me in waves of intense heat.

The locker hall was so packed today that the mass of moving students made it impossible to pass Ethan at his locker without bumping him. Then, just as I started to pass him, someone turned out the lights in the locker area. Of course the students whooped and hollered, getting rowdier. Instead of ignoring me like I expected him to do, Ethan quickly turned and clasped my wrist. Hauling me close, he ducked his head and commanded in my ear, "Unblock me."

I tried to resist and pull back, but the press of bodies only pushed me closer against his hard chest. "Why?" I asked, my mouth suddenly dry and my pulse racing like crazy.

His gaze dropped to my mouth and I swear I felt his heart thumping against mine as his fingers cinched tighter. His mouth was so close. *Kiss me, Ethan. Show me that you miss us.* When he didn't answer my question, I finally regained the ability to think rationally. "You think I should unblock you so you can *not* text me? Is that my father's idea too?"

As his expression shifted to a displeased scowl, I tugged my arm free. At least I had my answer. My father did say something to him. "I'm good."

Even now, I can still feel the warmth of him pressed against me, and for some strange reason, the way he's looking at me from across the parking lot hits me harder than it did earlier, shooting all the way to my toes. A part of me is relieved this wasn't Ethan's idea, but another part is angry that he let my father get to him. Grasping my open car door, I focus on my anger to help me shake off Ethan's charismatic stare. He doesn't get to look at me with such possessive passion or to expect me to comply. Not when he's the one who pushed me away.

I might miss his appealing smell and the comforting feel of his arms holding me close, but I also want to yell at him for quitting us, to demand to know what he's been doing. Where did he get the dark bruise marring his cheekbone and the two-inch cut slicing along his jawline? Those battle scars are new as of today. The last few days, he has appeared edgier, his stance more militant, his gaze aggressive as he sums people up in one judgmental sweep.

I can't help but question if Ethan's Corvus is staring back at me right now, or if this is just Ethan giving in to his Corvus's natural instincts? With each new change I've seen in him, he's been too far away for me to see his eye color and the dark hallway earlier didn't help. I can only hope that his gaze isn't black. Then again, Danielle's eyes hadn't been black, yet she turned out to be deviously evil. As a Corvus who'd been fully corrupted by demons, Danielle had scared me more than the demon she'd recruited to take over Drystan to kill me.

With the whole Danielle scenario, Ethan and I saw what could happen to a Corvus without a human to ground them. But what happens to the Master Corvus who thinks he's just a Corvus? Can the Master Corvus spirit be corrupted by all the evil he fights if he's not utilizing his full powers? Especially if he's without someone acting as a Paladin? That thought is terrifying.

No matter what Ethan thinks…he needs balance. He needs someone to keep the human part of him…human. *He needs me.* Even if I'm only allowed to act in an unofficial Paladin capacity and not as his girlfriend.

The "project" I mentioned to Kenny is Ethan's Corvus. Michael's warning has haunted me the last couple of days. Each night, I lay awake, racking my brain for ideas how to help while still protecting my family. Since Ethan seems to have shoved me to some dark corner, like a toy he can't have but also doesn't want others to play with, I've decided to focus on his Corvus. The only way I'll get anywhere helping Rave accept his true identity is by reaching out to the spirit directly.

And there's only one way that I know to do that.

Lifting my chin, I get in my car and drive home.

After I spend time helping Gran with her memory exercises, I retreat to my room. Closing my door, I sit on my bed and glance down at the ring on my finger. The Corvus symbol on it might protect me from demon possession, but it also keeps me from dreaming my next day, which I need for my plan to work. Ethan's ability to absorb other people's conflicted or negative issues has also worked on me in the past. Which means, as long as I'm not wearing the ring, he'll see my dreams along with his horrific nightmares. And Ethan's dream world is the only way I've been able to speak to the Corvus.

The idea to reach out to Rave came to me this morning when the sun shone on the crystal dangling from the necklace I'd wrapped around the raven statue sitting on my dresser. When I tried to use the crystal necklace my aunt gave me to help me get my dreams back, before I learned that Ethan was the one who had absorbed them, that's the first time I was zapped into Ethan's dream world. Not only did I experience Ethan's awful dreams, but whenever I was truly in harm's way, Ethan's Corvus has always protected me.

Even though Ethan's dreams are the only way I've been able to verbally communicate with his Corvus, getting an audience with Rave will be tricky. I've only been able to see into Ethan's dreams once without Ethan present and touching me, so I can't guarantee I'll be able to see into his dreams again, let alone find Rave. One thing's for certain, Ethan will immediately know that I took my ring off, since he'll dream my next day tonight. Of course, he'll be upset that I removed it, so I decide to challenge him. Stepping over to my mirror, I write on the glass with a dry-erase marker: COME AND MAKE ME PUT IT BACK ON.

Patch flaps his wings and squawks his disapproval, his gaze wary as he watches me twist the ring off my finger and lay back on my pillow. I'm just glad that Fate knows better than to mess with me. Not that he should be able to without Ethan touching me while

I sleep, but the last time I tangled with Fate in Ethan's dream world, he attacked me and Rave almost killed him. As much as my powers caused me to tangle with Fate, I couldn't let the spirit wipe him out. I couldn't imagine what would've happened to our world without Fate running in the background.

I definitely don't like what the self-serving, nebulous, sunken-eyed entity has done to try to destroy my family, but one thing I have learned through my run-ins with Fate is that…when you have the weight of the world on your shoulders, it's not always easy getting others to fall in line the way they're supposed to. Ethan's Corvus has been a huge challenge. He's steadfast in his refusal to believe that he's more than a regular Corvus, but also scary in how he so easily wields even a small portion of his vast power. In a fit of frustration or anger, with his powers raging, he could unwittingly destroy the careful balance between the Celestial, Mortal, and Under realms.

Curling my fingers around the crystal, I close my eyes and whisper, "Let me see my dreams," then give in to my lack of sleep from the past two nights.

*"Come on, asswipe, give me all you've got!" Ethan twirls his sword and catches it in a confident grip as he faces off against a guy close to his age.*

*Except the blond guy in a moto-leather jacket doesn't sound like he's seventeen when he belts out a maniacal laugh then snaps pointy razor sharp teeth together as he slowly reaches toward Ethan with talon-clawed elongated fingers. The ear-piercing sound of the demon's talons slowly drawing along the metal of Ethan's sword makes me wince.*

*He gives Ethan a confident smile. "Tsk, tsk. Now why would I do that when you're so obviously holding back?"*

*Ethan spins his sword in a circle so fast that the demon laughs once more. "I'm disappointed. With all your big talk and fancy sword, I expected so much more. I barely felt a thing."*

*Ethan doesn't speak, he just lifts his sword, tapping the metal tip on the guy's coat sleeve. The moment the metal connects, the fabric gives way and the creature's right hand drops to the ground. Blood spurts as the demon howls in pain. He quickly tugs his severed arm to his chest to stop the flow of blood, but at the same time lashes out with his other hand. A talon slices along Ethan's jaw before the demon digs his claws into Ethan's* shoulder, shredding his flesh.

"You'll die screaming in pain, Corvus!"

Ethan smirks and tilts his sword up, pressing it against the guy's throat. "You'll be in Under before you get a chance to act on that threat. I figure you've got about three minutes."

I gape at Ethan, shocked by his complete detachment. He seems eerily calm and smug in his ability to take the demon out, but the person's body the demon hijacked is also paying dearly.

The guy snarls and drags Ethan close. "Then I'm taking you with me."

This is the third fight I've witnessed in Ethan's dreams tonight. With each dream taking place in areas around town, and proof via the cut on Ethan's jaw, I realize that these are his memories, made even more twisted in his dream world.

"Let him go!" I call out, but the demon's ear-piercing wail as Ethan jams his sword into his chest drowns out my words.

I gag at the foul stench coming from the demon, but before I can call Ethan's name, I'm yanked from Ethan's dream into cold darkness. The sound of someone breathing next to my ear, the breath, just as cold as the air around me, makes my skin crawl. Even though I'm shocked to see Fate here, I still myself and address him in a tone as cold as the black space, "You have five seconds to return me to Ethan's dream world."

Fate's face suddenly lights up directly in front of mine.

It takes everything inside me not to cringe at the sight of his empty dark eye sockets no more than an inch from my face. The heat of the tiny flame flickering his smoky thumb licks along my chin, singeing my flesh.

Fate chuckles in a creepy baritone when I attempt to blow out the flame. He lets it die down then flare back to life like a trick birthday candle.

I narrow my gaze. "Do you have a death wish?"

His eye sockets shrink to slits and he pulls the fire away from my chin, but instead of dousing the light, he flicks his thumb and sends the tiny bit of light inside himself.

Staring at me like a creepy jack-o-lantern, he tilts his head. "Quite the opposite, Nara. I rather like living, so I brought you here to help."

I instantly tense, my suspicious hackles raised. "Help?"

Fate whirls away in a puff of dark fog, taking the tiny bit of light with him. When he turns back, the glow from his eyes reveals his foggy arms are folded. "You need to help Ethan's Corvus accept who he is, but you can't do that if you're not spending time with the boy."

I squint at Fate, distrusting that his goal is to actually help me, even *when it benefits him. He has always tried to hurt me in some form or fashion in every contact we've had. "I didn't think you could see Ethan's fate or any of my interactions with him."*

*Fate flicks his wrist, snorting his frustration. "Ever since the Master Corvus challenged me in the dream world, I've sometimes been able to capture Corvus-related glimpses as they pertain to you, but other Corvus moments throw off your timeline. So it's what I'm not seeing that tells me you need my help. If you were spending time with him, there would be pockets of unpredictability in your timeline. As much as I hated those unpredictable moments, the lack of them now is unacceptable. You must spend time together."*

"Now you don't want to see my daily activities? For all you know I could be playing with someone's fate during that time," I say, my eyebrow hiking.

"Don't even consider it, you silly girl. What I want is for you to keep that powerful spirit nesting in that boy's body balanced. He needs Ethan's human side. The Corvus mustn't go dark. And I have a plan."

"A plan?" I fold my arms and set my jaw.

Fate nods, the flame inside him showing with his up-and-down eye movement. "I can't always see you with Ethan, but what I can still see is whenever mortals are taken over by demons. That's when the person drops off my carefully laid course for them. All we need to do is draw some demons to you and Ethan will come to your rescue. Boom, you'll be back in business."

I grind my teeth, knowing I was right not to trust Fate. "You want to use me as demon bait?"

"You've been attacked by demons before," he says, shrugging his smoky shoulders.

And I nearly died! "That's the whole reason Ethan's staying away. He wants to keep me safe." I say this with confidence that I don't really feel. I've only seen what I thought was yearning in his eyes the first time he saw me after Gran came home.

"Exactly my point." Fate jabs a finger in my direction. "He'll be there to defend you the moment you're in trouble."

I shake my head. "I refuse to make myself a demon-beacon just to have Ethan back in my life. For now, I'm here to convince the Corvus who he is when I see him in Ethan's dream world."

"Like you've been able to do that so far." Fate's snide in his annoyance. "If you refuse to work with me, you're done here." Leaning close, he flicks *me on the forehead, his icy touch so shockingly frigid that my teeth begin to chatter. "Wake up!"*

I jerk awake from my nap, my breath fogging in the chilly air. Growling my frustration that Fate kicked me out before I could see my own dreams or connect with Rave, I try to close my eyes once more, but I'm too tense from shivering to sleep. The temperature in my bedroom has dropped considerably, and even with Houdini snuggled next to me, I'm still cold.

Lifting his head, Houdini whines and I give him a wry smile as I get up and slip on a zip-up jacket. It's probably warmer outside right now anyway. "Come on boy, I'll take you out."

Mom's pulling up as I walk out with Houdini. Pausing in the driveway on her way into our garage, she rolls her window down. "Wait for me and I'll take a walk with you and Houdini."

"Okay," I say, furrowing my brow slightly. *What's up with Mom? She never takes walks with me.*

Mom joins me on the driveway, buttoning her suit jacket. It's the first time that I noticed that she's lost weight. I guess the stress of Gran's recovery has affected her more than I realized. I glance down at her high heels. "Do you want to run in and change into your tennis shoes?"

Shaking her head, Mom gestures me forward. "Let's walk. I'll be fine, Inara. I just want to talk."

I wrap Houdini's leash around my hand to keep him from getting too far ahead of us and set a walking pace that my mom can keep up with. Once we're a couple houses away, Mom clears her throat. "Now that Gran's settled, I'd like to see that video your father left for you."

I pause while Houdini sniffs around a mailbox. "I can set it up on my laptop in my room later on tonight."

Mom pats Houdini as he looks up at her. "I'd like to watch it by myself if you don't mind."

*"Why don't you want me to watch it with you?" Then I can explain and fill in the blanks.*

"Because I want to watch it with my own thoughts." Mom pushes my hair over my shoulder, her fingers sliding along my hair. "I'll be happy to discuss it with you later, but I just want the time to be mine and your father's."

*But he doesn't really mention you at all. He just talks about protecting me from a force bent on making him pay for changing other people's fate by hurting his family.* If she does pick up on the fact he doesn't talk to or about her directly, I want to be there to ease the hurt. The video was meant for me only. "I kind of wanted it to be a mother/daughter moment," I say, trying to keep the concern from my voice. I might be angry with my father about Ethan, but I want my mother to be happy. She deserves that. I heard their laughter downstairs last night, and she seems less tense than she has been in a while. If she wants to give my father another chance by letting him back in her life on a romantic level, then I'll do whatever I can to support her.

Mom starts walking forward and Houdini and I follow. "We can still have that afterward." She casts me a sideways glance. "I hope you're not worrying that your father's reappearance in our lives will somehow weaken our bond. You will always be my first priority, Inara. Nothing will change that."

"Thanks, Mom. I know that. I just…" I pause, unsure how to get her to let me watch it with her. I would hate for this to set my parents' forward momentum back. "Feel like I could give you some insight."

"And you will," she says, nodding. "Afterward."

I exhale a sigh of frustration, and at the same time Houdini begins to snarl and bark. He's staring intently at a middle-aged man in a golfer's hat and trench coat standing on the opposite side of the street. The man pauses and stares at my crazed dog.

"Calm Houdini down," Mom says in a low tone, smiling apologetically.

He isn't someone I recognize. Then again, I don't know all our neighbors, but the way Houdini is sniffing the air and lurching forward, he's literally pulling me off the sidewalk toward the guy. Worry spikes and I squeeze my fingers together, expecting the comforting feel of the ring that protects me from demon possession. Panic wells when I remember that I left it in my room. Heart thumping hard while I yank back on the leash, I chance a quick glance at my mom in the hopes that she's at least wearing the locket necklace with the Corvus symbol hidden inside that Ethan had given her for Christmas.

"I'm trying," I reply, my voice strained. At least she's wearing his gift, but I still want to yell for her to run to the house. Not only would she think I'm insane, but even if she did listen to me, she wouldn't get very far in those heels. Demons can move extremely fast. Much faster than us mere mortals. And that's when it hits me what I need to do.

Reaching for Houdini's collar, I pull him close and pretend I'm reprimanding him, but I actually unsnap his collar and whisper in his ear, "Protect my mom, boy!"

The moment Houdini bolts forward, Mom screams my name, horrified by the thought of our dog attacking someone. The demon snarls at my dog, but before Houdini can reach him, Patch swoops in first, beak and claws inflicting as much damage as possible. Spouting an ear-piercing, inhuman roar at the surprise attack from the air, the demon thrashes his arms above his head, trying to knock the bird away. The raven pulls back, then dives in for more.

With Houdini almost upon him, the demon takes off toward the woods at a speed that's way beyond humanly possible. My dog quickly pursues, and Patch makes several angry *raaaaack* sounds as he flies after them.

I try to tug Mom around and get her moving toward our house, but her shoes are rooted as she gestures after them, clearly in shock. "Did you hear the horrible sound that man made? We need to do something!"

Gripping my mom's arm tight, I shake her to break her out of the haze of worry and confusion. "Let's go inside. For both animals to attack that man like they did, there was something really bad about him. They were defending us."

Mom's brow furrows and she clasps the Corvus pendant on her necklace. "You said it would protect us, but I didn't think it would be so literal. That bird was massive." She glances my way, a different worry creeping in her voice. "Now I'm worried about the dog. I hope he can find his way back."

"The other times he's taken off after rabbits, he's found his way back home." I keep my voice confident for my mom's sake. I doubt Houdini will be able to catch up to the demon, but I'm so glad I put a tracker on his collar. First chance I get, I'll go after him.

When we arrive back at the house, my father's car is sitting at the curb. As we walk up the driveway, I wonder if Mom knows that she just unbuttoned and re-buttoned her jacket, then smoothed her hands over it to straighten imagined wrinkles out.

My father is on his knees in his slacks as he slides a tape measure across the front porch. Taking the pencil from his mouth, he smiles at us as he writes down a measurement on a small pad he pulls from his dress shirt's front pocket. "I had some time and thought I'd get these measurements taken."

Mom smiles and nods her appreciation, and I glance up at Gran who opened the front door as we approached. Her face looks strained as she grabs hold of the door's edge and pulls herself up and out of her wheelchair.

"Gran!" I gasp and drop the leash to run up the couple steps and catch her just as her weak legs give out. Helping her back into the wheelchair, I brush wispy gray hair from her face. "What were you thinking? You could've gotten really hurt."

Heaving a sigh, Gran gestures with her good arm to my dad. "No!"

When she begins to pump her legs back and forth, the wheelchair wheels bobbing with her swinging movements, my mom steps forward. "Are you saying you don't want us to build a ramp?"

Gran nods, grunting, "My wings will mend."

I squat next to Gran and hold her gaze. "If you don't want us to build a ramp, do you promise to let me help you with your leg exercises now?"

Gran rests her hand on the top of my head and smiles, nodding. I look over at my dad. "You heard her…no ramp."

Dad zips the measuring tape closed and slides it and the pad in his pocket, muttering, "I'll just put the project on hold then."

Gran gives him a withering look. "Don't use old prunes to pluck young grapes."

While her words certainly aren't common phrasing, Gran's meaning shines through. Not only is this the closest she's come to her wacky sayings since she had her stroke, but she's telling my father in no uncertain terms to stop using her as an excuse to see my mom. I never thought I'd miss Gran's scrambled-metaphors with layered meanings, but I do. Suppressing a smile, I stand to grab hold of the back of Gran's wheelchair. "We're going to reheat leftovers. Do you want to stay and eat with us, Dad?"

My father clears his throat and gives me a thankful smile, the sudden paleness in his face subsiding. "Sure. I'll just cook up some more rice so there's enough for all of us."

I don't bother glancing my mom's way. Not only will they be

busy for at least a half hour preparing dinner, but that'll give me time to find Houdini's location.

Once I get Gran settled into a chair at the table, I pull up the tracking software on my phone and plug in Houdini's code. I'm relieved to see that he's only a couple neighborhoods away, but the fact his signal isn't moving jumps my pulse.

Glancing up from my phone, I hone in on my father saying that the rice will take twenty minutes as he pulls the box out of the cabinet and reach for my keys and purse on the island. "I'll just run to the store and grab a box of instant rice."

"It's fine, Nari," he starts to say, then frowns, glancing around. "Where's Houdini?" A part of me wants to stay and help smooth over Mom's version of what happened on our walk so Dad doesn't freak out, but Houdini's unmoving signal is more urgent. I would never forgive myself if something happened to him. I quickly open the kitchen door and step into the garage before anyone tells me to stay put.

After following the signal to a nearby neighborhood, my foot instantly eases off the gas to the point my car sits idling on the dark retirement community's street. Not more than thirty feet away, Ethan is standing beside Houdini underneath a streetlight's yellow glow. My dog is just sitting there panting and staring up at Ethan as if he doesn't have a care in the world.

The moment I pull over and cut my engine, Houdini's ears perk up. I move the baseball bat I'd set in my lap to the floorboard and open my car door. The moment my dog sees me, he starts to bound forward, but Ethan puts a restraining hand on his collar. "Stay, boy."

I pause a few feet away from my car. I can sense the tension in Ethan from here, and of course it's at this moment that I realize I hadn't gone upstairs and put my ring back on like I'd intended. The whole Gran/ramp thing distracted me. Tucking my keys in my pocket, I approach them.

Houdini looks at me and pants happily. He doesn't appear any worse for wear, but I can't help but wonder where Patch is. I don't hear the raven making annoyed sounds in a nearby tree. *Is he still off chasing that demon?*

As I stop a couple feet away, Ethan rests his hand on Houdini's head. "I got here to find an older guy bleeding from deep scratch wounds and walking in circles, babbling in confusion. I could smell the demon on him."

"Did Houdini hurt him?" I ask, my voice trembling.

Cupping his hand on the back of Houdini's neck, Ethan shakes his head. "He was snarling. I'm assuming because he could still smell demon stink, but he somehow knew the demon was no longer occupying the person. I called a cab and told the driver to take the man to Jefferson hospital so they could clean and stitch up his wounds."

I glance around at the trees behind the small ranch-style houses in the neighborhood. "Is Patch around here somewhere?"

Ethan's gaze narrows. "That vicious bird took off the moment I arrived."

"How did you know to come here?" I say, while stepping forward to rub Houdini's snout.

"I woke up from a nap and saw a brief flash of Patch attacking a man."

Gulping, I whisper, "You woke up?"

Ethan quickly clasps my hand. Pushing his thumb on the finger I normally wear the ring on, his eyes snap to mine, full of anger. "Why, Nara?"

*Fate kicked me out before I could see any of my own dreams, so Ethan couldn't have known I was in his dreams. But how did he see Patch? Wait...* I furrow my brow. "Did you just say that you saw Patch attacking the man *after* you woke up?"

"I saw the talons ripping at the man's skin. Felt the blood splatter and black wings flapping. You know how I'll get flashes sometimes. It was like that, but I felt the bird's defensive anger and knew it was Patch." Ethan curls his fingers tighter. "Why aren't you wearing your ring?"

"Are you saying you saw that scene from Patch's point-of-view?" I ask, trying to reason through what he's saying. *How is that possible? He never has before. He can't even communicate with Patch like he can with other animals.*

"Nara!"

Ethan's hand wraps fully around mine and his tone is so sharp, I'm yanked out of my own head. "I briefly took it off and forgot to put it back on when Mom and I went for a walk with Houdini."

Ethan's jaw muscle jumps. "What did the demon say to you?"

"Nothing. He didn't even look at us until Houdini started after him." I shrug, trying to remember. It had all happened so fast. As soon as I get the words out, it hits me why a demon, who didn't seem remotely interested in me or my family, would show up near my home. Fate! *Grrrr.* I refuse to play the damsel in distress to win my boyfriend back. "I think he was just squatting in that person for whatever reason, but the last thing he expected was for my dog to detect him."

"You must *never* take your ring off," he says in a softer tone as he slides his thumb along my finger, making my stomach dip. "It should be a permanent part of you."

My heart aches when I see that he's still wearing his matching ring with its protective symbols etched along the silver metal. I had my aunt create the rings for both of us. Ethan's was to replace his damaged dragon tattoo, but his tattoo is all healed now. At this point, the ring is unnecessary and probably gets in his way when he holds his sword. *Why is he still wearing it?*

"You mean *permanent* like us?" I challenge, summoning my anger from earlier today. He doesn't say anything, so I slide my hand from his and clasp Houdini's collar. "Let's go, Houdini."

As I start to walk away, Ethan sighs. "Nara..."

Flipping my hand, I call over my shoulder, "Don't worry. I'm never taking it off again."

The steering wheel creaks under my tight hold as I drive away. There has to be another way to speak to his Corvus face-to-face, but with everyone from Fate to Michael to my father and even Ethan trying to manage me in their own way, my choices are narrowing.

Finding a chance to speak with Rave in the past was challenging enough with Ethan in my life. Now that Ethan's acting like giving us up could very well be permanent, I've moved beyond feeling frustrated and hurt. I'm pissed, which makes me more determined than ever to succeed.

If Ethan thinks I'm stubborn now, he hasn't seen anything yet.

# Chapter Eight

*Nara*

As soon as I walk in from the garage with a box of instant rice and Houdini, Mom and Dad turn from finishing up the dishes. Dad slides a stack of plates into the cabinet then turns toward me, worry lining his face. "Why didn't you answer your phone? It kept going straight to voicemail."

"I'm so glad you found Houdini." Mom steps forward, her expression tense as she dries her hands on a towel. "I told your father about what happened and how a raven attacked that man."

I shift my gaze between them, wondering how much to say. Dad's staring at Mom's locket, a frown on his face. In his mind, anything associated with Ethan can't be good. He might know that Fate is real, but he doesn't have a clue about the whole demons-and-Corvus-exist-in-our-world part. If I tried to tell my mom the truth, she would probably take me straight to see a psychiatrist, so I keep as close to the truth as I can without freaking them out.

Glancing down at my mom's necklace and then at my father, I say, "I told you that yin-yang raven symbol inside the locket was for protection. "

His mouth thins. "Your mother said Houdini attacked that man."

"And so did the raven," I remind Mom as I unhook Houdini's leash and let him bolt into the living room. "Two completely different animals don't go after a person for no reason, Dad."

"What *was* that reason exactly?" My father crosses his arms, his brow furrowed. "The last thing your mother needs is to be sued."

"I can speak for myself, Jonathan." Turning to me, my mom's tone softens. "He has a point, Inara. That man might've growled like some kind of strange animal when Houdini went barreling after him, but he didn't threaten us in any way."

I open my mouth, then close it. Technically, the demon didn't *do* anything. Damn Fate and his meddling. "I'll get Houdini a new collar tomorrow that he can't escape from."

My father starts to speak, but my mother cuts him off. "I think that'll be for the best." Gesturing to the foil-covered plate on the island, Mom tucks a hank of her blond hair behind her ear and continues, "While you eat, your father and I want to discuss something with you."

Mom's tone is so uncharacteristically excited, my shoulders tense. *What are they up to?* "Okaaaaay," I say, then grab a fork and sit down with my plate of food.

As soon as I put a forkful of rice and vegetables into my mouth, my father slides a flyer for a class trip to London across the island and leaves it in front of me. "I was in the copier room while Mr. Hallstead was making these copies for tomorrow's class. I snagged one for you. I think it's a wonderful opportunity to see another part of the world and experience history."

Twenty-eight hundred dollars for a seven-day school trip to London in three weeks.

My father pushes the paper even closer when I take a few more bites of my dinner without commenting. I look up at him, and while I see excitement in his green eyes, I also note something else, urgency. He wants me to go out of town. I can only guess that he's hoping this school trip will help me fully break from Ethan and our past together. "I know what you're trying to do—"

"Didn't you say London is where your friend Drystan moved?" Mom interrupts me, keeping me from finishing.

"Yes," I say, then quietly chew my way through several forkfuls of food so I can think.

School trips usually keep students on a very strict tour schedule. I don't know if I'll be allowed enough exploring-on-my-own time to get a chance to see Drystan. I was all for going to London until everything happened with Gran. Now, the last thing I want to do is leave Blue Ridge. Gran is still recovering, and Ethan…God, I don't want to think what might happen to him if I'm gone for a week or more. Will his Corvus completely take over? He might be trying to keep me at a distance, but at least if I'm here I can see how he looks everyday and try to gauge how he's doing. I hate feeling so helpless.

"History is there. You must go," Gran says from the entrance to the kitchen.

I blink to see her standing there all wobbly on her own with no wheelchair in sight. "You're up!"

"She insisted that I put the wheelchair away for the evening," Mom says when I move faster than her to help Gran over to sit on one of the stools next to me.

"She's determined. I'll give her that," my father murmurs.

The moment Gran rests her casted arm on the island and I see the strain that putting on a good front is taking on her, I shake my head. "A trip to London is expensive."

"It'll be my gift to you, Nari," my father says. "I'll put any money you use back in your savings account. You've worked very hard and deserve this. This is a great opportunity. You shouldn't pass it up."

"Thanks, Dad, but I've got a lot going on at school, from meetings about colleges with my counselor, to a couple of big tests. It's just not a good time for me."

I'm surprised by the disappointment showing in Gran's face. She seems truly upset that I'm not going. I pat her hand. "This will give me more time to work with you. Lots of Nara/Gran time."

Gran snorts, then shakes her head. "Birds fly home."

One thing I'm starting to understand with Gran is that when she's tired, her progress degrades and she reverts back to gibber-talk, but I can tell she wants me to go too. "No arguing," I say. Kissing her cheek, I stand and sweep up my plate. "And with that, I'm outta here to do homework."

As annoyed as I am with my father for trying yet again to control me and at Ethan for trying to tell me what to do, I put my Corvus ring back on the moment I walk into my bedroom. My family's overall safety is more important than my own need to assert my independence.

While taking a homework break an hour later, I remember

Mom's request to see the video Dad made for me. My stomach churning, I slide the CD from between the two books on my desk, my fingers tight on the jewel case. Maybe if I watch it again, it won't be as bad as I think and I'll feel better about letting Mom watch it alone. I open the case and stare in shock at the ruined disk. Someone has taken keys or something sharp and scratched the CD. *Who would do this and why?* I quickly close the case and set the CD inside my desk, my face hot with worry. Since I didn't want her to see it without me, Mom will never believe that I didn't ruin it on purpose.

Ugh, I need a distraction from my worries. Maybe Drystan's in a better frame of mind. He doesn't answer my attempt to video chat, so I sigh and turn back to my homework. A couple minutes later, the ringing sound of a video call comes through. I quickly push aside my homework and pull my laptop in front of me. I don't recognize the avatar or handle, but for all I know Drystan has changed his or is using a friend's phone.

The last face I expect to see on my screen is an older man with gray hair, his salt and pepper goatee curved with his greeting. "Hello, Nara."

*Why is Drystan's uncle calling me? I'm sure running the Order's sanctuary keeps him super busy. Oh God, is he calling because something has happened?* "Hi, Mr. Wicklow. Is everything okay with Drystan?"

He lifts his hands, his tone calm. "Drystan's fine. He's not here right now, but when I heard someone trying to video conference him just now, I popped in to see who it was. I want to know what friends he's been spending his time with lately."

I furrow my brow. "He told me about a couple of Paladins, a guy and girl, he'd made friends with. Maybe they're out together?"

"Sadly, I know for a fact he's not with Phillip and Chloe." Mr. Wicklow's upbeat expression fades. "A tragic accident happened last week. Phillip's ability to heat objects with his mind got out of hand. A fire started in his room, raging out of control and he was killed. We've asked Chloe to stay here in the sanctuary under constant care while we work with her to teach her how to control her suddenly growing gift. She isn't as potentially lethal, but we're erring on the side of caution after what happened to Phillip."

"How horrible," I say, my heart sinking. "Are you sure Drystan's okay?"

Drystan's uncle's short-cropped hair shifts forward with his creased brow. "Phillip's death was a blow to all of us, but Drystan took it especially hard. He's been spending more time away from the sanctuary lately. I have no idea who his friends are or where he goes. His mother feels that he just needs time to process. Of course, I would prefer that he do that here."

I sigh my frustration that I haven't been able to connect with Drystan. The last thing I want to do is worry his uncle as to what I heard from Drystan in the hall at school. "I wish there was some way I could help. It's times like this when the distance seems especially far."

"I know a visit from you would cheer him right up," Mr. Wicklow says, nodding. "Have you considered my invitation? Maybe you could come sooner? How about over spring break? Drystan would love to see you and take you on a tour. You should bring Ethan too. His Corvus might be resistant. I know how stubborn they can be, but I know he would find the Order's sanctuary interesting, if for no other reason than to see the place that nurtures Paladins who can make Corvus' lives easier."

His expectant expression ups my concern and my dinner conversation with my parents flickers through my mind. With all he has going on, Drystan really could use a friend right now. I know he would do everything he could to be here for me if he thought I needed him. I'll have to push harder for him to get in touch with me.

"My history class will be taking a trip to London in a few weeks, Mr. Wicklow. The student tour stuff is usually pretty packed in with very little breaks, but I'll check if my parents will let me come a day early so I can spend a bit of time with Drystan at the sanctuary."

A pleased smile curves his lips. "I hope you'll do your best to convince them. My nephew misses his friends, but especially you. Carrying Corvus secrets around can feel like a heavy load at times, especially for someone who's stubbornly keeping himself on the outside. Call me at the number I gave you once you know your plans. You and Ethan surprising Drystan would be brilliant."

I don't miss his uncle's disappointment that Drystan still hasn't decided if he'll become a Paladin. A surprise visit would be fun. "If I'm able to visit, it'll just be me."

Mr. Wicklow's eyebrows hike. "Ethan wouldn't want to come?"

I know cost would be an issue for Ethan, but that was before he started distancing himself from me anyway. "He, um…has a lot going on right now, and I'm pretty sure the last place he'd want to visit is the sanctuary," I say with an apologetic shrug.

"Ah, I see. But no matter how he feels, I've seen how protective he is. He wouldn't want you coming to London without him," Mr. Wicklow says with a knowing nod.

*That's a very good point.* I offer a hopeful half-smile. "We'll see. I'll be sure to let you know if the London trip is a go and whether my parents will let me come a bit early."

"Wonderful, Nara. I look forward to hearing from you."

Once I hang up, I take a deep breath. With my parents' heavy push for London during dinner, I'm pretty sure that convincing them to let me go a day early to see Drystan won't be an issue. But even better, I now have a plan that Ethan can't ignore.

# Chapter Nine

*Nara*

"You're Matt's least favorite person at the moment." Lainey nudges her tray against mine, nearly knocking off my milk as she steps into place next to me in the lunch line.

I glance over my shoulder until I see Matt's blond head. He's already sitting at the table he normally shares with Lainey, but he's definitely giving me an impatient look. "I haven't had a chance to talk to Drystan," I say to Lainey. "I promise I'll ask him to call Matt when I finally get through to him myself."

"That's not it." Lainey huffs as we move into place to pay. Reaching around me, she tells the thin cashier with a bored look on her face to swipe her card twice for both our lunches. I grunt, but Lainey just waves and slides her card back into her purse after the lady returns it. "It's faster, Nara. Matt wants to talk to you about London. He's so mad that he's not in Mr. Hallstead's class."

I didn't think about how Matt might react when he learned I would be going to London. There's only one person I wanted to notice when I went up to the front of History class and signed the interest form for the trip. And so far, Ethan hasn't said a word to me. Two classes, two locker visits and now lunch without a peep from him. Did I overestimate his interest that I'll be going to the country where a library claims to have another copy of the raven book that demon stole from us? Just because Drystan couldn't find it, doesn't mean that the book isn't there. He's not as determined as I am.

The idea that another book might exist—hopefully one with a scroll in the spine like the paper that disintegrated on me—makes my heart race. If there isn't a scroll, I can only hope that holding the book in my hands will trigger a memory of what that paper looked like.

Just when Lainey and I sit down with Matt, my phone beeps with an incoming text.

*Ethan: Don't go there.*

I gape at my phone, knowing that I'd blocked him.

"Who's texting you?" Lainey asks, but Matt talks over her.

"Is it Drystan? Tell his sorry ass to call me."

I shake my head. "No, it's not Drystan, but trust me if I don't hear from him soon, I'm going to personally kick his butt from all of us once I get to London."

While Matt rambles on about the many texts he's sent Drystan with no response, I check the settings on my phone for Ethan's contact info. His number is no longer showing as blocked, but I know I blocked him. Even though I'm relieved that he's texting, I'm still annoyed as to how he managed to unblock himself, so I pretend ignorance.

*Me: Go where?*

*Ethan: Graphic novels. Trust me, they're not your thing.*

Huh? What is he talking about?

"Is that Ethan?" Lainey asks, her lip curling with irritation. "He's getting on my last nerve lately. Did you know he ditched meeting up with Matt last night at McCormicks for some *thing* he couldn't miss? I just don't get him."

"It's cool, Lane. He said it was important. I still hung out and enjoyed Weylaid's sound."

"You should've called me." She frowns her worry. "And here I thought you were getting in some 'guy' time."

*What was so important last night that Ethan ditched Matt?* Oh…that would've been standing there waiting with Houdini until I arrived. Oh boy. Another text from Ethan pops up on my screen.

*Ethan: Especially now.*

Of course graphic novels aren't my thing. They're his. But why does 'now' matter? Ah…that's a signal!

I quickly stand. "Ugh, I just remembered that I'm supposed

to meet with the teacher during lunch to go over a couple math problems I missed on my last quiz."

"So can I have this then?" Matt says as he reaches for my tray before my chair is fully pushed back.

I laugh, gesturing to my untouched food. "Yes. Am I forgiven?"

"Nowhere near." He downs my milk in one quick gulp, then mock-glares at me. "Tell Drystan I'm so pissed at him that I might not answer his call if he ever bothers to 'ring' me."

"Really?" I say, my eyebrows shooting up.

Lainey bursts out laughing. "Of course not! I swear the way he's talking about missing Drystan, I'm starting to get a little jealous. Just get that Welsh boy to call his friend!"

Nodding, I leave the cafeteria and head for the first place Ethan brought up the subject of graphic novels.

Mrs. Wilhelm, the new librarian is busy with a student when I walk in, so I immediately go for the fantasy book section. I turn down the aisle to find Ethan leaning against a shelf, casually flipping through a graphic novel.

I start to speak, but he shakes his head and presses his mouth together. Setting the book on the shelf, he jerks his chin for me to follow him into a quiet space between extra tall bookshelves in the back corner.

The moment he turns to face me, I let my annoyance at myself for trailing behind him, inhaling his amazing smell like a sappy puppy, come through in my crisp tone. "So now we're talking in code? How did you manage to unblock yourself?"

"You got the message. That's all the matters."

I catch the flicker of confusion in his blue eyes, but he quickly shrugs it off and slides his hands into his jean pockets. As much as my heart is racing while standing here with him and talking in low tones, I'm also angry. How can he act like he doesn't want to touch me? My fingers are twitching so much that I have to curl them into my palms. If he can pretend, so can I. Whatever he has to say, I'm not going to make it easy. "I'm only here because I want to know *how*, Ethan," I whisper.

"Don't go to London," he says, ignoring my question.

I roll my eyes and fold my arms. "You took yourself out my life, so you don't get any say in what I do."

When he doesn't look the least bit regretful, that pisses me off. I start to walk away, but Ethan grabs my elbow, his grip unyielding. "This isn't a joke, Nara."

"I'm well aware what's at stake. Now that the book is gone, I have a responsibility to find out if a second one truly exists in that London library. Whether you want to admit it or not, the demons might finally get the upper hand over your Corvus if they discover a secret we never did within its pages."

He smirks "That will never happen.

I don't care if it's Ethan's or his Corvus' arrogance bleeding through. I snort. "Cocky much?"

"Have Drystan go back and search the library for you," he says, his eyebrows pulling together.

"Drystan's got enough on his plate."

Ethan instantly tenses. "In what way? Has he become a Paladin?"

"No." I'm not going into detail about Drystan's issues. For all I know it could be his uncle's perception and not reality. I can't mistake the drunken Drystan I overheard, but maybe there is another explanation. "The book is my responsibility." I pull free of his hold. "There's only one way to find out. I'm going to London."

I pivot away, but Ethan moves so fast, he's blocking my path. "If you're going to be stubborn, then you won't go to London without knowing how to protect yourself. I'll continue the defensive training that Drystan started with you. Meet me at Studder's gym at six."

*Ugh, what terrible timing.* "I can't tonight. I promised Lainey I'd go shopping with her."

"Reschedule," he says in a clipped tone. "From now until you leave, training is your only priority."

The strong, independent girl in me wants to tell him to shove his attempt to dictate my entire schedule, but I keep my mouth shut, because this is exactly what I hoped would happen: Me, him… working together. It's a step in the direction of finding out the book's secrets and hopefully helping the Master Corvus acknowledge himself.

When I nod and start to go around him, Ethan clasps my arm. He leans close, and my heart jerks so hard I'm surprised he can't feel my whole body vibrating as his warm breath stirs my hair near my ear. "Make sure you're not followed to the gym. No one can know that we're working together."

Even though he's being all business, I suppress a shudder at the feel of him so close. "But—"

"*No* one, Nara. Understand?"

I nod, frustrated that I can't at least tell Lainey. She has really jumped on the "dislike Ethan" bandwagon. Considering she doesn't have all the facts, I understand how she feels, but the quickest way to get her to chill about him would be if I told her he was helping me with my defense lessons.

I'm nervous about my upcoming training with Ethan this evening, so after school I drive a bit out of my way to my favorite carwash place. There's just something about a carwash that I find relaxing. I love the flashing neon lights and the pretty sudsy rainbow of colors that splatter on my windshield while wonderful citrusy scents waft through the vents, but if I'm being honest with myself…it's the five minutes of quiet space where I let my foot off the gas and total control is taken away as someone else drives that settles my anxious thoughts.

I pay at the drive-up kiosk, then pull into line behind another car. The lanky-haired carwash attendant directs my wheels onto the automated skids, then picks up a fire-extinguisher sized spray container. Lifting a wand, he applies a thin layer of suds across the passenger side window, the back and then along my driver's side glass.

Movement in my window draws my attention.

I glance at the glass and see a circular shape being drawn in the foam. My stomach tenses when I realize that I can't see anyone touching the glass. Dread knots my belly as a sudsy version of the Corvus symbol forms on my window. Once the symbol appears to complete itself, my widened gaze locks with the carwash attendant standing outside my car, and my pulse jumps into panic mode at the glare of recognition in his gaze.

I don't have time to curse Fate for antagonizing the demon, because he reaches for my car door handle at the same time I hit the door lock button. My heart hammers like a cornered rabbit's as he sneers at me. Growling his frustration, he moves with lightning speed, grabbing the spray container from the ground. The moment he lifts it in the air, my car jerks forward into the carwash where the massive sponges and sprayers fold around my car.

Panting, I try to look and see if he followed me into the cramped space, but pastel suds splatter and spread all over my windows at once, blocking my view. I'm trapped in this peaceful, sweet-smelling pocket, waiting for the carwash to end and the violence to begin. My pulse races and I'm breathing so hard, I'm worried that I might actually pass out.

When I lean forward to attempt to calm my breathing, my phone rings.

I quickly punch the answer button. "Ethan, I can't see him—"

"Where are you?" he commands in a sharp tone.

"I'm at the Clean and Go carwash."

"Where's the demon? Is he in there with you?"

I jerk my gaze around once more. "I don't see him, but he'll be waiting—"

"As soon as the wash ends and your wheels are free, hit the gas and get out of there,."

"But—"

"I don't care if he's standing in your way, gun it. Then take the highway to Bayberry Farm."

"You mean that abandoned farmstead?"

"The carwash isn't far from there and there will be less chance of other people getting hurt. Hang up and get ready."

The click of silence on the other end of the phone kicks me into gear. As the industrial dryer moves across the front of my car, I can see the guy standing directly in my path with a piece of pipe in his hand. I swallow hard as I feel the equipment release my tires. Setting my phone down, I put my left foot on the brake and shift the gear from Neutral to Drive.

The demon smacks the pipe into his hand, leering gleefully at me.

Palms sweating, I grip the steering wheel and push on the gas, revving the engine to warn him that I'm not messing around.

The man ignores his manager, who's standing in the background at the doorway of the building. He's yelling for his employee to move away from the carwash exit.

Instead, as the industrial dryer arm begins to lift, the carwash guy holds three greasy fingers up, then slowly counts them down.

Three

Two.

One.

He might be blowing off his boss, but he can't ignore the raven suddenly dive-bombing him. The guy swings the metal pipe wildly and manages to clip an edge of Patch's wing.

I scream, worried for the bird who's still trying to protect me despite taking a hit. That pipe might *kill* Patch at any moment.

The instant the dryer arm elevates, I lift my left foot off the brake and slam my right foot down on the gas. My wheels squeal and my stomach clenches at the idea of hitting a person with my car, but I don't let up the pressure. I'll defend that bird as hard as he does me.

When the demon dives out of the way at the last second, I sigh my relief at the near miss, then press my lips together when I see him bolting toward a truck in my rearview mirror. I lay on the brakes briefly to make sure I'm not going to hit any oncoming traffic, then gun on the gas once more.

The demon wastes no time coming after me, so I keep my foot down and my eyes on the road, hoping to put distance between us.

While speeding along the open highway toward the farm, I can't help but wonder if Fate has a death wish, or if he only pretended to give up his goal of destroying me, and this whole idea he concocted is really a two-birds-one-stone kind of deal for him.

Ethan calls and I quickly answer, putting him on speaker. "He's right behind me."

"I see you. Speed up."

"This is the last push I've got." I grind the pedal to the floor and squint far into the distance, looking for Ethan's car. Nothing. I quickly glance in the rearview mirror, but his shiny black car isn't following the beat-up red truck a few car lengths behind me. *How can he see me? Where is he?*

I dart a glance at a cloud of red dust surrounding an approaching car. From a dirt road ahead of me, a dark car flies directly toward the highway. My heart races, but I keep my foot pinned to the floor. Just as I pass the dirt road, the Mustang bursts onto the highway directly behind me. I glance in the rearview. Wheels squealing, Ethan jerks his car to a dead stop, facing the on-coming truck.

I hit my brakes and come to a jerky stop. Panting and shaky, I spin to see the guy's truck brake hard.

His truck fishtails as he tries to gain control of his vehicle. Panicking, I yell for Ethan to reverse his car out of the way, but he doesn't. His brake lights aren't even on. I grip the back of my seat, my stomach churning. Shit. That truck can't stop in time.

But the truck comes to a hard, lurching halt no more than five feet from Ethan's car.

Ethan doesn't even hesitate. He jumps out of his car, then kicks the door closed with his foot while a sword begins to lengthen behind his hand, forming from the tattoo moving along his arm and down his wrist. The lanky-haired guy curls his lip in disgust behind his windshield, then puts a hand out his window. The second I see what looks like a handgun, it takes all of my willpower not to lay on my horn, but I don't want to distract Ethan. I have to trust that he sees the gun too.

The second the guy pops off a couple of shots, Ethan moves with smooth, lightning speed, using his sword to deflect the bullets. The moment one of his own bullets whizzes past him, the guy throws his gun down and quickly puts his car in gear, hits the gas and begins to back up at a rapid pace.

Ethan spins his sword once, then slams his foot on the ground.

The ground rumbles, my car shakes, but most of the impact must've gone forward, because the truck's front end actually comes off the ground and swerves a bit before the guy gets control once more. As he continues screeching backward, Ethan calmly rolls his head from one shoulder to the other, then takes two running steps and leaps impossibly high and wide. Landing on the truck's hood, he slams his sword straight through the windshield and into the guy's chest.

Holy shit!

A few seconds later, the truck rolls to a stop in the middle of the quiet highway. It's now eerily quiet, empty. I don't know what happened, but I know Ethan wouldn't have turned that person to dust unless absolutely necessary.

I slowly turn my car around and drive up beside the Mustang. Once Ethan moves the empty truck to the side of the road, he walks over to my side of the car.

Ethan's face is set in hard lines and I can see the question in his eyes, so I answer. "He saw the Corvus symbol and came after me."

Glancing down at my hands still wrapped around the steering wheel, Ethan stares at my ring and shakes his head. "It's supposed to protect you, not make you a target. I thought I had the jeweler engrave it small enough for most people not to notice."

Regret and other unfathomable thoughts swirl in the blue-black gaze scanning my face, and as much as I desperately desire to have him back in my life, the last thing I want is for his need to constantly protect me be the only reason why. Not only would that crush my heart, but that would give Fate exactly what he wants. After the narcissistic entity painted a target on me, I refuse to keep his involvement a secret.

"It wasn't my ring. Fate drew a Corvus symbol in the soapy foam on my car window right in front of a demon working at the carwash."

"What?" He curls his hands into fists, his eye color shifting to all black. "Fate knows what'll happen to him if he attempts to hurt you."

I hold my hands up. "There's no need to go after Fate."

"He nearly got you killed. Why are you protecting him?" Ethan asks, his gaze narrowed in suspicion.

"I'm not," I huff. "Trust me. He's done messing with me."

Ethan frowns and crosses his arms, his biceps flexing. "And you know this how?"

"Because he only did it to draw you back into my life. He thinks I help balance your Corvus."

"You spoke with Fate that day you removed your ring," he states in a flat tone, his jaw muscle flexing. "You took it off on purpose and what…took a nap?"

I lift my chin. "I figured Fate wouldn't be dumb enough to attack me after his last encounter with your Corvus."

"His arrogance is only surpassed by the spirit's squatting in my body. You know this!"

"I needed to talk to Rave. I thought I could help him understand that he can't keep hiding from who he really is."

"Nara—" Ethan pauses and closes his eyes, his body completely still as he takes several breaths.

Coming clean about Fate probably wasn't the best idea. The way Ethan is clearly trying to keep his cool, his whole body tensing so much he's starting to shake, makes me feel like crap. I fold my fingers around the TTTWFO tattoo on his arm. "I'm sorry, Ethan. I know trying to reach Rave through your dreams was a mistake. That's why I put the ring back on. The fact that we'll be training should be enough to make Fate back off." Ethan needs to believe Fate will leave me alone now. I refuse to be responsible for his Corvus ending Fate's existence.

Lifting his head, Ethan exhales slowly, his gaze locking with mine. "I can't do this if I know you're not safe, Nara. You understand that?"

Many unsaid thoughts lurk in his eyes, but understanding finally dawns and I lift my hand away. He's telling me that I need to accept that we truly can't be together. While my heart feels as if it's being shredded to bits, I blink back the mist clouding my vision. "Yes, I get it. I'll be at the gym on time."

# Chapter Ten

*Ethan*

As Nara stares after me, I force myself to walk back to my car with determined strides. Which is far harder than it looks with an angry spirit bellowing in my ear. The pain in my head is so excruciating I nearly drop to my knees. Twice.

*Don't you dare walk away! You heard her. She wants to talk to me.*

*She can't talk to you,* I snap as I get in my car and slam my door shut behind me. Since Nara needs my dreams to speak to the Corvus...I can at least control that.

The spirit waits until Nara drives off to continue his rant. I feel his tense resentment as he stares after her car's taillights. *Just admit you're doing this because you're afraid her father will file that report. Acknowledge that you're a coward, so I can fully stamp out the rest of you. You are not worthy.*

I ignore the Corvus' snide comments as I start my engine and head back to town. He's trying to rile me and if I haven't learned anything in all my interactions with him, it's that I have to keep myself in constant check. Every time I relax or allow myself to get emotional, the Corvus gains another millimeter of control. I sense him worming his way into my DNA, imprinting himself. As if he's trying to completely absorb and rewire me.

When my chest puffed with pride as I took out that demon, I knew it wasn't my pride...it was the Corvus', but the physical reactions occurred as if they were mine. The Corvus was proud that Nara got to see him defend her. I wasn't surprised by his arrogance and swift attack on the demon, but when the man suddenly convulsed from the force of the sword's blow, and his body shifted on the sword, turning to ash...the Corvus' smirk of satisfaction set me on edge. Yes, the person was a nasty individual, but the fact the Corvus felt no guilt over the man's unintended death worries me.

I'm pretty sure Nara couldn't see everything that happened from her position in her car, but the Corvus' powers are definitely growing stronger, right along with his need to showoff.

Not only did he stomp the ground to disrupt the demon's flight, but the moment I jumped down from the truck after the demon was gone, the Corvus forced my left hand to grasp the truck's wheel well.

*Put it down,* I commanded as he started to lift the truck off the ground. *The demon is gone. This is overkill.* Nara didn't need to know just how reckless he had become.

The spirit's amused laughter vibrated in my eardrums. My arm muscles continued to tense, my fingers already bending the metal. I felt his intention to send the vehicle rolling into the open field across the street like a run away tumbleweed. The destructive desire vibrated through my body as if it were my own, even though the thoughts weren't mine.

So I focused my mind on the one thing that has kept me firmly in control whenever he started acting like a kid with a new toy. I recalled the warm press of Nara laying her head on my chest and her sweet smelling hair brushing my jaw as she curved her leg over mine. This was where I went in my head...a place that the Corvus couldn't see. The spirit hated whenever I did that. An arrogant bit of satisfaction flickered through me that I managed to knock him out of control without him knowing how I did it.

The truth is, I might be able to regain control of his actions for now, but he's challenging me more and more. Keeping my mind highly focused is a requirement every single day. But the one downside of partitioning my thoughts from the Corvus is that it's a two-way street; his are also kept from me. I don't have a clue as to his motivations.

I can guess what he's thinking, but the Corvus is ancient. I can't come close to understanding the emotionless, logic-filled thoughts that rumble around in his elevated, spiritual mind.

The second Nara said she had tried to reach him, the Corvus snapped to attention and a jolt flashed through my body.

*Let me speak to her. Drop your guard.*

Once he had a taste, I knew he wouldn't back off. *No.*

*Do you want her to be unhappy? She needs to speak to me. Let her.*

*No.*

*Your stubbornness needs to end. She deserves so much better than you.*

He continued his rant the entire time Nara and I talked, berating me for my refusal to let him communicate with her. Nara was the only person he even tried to relate to. Why else would an entity, whose sole purpose is to protect mortals from demons, allow himself to be given a name by a mere human, much less insist that I also use it?

Nara is far from insignificant to my Corvus.

His need to be close to her seems to be growing right along with his anger at me for not giving in and letting him have free rein. He's definitely dangerous, but now that Fate is playing games with Nara's life, my internal rage jacks. All this is happening because the spirit inside me won't get with the program and accept who he truly is—omniscient powers and all.

Knowing that I put that shattered look on Nara's face just now crushed a part of my soul. I'll despise myself forever for having to do that to her, but she has to believe that we're done. It's ironic that the Corvus hounding me constantly in her presence is what gave me the strength to resist folding my fingers around hers and asking her forgiveness. The spirit might want her in his life, but she's far safer without him in hers.

Above all else, I must protect her, even from myself.

# Chapter Eleven

*Nara*

After the initial shock of Ethan making it super clear where we stand as a couple, I spend the rest of the afternoon with brewing anger setting in. Once darkness falls, I tell my family I'm heading to the library. Thankfully Dad had a late meeting at the school. The last thing I want is the third degree from him. Mom absently waves goodbye from cleaning dishes at the sink, but Gran silently raises her eyebrows once her gaze sweeps past my backpack, long sweater and black leggings, to my workout tennis shoes.

Snapping my seatbelt around the zip-up thermal shirt I have on underneath the sweater, I drive a circuitous route to the gym with gritty determination fueling me.

The last thing I expected was to get a video call from Drystan right as I pull into the gym's parking lot.

"Hey, stranger!" I say, holding my phone up so I can see him better. Only Drystan's screen is completely blacked out. "Wait... why can't I see you?"

Letting out a low laugh, Drystan snorts. "Because I'm knackered and it's dark in my room. But I can see you. That's all that matters. Where are you anyway?"

I glance behind me at the stand of trees that line the back of the gym. I start to tell him, but then remember my promise to Ethan. "I'm running errands and just pulled off into a random parking spot when you called me." I hate that I can't see his face and crinkle my nose, feeling goofy just looking at myself. "So are you going to tell me what's going on with you? I got a 'mental message' from you the other day while I was at school. You didn't sound like you were in a good way."

Drystan heaves a sigh and then flips on a light switch. Digging his fingers into his spiked light brown hair, he shakes his head. "Sorry, Nara. I didn't know that I was broadcasting. I'd just found out that one of my friends died and I needed to get away from the sanctuary."

I'm glad that I can finally see him, but he looks like he hasn't slept much. I feel so bad that he lost a friend. I open my mouth to say something when he says, "And I feel partially to blame. I was the one encouraging him to see how far he could take his powers. Yes, his ability to super heat things could be considered dangerous, but he'd been warming food and lighting candles and such with his mind for years. I know setting his room on fire was an accident, but yeah, it's been hard this past week."

"It's not your fault, Drystan. I'm so sorry that you lost a friend. That's truly horrible, but you didn't make him experiment in an unsafe environment. You were just excited for him."

"Yeah well, I'll still always feel guilty. I definitely encouraged him and Chloe."

"Is your other Paladin friend okay?"

"I haven't seen Chloe since Phillip's funeral. One of the main instructors is keeping her schedule queued up with carefully monitored experiments to control the strength of her auditory power until she can learn to fully manage it. At least Warren's someone I trust to work with her. He's well-respected here." He shrugs. "'Nuff about me. How are you?"

I decide to skip telling him about Gran. I know the subject of demon possession would upset him, so I just say, "My Gran moved in with us and my dad and mom seem to be getting along well."

Drystan smiles, then his eyebrows pull together. "What about the Dark One? That Corvus had better be treating you well."

The last thing Drystan needs to hear is that Ethan and I aren't dating, especially since I plan to visit him in a couple of weeks. I know he wanted more between us than friendship, so I don't want to give him false hope. "Ethan's been busy doing Corvus things, but enough about me, I wanted to let you know that…drum roll…I'll be coming to London on a school trip soon. I'm planning to come a day early so I can see you and tour the sanctuary."

Drystan sits up, his green gaze full of light. "Are you serious? How soon?"

I nod. "Two weeks! Isn't that exciting? I've never been to London. I'm looking forward to visiting the city and seeing you."

Rubbing his hands together, he grins. "This is brilliant, and the best news I've heard since I got here. Be sure to text me your arrival dates and itinerary."

"I will. I need to go. I have an appointment that I'm already a few minutes late for. I'm so glad we got to talk. I'm looking forward to seeing you and touring the sanctuary to see where Paladins live."

"Take care of yourself, Nara. I can't wait to see you."

"You too. Oh, and Drystan…"

"Yeah?"

"Please, for the love of my sanity, contact Matt. He truly misses you and would never forgive me if I didn't get a promise from you to call him."

He sighs and rubs his forehead. "I know. I've been terrible about keeping in touch. I'll ring him."

I nod my appreciation. "Night, Dryst."

"Night, Nara."

Feeling better that he seems to be doing okay, I smile when I hang up. Of course I lower my phone in time to see Ethan's frowning at me before he closes the gym door behind him. Great.

Ethan looks up from his position in the middle of the gym as I open the door. "It's not too late to change your mind about London. If your video chatting with friends cuts into your training time, you're obviously not focused on this."

He doesn't need to know that Drystan is having a hard time adjusting. If he did, he'd insist that I not go. "That was a call I needed to take," I say lightly and walk inside. "Why are the lights so low in here?"

Turning his back to me, Ethan finishes sliding a mat into place, creating a large square in the huge open gym. "No one can know what we're doing."

I force my gaze up from appreciating how well his athletic pants fit his butt, past the play of muscles under the sword tattoo slicing diagonally across his bare back to the dim glow coming from the lights above. "Are these emergency backup lights? Do we even have permission to be here?"

"I chose this place because no one is scheduled to be here for a few weeks, but using the full lights will draw too much attention." Ethan lifts a two-inch wide, five-foot long wooden stick from the mat with his bare foot, easily tossing it up to his hand. "Take off your jacket and shoes."

I hadn't planned on removing my workout jacket, but I smirk and tug it off while I step out of my shoes and socks.

Ethan's jaw muscle jumps as his gaze glides over my body— from my bare midriff, to my cropped sports top, to my face. Instead of saying anything, he just tosses the stick to me.

Capturing it, I grasp the center and frown when he bends to pick up a matching one from the stack of wood weapons, including bats and swords, he'd brought in to train with. "Why are we training with sticks and swords? It's not like demons carry around swords on their backs."

"Ethan adopts a ready stance and lifts his own wooden stick, then taps mine silently telling me to do the same. "Tomorrow... wear a T-shirt."

"Only if you do." I smirk and give him a smartass salute, then mimic his stance.

His gaze narrows on me. "Drystan had the right idea training you how to evade demons using parkour moves. If you're backed into a corner, your goal is to use anything you can find to keep some distance between yourself and the demon until you can get away." He leans forward, knocking the end of my stick with a hard, fast swipe of his.

"Sometimes running isn't an option. And the only way is to face your opponent," I say, swinging my stick back around to whack hard against his.

He holds my gaze for a split second, then surprises me with a fast hit that knocks my weapon against my shin. "Demons are too fast and strong for you to even consider trying to fight them. So don't," he finishes as he moves to swing toward my shoulder.

Taking a firmer grip on the stick, I counter his move, knocking his weapon away.

"Come on, Nara. Show me you can do this," he challenges,

stepping forward with an onslaught of rapid hits. I move backward, countering his attack while breathing hard to keep up with his relentless pace.

"Slow down," I snap. Tapping out three good jabs of my own, I look for an opening, then aim for his belly.

He knocks my jab aside with a fluid upward swing. "Do you think demons will give you a chance for a breather?"

Ethan spends the next hour drilling me, using various weapons until my arms feel like jelly.

When I drop the wooden sword on the mat and declare, "That's enough for tonight," Ethan leans over and picks up the long two-inch wide stick we'd started the hour with once more and tosses it my way.

"You're not done yet."

"I'm not kidding. I'm toast, Ethan."

Picking up his stick, he shakes his head and quickly raps my knuckles with it.

Gritting my teeth, I ignore the pain and draw on the anger and hurt I felt earlier today and go after him with renewed force. Sending him backward with a barrage of rapid-fire hits.

When the mats under Ethan start to slide apart, his feet quickly separating, I take advantage of his unsteady footing and jab the end of my stick into his shoulder.

The moment he goes down, I step between his splayed legs and hold my stick against his chest, gloating, "And the student schools the teacher."

A split-second later, I'm flat on my back with Ethan straddling my hips, his stick hovering across my throat. "Never get close to your opponent, Nara. If I were a demon you'd be dead."

I vaguely recall his legs tangling in mine to take me down…but right now, I don't care how I got here. My vision blurs as I try to speak, but I can only gasp as I try to take a breath.

"Shit! I'm sorry, Nara." Ethan throws his stick and moves off me. Lightly pressing his hand to my belly, he holds my panicked gaze. "Push your stomach out as you take a deep breath, then try to suck in as you breathe out. It'll force your diaphragm to start working faster."

White-hot heat flashes through me as I struggle to focus on his instructions, but his touch at least takes away the sheer terror that

I'm going to die. After a few more painful seconds, I'm finally able to take deep breaths once more.

"Are you okay now?" Ethan's looking down at me, concern etched on his face as his thumb strokes along my skin.

Heat curls in my belly at his touch. The last thing I want him to do is stop, but I nod and take a couple more deep breaths. "I'd forgotten how much it hurts to have the wind knocked out of you."

Silence descends as his gaze holds mine. For a brief second I think I see the same yearning in the blue depths that I feel every time we're together. I miss him so much. I start to speak when a glowing light shines where his hand lies on my stomach. Our gazes lock and I know he's remembering that the only time that has happened between us was when passion was high.

Just as hope blooms in my heart, Ethan jerks his hand away. Standing, he pulls me to my feet and says in a gruff tone, "You're right. It's time to go. I have an appointment that I can't be late for."

His tone is so brisk and matter-of-fact that I wonder if I imagined what I saw in his eyes just now. I glance down at my stomach, and when I don't see a trace glowing handprint—which has always happened before—my excitement dies. Did I imagine it? Is my wishful thinking playing tricks on me?

When I look back up at Ethan, he's already collecting the practice weapons. As I help him load them in an oversized canvas bag, I can't help but wonder where he's going. *Who is he spending so much time with?*

Zipping the bag closed, Ethan nods to the back entrance. "You go first. I'll follow in a few minutes. Meet me back here tomorrow night at the same time ready to work."

"See you then." I keep my tone light when all I want to do is ask about his *appointment.*

I leave first, but I just drive around the corner to a side road and turn off my lights. I don't care if it makes me lame that I plan to follow my ex-boyfriend to his secret rendezvous; I have to know where he's going. And who he's meeting.

He'd better not be seeing someone else or I'll insist we use real weapons for tomorrow night's lesson.

The last place I expect to follow him is to Barboursville. But when Ethan's Mustang turns down the road that leads to my aunt's house, then he zips up Aunt Sage's driveway, I drive past it and pull over to the side of the road, my heart hurting as I shake my head. *He's cut me out of his life, yet he has appointments with my aunt? Why is he here? And why hasn't my aunt told me?*

After an hour passes, Ethan walks outside. He faces the doorway and pets my aunt's dogs, who're running all around him, while he talks to her for a minute. I can't see my aunt from this distance, but once he gets in his car and heads back toward town, I text my mom.

*Me: I'm at Aunt Sage's. I'll be home later.*

*Mom: Your dad stopped by. I'll be sure to keep him here for a bit longer so you can have some alone time with Sage. I know you miss your girl visits with her.*

*Me: Thanks Mom!*

Ten minutes is about all I can wait until I pull into my aunt's driveway. The moment she opens the door, my aunt's auburn eyebrows shoot up in surprise. "Inara! I wish you had called ahead, I could've made a pie."

My plans to confront my aunt are completely obliterated as I blink at her in shock. "You cut your hair off...all of it."

Laughing softly, she self-consciously runs her fingers through her pixie-style cut. "Yes, I did. Do you hate it?"

I swallow and shake my head. "No, it looks fantastic on you." Actually, now that she's ditched her flowing maxi dresses for distressed skinny jeans, a soft Kelly green cashmere sweater, cat-eyed eyeliner and a new haircut, she's gone from attractive to drop dead gorgeous, looking much younger than her age. With my hair in a ponytail, no makeup and workout clothes, I feel frumpy in comparison. My brain is suddenly going in a direction it wasn't before, leaving the questions I was going to ask about Ethan stuck painfully in my throat. "I hope you don't mind that I just stopped by. If it's a bad time, we can schedule a time to meet in town."

"Don't be silly, sweetie. I miss not seeing you. Just let me make a quick phone call and then we can chat."

I follow Aunt Sage into the kitchen, her Jack Russell, Rottweiler, and Shepard dogs trotting along and nudging my hands for attention. While she picks up her phone and dials a number, I give Bo, Luke, and Duke lots of pets and kisses.

"Hey, I hope you don't mind, but my niece just showed up. I haven't seen her in a while and I'd like to catch up with her."

When she pauses while the person on the other end speaks, I

jerk my gaze up and jiggle my keys, thumbing toward her front door to let her know I can go.

My aunt quickly shakes her head, then smiles broadly at whatever the deep voice—a man—says on the other end. "Thank you for understanding, Russell. I'll bring your favorite by tomorrow. We can eat and talk about the next show coming up."

When she hangs up, my thoughts about Ethan briefly shift to the back of my mind. I grin at her, my eyebrows raised. "You're seeing someone?"

She presses her lips in a rueful smile. "In case you're wondering, I cut my hair and changed my dress style as part of a bet I made with your father. This was *before* I met the hunky guy. Russell and I crossed paths at a tradeshow last week. We had so much in common, we just really hit it off, but since I've got a few projects going right now, I'm trying to take things slow. It's probably a good thing he can't see me tonight."

"What did you have in common with Russell?" I ask as she pulls down a set of coffee cups.

"Decaf?" she asks while reaching inside the cabinet. I nod and she answers, "Russell owns a jewelry store on the downtown mall. He wants to carry some of my pieces in his 'local artists' collection."

"That's wonderful, Aunt Sage!"

She smiles as she measures out the coffee and adds water to the pot. "Maybe, but I turned him down."

"Why? Isn't that what you've always wanted? To be in jewelry stores?"

My aunt pauses while sliding a glass-domed dish across the counter. "I used to think so, but there's something incredibly satisfying about running this business myself. Also, I'd rather just have the relationship part right now without the business stuff getting in the way, you know?"

I nod. Sadly, I have the opposite problem. With Ethan and I, it's all business all the time.

My aunt cuts a slice of chocolate cake with white icing for me, then one for herself. Handing me a fork, she holds onto it when I try to grasp it. "By the way, your dad doesn't know about Russell. I don't want Jonathan getting all protective brother-y and having his DC people run a background check on the poor guy. The last thing I want to do is scare him off before he gets to know me."

"I promise I won't tell Dad." When she releases the fork, I take a bite of my cake, then moan at the melt-in-your-mouth dessert. After I down most of the cake, I point to the long, gold chain around her neck with gold fleur-de-lis stations inset with mother-of-pearl. "This is new. Is that one of your designs? Don't you usually work with silver?"

My aunt lifts her necklace. "Russell asked why I didn't offer gold pieces in my store, so I thought I'd see what I could come up with for a new line. Do you like it?"

"Very much. I love how striking yet delicate it looks."

Beaming, my aunt releases her necklace to stand and pour us some coffee. "I can't wait to make something for you in rose-gold. It'll look perfect against your peach-toned skin and blonde hair."

Once she gives me my mug and sits back down with hers, I twirl my fork in the gooey frosting left behind on my plate. Licking it off the tines, I casually ask, "So what other projects are keeping you so busy?"

Aunt Sage's hazel gaze scans my face and she raises an eyebrow. "Did you think I believed that you just *happened* to stop by not long after Ethan left?"

I frown at my aunt. "Are you going to tell me or will I have to drag it out of you?"

My aunt sighs. "After I made those rings for you and Ethan so you could help pull him out of the nightmare dream world he was stuck in while in his coma, I never stopped worrying about him. So when your father told me that he threatened Ethan with a restraining order—" She breaks off and lays her hand over mine when I scowl my anger. "I called Ethan and asked him to come work with me. If I could help him learn to control his dreams, then maybe I could get your father to back off. It's been harder than I expected."

I tense, worried that Ethan has told her about his Corvus and demons. That truth is one my father would never get over. "How has it been harder?"

"I know that Ethan is a good person, but the evil in his dreams is scary, Inara." She squeezes my hand. "Your father told me what he saw in Ethan's dreams, so I understand his concern. Sometimes when Ethan comes to work with me, he looks so tired and drained. I worry for him, but he's as determined as I am to help him learn to control his dream world. I'm happy to report that I think we're making progress. Tonight he seemed especially single-minded in his focus."

Nagging suspicions have hounded me since Ethan pushed me away, but what my aunt just told me worries me deeply. The only reason he would be here working with her isn't to control his dream world like my aunt thinks. It's to control his living one, which centers entirely on one powerful, yet volatile raven spirit.

Ethan thinks he's losing the battle.

"How are you helping Ethan learn to control his dreams?" I ask, trying to keep the rising alarm from showing on my face.

"I'm teaching him lucid dreaming techniques," she says, nodding confidently.

"How does that work? Does he take a nap?"

"No, we work on inducing a dream state while he's awake, using breathing exercises, then layer in visualization techniques. It's a way to settle his mind as he falls asleep. The goal is that when he's in his dream world, he'll be able to maintain that same kind of calm mental state where he can manipulate the world he sees. This will allow him to do reality checks and recognize that it's a dream so he can control the outcome."

As my aunt rattles off more details of breathing techniques, I can't help but wonder: *But how does that help him control his Corvus?*

I spend another forty-five minutes chatting with my aunt, but I have to leave for home before it gets too late.

My father is just pulling into the her driveway when Aunt Sage wraps me into a tight hug and whispers in my ear, "Your father doesn't know about me helping Ethan. For now let's keep that between us."

She pulls away right as my dad walks up the sidewalk. "Come back soon. I've missed you, sweetie."

"I hear you've signed up for the London trip," my father says, a pleased smile on his face.

I shrug. "I gave it more thought and decided you and Mom are right. It'll be great for me to go, but I want to make sure I get to spend some time with Drystan, so I'm going to leave a couple days early and meet my class at the hotel."

My father shakes his head. "You need to go with your school—"

"*Tsk, tsk*, Jonathan. The trip was your idea. You can't dictate every little aspect," Aunt Sage cuts him off. "Inara's almost an adult.

How will she learn if she can't make her own decisions?"

"We're talking about another country," my dad blusters.

"She'll be fine. For all you know she'll decide to go to college abroad. Think of this as a mini test run for her. Now let your daughter get home so Elizabeth doesn't blame me for her arriving home so late."

Dad grunts his agreement. "It is late. Text me when you get home."

"I will. Night you two," I say, relieved my aunt helped sell those extra couple of days in London. I'll need them to see Drystan and to hunt for the other *Ravens* book in the library.

The sound of Houdini's low growl quickly shifting to a whimper wakes me. *Is Patch tapping on the glass? He wasn't around before I went to bed.* I sit up in bed and start to look toward the window, but my gaze snags on Ethan standing just inside my closed door.

Blinking away sleep's grogginess, I wonder if my imagination conjured him. I'm afraid to speak, because I don't want the surreal moment to disappear with reality's intrusion.

But when he takes a step forward, Houdini jumps down and walks over to sniff him. I immediately push the covers back and stand, my long sleep shirt too thin a barrier.

"What's wrong?" I ask, stepping to the middle of my room.

"Nothing." His voice is low and quiet. When he doesn't move any farther or attempt to pet Houdini, my dog loses interest and jumps back up onto the end of my bed. "I just wanted to make sure you're okay…from earlier."

"I'm fine." I sigh that he's chosen to remain by the door, like he plans to bolt any moment. "I stopped by my aunt's this evening…" I trail off, hoping that Ethan will share his reasons for being there too and why.

He tilts his head as if surprised I mentioned her, then slides his hands into his jean pockets. "You're aunt's a very soulful person."

So much for getting him to open up. "Yes, she's beautiful through and through. I was surprised by her super short haircut, but it looks stunning on her." I don't know why I'm rambling, but Ethan's making me nervous. I don't want to read too much into him showing up in the middle of the night. Pushing my bedhead hair away from my face, I grimace. "I wish I could pull off that kind of style."

"Don't cut your hair."

His adamancy makes my heart race. I want to see his eyes, to know if the yearning I've never stopped feeling for him is reflected in his expression right now. I step forward and see an oozing gash across his cheekbone. "What happened!"

"Stay there," he says, but I ignore him and rush forward. Throwing my arms around his solid frame, I bury my face in his leather coat.

He lets out a grunt, and I ease my tight hold, my voice muffled against his chest. *Please tell me about your Corvus, Ethan. Are my aunt's breathing techniques working?* "Whatever it is...let me help you."

Ethan presses his nose in my hair and inhales deeply, then runs his hand lightly down my back. I look up at him and he tucks my hair behind my ear, his expression hard to read.

I'm a little disappointed that my skin doesn't light up as his fingers linger behind my ear, but if he'd just kiss me...I'm sure we'd be as bright as Times Square. My heart is beating triple time. I know he feels it.

"What would you say to my Corvus if you could speak to him?"

I'm so surprised by his question, that instead of the speech I practiced over and over in my head to give to Rave, where I'd tell him that the world depends on him to protect us from Lucifer, I speak from my heart. "I would make him promise that he'd always protect you."

He lowers his hand and frowns. "You're supposed to convince the Corvus how important he is, not talk about me."

"He can't exist without you."

"He's existed for eons, Nara."

"Not physically." Shaking my head, I put my hand on his chest, right over his heart. "He needs this right here, because without it, what is he really fighting for?"

Ethan holds my gaze, then presses his mouth together and takes a step back into the darkness.

Whispering his name in frustration, I follow him into the shadows, but he's gone.

# Chapter Twelve

### *Ethan*

"I leave you alone for one day and look what happens. What did you do at school to deserve this level of defiance?" I ignore the gleeful undertones in the Corvus' snark as I watch Nara toeing off her tennis shoes next to the mat. She walked into the gym right on time this evening wearing skinny jeans and her gorgeous blonde hair bouncing around her shoulders. She knows I love her hair down and now it'll be wafting her sweet, arousing scent all around me every time she moves. But it's the T-shirt with KISS ME, I'M IRISH in bold white letters across a green Saint Patty's Day shamrock on her chest that makes my head feel like it might explode. It's bad enough that the tight black shirt and painted on jeans accentuate every curve in her body, but the whiteness of the letters on her chest are like bright lights and I'm completely drawn in. The fact I'm seeing less skin today is only making me want to see more. Damn, this training session is going to be ten times harder than yesterday's.

*It'll be vastly entertaining, me thinks.*

The spirit begins to chuckle in my ear, but I bark, *Enough*, and close my eyes to cut off the inviting image of Nara's T-shirt riding up her back just above her black jeans as she wiggles out of her socks. Focusing on my breathing, I manage to cut the Corvus off just when he tries to say something else equally annoying.

Once he's no longer harping in my ear, I walk over and drop the bag of weapons next to Nara and cross my arms.

"If you can't come prepared, then that's another indication you should back out of the London trip."

Glancing up, Nara drops the sock she was holding, her eyebrows arched. "For your information, I have two minutes to spare, which makes me *early*. What exactly makes you think I'm not taking it seriously?"

"Those, for starters," I say, gesturing to her pants. "Jeans will restrict your movements."

Looking at me, she hooks her thumb in the waistband and pulls it a good four inches away from her hip. "These are jeggings made to look like jeans. As you can see, they're plenty stretchy."

I cough and nod curtly, relieved when she lets the material snap back into place. The sight of the two thin strings barely holding her underwear together across her hip painfully reminds me how much I miss folding my hands around her curves, and the feel of her soft skin and curved body molding to mine as I pull her close.

*You could press her against you any time you want. You're the only one holding yourself back.* I don't like how the Corvus has wormed his way back into my consciousness, nor do I trust his sudden civil tone. Now he wants us together? What's his angle? He's spirit; it's not like he gets anything physical out of it. *Bite me, you self-important bird. Go back to the dark where you belong. Training Nara isn't a joke. I want to know she can defend herself enough to get away from a demon.*

"Helllllo? Anything else you disapprove of?"

Nara's comment quickly draws me out of the argument in my head. Snapping my gaze to her, I gesture to her hair. "I said to wear it up, remember?"

She lifts her arm and snaps the band around her wrist, then quickly ties her hair back into a ponytail. When I frown, she sighs and tucks the hanging ends inside the elastic, creating a messy bun.

Lowering her arms, she gestures to me. "Just so you know…if your shirt comes off, so does mine."

As the Corvus barks his laughter at her snappy comment, my gaze instantly drops to her chest and the words: KISS ME. "I'll keep my t-shirt on," I say gruffly. I feel every bit of her presence—from the tempting way she smells, to the body heat emanating off her skin—all the way to my toes. I want to touch her so badly my jaw hurts from clenching it so hard.

Lifting the two wooden swords, I toss Nara hers. She easily captures the weapon and smirks as she swipes it once to the left of her body. "I don't understand why we don't use real weapons. Then you could use yours."

*Yeeeeeah, use your sword with Nara. Go ahead. You know you want to.*

"I won't use my sword with you, Nara. Not even mock fighting," I say, while answering the Corvus, *You sound like a dirty old man. Shut the hell up.*

*What?* The Corvus adopts an innocent tone. *I was just agreeing with Nara's suggestion. What were you thinking?*

"Why?" Nara says at the same time she suddenly lunges and knocks my sword out of my loose hold. Glancing at me, she smirks. "You afraid I'll beat you?"

I bend to retrieve the wooden sword from the floor, then shift my gaze briefly to her free hand. "That scar on your palm proves that my sword can hurt you. I refuse to take that kind of risk just to have a more realistic sparring session."

Nara lifts her hand and stares at the raised scar. "It's not like you meant to. My hand just happened to be on your back as you were coming out of your dream in battle mode. It seems to be slowly getting better." Turning it toward me, she continues, "Touch it. It's barely raised any more."

My gaze snaps to hers and I'm instantly on alert. She's definitely in a mood. The scar looks the same to me. *Why is she torturing me like this?* The possessive part of me wants to take her hand and slide my thumb across that bit of marred skin on her palm to assure myself that my touch there still makes her body tingle all over. But the responsible half of me feels relief that she might finally be healing, which means that a Corvus sword couldn't be used to kill her the way Danielle had believed.

So I touch her scar, and even though Nara's fingers involuntarily curl around my thumb, she doesn't utter a gasp or react in any way other than to blink calmly at me and say, "See?"

She might not be affected anymore, but my heart is pounding so hard I can hear every rush of blood in my own veins. Territorial tension rolls slowly through me and a loud grunt of annoyance erupts in my ear.

*See? See! You're seeing what happens when you walk away from someone as special as Nara? She moves on.*

*No,* I bark at the stupid spirit.

*It's your own fault.*

*Stop* talking. I sound menacing even in my own head, but I'm too tense to find the calm I need to shut him out.

*I won't. You need to hear this. You were an idiot to push her away. Now you may never get what you had back.*

The brush of Nara's fingers against mine suddenly silences the Corvus. "Are you all right, Ethan?"

The smart-ass look completely vanishes from her face, worry taking its place.

But my brain is stuck on why the Corvus is now encouraging *us.* I could've sworn the spirit had every intention of taking over my body and replacing me completely. I don't trust his motives at all. What's his end game?

"Ethan?" Nara's hand squeezes mine, bringing my thoughts into focus.

"I'm good," I say, shaking my head to clear it. While the Corvus is gone, I'm determined to focus and give Nara a thorough lesson for the evening. "Let's get started."

### *Nara*

Ethan's entire demeanor changes when I attempt to ask him how he's doing. I can tell he's having some kind of internal struggle, and just as I'm about to ask him about his Corvus, he ruins the moment by lifting his sword and insisting that I do the same.

We spend the next hour working on different defensive techniques with the various weapons. Every move he teaches me is meant to help me gain some distance between myself and my attacker so that I can try to get away, but after a while I start to get tired of his one-sided approach. These training sessions feel too much like a metaphor for our current relationship. Except it's me trying to get close while he continues to keep me as far away as possible.

I can tell he's winding down the lesson, but the last thing I want to do is leave. As frustrated as I am about us, even without using his powers on me, he still calms me in ways I can't explain. When he touched my scar earlier, my knees almost buckled, but I was so irritated at him for just leaving last night, then pretending like nothing had changed at school during the day today, that I wanted him to feel some of what I've felt: rejected. So yeah, I pretended like it didn't affect me at all. Just like I chose my outfit and wore my hair down to tick him off.

Only, none of that seems to work. If anything he grows more distant with each new lesson we go over.

"We should probably wrap it up for the evening," he says, pulling me out of my own head.

Frustrated, I grab the wooden sword, I tag him on the arm, determined to change things up. "Come on. Spar with me a bit longer. But this time, I want you to really spar, Ethan. None of this… defensive stuff."

I smack my sword hard against his hand, making him frown.

He turns his wrist, swiping the sword between us twice. "That's not a good idea."

"Why not?"

Flexing his hand, he curls his fingers tight around the sword's handle. "Because I'm stronger than you without the Corvus' help."

I point my sword at him. "We'll see about that." Holding the blade steady, I angle my chin upward, letting him know I'm serious. "I want you to come after me like you would a demon." *And what was that visit really about last night?*

"Be careful what you wish for," he says as he drops his sword, and in the matter of a fast beat, a very real sword's blade whacks my wooden weapon so hard that it slams to the floor.

Annoyed by his arrogant laugh, I quickly bend to retrieve the weapon. As I move to straighten, the tip of Ethan's sword lifts my chin up.

"This isn't a game, Nara. This is life and death. I don't use this weapon's power lightly. I want you to understand *exactly* what you could be up against if you go looking for a book that most likely doesn't exist, but if it does…it probably carries no more value than the paper it's printed on."

When I start to push his sword away with the back of my hand, he quickly drops it from my chin, bringing it to his side.

"Its value is in the belief behind it…at least to the demons. I want to make sure the book doesn't end up in the wrong hands."

"Too late for that," he mutters with a derisive twist of his lips.

My back stiffens and I sweep my sword in front of me a couple of times, then tilt it toward him. "If you're so worried, you should come with me."

His mouth presses together in frustration. "Even if money weren't an issue, I've got stuff I need to take care of here. I can't guarantee how long it'll take. It's for the best if you don't go at all."

"Like what stuff?" My hand tightening around the sword's handle, I jump on his casual comment, hoping that he'll finally share about his struggle with his Corvus.

A quick smirk tilts his lips as he swipes his sword up and strikes at mine. The sensation jarring along my arm is so extreme, I nearly drop my weapon again. Gritting my back teeth, I refuse to give him the satisfaction of seeing how much my right shoulder is screaming in protest. "What stuff, Ethan?"

"Right now...training." His dark blue eyes suddenly narrow. "Better run, *demon*."

I'm not exactly sure what I just unleashed, but I know he's serious. I asked for it, so I refuse to go down easily. Swinging my sword wide, I let out a loud battle cry and slam my sword against his, then turn and run toward the bleachers because it's the only place I can get some height on him.

Ethan bolts after me, but it's really no contest because he moves so fast he's on the same step as I am in two seconds. Jumping up two more steps, I hold my sword with two hands and face him in a defensive pose, ready to battle.

Standing below me, he gives me a confident smile as he slowly slides his sword along mine. Even though I'm holding my sword with all my strength, he uses the tip of his to easily push my weapon out of the way as if it's no stronger than a feather. "You might have chosen a very beautiful vessel, demon, but that won't stop me from sending you to Under in the most painful way possible."

If Ethan wants to keep this role-playing thing going, I'll take it to a new level. Shifting my sword to my right hand, I quickly pull the elastic band from my hair and let it tumble across my shoulders. "Then I'm not going to make it easy for you, *Corvus*." I throw the elastic band in his direction. While he reaches out for it with his free hand, I use the distraction to bring my sword's handle down on his weapon hand. The moment his sword flies across the bleachers to land on the hard gym floor with a loud, reverberating clatter, I don't bother to wait for him to go after it. Instead, I sprint up the bleachers as fast as my legs will take me.

By the time I reach a few stairs from the top, Ethan is right behind me shaking the whole bleacher staircase at a frighteningly fast pace.

When I'm instantly halted by a big hand sliding into my hair and palming the back of my skull with a vise grip, I yelp, not because it hurts me, but because his hold on my head makes me feel like a weak child who will never, ever win. As his fingers curl into my hair and he slowly tugs me back against his chest, the bit of pain in my scalp is nothing compared to how much his nearness makes my heart ache. His warm breath rushing across my temple is almost my undoing until he whispers against my ear, "And this is why you wear long hair up."

I'm so angry that he keeps putting everything else before us— even when he knows we're the strongest weapon as a team—that I decide to remind him what that feels like.

Calming my labored breathing, I lay my hand lightly on his muscular forearm and lean my head closer to his. "You know, there are lots of weapons we still haven't used."

"We've covered most things you could use in a pinch to defend yourself," he murmurs, his fingers flexing against my scalp as he tilts my head slightly and takes a deep breath.

I smile when I hear him inhale once more, then curl my fingers around his arm and lean into him. "I know, but there's something to be said for less obvious defense tactics."

"Like what?" Ethan stiffens when my butt connects with his hips, but just as he starts to pull away, I stomp on his toe and quickly pull free of his suddenly loose hold.

"The element of surprise," I call over my shoulder as I take off toward the top of the bleachers.

The second I land on the top step, I barely get a chance to pivot and hold my sword up before he's right in front of me. And of course, here I am once again on the last stair of the bleachers with maybe three feet of room until they end. At least this time around I'm in a pretend scenario instead of being chased by a demon out for my blood. Then again, the hard look on Ethan's face makes me instinctively tighten my grip on my sword once more.

"*Never*, ever go high unless you have a guaranteed escape

route." He takes a couple steps forward and I immediately take the same steps back to keep some distance between us. "Up high, you'll always be trapped. So what are you going to do now?" he says as he takes another aggressive step.

The bleachers are so tall that Ethan has to duck a couple inches to keep from hitting his head on this old gym's metal rafters. He's close, but I'm not down for the count yet. "I always come up with a plan," I say, then drop my sword and jump up to grab onto the metal rafter above my head. Swinging, I slam the flat of my feet into Ethan's chest and send him stumbling back onto the bleachers.

Before I can release my hold and run like hell back down the steps, the metal piece I'm hanging from suddenly telescopes four feet away from the edge of the bleachers, leaving me dangling twenty feet in the air.

Once my initial scream settles into fearful pants, I re-clench my hold on the rafter and refuse to look at the twenty-foot drop below. Instead, I send a "please help me" glance Ethan's way.

His menacing expression is gone, replaced by a concerned one. "Can you inch your way back?"

When I try to walk my hands along the rafter and a loud creaking echoes in the ceiling, he quickly shakes his head. "Don't move, Nara. Just stay there."

"Where are you going?" My pitch elevates as Ethan zips down the bleachers. I hate that I can't see what he's doing. If I turn to look, I'm worried I'll jar the beam and the rafter will detach completely.

The sudden sensation of air blowing my hair around my face spreads goose bumps across my skin, right as Ethan speaks diagonally behind me. "I'm here, Nara."

I turn my head slowly and stare at Ethan's massive raven wings moving in a rhythmic beat to keep him even in the air with me.

"We need to do this slowly so that rafter doesn't come down on your head." Moving a bit closer, he slides a hand along my upper back. "I need you to follow my directions, okay?" When I nod, he bends one knee. "Anchor your left foot on my thigh."

As soon as I do that, he says, "Now put all your weight on that leg."

The second he feels my weight shift to his thigh, Ethan moves his hand from my back up my ribcage to just below my armpit. Clamping his thumb and fingers around the inside of my upper arm, he says, "You're just going to have to trust that I won't drop you with this next part. When I say *now,* I need you to do two things: Release your hold, then let my hand under your arm be your guide toward me as you spin in my direction. Ready?"

"Yes," I say in an unsteady voice.

"Now."

I hold my breath and close my eyes, releasing my death grip on the beam. At the same time gravity takes over, Ethan's hand turns me toward him. I instantly reach for the one person who always makes me feel safe, even hanging twenty-five feet in the air.

"I've got you, Sunshine," he murmurs as he quickly folds his arms around me and pulls me against his chest. I instinctually wrap my arms and legs around his warm, muscular frame, and I don't let go until we land on the ground.

As soon as my feet touch the floor, Ethan vaults back up in the air. With his wings holding him up, he uses his Corvus' brute strength to lift the metal rafter piece and slide it back where it came from. Once he bends the metal ends of the other rafter against it to hold it in place, he returns to the floor next to me.

His expression is so intense I think he's going to lay into me once more for not taking the training seriously. Instead, he takes a step into my personal space and pushes strands of my hair back from my face. "Even without me saving you just now, somehow I think you would've found a way to save yourself. But for my future sanity, can we please just stick to the ground."

While Ethan talks, his wings are still fully spread. They're massive and so impressive I desperately wish the main lights were on so I could see every blue and purple streak. One thing the lower lighting doesn't hide is his wings reflecting his true emotions. They're quivering with tension. As my accelerated heart rate settles to a normal beat, guilt rests heavily on my shoulders. No matter how much it upsets me that he's being so stubborn and I can't seem to break through to him, one thing I can never question is whether he has my best interests at heart. Because he always has.

"I'm sorry, Ethan. I promise to be more focused during training."

"Nara…" Ethan sighs as he reaches up to slowly push my hair behind my ear. The moment his fingers curl to the base of my ear, he frowns, his gaze drawn to his hand. "I haven't been having your dreams, but that just felt really familiar."

"That's because you did it last night," I say, hoping he'll want to finally discuss his nocturnal visit.

At the same time his blue eyes snap to mine, a bright light begins to shine where he's touching me, but Ethan instantly drops his hand. Stepping back, he shakes his head as if stunned, then glances at the clock on the wall. "We've gone longer than we did last night. It's probably best to end the lesson here."

It's bad enough that he ignored my mention of last night, but my heart sinks that he cut off the passion flaring between us just now. I don't understand why he's being so hot and cold. "Are we meeting at the same time tomorrow?"

Ethan glances away, his jaw muscle working. "I'm not sure."

"Do you have other plans?" I tilt my head and try to gauge his expression, worry sinking in. *Does he still think I'm not serious about this training?*

His brow furrows and he clenches his hand into a fist next to his thigh. "I have something I need to work on."

My chest tightens as his expression continues to shut down, which means he'll keep whatever's going on to himself. "Okay, let me know." It takes effort to sound upbeat when frustration churns in my belly, but I force myself to appear nonchalant and turn toward the bleachers to retrieve the wooden sword that fell through.

"Don't worry about that. I'll get it," Ethan says, stopping me. "Go get your homework done. I promise to let you know about tomorrow."

I can't believe how detached he suddenly sounds. I thought we were moving a bit closer, then, *bam,* he shuts us down. He might be a brick wall, but *my* emotions are pinging all over the place. I'm so confused I want to scream, but if he's determined to shut himself off about *us,* I want him to know that I do appreciate his efforts for my safety. "The next time we train, I promise no more aerial antics."

When a half smile breaks his stoic expression, my heart leaps. I want to ask him about my aunt and if she's helping him with his Corvus, but the bit of humor in his expression disappears just as quickly as it surfaced. Pasting on an unaffected smile as I tell him goodbye, I leave without asking him anything, my heart heavy and my concern growing.

# Chapter Thirteen

### *Nara*

Once I turn off the light to go to bed, a familiar tapping sound pings my window. Houdini lifts his head from the end of my bed. Growling once, he stands and turns his back to the window, then settles on my bed once more. I chuckle at his obvious rebuff. He's never forgiven Patch for slicing his ear with his sharp beak. The sight of the raven's white eye feathers standing out in the darkness as he hangs out on my sill bolsters my spirits and I quickly lift the glass, smiling.

"Good evening, Patch," I say, my breath billowing in the cool air. "I wondered where you went off to. I'm so glad to see at least one raven hasn't abandoned me. I know it's not your preference, but," I pause and retrieve a quarter from my wallet hoping to entice him. "Do you want to come in tonight?"

Patch fluffs his wings once, but just taps at the quarter a couple of times. Lifting his head, he makes low *tock, tock* sounds and starts to rock his body back and forth, completely disinterested.

Sighing my disappointment, I set the quarter down, then pull on a thick sweater and drag my chair up to my windowsill. "I guess I'll join you here for a few minutes then. Do you have any words of wisdom on how to deal with temperamental Corvus—both the spirit and his host?"

When I slowly set my hand on the sill next to him, Patch lifts his head and lets out a couple guttural noises, then nudges his beak under my fingers. I smile at his forthright way of asking to be petted and gently run my fingers over his head and down his back. "If only Ethan and Rave were this easy to figure out, I'd be set."

"Inara?" Gran calls quietly from behind me.

I lift my hand and quickly glance back, surprised to see her there. Gran's like a stealthy ninja in that wheelchair. She's been making great progress, only using the chair upstairs at the end of the day when she's worn out. "I thought you went to bed?"

Gran maneuvers her chair closer, her attention locked on the window behind me. "Statue?"

I slide my gaze back to the sill, surprised to see Patch hadn't taken off like he normally does whenever anyone else approaches. Instead, he's staring intently at Gran.

As still as Patch is being it would be easy to pretend that I had set the raven statue my grandmother—and Gran's sister—had created in art class years ago out on the ledge, but I'm fascinated by the fact Patch seems to be equally interested in Gran.

"No, this is Patch," I say and lower my arm down for the raven to climb on. "I guess you could say he's kind of adopted me."

She gasps, her eyes sparkling in delight when he immediately hops onto my arm so that I can bring him into the room.

Patch hasn't stopped staring at Gran. He's making a humming sound and bobbing his head back and forth as if he's telling me he wants to move closer. I laugh and step forward. "I think he wants to meet you. Is that okay?"

When Gran grins, Patch spreads his wings and quickly takes flight, landing on the thick blanket Gran has spread across her knees.

I've never seen my grand aunt giggle in delight, but she does just that when the big bird lowers his forehead to the blanket as if he's bowing deeply, then he walks up to her chest and presses his whole body against it. I can only stare in shock. He doesn't even flinch or peck at her hand when she lowers her gnarled fingers to stroke his feathers. Instead, he lifts his head to ask her to pet him there too.

"I—I've never seen him act like this. It's like he deeply respects you, which is unusual. He's totally alpha among other ravens."

Gran looks up at me, her eyes glistening. "Margaret."

I squat down beside her chair and watch in awe as Patch displays his reverence to her in every move he makes. "Your sister would be happy and probably a bit jealous like I am. Patch has never acted worshipful. It's actually very sweet to see."

Gran looks up at me and points to the raven, who's now walking around on her lap, examining every bit of real estate. "Pack."

I smile and correct her. "Patch."

She shakes her head, then stutters out the phrase. "Patch...is... pack. Ethan's pack."

I let out an honest half-laugh. "The last thing Patch would ever do is follow Ethan."

Gran frowns at me in confusion.

"Corda? Are you in Inara's room?" Mom's voice floats down the hall, sending Patch flying out the window.

I jump up and close the glass pane just as my Mom walks into the room and flips on the light switch. "What are you two doing sitting in the dark?"

When Gran and I look at each other and burst into secretive laughter, Mom frowns and wraps her arms around herself. "It's freezing in here. Do you want me to call the heating guy, Inara?"

"No, I just had my window open for a minute. I like it a little cool in my room."

"I prefer not to heat the outside, sweetie." Mom shivers, then briskly walks over to grab hold of the handles on Gran's wheelchair. "And it's entirely too cold in here for you, so say goodnight, Corda."

"G'Night, Corda," Gran says, her eyes full of mischief.

Snickering, I lift up to my knees and press a soft kiss to Gran's papery cheek. "Night, Gran."

She pats my jaw and nods toward the window. "Protects."

"Only if she keeps it closed and locked," Mom mutters as she pushes Gran toward the doorway. "Come on Houdini, I'll take you out before I lock up for the night."

While Houdini follows them, I notice the way Gran cranes to keep her gaze locked on the glass until she's out of the room. I know she wasn't talking about the window earlier. Gran had called Patch part of Ethan's pack. It's logical that she would make some connection between the Corvus symbol on her headphones. Maybe she heard Mom tell Dad the story about a raven helping Houdini go after that man to protect us?

She showed no fear of Patch, only delight at his presence. The way they connected surprised the heck out of me. I feel like she knows more, yet she also seemed confused when I said that Patch wouldn't follow Ethan. I wish she could tell me what she's thinking or at least use the tablet to convey her thoughts.

I turn off the light and let my churning thoughts go at the sight of Patch landing on the sill outside to resume his evening sentry ritual. He makes me feel safer than a lock ever could. "Thanks for being so sweet to Gran and distracting me from Ethan worries. Night, Patch."

I can't help but snicker when the raven puffs up his throat feathers, then bobs his head up and down. Apparently the cocky, temperamental bird is back.

The sensation of fingers sliding along my forehead pull me from a deep sleep. The touch is light, but purposeful. My heart jumps when I see Ethan sitting on the bed beside me.

"What is it?" I ask, my brain foggy as I move to a seated position against my headboard.

"What else would you say to the Corvus?" Ethan's brow is furrowed, his expression focused.

"Whaaat?" Pushing my hair out of my face, I blink and yawn as my body tries to wake up. *It's good that he's trying to help his Corvus, but why is he here, making my heart pound to feel him touch me again? He made it perfectly clear he's not interested in renewing our relationship.*

When Ethan just stares at me intently, but doesn't say anything else, I let my frustration get the best of me. "I would tell Rave to stop hiding from who he really is, that lives—including yours—are at stake and he can't keep ignoring the obvious in the hopes it will go away. Lucifer certainly won't. Michael told me he's coming."

"What?" Ethan's gaze narrows, his whole body tensing. "When?"

I shrug. "I don't know, but he's worried, Ethan. An *angel* is worried. That has to mean something."

"What if he's wrong?" His profile is barely visible in the darkness, but the strain in his tone comes across as he stands and glances away. "What if my Corvus really *isn't* the Master?"

My worry from earlier rushes back. Ethan believes his Corvus is the Master just as much as I do. He told me this, so what has changed his mind? What has happened that makes him believe differently? I quickly push back my covers and stand. "You're scaring me, Ethan. What aren't you telling me?"

Just as he turns to face me, a phone alarm starts beeping on full blast.

Ethan frowns and glances down at the sound coming from his army jacket's pocket. Heart racing, I rush forward and grab his phone out of the pocket, then quickly shut it off so it doesn't wake my mom.

"Are you trying to get me grounded?" I huff in a low tone.

Ethan grabs my wrist as I start to slip his phone back into his pocket. "Nara?"

I jerk my gaze to his, surprised by the alarm in his voice. He quickly clasps my face, his gaze scanning mine. "Are you all right?"

"Huh? I mean, yes, I'm fine." When he lowers his hands to my shoulders and squeezes them, then slides his fingers down my arms as if to assure himself that I'm telling him the truth, I put my hands on his, halting his movements. "What's wrong?"

Exhaling a harsh breath, he narrows his gaze and his face hardens. "I'm going to kill the sneaky, conniving bastard!"

I've never seen him this angry. "What are you talking about?"

"My Corvus!" Jamming his hands in his hair, he begins to pace, his tone low and angry. "I knew letting him fight was a risk, but I was learning new ways to go after demons each time he got involved in battles. I'd hoped it would be a way for us to be less combative. I foolishly thought that taking his aggression out on demons would make him more agreeable, and we could peacefully co-exist. Instead he became more insufferable. And now," he pauses, his chest heaving. "He's hijacking my body while I sleep to spend time with you."

"Wait…are you saying that I was just talking to your Corvus? Did you set that alarm on your phone to jar yourself awake?"

"Yes, I set the alarm after that déjà vu moment from the gym earlier. I had to know." Ethan's jaw flexes and his expression turns hard, unforgiving. "How long, Nara?"

"How long, what?" I fold my arms and focus my attention on Houdini so he can't see how hurt I am that he wasn't the one sneaking in to see me.

Stepping forward, he hooks his finger under my chin and forces me to meet his gaze. "How long have you been letting my Corvus replace me in your life?"

The betrayal, confusion, and anger lurking in his dark eyes makes my heart hammer. "I didn't *let* him do anything; he was just concerned."

Before I can say more, Ethan presses his thumb over my bottom lip and lowers his face close. "You're *my* Sunshine." His dark, territorial tone slides over me like a seductive caress. "I protect you. Not him."

The fact that he's talking about protecting me, but not loving me, crushes my heart even more than when he made it clear we couldn't be together. After his visit last night, a part of me held out hope. But then again, that wasn't him. Wait…all those inexplicable dirt stains in my room? Crap…*how long has his Corvus been doing this?* All these questions fly through my head, which only highlights the fact that *Ethan* didn't sneak into my room.

He truly had distanced himself from *us,* and that stark reality makes me curl my hands into fists. Our breathing revs, hiking my emotions, but when a light begins to glow between us and Ethan quickly releases me, I lose my temper.

I shove at his chest. As he stumbles back in surprise, I step forward and unleash my fury. "I'm only 'your Sunshine' if you're *all* in." This time I hit his chest hard. "You can't pretend I didn't see that light this time. How could you walk away from us? You broke my heart, Ethan. How could you do that to me?"

Ethan clasps my shoulders, his fingers flexing. My heart hammers as his tortured gaze searches mine and then I'm yanked against him. "I can't." Pulling me close, his voice is hoarse as he slides his fingers into my hair and presses his mouth against my temple. "Not any more. I miss you so much, Nara. I tried to do it without you, to keep away so you'd be safe, but he's too strong. Even your aunt's breathing exercises couldn't keep him from wearing me like a skin-suit while I slept. It's like he's seeping into every part of me. I've had blackout moments…spans of time I don't remember." His voice lowers. "I don't know what he's doing."

I wrap my arms around his trim waist and inhale his masculine smell, elation and worry raging through me. It feels so good to press myself against his muscular frame, but I'm terrified that the Corvus now has too much control over him. While I know Ethan will need the spirit's powers and skills to battle Lucifer, the lack of his overall control scares me. That must be why Michael said Ethan needed my help. "I think your Corvus is starting to realize that he *is* Master and it scares him, Ethan."

He looks down at me, his brow furrowed. "How long has he been seeing you? And is that what he talks to you about?"

"That I'm aware of, he's only been here as you twice…last night and tonight. Last night, he asked me what I would tell your Corvus if I were able to talk to him face-to-face. Then tonight, he asked if Michael was wrong about him being the Master Corvus."

"Has Michael talked to you?" When I smile sheepishly, Ethan exhales a heavy sigh. "I never could keep you out of this, could I?"

I squeeze him until he grunts. "I told you that I'm as knee deep as you are."

Shaking his head, the tension eases from his body as he brushes his lips against my forehead. "I've missed doing that. We'll have to be careful, Nara. No one can know we're together. I'm a walking target for demon attacks. I won't let you or your family be ones too." When I nod my understanding, he says, "So what did Michael say?"

"He asked me to help your Corvus remember who he is. He said that you couldn't do it by yourself and that you needed my help because the Corvus is more settled with me around. Did he cause that earthquake in Richmond?"

Ethan shakes his head. "I honestly don't know. If he's been sneaking off while I was supposed to be sleeping, then it's possible. At least now I know why I've been falling asleep in my classes." He trails his fingers along my hair. "If the Corvus could turn me off completely and have you to himself, I'm pretty sure that's what the dang bird would do."

I snicker and shake my head. "It's true that we have a rapport, but honestly, I think his affection for me is coming from you. He knows you're settled and happy with me in your life. He feels what you feel and is projecting it."

Ethan snorts. "By wielding his vast powers like play toys to try and impress you?"

My eyebrows shoot up. "So you were trying to impress me, huh?"

"No, the bird was—" He stops and sighs. "Never mind."

I give him the side-eye, but finish telling him the rest. "Michael said that Lucifer is almost here and that your Corvus would be vulnerable if he goes up against the demon without his memory of the entire Mortal world history intact. He said Lucifer will use every advantage in his arsenal to beat the Master Corvus while he's at his weakest."

"Did he say when or where Lucifer will appear?"

"No. I get the feeling he just senses the threat coming. Maybe it's angel mojo or something. But that's why I must go to London. If Rave doesn't get his memory back, we have to be as prepared as possible. That means making sure that if another *Ravens* book does exist with a scroll inside, that I get to it before the demons do."

Ethan shakes his head and wraps his arms tight around my waist. "*We* get to it before the demons do."

"You're going?" My eyes widen and I try not to cry, but tears leak out anyway. I need him as much as he does me. "I thought you couldn't afford to go to London? Do you even have a passport? Doesn't it take forever to get one?"

Ethan clasps my face to calm my rising worry. "I'm coming, Sunshine. I won't let you go without me." He leans close and kisses each cheek, his warm lips swiping away my tears.

I lift my face so his mouth is hovering over mine. "You missed some tears right here."

Smirking, he tilts my head, his fingers flexing against my jawline. Light begins to glow from his hands, and his smirk softens as he inspects me thoroughly. "Your lips look dry to me."

I cherish that we're glowing. And it hits me, that's why we didn't glow when he touched me last night. Ethan wasn't touching me; his Corvus was. My heart swells as the realization that his love shines through, even when he's teasing me and pretending to be unaffected. "Ethan, just kiss—"

His lips claim mine with such toe-curling longing and sizzling heat that my feet feel like they're melting into the carpet. As his tongue twines with mine, I let out a happy gasp and slide my fingers up the back of his shirt. Ethan fists his hands in my hair, his fingers digging deep as he murmurs against my mouth, "No more tears, Sunshine."

I cling to him and kiss him with every bit of pent up emotion I've held back. Breaking our kiss, he exhales in frustration, then presses his forehead against mine. "I wish we had all night together."

I brush my fingers against his jaw, then lean back to meet his gaze. "I want that too, very much, but right now…I need to ask you a favor."

He cups the back of my neck and folds my body fully against his. "You know I'll give you anything. What is it?"

I can feel him pressed against me and it makes my heart race and my stomach knot as I hold his sincere gaze. "I need you to let me talk to Rave."

# Chapter Fourteen

### Ethan

"Anything but *that*," I grate. Nara winces and I realize that I've subconsciously fisted my hand in her hair. I instantly release her and take a step back to get a grip on myself. "You can't possibly be serious? He's already creeping in while I'm sleeping and now you want me to give him access while I'm consciously awake?" I shake my head in a fast jerk. "I can't risk letting my guard down and giving him access to my mind." Intuition tells me that's the only way he'll be able to have a truly personal conversation with Nara, and that scares the shit out of me. He could completely shut me out and I would lose her forever.

Worry flickers in her green eyes and she steps close to me once more, folding our fingers together. "You said that you don't want me to have to face Fate anymore. Other than through your dreams where Fate can get to me, face-to-face is the only other way I can talk to Rave, Ethan. I need to try to reason with him so that hopefully I can convince him to let us help him."

My stomach churns with worry as I reach up and trail shaky fingers down her hair. "I don't want to lose you, Sunshine. If I let him in…I might not be able to shove him back out again."

Nara bites her lip, her eyes watering with renewed tears. "I don't know what the right answer is, but this is bigger than us, Ethan. If we can't get your Corvus on board…to help him remember, there won't be an 'us' for long." Her hand shakes a little as she lays it on me. "Please let me help, Ethan. I won't let Rave take over."

The pressure of her hand affects me so much I have to swallow the lump of emotion jammed in my throat. Sliding my thumb over the back of her hand, I keep my gaze locked with hers. "You're the only person I completely trust." My lip curls in dislike as I continue, "I distrust the Corvus' intentions when it comes to you. He could fool you into believing he let me back in when he really didn't."

Nara takes my hand and presses it against her cheek. "Think of us together as if no one else was in the house."

My fingers intuitively curl against her cheek and my body aches at the mere suggestion of being with her again the way I want to. Nara's skin is so soft...I want to touch every part of her. The room suddenly lights up so bright from the glow of our touch that Nara lets out a soft laugh and squints against the intensity. "Well, then... thanks for showing me how you really feel."

I shrug, unapologetic in my desire for her. "I could power an entire city." When I lower my hand to her hip, I chuckle. The glowing impression my fingers left behind on her face reveals suddenly red cheeks. Seeing her cheeks bloom never gets old.

Nara shakes her head and smiles as she points to the handprint that's already starting to fade. "This is how I'll know. Whenever the Corvus touched me, this didn't happen."

I scowl, my hand flexing on her hip, pulling her closer. "I don't like him touching you at all."

"The point is...I'll always know the difference," she says earnestly. "He won't be able to fool me."

Nara's confidence eases the tightness in my chest somewhat. The last thing I want is my refusal to then push her to attempt to talk to the Corvus through my dreams again. I don't trust Fate at all. He's already put her in harm's way too many times to count. His agenda is fully self-serving. Maybe if I allow the Corvus to have a conversation with Nara as himself and not while he's pretending to be me, he'll back off my life and start focusing on being *him*.

"All right. I'll try to let go and allow him to speak to you, but I'll only do this once. If it doesn't work, we'll find another way to get the Corvus to accept who he is."

Nara quickly nods. "I know that lowering your mental block is risky. London will be our only other option. I just hope he doesn't give you a hard time about the sanctuary. I really want you to see it."

My body stills. "You're going to the sanctuary? Why?"

Nara's eyes widen and her pulse jumps. "I want to see Drystan in his new environment."

"I thought the London trip was about getting the book."

"It is." She nods. "But you don't expect me to go all the way to London and not see Drystan, do you?"

The fact Nara seems suddenly tense raises my protective hackles. I trust her, but I know Drystan wants her to himself. "You're not planning to become a Palidin, are you?"

"No," she says on a laugh. "I truly just want to see the place. Drystan said it's impressive. I hope you won't let your Corvus' issue with it keep you from visiting with me."

Nara told me the story that Drystan's uncle shared with her about the Master Corvus destroying the sanctuary thirty years ago. The powerful spirit might not remember what happened or why he did that, but he obviously has an aversion to it since the mere mention of the place makes *my* blood pressure rise. No matter how apprehensive I feel, I won't let Nara go without me by her side. "He won't have a choice. Where you go, I go."

Nara smiles her appreciation, her blonde eyebrows hiking. "Are you ready to try to let me talk with Rave?"

"I really wish you hadn't named him," I say, grunting my annoyance.

A blonde eyebrow hikes and I sigh. "I'm as ready as I'll ever be."

She nods and the second she releases me, the Corvus slams against my skull like he's been using a sledgehammer this entire time.

*Let me talk to her,* he commands in a fierce tone.

I set my jaw at the sudden excruciating pain flooding my head. "Are you all right?" Nara asks, placing her hand on my arm.

The sudden lack of pain and utter silence in my head makes me blink at her and smile. Somehow…our physical connection blocks him. "I'm good, Sunshine. Just give me a minute."

"Oh, okay."

This time I'm prepared when her hand falls away. *Stop acting like a spoiled child and screeching in my ear. You sound like a magpie.*

I can literally feel his fury at my insult, but he reins in his temper.

*Stop cutting me off! I want to finish my conversation with Nara.*

I get the sense that he's reluctant to forcefully take over my body while Nara is staring directly at me. Or maybe...he can't until she lets go. I can also tell by his reaction that he has no idea that I'm about to finally grant him his wish. And since he's toyed with and manipulated my emotions on numerous occasions, it's my turn to mess with him. *Why should I trust you at all right now, Corvus? You've been pretending to be me to the one person who means the most to me. All for what? Just for kicks? What was the purpose? For a dawn-of-time "Master Corvus," you sure act like a juvenile.*

*Watch your mouth, boy. I could destroy you with a thought. Keep that in mind the next time you dare to question me.*

The shock of power surging through me right now is what scares me more than anything. The way this spirit wields his supremacy so frivolously, throwing his figurative weight around. In an instant, he could lose his temper and rip me to shreds. But what worries me most is him putting Nara at risk. I have to let her try to reason with him. I don't have a choice. He's out of control. He needs to know this willful abuse of his power must be controlled.

*To be clear, Corvus, the only reason that I will allow you to speak to Nara directly this one time is because she believes that you're worth trying to help. She thinks that you aren't so broken. I wonder if you're so damaged that you could be considered a Corvus who's going dark. As a matter of fact, the more I think about everything you've put me through, I'm more inclined to believe that scenario.*

*I am not...dark.*

The hesitation in his adamant statement sends up an internal alarm. He has never hesitated. Not once. He's worried about something. *You have ten minutes.*

The Corvus snorts rudely in my ear. *To be clear...Nara is the only reason that I haven't completely obliterated you for your constant insolence.*

*Good to know where I stand in the pecking order of things. In case you need to be reminded...you are and will always be a bird.*

*Do you want to die?* the spirit booms inside my skull, his fury vaulting to new levels.

I stare at Nara, who's watching me intently. By the look of concern on her face, she can tell I'm having a mental battle of wills with this stupid raven.

*I very much want to live, Corvus. But I will do it on my terms, not yours. You now have nine minutes and thirty seconds before I kick your overbearing ass out of my head.* I ignore his growl of irritation and close my eyes. Taking a deep breath, I force my body to relax and let down my defenses. As the flood of the Corvus's immense power crashes over my mental walls and begins to drown out my consciousness, I tense every muscle in my body to suppress my natural instincts to fight it. I have to trust that Nara will be able to pull me out of the deep hole the Corvus will definitely shove me into.

### Nara

The second Ethan opens his eyes, I know I'm looking at the Corvus. How did I not see that arrogant, weary-wise look and slightly stiffened stance in the past? Was I so desperate for Ethan's attention that I ignored all the signs?

"It's good to finally meet you in the real world," I say, then purse my lips and narrow my gaze. "But the underhanded way you did it makes me angry. You put Ethan's well-being at risk for your own personal gain."

Folding his arms, he shrugs. "I needed answers. You've always been honest with me, yet he refused to let me anywhere near you."

When he snorts his annoyance and I hear the words *insolent, arrogant,* and *closed off* muttered in my mind, I sigh. "We're not in Ethan's dream world. Here you're able to use Ethan's voice, so use it, Rave. You need to learn to get along with your host. Ethan is a good person, who just happens to be incredibly strong-minded and just as stubborn."

Rave sneers, "That's an understatement."

"You might not be used to a host as strong as Ethan, but maybe there's a reason you chose him, even if it was subconscious. Have you considered that?"

His only answer is to grunt, so I continue. "Instead of battling Ethan for dominance, why don't you accept his help? He could be your greatest asset. Now that a demon has the Raven book—"

"Asset? It's *his* fault the book was taken in the first place." He sniffs disdainfully.

"Actually, it was my fault. I'm the one who told the demon where to find it to save my Gran's life."

"You're allowed human emotions. *He's* not."

I roll my eyes at that. He won't let me take the blame for losing the book. "All that matters now is that we have to assume the demons might discover a way in that book to help Lucifer defeat you. That's why you must work together with Ethan. Then we can focus on trying to help you—"

"Why do you think I'm the Master Corvus?"

I blink at his blunt question. "Because Fate and Michael both said—"

Rave steps forward and clasps my hand. "Why do *you* think I'm worthy of such a role?"

I quickly shake my head. "I—I'm just a girl who can dream her next day. I can't say if you're…"

Rave flattens his palms around my hand and the power suddenly humming through me is so strong, the top layer of my hair begins to rise all around me. As I glance up at my hair, my gaze is drawn to the darkened room in general where subtle layers of colors overtake the normally monotone darkness. Somehow his higher frequency is enhancing my vision. I can literally see little colorful bits of particles floating in the air and hear every breath my mom, Gran, and dog take. I smirk. Houdini is sleeping on Mom's bed. He's been trying for a while. I can't believe Mom finally let him.

I turn my head and take in the sound of the bugs and worms in the dirt beneath our house. I try to look at Ethan to express my wonder and hope he's in there witnessing this too, but instead I see right through his face, past his dark hair and skull. I glance up and blink—I can see through the ceiling, rafters and rooftop into the night sky and far, far beyond where the twinkle of stars turn a misty white. It's raining outside and even though I'm dry, I blink against the drops that feel as if they're falling right through me. Am I seeing through Rave's eyes, where the layers between physical reality and spiritual existence are merged?

"Holy wow…is that what the veil looks like?" I ask of the misty white where my seemingly endless vision appears to stop.

Rave's hold on my hand suddenly tightens and my vision swiftly narrows to the current plane. I come back to myself to see he's staring at me with a curious expression. "What did you just see? You appeared to be staring right through me."

It feels so surreal to be experiencing this with Ethan, but it's not Ethan. "I um, was. You don't see through me, then outside and beyond?"

"A Corvus can walk through walls, but he can't see beyond them like what you're describing." When he releases me and I see his jaw muscle jumping in frustration, my stomach bottoms out. How can he discount the power his touch alone elicits? It feels deep and electrifying...and very spiritual. It's incredibly powerful and vast, even if he doesn't mentally acknowledge it.

Shaking off his frustration, Rave holds my gaze with mesmerizing intensity. "I want to know why you believe it's true."

He's staring at me as if every breath I take and every minute movement is being scrutinized. There are so many things he consciously does that I could point out: from his inexplicable ability to move from one place to another so fast I can't track him, to his strength of shaking the ground by slamming his foot down, to that time he "captured" Fate's shifting vaporous form in his bare hands and threatened to annihilate him, but instead of recounting what he knows, I take a risk and ask the one thing I don't think he can answer. "Tell me about your history. Go back more than thirty years ago."

He huffs as if he's not going to bother to answer, his black eyes piercing into me. If he wants a staring contest...I fold my arms and raise my eyebrows, my expression hardening to let him know I'll do this all night.

Eventually his resistance dissipates and his eyebrows pull together. "I don't remember."

"I think you have your answer then," I say as I walk over to my desk and open my laptop.

"Why can't I remember?" he asks from directly behind me.

Other than my hair lifting in response to his swift speed, I never even heard him move. "I have no idea, but we're going to find out by digging into your past as best we can. Maybe doing a bit a research will help you remember."

Rave leans over my shoulder and reads the heading of the news article I pulled up on my laptop. "Crows and Ravens All Over the World Fall Out of the Sky: Biologists Speculate."

I glance up at him. "Does this particular event ring any bells? I found it a while back."

"That's significant." He stares hard at the screen, his brow creased. "I don't understand why I didn't know about this?"

"Maybe you can't remember it or...you don't want to," I say, closing the document. In re-reading over the document just now, I realize that the birds dying happened right around the time frame that the Master Corvus destroyed the sanctuary. Whatever happened at the sanctuary must've been pretty bad. I don't want to freak him out, so I keep my thoughts to myself and my expression perfectly schooled. "Hopefully if we dig deep enough we can find something from the past to help you remember."

Rave's lips quirk upward slightly "You really do look at the positive side, don't you?"

I smile. "I try my best. So will you please make an effort to work together with Ethan? It'll make things a lot easier if I knew you two were getting along."

He glances down at Ethan's body. "I rather like having complete control of this physical form instead of borrowing it from time to time. I don't want to have to wait for Ethan to share what you two have learned."

Ethan's mind must be pretty strong if Rave can't always hear us. I like the idea that we can have private time without the spirit constantly listening in, but Rave's sudden declaration makes my stomach knot.

Turning, I poke his chest. "Don't even go there. You had your fun running around without Ethan's permission for who knows how long. You need to give his body back to him and only surface when it is truly necessary. I promise you that he will share any important details we discover."

He captures my finger and shakes his head. "As for me being the Master Corvus...that remains to be seen. I concede there's some kind of block in my memory that needs to be lifted. How will you know if the research you unearth is important or not? The tiniest detail may trigger a memory for me." He releases me and straightens, his expression determined. "I will remain so I'm constantly aware of everything."

I try not to panic. Maybe sharing details I already know will prove to him that I won't hold back, no matter how much I think he might not like what I discover. "For now I can tell you what I learned from Drystan's uncle about the Master Corvus and what happened at the sanctuary thirty years ago. I believe the timing is around when the ravens and crows fell from the sky."

He releases my hand and walks away. "I don't want to talk about that."

"I don't care." I follow him, refusing to let him hide from his past. "We have to talk about it. It might help trigger a memory for you."

He turns to face me, his gaze narrowed. "What if you tell me and it still doesn't help?"

"It might not. But all we can do is try."

A scowl forms on his face, but he folds his arms and gives a curt nod. "You may proceed."

I take a deep breath. "Drystan's uncle, Mr. Wicklow, told me that the Master Corvus came to live at the sanctuary. That it was the first time he had ever shown himself to mortals. Mr. Wicklow said the Master Corvus usually worked alone and didn't know why the spirit just showed up there, but he was honored to have him."

"Why would I do that?" he says on a doubtful snort.

I throw my hands out. "Why are you talking to *me*? Why do you like being called Rave? Maybe there was a reason you decided to interact with humanity at that point in time." I shrug. "All I know is that according to Mr. Wicklow, the Master Corvus got into an argument with the leader of the sanctuary. Back then Mr. Wicklow worked as the leader's right-hand man. He said he didn't know what the argument between you two was, but he did remember that it was heated. And then the next thing he knew, the Master Corvus…" I pause, apprehensive about telling him the rest.

Rave gestures his agitation. "Finish. What happened?"

"According to Mr. Wicklow…" I exhale a deep breath. "The Master Corvus killed the leader and then he destroyed the sanctuary."

*No!* The Corvus's voice booms in my head. "It didn't happen like that."

My eyebrows shoot up, excitement thrumming through me. "Do you remember?"

Dropping his hands to his sides in clenched fists, he shakes his head. "Of course I don't remember. But I know that I would never have willingly killed a human. Protecting humanity is the very reason I exist. It's fundamental to who I am."

I sigh and shake my head. "That's all I know. I think it might help if you talk to Mr. Wicklow directly. And…" I pause and nod, liking this idea. "Meeting him in person would be even better."

"I have *no* intention of going to the sanctuary," he growls and the electric tension in the room rises.

I cross my arms, just as determined as he is. "Oh, you're going, because we are. You won't have a choice."

Rave's expression hardens. "My *choice* is to take over this body and guarantee that I'll never enter that place."

"You must *not* push Ethan out." Panic lodges in my throat. "He is the very essence of the body that you're in. You cannot completely overtake him."

The moment I see his expression shutting down, I grit my teeth and take a couple of calming breaths so I don't raise my voice and wake my Mom. "You will *not* keep him out of his own body."

When Rave slowly rolls his head from one shoulder to the other, then says, "I can do whatever I want," I realize that meeting his bullheadedness with my own isn't working. I need to find another way.

I step close and lightly rest my hand on his arm crossed over his chest. "London is where it all started. It's the key to your past. You have to release Ethan. We work best together and will do everything we can to help you unlock those lost memories. Whatever you've buried, Ethan's strong mind could help buffer the darkness. He can be someone to lean on too."

Rave smirks, a low laugh rumbling. "If he could physically punch me in the face, he would. *You're* the buffer. He's the fist."

As I try to think of something to say to convince him he can trust Ethan, Rave takes my hand and turns it, palm up. I can't tell what he's thinking when he places his palm on top of mine and clasps our hands together, but I'm afraid to move or pull away. I *need* him to release Ethan. "Please, Rave..."

When he stares at our hands, then slowly shakes his head, my stomach plummets.

"Whatever you and Ethan have, it's pure and unique."

Rave has always spoken with arrogance and, at times, age-old amusement, but always with authority. The wonder in his voice now pulls my gaze to our clasped hands. Just as it hits me that he's talking about the glow that happens between Ethan and me, hope blooms and I speak from the heart, lifting my gaze to his. "He means everything to me."

The shine in the Corvus' dark eyes dims. "As much as I hate to admit I need him. I will consider lettin—" He sucks in a deep breath and his fingers cinch mine tight.

I gasp in pain and he quickly glances down at our clasped hands, then yanks me against his chest, folding his arms around me. "Never, *ever* again, Nara." Breathing heavily, Ethan inhales against my hair and cups his hand tight against the back of my head as if he's worried someone will try to rip me away from him.

He's shaking and the rasping roughness in his voice twists my heart. He sounds both tortured and relieved. I wrap my arms around him and press my face to his warm neck, holding him just as tight. "I'm so sorry. For what it's worth, I think I did get through to him. You sound like you've been running. Where did you go?"

"I was fighting through a powerful wall of control trying to hold me down." Ethan cups my face and kisses my mouth, then my nose before pressing his lips softly against my forehead. As the light between us begins to shine where he's touching my face, he says, "I need to try something."

"What—"

His lips cut off my question, and as his tongue slowly traces along mine, sending shivers of delight along my spine, I hear his voice in my head. *Can you hear me?*

I gasp, then nod, kissing him once more as excitement tingles all the way to my toes. I didn't imagine hearing his voice in my head that snowy day in his car.

Ethan pulls back and stares at me, but I don't hear anything. Shaking his head, he trails his hands down my back to my butt. *Can you hear this?*

His familiar touch makes my stomach flutter and my eyebrows hike. "You're such a guy." *Can you hear me? I love you even when you grope my butt to prove a point.*

An unapologetic smirk tilts his lips as he cups my rear in a firm hold. *If you said something to me mentally, I didn't hear you. Apparently this mental speak only seems to work when we're intimate, and only from me to you, like the glowing thing.*

I nod that I'd tried. "This is so not fair, but I do like how you prove a point," I say on a sigh as I wrap my arms around his neck, appreciating this new way to communicate, no matter how one-sided.

"Remind me to thank your aunt. Her mental exercises definitely helped." *I'm pretty sure the Corvus doesn't feel us when we're close like this. I don't sense him, but from now on we have to assume he can at least hear everything we say, Sunshine. My mind is the one part of me he hasn't cracked, and now that I know I can speak to you this way, it'll be the only place we can talk freely. He sent me to a place of pure darkness, Nara. Our connection is what led me back. I couldn't see anything and didn't even know where to concentrate my effort on breaking through, until I saw the glow around my hand holding yours in the darkness. Do you think you can act natural while I tell you what happened in that dark space?*

I nod and answer his other comment. "That's great to know she's helping." Exhaling slowly, I press my face to his jaw so he can tell me. Ethan moves his hands up to my waist under my shirt, trailing his warm fingers tenderly over my skin. Even though his touch along my spine and ribs makes my skin prickle and my heart thump, his muscular chest feels tense against me as his deep voice filters into my head.

*I think the Corvus sent me to the furthest recesses of his mind, a place even he doesn't go. It felt heavy and thick, cut off from everything. Whenever I took a breath, I tasted, felt, heard, and smelled sweeping waves of rage, a deep sense of betrayal, and utter disdain for all of humanity's sins. Backstabbing, lying, cheating, stealing, murder, torture, horrific atrocities and depravity played over and over. All things the Corvus has witnessed across eons filled my mind. You have no idea what it's like to feel violently ill, but not have a body to expel the vileness rushing through you. The anger emanating there was a soul-sucking flood of emotions so magnified that it felt like I was being torn to shreds from the inside out. If it weren't for your aunt helping me with visualization techniques to distract me from the destructive bombardment in my head…*When he trails off, I look up and meet his gaze. So much emotion swirls there, but the last one I expect to see is disillusionment. *How can the Master Corvus feel this way about the people he's supposed to protect, Nara?*

I blink so the mist in my eyes doesn't turn into tears. It's hard to remember not to react to what Ethan just mentally told me, especially while feeling such love for him and sadness for his Corvus. The emotional roller coaster is making my heart speed up and slow down erratically. But there is at least one thing I can convey out loud. "Rave admitted that his memories are only thirty-years old. My guess is they started after the event at the sanctuary since he has no memory of that day other than his sheer hatred of the place. Also, the timing of that article about the crows and ravens falling from the sky lines up. He acknowledges that he needs to remember what happened so he can recover his past memories, and I promised we would help him."

Ethan traces his fingers along my jaw, worry reflected in his gaze. "Then we will."

As I let out a breath of relief, he says in my mind. *But what if the only thing keeping the Master Corvus stable and protecting humanity is the fact he can't remember that he despises the entire human race?*

I'm so shaken by this revelation that I glance up at him, but Ethan must be worried I'll respond to that, because he quickly turns my back to his chest and wraps his arms around me. *After what I felt, I don't know if helping the Corvus regain his memory is such a good idea. He has lived thinking he was just a Corvus for thirty years with no human Paladin to help balance the evil he fights every day. What happens when all that hatred comes back to him? He and I might have our differences, but instead of helping him recover his past, I can be the Corvus' conscience and keep positive thoughts about humankind in the forefront of his mind.* Pulling me closer, he kisses my neck, whispering in my ear, "I love you, Sunshine."

I fold my arms around his on my waist and squeeze my eyes shut. If the spirit never regains his memories, that would mean that the Corvus wouldn't fully become the Master and all that entails. Ethan would be at a much greater disadvantage going up against Lucifer. Just thinking about that scenario gnarls the knots in my stomach even more. Taking a few calming breaths so I don't blurt out something that would alert Rave of my deep worry, I give an answer that the Corvus would appreciate and one I truly believe.

"Rave didn't have *us*, Ethan. I believe in your Corvus, and deep down, despite your dominant personalities constantly butting against each other, I think you do too. We must go to London. No matter what we uncover there—memories or not—it doesn't change the fact that Lucifer is still coming, if he's not already here. We need to help prepare Rave so he can make sure Lucifer doesn't make our world his permanent playground."

"We'll figure it out. For now I need to go before the sun rises." But instead of moving away, he presses his lips to the spot where my oversized T-shirt has slipped down, exposing part of my shoulder.

His mouth lingers, his breath warm and inviting. *I miss your soft skin and sweet smell. I could bask in you all night, Sunshine.*

Releasing me, he murmurs huskily next to my ear, "You make it hard to leave."

"Then don't. Not yet," I whisper desperately. Smiling, I quickly turn around to hug him close, but he's already gone.

### Ethan

"Take me back, I'm not done talking with Nara." The Corvus' command has boomed over and over in my head from the moment I released Nara.

I slide into my car down the street from her house and put my key in the ignition. I need to get home and take a shower for school before Samson wakes up. The last thing I want to deal with is a lecture from him about grades and school coming first. "The *Ethan* express is over, bird." When the engine rumbles to life, I have to use both hands and my own stubborn determination to counter the spirit's strength as he tries to force me to turn the engine back off. Yanking my car into gear, I push on the gas so the spirit can't try to physically eject me out of the vehicle.

"How were you able to overcome my block?" he demands as I turn onto the road that'll take me home.

The fact he sounds both disgusted and curious that I was able to break free of his mental hold gives me a measure of grim satisfaction. Despite the knowledge that he could rip me apart with a mere thought, he needs to know where I stand. *The rest of the world might be yours to protect, Corvus, but Nara's mine. If you ever want her help again, you'll have to go through me.*

*I can take over whenever I wish, you impudent bag of flesh. Then you will cease to matter.*

Gripping the steering wheel tight, I meet the black eyes staring back at me in the rearview mirror and sneer, *Go ahead and try.* As a surge of energy tightens my chest, I set my jaw and focus on keeping him out of my head and my car on the road.

His laugh is low and confident. *It's much easier to go where I've already been.*

Nara might be my Achilles heel, but if I learned anything while being held in that dark hole in the Corvus' subconscious, it's that she's his weakness too. Trying to stay sane while surrounded by a maelstrom of destructive emotions, I learned that the strongest muscle we humans have is our mind. With this entity, mine will definitely have to be sharper than my sword.

*How soon you forget that Nara can tell the difference, Corvus.*

# Chapter Fifteen

### *Ethan*

*It's about time!* The Corvus snarks in my head as I leave Central Virginia Animal Shelter.

*Shut up, bird! If you continue to harp in my ear, I'll walk right back in there and ask Sally to schedule me for a few more days. She'd be happy to shorten my three-week request for time off.*

"Mr. Harris?" I shift my gaze to Grant Rockford exiting the gleaming black pickup truck wearing his custom Italian suit and grin at the two completely different styles.

Glancing over my shoulder to make sure none of the other employees are around, I say, "Thanks for meeting me here. My house isn't the best place."

"Per your request, the multi-year lease paperwork is in the glove box ready to be signed." He drops the truck keys into my hand, then twitches his tie. "In the future, we could meet at your apartment downtown if you prefer."

I stare at him for a second, still floored by the Gaston estate's vast holdings, but glad I spent the time heavily researching finances to prepare for this meeting. "Actually, sell it."

"What?"

"That's what I'd like you to do. Sell the current place. Then set up a new company name that can't be traced back to the estate. Have the new company purchase another apartment of similar value. I want a third party to handle the transaction in cash, furnish it and for them to send me the address when it's done. They can mail you the key, which I'll collect later."

The lawyer swallows and blinks at me as if I've lost my mind. "So you want to meet there in the future for any business or estate transactions you need taken care of?"

I shake my head. "You're never to go to that address. Consider it my personal space."

He eyes me for a second. "Okay. Anything else?"

"Buy a new phone and only use it to communicate with me. No other incoming or outgoing calls should go to that phone. Did you bring what I asked for?"

Nodding, he pats his suit jacket, then slides a thin envelope out. "Everything you asked for is in here. The tickets you requested are in there as well. Is there anything else you require?"

I hold his gaze and try to measure the quality of his trustworthiness. "What did you think about Danielle?"

He swallows, but answers without hesitation. "She was a cold-hearted person."

Grunting my agreement, I take the envelope. "Thank you, Grant. For now, that's all I require."

"But your other holdings…would you like me to hire a financial manager?"

We stare at each other for a beat. "I don't want any more people in my affairs than necessary. Can you handle it?"

"Beyond my law degree," he begins, straightening his shoulders slightly. "I also hold an MBA from Central University."

I nod. "For now…as long as you don't ask any questions and are able to maintain the family businesses, I'm fine with you overseeing the management. You'll receive commission based on performance. The better the overall business does, the better you do. Is that agreeable?"

He nods, smiling. "I'll be happy to take on the expanded role, Mr. Harris. Thank you for your trust."

"Ethan," I correct him, then narrow my gaze. "From this point on, I consider you part of the family. I might look young, but my beliefs are old-school. Don't betray my trust. As you know, people in the family haven't stuck around very long."

When Grant audibly swallows, I realize I've probably scared the guy to death. I should back off a bit. I glance at the building. "Have you ever been to this facility?"

"I got my first dog from here when I was ten," he says, eying the animal shelter.

Knowing that Danielle resented the time I spent here volunteering instead of Corvus training with her twenty-four/seven, I nod toward the building. "This place needs to expand. Please go inside and make a generous donation. Make sure it's enough to allow them to double their current space, and I want the donor to remain anonymous."

Grant nods and grins broadly, buttoning his suit jacket. "It'll be nice to do something charitable for a place I personally know."

I frown. "The Gaston estate doesn't donate locally?"

"Just at the national level."

"Then we need to mix it up some." I smile for the first time since he walked up. "Go make the animal shelter's day."

Once he disappears inside the building, I let out a deep breath and thumb through the envelope he gave me, moving the spending money out of the way to check my name and tickets.

"Let's go already," the Corvus complains. I know seeing the passport is making him edgy. Just to annoy him further, I put my hand on my car door's handle and take a deep breath as I glance back toward the CVAS building. Volunteering at the animal shelter the last couple of days has been my way of dealing with the Corvus' tantrums. Each day at school he ranted and fumed in my ear during every class, but in the afternoons, I escaped to the animal shelter and stayed busy. The moment I walked into CVAS, the animals' positive energy muffled the spirit's voice until I could pretty much ignore his constant haranguing.

I might've been able to control these past two days, but the Corvus owned my nights. He filled my dream world with every hellish thing he could think of to punish me for keeping him from Nara. But this morning, the moment I rolled over in bed, instead of starting in with a rant, he tried a different tactic.

*You're interfering with my progress in remembering and putting the world in danger. There are bigger issues at stake than your bruised pride.*

The world had been in danger every single day since the beginning of time, yet *now* the spirit is talking like he cares about the entire population? After battling wills for two days, the weight of sleepless exhaustion was starting to wear on me, which only amplified my need to gain control. Folding my arms behind my head, I stared at my bedroom ceiling and refused to rise to his bait. *Nice try. I call bullshit, Corvus. You know what I'm waiting on.*

As much as I desperately missed seeing Nara the last two days, staying away was necessary. Until the Corvus acknowledged that he wouldn't attempt to take over my mind again, he wasn't going anywhere near the most precious thing in the whole world to me. To assure this, I refused to hunt for demons and set alarms at night to wake me every hour. I didn't trust that he wouldn't take off to Nara's. The alarms annoyed him, but the inability to hunt *really* ticked him off.

During our standoff, I was never more thankful for my newfound ability to communicate with Nara mentally. As I passed her in the hall yesterday at school, I whispered in her mind, *I think I'm wearing him out. He's still pissed at me, but we're coming to an understanding. Expect to resume training soon.*

Nara pushed her hair behind her ear and pretended to smile at someone behind me, but I knew that move was meant for me. It made my heart soar. *I've missed her too.*

I haven't had a chance to text Nara yet, so I beep the key fob and climb into the truck, then retrieve my phone to invite her to the gym. Just because we'll be together in London doesn't mean she should stop learning to defend herself. I start to type her a note when my phone rings.

I'm surprised to see it's my mom calling.

"Hello?"

"Ethan, I'm…calling—"

"Mom? What's wrong?" I instantly sit up straighter and feel the sword tattoo on my back start to harden. She's sobbing. I can't remember a single time that I've ever heard my mom cry.

"You're father's in the hospital. I came home to find him on the floor in the living room."

"I'm on my way," I say and quickly start the engine.

"Someone attacked him…badly. There was so much blood! He's in and out of consciousness, but hasn't been able to talk. The doctors are with him now." She breaks into another sob. "They're running tests to see if he has any internal bleeding." As I pull out onto the road, Mom says, "I tried to call your brother, but his phone went straight to voicemail. I was going to try again—oh, a nurse is here with paperwork—but can you call him?"

"I'll take care of it, Mom. You're at Jefferson, right?"

"Yes, Jefferson. Thank you for calling your brother."

"Don't worry. I'll get in touch with Samson. We're coming."

My hand shakes slightly as I hit the button to call Samson. The moment I press the phone to my ear, my brother picks up. "I hope you're on your way home. You'll be just in time."

Samson's tone is so jovial, I instantly snap. "Why didn't you pick up when Mom tried to call you earlier?"

"I was busy answering the door—Oh, not that cabinet, the other one. Yeah, the wooden bowl."

*Did his girlfriend get back early from her trip?* Just when I start to cut him off, my brother speaks into the phone again. "Dinner will be served in ten minutes, so hurry up, bro."

"Samson, Dad's in the hospital. That's what Mom was trying to call you about. Someone beat him up in their home. He's barely conscious and so far he hasn't spoken. I'm on my way over to the hospital right now. I'll meet you there."

"Nah, I'll pass," he says, while the sound of running water floats across the line. "Dinner's almost ready."

"I just told you that Dad's in the emergency room and you're rambling about dinner?" I growl into the phone. "What the hell is wrong with you?"

"I saw him earlier today and left their house feeling *very* satisfied." My foot eases off the gas and my chest tightens at the almost gleeful gratification in Samson's tone. "So you can go do that if you want, but if I were you, I'd come home for dinner instead."

His lack of human decency knocks me in the gut. *Shit, shit, shit!* My hand grips tight on the phone. A demon has Samson.

*Beating up your father with your brother's fists? This demon is beyond twisted.* The bit of sympathy edging the Corvus' sharp comment surprises me. I fold my fingers tight around the steering wheel and try to reason what to do—my father is fighting for his life. I can't abandon my mother, but doctors are taking the best care of my dad and Samson's at greater risk right now. The Corvus' voice booms in my head just as my car veers into another lane. *Pull over before you wreck!* He doesn't give me a chance to react; my foot suddenly pushes hard on the brake and my hand turns the wheel, yanking the truck to the side of the road.

The screeching wheels hikes my adrenaline, jarring me into fight mode and I bark into the phone, "I'm going to rip you to shreds, demon—"

"We're having steak," he cuts me off in a pleasant, unaffected voice. "Our guest is going to be disappointed if you can't make it." His voice moves away from the phone. "Tell him to get his butt home."

As dread slows my jacked pulse to a sluggish *whoosh*, the Corvus snarls in my head, *He has Nara.*

"Surprise! I'm making salad," Nara calls from a distance in the background.

My heart rate vaults at the happiness in her voice. She has no idea a demon has taken possession of my brother. I might hunt and battle demons daily, but there's only one demon who knows about Nara and me—the Inferi who nearly killed her Gran and stole the *Ravens* book—Harper's demon. "If you touch one hair on her head, you'll wish all I did was send you to Under—"

"See you soon, Ethan," the demon says cheerfully then hangs up.

# Chapter Sixteen

### Nara

"I'm going to check on the steaks." Samson sets the phone down, then puts away the spices he'd seasoned the meat with.

"How much longer?" I ask, excited to see Ethan. Samson called earlier, inviting me for dinner and I immediately accepted. I was so disappointed that I hadn't been able to at least train with Ethan the last couple of days, and though I knew why he'd been keeping his distance, I thought his brother would be the perfect buffer for us to spend some time together as a couple without worrying who might see us. Not to mention, Samson's presence should keep Rave firmly tucked away.

Pulling open the backdoor, Samson glances my way and chuckles. "Now that Ethan knows you're here, he'll probably break the sound barrier getting home."

I laugh and pull my phone from under the cookbook Samson had set on it. Moving back to the bowl, I toss the fresh vegetables with the salad fork and spoon. "I meant for the steak. How much longer until they're done?"

"It won't be long now." Samson retrieves the spatula and plate from the counter. "Probably five more minutes."

I nod and grab up the carrot bits, tomato ends and celery stalk leaves and toss them all into the sink. Turning on the water, I push some of the celery stalks into the disposal and hit the light switch to turn it on.

When the disposal makes a distinct metal-on-metal grinding sound, I instantly turn off the switch and tug the rubber stopper out. All I can see are partially chewed up celery leaves, so I grab a pair of tongs and start pulling the leaves out, a few chunks at a time. Nothing comes out but leaves. I turn to grab my phone to shine the flashlight, but it's not where I thought I left it.

I give up looking for my phone and blindly fumble around in the disposal a couple more times, but I can't seem to grasp onto whatever is down in there. Setting the tongs down, my stomach tenses as I carefully reach down in the disposal to grab the culprit.

I'm surprised that I latch onto something supple. I tug but it doesn't give, so I twist my finger around the flexible piece once more and yank harder this time. *Yes*, I smile as I pull out the offender only to stare in surprise at a man's watch.

Frowning, I turn the mangled timepiece around by the sliced up leather strap. As I finally make out the destroyed Corvus symbol and inscription from Ethan to his brother on the back, my stomach pitches. *Oh no...Samson.*

"And here I thought you'd be clueless until Ethan arrived."

I glance up at Samson shaking his head, but I know that a demon is hiding behind his amused smile.

"You should never underestimate me," I say at the same time I fling a handful of wet vegetables at his face. I don't stop to see if I hit him. I just run out of the kitchen and into the living room, looking for anything I can use to slow him down.

Grabbing the first thing I can find, I yank the floor lamp out of the socket and run back to the wall next to the kitchen. The moment Samson bolts through the doorway, I swing the lamp and catch him in the chest. After the demon goes down, slamming onto his back with a furious roar, I toss the lamp on top of him and bolt for the door.

Just as I start to yank it open, I'm lifted off my feet by the back of my sweater.

"Nice try, you little bitch. I only need you breathing to get what I want. The rest is up for grabs," he growls and then throws me across the room.

I hit the back of the couch, my body spasming from the impact. Arms flailing, I try to grab onto something, but I'm moving too fast.

Momentum pulls me over onto the cushion, where I bounce right off to land on my stomach on the unforgiving hard wood floor.

Blinking through the pain, it takes several seconds for my vision to stop blurring in and out. Just as everything comes back into focus, I'm lifted off the floor by an electrical cord wrapped around my neck like a noose. I stumble to my feet, gasping for breath once more, but Samson yanks hard, a sneer of satisfaction on his face as the noose cinches tight. Choking, I try to elbow him while pulling at the cord with my other hand, but he quickly wraps the cord's length around his fist, laughing his delight. "Go ahead, fight me. The more you tug, the tighter it'll get."

I quickly lower my hands, my gaze pleading with him to loosen it. His sneer turns into a broad smile as he takes his time slowly easing off the cord's tightness.

While I gulp in long drags of air and tears streak down my cheeks, he pats the top of my head. "If you behave, you breathe. Simple as that." As he glances toward the front door, I feel something hard and metal press against my ribcage. "Once the Corvus arrives, the three of us are going to have a nice little chat about what happens when you try to screw me over."

"I'm already here," Ethan says from directly behind us, his deep voice full of barely checked fury. "Release her, *now*. Or I'll eviscerate you where you stand."

The demon briefly stiffens next to me, but then he smiles. "You're not going to send me to Under just yet. You want to know why I did what I did, don't you?" When Ethan doesn't speak, he continues, "Step around so I can see you. By the way…how's the boy's father doing?"

Fury laces every crease on Ethan's face as he slowly steps around Samson, the point of his Corvus sword sliding lethally around the middle of his brother's neck. "You'll pay for what you did to him." Stopping in front of Samson, Ethan flicks his gaze to the gun jammed against me before he presses the sword's tip just below the hollow of his brother's throat. Several beads of blood trickle down Samson's skin, staining the collar of his shirt as Ethan's gaze narrows. "If you don't release Nara and my brother unharmed, there will be no Under for you. Only excruciating pain unlike anything you've ever felt. I'll send you to a place you'll never escape from."

The demon snorts. "Nice try, Corvus. We both know sending me to Under is the extent of your capabilities. Let me speak to Ethan. While I can see you seem to care for this one as well..." he says, releasing the cord to hook his arm around my shoulders in a tight grip. "He has far more to lose in this transaction. I want what was hidden in the spine of that book."

*What happened to his father?* I glance between them. *What did the demon do?*

"You're talking to Ethan, you demon piece of shit." Ethan's blue-black gaze flicks to mine, and the retribution covering the worry for his family makes my heart hurt. I know the Corvus can hear what's going on. I shake my head and press my lips together, telling him not to give any details confirming the demon's suspicion there was something hidden in the book. I don't want to give the Corvus a reason to take over, because if it came down to a choice between Samson or me, he'd choose me and I can't allow that.

The demon cocks his head, eying Ethan up and down. "How interesting that the Corvus is second. I've never seen that."

Ethan's hold suddenly tenses on his sword and more blood seeps down Samson's chest. Samson laughs, his eyebrows shooting up. "Good to know you're not a total wuss, Corvus. In case the boy isn't aware that what he's seeing isn't normal, you can tell him."

I blink in confusion, but then it hits me what the demon is referring to. Ethan's sword shouldn't hurt a human at all. It should go right through the person, leaving them unharmed. The only time a Corvus' sword would also harm a mortal is if the Corvus turned the blade once he'd stabbed the person. Not only would that send the demon to Under in the most excruciating way possible, but it also turns the person to dust if the person's soul has been corrupted by the demon inside them. As far as I know, I'm the only person who's been hurt by a Corvus sword and I've never been possessed by a demon. The small knick on my hand took forever to heal and it's still a tiny scar. So what does it mean that the sword's tip is making Samson bleed?

"I'm going to tear you to pieces for what you've done to my brother," Ethan vows in a slow, lethal tone.

The demon *tsks* and shakes his head. "I only took away your brother's conscience. He's the one who unleashed all the rage he'd bottled up for years against your father. It's amazing how completely primal a person can be when all that concentrated pressure is uncorked. Samson's fists, Samson's fury, Samson's...*guilt.*"

*Is he saying that the blood on Samson's shirt means he's on his way to full corruption?*

"That is *not* who Samson is," Ethan says sharply.

"In order to send me to Under..." The demon glances down and smirks at the blood the sword has already caused. "Apparently that'll mean hurting your brother. Is it worth the risk? Will his wound heal?" His light blue gaze searches Ethan's. "The doubt is killing you, isn't it? You don't know what will happen to him. *Good.* Now fucking tell me what I want to know! What was in the book's spine? Are you going to London because of it? Answer me! You don't have a choice if you want me to leave his body."

Ethan snarls, then says, "The spine contained a scroll that disintegrated—"

"No, Ethan!" I cut him off, but the sudden click of the hammer being pulled back on the gun in Samson's hand makes me gasp.

"That's your only warning." The demon snaps at me, but Ethan growls and shoves his sword deep.

I gape at the blood-soaked sword sticking out of Samson's back, but worry more about the vengeance on Ethan's face. Knocking the gun from the demon's hand, he uses his sword to walk Samson backward away from me.

I quickly yank the cord from my neck and follow them. Ethan's arm is like steel when I touch it. "Ethan...stop!"

Clasping Ethan's shoulder with a tight grip, the demon's expression alternates between flashes of pain and jeering amusement. "You're trying to figure out why I'm not a puff of smoke, aren't you? A stab from your sword should've done it, right? I'll let you in on a little secret. I added a special ingredient to my food this week: charred Corvus." He gives a triumphant laugh. "The *only* way you're getting rid of me is if you turn your sword. The last thing you want is me telling other demons that consuming Corvus ashes makes us invisible to other Corvus while we're inside mortals."

When Ethan lets out a furious roar, I squeeze his arm and try to get him to calm down. He's shaking, his muscles hard and tense under my hand. "Ethan!" I yell to snap him out of it and he finally slides his attention my way. Blue swirls in his glassy black gaze. The tortured pain in his eyes makes my stomach drop.

"I can't stop him, Nara. I don't know what this will do to

Samson." *I can feel my brother's soul spiraling on the edge of corruption,* he says in my head. *The Corvus is so angry. He's too strong.*

"Uh oh...it looks like big brother just graduated to the dark side," the demon sneers. "I just felt dear old dad take his last breath. I rather enjoyed giving your brother the backbone he needed to beat the shit out of your father. And the added bonus is...if I'm going back to Under, you're going to crash and burn with me. A brother killing another?" He exhales a pleased chuckle, even as his face contorts in pain. "That should destroy what's left of your humanity and the Corvus right along with you."

Tears mist Ethan's eyes, but when the black in his irises suddenly swallows the blue, my heart seizes. If I can't stop Rave's vengeful wrath, I have to do what I can to buffer it.

I quickly wrap my hand around Ethan's on the hilt at the same time I press the flat of my other hand to Samson's chest.

"Rave!" I yell, trying to get the spirit to look at me, but he's being driven purely by instinct.

When Rave turns the sword, I squeeze Ethan's fingers and channel all the love and sacrifice I know that Samson has given for his little brother.

"He's worth saving," I say as I push all that positive energy down my arms and through my fingers. I ignore any nagging doubts that this will work and *believe* the power of my own words, "Get out of him now!"

The exploding cloud of vapor forces me to squeeze my eyes closed, but I'm unprepared for the nausea and dizziness. My legs begin to wobble and darkness completely consumes me.

"Wake up, Nara! Can you hear me?"

The leather under me creaks as Ethan's hold on my hand tightens. Wincing, I croak, "Ow, my fingers."

"Sorry," he murmurs and leans forward to press his lips to my forehead. "Look at me. I need to know you're okay."

As soon as my eyes flutter open, everything comes back to me. My teary gaze instantly locks with his. "Samson?"

Ethan silently glances over his shoulder to his brother, who's face down and unmoving on the floor next to the coffee table.

I'm so relieved that Samson wasn't obliterated along with that demon, that a soft sob escapes. Ethan returns his attention to me and slides his thumb along my cheek, capturing my tears. "I don't know what you did, Sunshine, but he's only here because of you. The Corvus would've destroyed him otherwise." His gaze turns shadowy as he blinks back emotion.

"He was acting on instinct with an impossible choice. You can't blame him."

"Yes, I can," he snaps, then takes an unsteady breath. "But no more than myself. Thank you for saving my brother...from me."

I fold my fingers around his. "All I did was believe in him. You're not responsible, Ethan. The *demon* threatened your brother's life."

Ethan's jaw muscle clenches and his body stiffens. "Not any more." When he releases me and stands to pull his phone out of his pocket, I quickly slide off the couch to check on Samson. I'm shocked to see the only thing left of his sword wound is the ripped bloody hole in his shirt. The skin on his back is completely unharmed. While I lean close to check that his breathing is fine, Ethan speaks into his phone in a calm and controlled voice.

"I have a job for you." His hand curls tighter around his phone. "No questions asked. Just do the work and you'll get paid well. You've worked with the UV kind before, right?" The person answers and he nods. "That's all this one will be. Can you come to my house now? Take a cab. You'll have a ride home."

While he gives the address, I wonder who he called as I gingerly touch the side of Samson's throat. His strong pulse makes me feel better, but I glance at Ethan as he hangs up. "Why isn't he waking up?"

Ethan shakes his head. "I don't know, but I hope he stays out for a couple hours."

"Why?" I ask, confused.

He glances down at his brother. "I won't lose Samson to a demon again."

Whatever he's planning, the determined look on his face tells me I won't be able to change his mind. "What about your dad?"

He shakes his head. "I don't know. My mom is at the hospital with him."

"Wait...you haven't called to check yet?"

"Samson is my priority." He sets his jaw at a stubborn angle. "I won't leave him until this is done."

"You need to call her, Ethan," I say, gesturing to his phone.

Ethan looks down at his phone as if he forgot it was in his hand. When he doesn't dial, my heart squeezes for him. I stand and step close.

His deep blue eyes meet mine, full of angst. "If I don't call, I can keep hoping that the demon was lying."

I put my hand on his arm. "Either way, your mom needs to hear your voice. She's all alone right now."

Blowing out a breath, he nods and dials. "Hey Mom. How's... Dad doing?" She says something and I can tell she's crying, but Ethan's gaze jerks to mine, brimming with relief. "I'm sorry we weren't there, but I'm glad they got his heart going again. I called to let you know I swung by to pick up Samson. Unfortunately my tire blew on the way there. Yeah, it was a bad time to discover I don't have a jack in this car. We're waiting on the tow truck now. It'll be a while before we get there."

His mom says something and he swallows, then looks at the ceiling. I can tell he's choking up, so I clasp his hand and slip my fingers between his, giving him my silent support. "I love you too, Mom. See you in a little while."

Ending the call, he exhales a long breath. "Dad's stable now, and there isn't any broken bones or internal bleeding. Mom said that he woke up asking her why he was in so much pain. I'm thankful he doesn't seem to remember any of it." He releases my hand and squats down next to his brother, his mouth set in a grim line. "The only saving grace about a demon possession is the memory wipe. Samson would never forgive himself."

"I truly hope so for Samson's sake, but not *everyone's* memory is wiped."

Ethan's gaze snaps to mine. "What? Did Mr. Dixon remember being possessed later?"

I shake my head. "Not that I'm aware of. I was referring to Drystan. He remembers everything."

Ethan's gaze narrows. "If he remembered, he had a lot of nerve even talking to you afterward, let alone continuing to call you."

"He had to know I forgave him before he left for London. It tore him up what the demon had tried to do to me, but I'm more worried about what he didn't tell me. I think something else he did while he was possessed is really bothering him. If he doesn't want to talk about it, it must've been really bad."

"And you *want* to go see him?"

"He's a friend!"

Ethan starts to say something when someone knocks on the door.

A tall, thin guy with straw-colored dreadlocks walks in with a messenger bag slung over his shoulder.

"Where's your equipment?" Ethan asks, frowning.

The guy grins and pats his bag. "In here. I brought a brand new machine and the UV you requested." He eyes the both of us. "Which one is getting it?"

"Hi, I'm, Na—"

"No names. Just call me Z," he says, gruffly.

I shift my gaze to Ethan as he tilts his chin toward Samson. "He's getting the tattoo."

"You *can't* put a tattoo on him without his permission," I say, trying to reason with him.

"Watch me." Ethan's completely unapologetic and ruthlessly focused as he walks over and points to the area between Samson's shoulder blades in the center of his back. "I want you to put a tattoo here on my brother's back. No bigger than a baseball. Do you have a problem doing that while he's passed out?"

Z raises an eyebrow at the bloody tear in Samson's shirt. "Is he drunk or on drugs? He'll bleed too much if he's been drinking." When Ethan shakes his head, Z snorts his confusion. "Did you knock him out and this tattoo is because he lost a bet?" Before Ethan can respond, Z holds his hand up. "Never mind. The less I know, the better. For the record, if he wakes up during the process, I'm handing *you* the machine. Otherwise, as long as your money is green, I've got no issue doing this."

Why is Ethan trusting a tattoo artist with questionable moral code with his brother? But when Z pulls his bag off and opens a brand new tattoo machine, takes out sterilization cleaner and gloves, and then even sterilizes the scissors before he asks Ethan's permission to cut his brother's shirt, I kneel beside him and help pull Samson's shirt out of the way to give him the space he needs. I know Ethan's heart is in the right place, but I'm just glad he insisted on UV only ink. That's smart. The symbol will keep demons away, but will only be visible to anyone else under black light.

Once Z loads his portable tattoo machine with UV ink, he glances up at Ethan. "Show me the design you want."

Ethan turns and lifts his shirt, revealing his sword tattoo on his back. "I want you to put this raven yin-yang symbol you see near the hilt of my sword on his back."

Z moves close and eyes the symbol, then nods as he slides on a pair of protective eyeglasses. "Grab that black light and extra pair of glasses out of my bag, then turn out the lights," he says to Ethan.

He works efficiently, only asking Ethan once if the design outline is to his liking before he fills in the shading areas with more UV ink.

Once he's done, Ethan pulls a stack of cash out of an envelope and hands it to him. As Z tucks the money away, he reminds Ethan about the care his brother will need to do for the tattoo. Ethan nods and says, "I'll make sure he keeps it clean. Thank you for coming on such short notice. I really appreciate it."

The guy cracks a smile for the first time as he hoists his bag across his body. "Anytime."

Ethan pulls a key from his pocket and hands it to Z. "Take the black truck to Shaun's. Let him know it's leased to him for as long as he wants. He'll give you a ride home."

"You doing this so his shithole father can't sell it out from under him like he did the last one?"

Ethan's gaze narrows. "He can't sell what he doesn't own. Tell Shaun I'll see him at McCormicks in a couple weeks."

Curling his fingers around the key, Z points at Ethan as he grins at me. "*This* is why I've got his back, no matter what."

I smile my agreement and after the tattoo artist leaves, I ask, "How are you going to do the daily care for that tattoo without cluing your brother into the fact it's there?"

He smirks. "I have a feeling that with 'charred Corvus' still in his system, the tattoo will be fully healed and completely invisible in twenty-four hours. If not, I'll treat it the same way I dealt with feather tattoo that formed on my back without me knowing it. I'll just point out that he has a rash on his back and offer to put the cream on for him since it's in a place he can't easily reach. My brother is lazy when it comes to stuff like that, so he'll let me play nurse for him, especially since Emily is still gone. I'll just switch out the cream for a salve when he's not looking."

When Ethan tucks the envelope away inside his backpack, I

raise my eyebrows. "Do I want to know where you got that truck and wad of cash? As far as I know you haven't had time to sub in with Weylaid, nor does the band pay *that* well."

"Danielle," he says casually before walking back over to his brother's side.

When I stare at him in shock that he's receiving money from a dead girl, Samson's moan of pain draws our attention. Before Ethan bends down to speak to his brother, he says in a low voice meant just for me, "You're looking at the executor of William Gaston's estate. As sole heir, I'm going to make sure all that money is put to good use."

# Chapter Seventeen

*Ethan*

"Thanks, Ethan," my father says, clasping my proffered hand to help him get out of Samson's car. I easily pull him to his feet, my chest tightening. It's hard to watch him struggle. I've only ever known my father to be a tough guy who would never ask for help.

"Sure thing, Dad." While I hand him his cane, then walk beside him along the sidewalk to make sure his right leg doesn't give out, Samson carries Dad's bag and follows Mom inside. Other than a few bruises that are still healing, the limp is the only leftover remnant of his attack. The doctors say he'll eventually be able to ditch the cane, but that a hitch in his step will most likely be permanent.

I know Mom's in there fluffing the pillows in the left corner of their leather couch. It's my father's favorite spot, where he usually watches the daily stock news while working on his laptop. Now, it'll be where he binge watches The Ranch, a show he hasn't stopped talking about wanting to see since one of the nurses mentioned it.

This past week has been a whirlwind of Samson and I taking turns visiting my father in the hospital so we could force our mom to take a break. The doctors have been extra cautious about monitoring my father's heart, which freaked her out, but honestly beyond my father healing well, the most miraculous change has been to my family in general.

I think the fact that his heart stopped and he was brought back has completely changed my dad's perspective. My mom's too, but Gerald Harris's overall demeanor underwent a true transformation. From the moment Samson and I walked into his hospital room, it's like we were talking to a different man. Maybe experiencing his own mortality made my father realize that he'd put too much emphasis on things that didn't really matter in the scheme of things.

I help my dad inside and guide him into the living room where Mom and Samson are grinning at the surprise we'd kept from him.

"Holy mother that's a big TV," my father says, his eyes lighting up like it's Christmas.

"It's actually a projector, Dad." Samson walks forward and sets a slick remote with all the bells and whistles into my father's hand. "Check it out."

When he clicks the ON button and bright football helmets and uniforms pop onto the massive screen, followed by the booming base of the pregame theme song, Dad whoops and loses his balance. "This is awesome!"

I quickly latch onto his arm, catching and directing him onto the couch. Dad's too preoccupied to even notice that he almost fell. His gaze is glued to the sixty-inch screen as he clicks the remote like a video game controller to see what all it does.

But Samson noticed. I see it in the way he swallows and moves over to pound the pillow extra hard next to Dad, fluffing it as he rambles about the settings. "There are a ton of extras with this sound system, Dad. I'll be happy to help you go through them."

I glance up and notice Mom standing in the kitchen doorway, a tray of snacks in her hands and tears glistening in her eyes.

"I'll take that." Walking over, I stand in front of her. "Is everything okay, Mom?" I can't tell if she's happy or sad...or somewhere in between.

She looks at me, her blonde eyebrows raised high as she blinks back her tears. "I'm just so thankful he's home, Ethan. Having you boys here means a lot. I hope that you'll come and visit with us more now that he's out of the hospital."

When we weren't at the hospital, my brother and I worked together installing the speakers, projector and screen for our dad, but Samson was the one who did all the research into the latest technology, the best projector, sound system, and he paid for it all. I glance back to see him sitting next to Dad and pointing to the remote, their heads together in deep discussion. "Yeah, I don't think you'll have to worry about that. At the very least he's going to be over here every Sunday for football."

"And you?" Mom asks. "Will we see more of you too?"

When I return my gaze to her, she's biting her lip. "This past week has really shown your father and me how screwed up our priorities were. Life…can be taken away so easily. If you'll let us, we hope to make up lost time with you, Ethan."

"Touchdown!" Dad and Samson yell at the same time. I smile and take the tray from her hands. "You already are. Let's go watch the game."

Mom follows me into the living room and as soon as I set the tray down, she says, "Your father and I have a surprise for you boys as well."

I grab up a handful of pretzels and sit in a side chair. "Oh yeah, what's that?"

My father clicks the remote, muting the game, and the sudden silence in the room has me glancing Samson's way. He'd been in the process of popping a chip into his mouth, but he pauses and shifts his attention to Dad.

"I've decided to retire. Your mother and I are moving here permanently."

"We want to be wherever our boys are," Mom chirps, resting her hand on my shoulder. "Once we've redone the kitchen and extended the breakfast nook area—construction should be done in a month—we want you boys to bring Nara and Emily over for a celebratory new house-warming dinner."

Samson looks at my father, his expression serious. "Is retiring what you really want, Dad?" He gestures to the cane leaning against the couch. "The doctor said that you won't need that forever. That you'll get most of your mobility back."

My father's laughter surprises me as he gestures to the cane. I don't remember the last time I heard him laugh so freely. "That cane is a physical reminder that I need to slow down, son. Even when I don't need it any more, I'll never put it away."

"Why?" I ask, exchanging a baffled look with Samson.

He spreads his hands wide, his blue eyes sparkling. "Because it'll remind me that I'm not invincible, that I won't live forever, and why the hell am I working so hard if I never take the time to enjoy or share any of it?" Glancing between Samson and me, he continues, "Thank you, boys, for the surprise gift and for your support this week. Your mother and I appreciate it so much."

Dad might've been talking to both of us, but the rest of the time he spoke, he'd laid a hand on top of Samson's in a firm grip.

Samson's smiling, but it's forced. I can tell by the tension lines around his eyes.

*What's wrong?* The answer hits me harder than a demon's punch—I'm usually prepared for those. My father *remembers* what Samson did. By the sudden paleness in my brother's face, he's just now realizing that upsetting fact too. Nara was right. Samson might not remember everything, but his telling reaction means he remembers bits and pieces. Did he think the awful imagery in his head was some kind of Freudian dream that freakishly paralleled reality? Whatever my brother's mental rationalization, now that Dad just silently confirmed he remembers, I hold my breath while I watch their interaction.

It seems like an eternity before my father nods and pats Samson's hand. Exhaling sharply I notice Samson's blue eyes turn glassy as he looks away and reaches into the chip bowl.

Neither man is going to admit what they know about the other. All I know is…this father, one who smiles more and judges less, I actually like. And I think my brother does too.

Oblivious to the undercurrents in the room, Mom heads back into the kitchen, calling over her shoulder, "Who wants a drink?"

As we all ask for one, I catch Samson looking at me.

The pretzel in my mouth suddenly tastes very dry. *What else does he remember? Does he know about the demon? About the Corvus and me?* If so, why hasn't he said anything?

Mom walks in and hands Dad and Samson each a beer, then gives me a soda. I take it with a wry smile and Samson points his longneck in my direction. "Don't wish your youth away, little brother."

I raise my soda can in salute, giving him a "too late for that" smirk, but the probing sympathy in his eyes has me nodding my acknowledgement before I take a sip. He remembers enough to finally believe that my horrific dreams weren't just me confusing reality with my dream world. He now knows that true evil does exist.

With his gaze conveying so much, I'm truly thankful the men in my family don't discuss their feelings. The amount of therapy my father and brother would need if they demanded the whole truth from me would weigh them down far more than the benefit of just accepting each other's past mistakes and moving forward in a positive direction. Not to mention, they'd probably try to lock me up to protect me from a responsibility I can't walk away from.

I don't want to think about what the future means for me, or how the idea of facing Lucifer without the Master Corvus' full memory and power to back me up scares the hell out of me. I only share my worries with Nara, because if anyone can understand facing crazy odds against inhuman forces and surviving, it's my Sunshine.

I've missed not being able to talk, text, or train with her this week, which at this point would be just an excuse to pin her sweet body to the mat and do things to her that would make her blush and then beg me for more. I love her even more for understanding the time I needed with my family, but now that my father's back home and on the mend, I'm truly looking forward to our trip to London in a couple of days. Even though we have a mission to accomplish, we'll finally get some much needed alone time together.

*Finally is right. It's about damn time,* the Corvus grunts his annoyance. *I'm even willing to get on that plane now. If I didn't know better, I'd think you planned this* Nara-abstinence *on purpose to gain my full acceptance of this trip to London.*

I don't let the fact he was able to hear the last part of my thoughts about Nara bother me. Apparently a mellow mood lowers my mental barrier. Bolstering my mind once more, I snort. *Good to know you're not dead in there. I was beginning to wonder.*

*Don't you mean hope?*

*Tomay-to, tomah-to.*

I'm pretty sure he's surprised my comment lacked its usual hostile bite, but I appreciate the fact that he'd left me alone this week. Not that I would ever admit that to the ornery bird, but his complete silence for several days was starting to worry me.

As we settle in to watch the game, a text coming through on my phone draws my attention. I glance down, then my gaze snaps to my brother's serious one across the living room.

*Samson: I want you to move back in with Mom and Dad.*

# Chapter Eighteen

*Nara*

I pull into Studder gym's parking lot, my thoughts instantly turning to Ethan. Even though I've missed seeing him this week, I focused on finishing a project I started for Central Virginia's Animal Shelter. Every day I uploaded new pictures of adoptable cats and dogs along with an accompanying story about the animal on CVAS' social media's *Virality* page. Between keeping the CVAS's site updated, helping Gran with her therapy, and dealing with Lainey's extra need for girl time, I've been swamped.

"Why'd you choose Studder's?" I say into the speakerphone in my car. "It's not the best set up for an indoor soccer scrimmage." Only Lainey would plan a last minute co-ed scrimmage as a way to relieve stress. Most people would consider coordinating gym space, sending out email invitations and keeping track of responses stressful enough, but not my best friend.

"It was the only place that wasn't already booked with other on-going events," she huffs across the line. "I just need an outlet to take out my frustration, Nara. Does it really matter where?"

"No." I eye the building with wistful thoughts of Ethan. Being here makes me think of him and how excited I am that we'll be able to "be a couple" in London even if we'll be there on a mission. It makes me sad that we have to hide our relationship in our own hometown to protect the ones we love. "Love *is* sacrifice," I mumble.

"Really, Nara? Don't you think I know that?"

I jump when Lainey knocks on my passenger window and thumbs for me to unlock the door.

Cold air rushes in as she sits down and zips her sweat jacket tighter around her neck. Tucking her phone in her pocket, she faces me and doesn't skip a beat in our conversation. "I've done everything I can to calm Matt down short of kidnapping Drystan and bringing him back to Central Virginia. It makes me so angry that Drystan's idea of finally calling Matt was a quick two-minute video call in the middle of the night."

"I'm sorry, Lainey. When I see Drystan, I'll have him call Matt while I'm there."

"Actually, what I want is for Matt to forget about him completely."

"What?" I frown at that comment. "Why would you say that?"

"I wanted to wait to see you in person before I told you this part." Lainey bites her lip. "I think Matt may truly be losing it. He called me last night about a dream he had featuring ravens, and then he swore up and down that his tattoo has changed on his back. That he actually *felt* it morphing."

"How is he saying it's changing?" I ask, my breath catching.

"That's what you're focusing on?" Lainey snaps, flinging her hands out. "Not the fact he might be off his rocker?"

"Um…I mean…I'm just trying to understand. What did Matt say exactly?"

Lainey blows out a breath. "Remember the dreams Matt had been having? You know, where the ravens were flying off that raven yin-yang symbol. The one that made him want to get that tattoo? She continues after I nod. "Well, he called the other morning ranting about a new dream…where all the ravens on his tattoo had turned inward and were flying toward it."

*That's not necessarily a bad thing.* "And?" I encourage her to continue.

"That's not the craziest part. Then he went off about how hot his back felt, like it was on fire. He wanted me to come over and look at his tattoo, since he can't see it as well on his shoulder blade. He needed to know if it looked like the flying birds were turning back toward the overall raven yin-yang symbol?" She pauses and rolls her eyes. "I told him it was just a dream, but he insisted so I went."

"Wait?" Worry grips me. "He didn't get the tattoo like the symbol on the charm bracelet I gave you? Where the ravens are intact? Ethan told him *that* symbol was for protection."

Lainey blows out a frustrated breath. "No, he got the one he's been dreaming about. He said that one spoke to him, so that's the one he had inked."

"Did you go to his house?" I ask, trying not to let her see my concern about the tattoo he chose to get.

"Of course I went! The guy I've finally decided to give my virginity to is losing it. I don't want a broken Matt, Nara. This is freaking me the hell out."

My eyebrows hike. "You and Matt finally had sex?"

"No! Ever since Drystan left, he's been so preoccupied with this raven stuff that—" Lainey shakes her head in fast jerks. "Never mind that. So I went to Matt's and he's all agitated and tense when I get there, his eyes wide and his skin flushed. I put my hand on his shoulder to turn him around and look at his back and he instantly stiffens and says, "It stopped. The heat and pain are gone."

I furrow my brow. "Was his tattoo fine?" I stop just short of asking if it *had* changed. Otherwise Lainey would think I'm as crazy as Matt.

"Of course it was," she says, snorting. "It looked the same as it did the day he got it. It was really hard not to shake some sense into him, Nara. Instead I just told him he was having a waking nightmare, but honestly I'm truly at my wits end with this strange stuff that's been going on with him."

I feel sorry for Matt. It's hard not to blurt out the fact he might actually be experiencing what he says he is. "I admit it's a bit different, but what does this have to do with Drystan? Why do you want Matt to forget his friendship with him? It sounds like he could use a friend right now." *Sheesh, the poor guy needs someone who can understand what's going on with him.*

Lainey cuts me a "are you kidding me?" look. "This happened to Matt the same night that Drystan called him, so of course now Matt believes Drystan is connected somehow."

"Wait…that was a week ago, right? Why are you just now telling me about it?"

"Because he's had the same dream every night since, Nara. And of course Drystan hasn't returned any of my calls now either.

'TheWelshArse' is an appropriate handle as far as I'm concerned."
Lainey's shoulders slump and her terse tone changes to a shaky one.
"It's been hard having to constantly be supportive over something
that isn't real. If things don't change soon, I'll have to tell his parents
so he can get an intervention of some kind. He's not sleeping and his
grades are taking a hit."

"I'm sorry, Lainey. I had no idea. Would it help if Ethan talked
to him? You know...guy to guy?"

Lainey suddenly straightens and hope fills her teary gaze. "It
wouldn't be awkward for you to ask Ethan for a favor? I know you
two aren't together anymore, but Matt likes Ethan. He's convinced
I'm not seeing it because I don't want to. Maybe he just needs a guy
to tell him to get the hell over himself, you know?"

I clasp her hand and squeeze, wishing I could tell her that the
world isn't black and white, but for some reason I think Lainey *needs*
it to be. I hate that I can't tell her that Ethan and I are back together,
but I know this is to protect her. "Ethan likes Matt too and I'm sure
he would help in any way he can. I'll ask him to call Matt."

"Thank you, Nara! I knew you'd come up with a plan to help
him." Swiping away her tears, Lainey smiles and nods toward the
cars arriving in the parking lot. "I guess we'd better get inside."

"I'll see you in a few minutes." I wave to her before she closes
the door and runs off to get her soccer bag from her car.

I immediately pull out my phone and try to video call Drystan,
but he doesn't answer. Sighing, I hang up and dial his Uncle. I owe
Mr. Wicklow a call anyway.

"Nara, it's so wonderful to hear from you. I hope you're calling
with good news about coming to London..."

I'm a little surprised Drystan hasn't told him already. "Hi, Mr.
Wicklow. Yes, that's exactly why I'm calling. I tried to call Drystan
to let him know that we're definitely coming and when. Since I
couldn't reach him, I'll text him the information, but I wanted to let
you know too that I was able to convince Ethan to come on the trip
with me as well. We'll be arriving on Monday morning, a couple of
days ahead of our class, which should give us a chance to visit with
Drystan and tour the sanctuary."

"That's brilliant news, Nara. Drystan will be so pleased. Would
you like us to pick you up at the airport? We can bring you straight
away to the sanctuary. We have plenty of room for you to stay before

your class' arrives for their tour and you have to move over to the hotel."

*Getting Ethan to set foot in the place will be hard enough. He'd never go for staying there.* "Thank you for the offer, but that won't be necessary. We have some sight seeing we want to do. I'll be sure to text you once we're ready to venture out to the sanctuary. I'm looking forward to another Order/Corvus/Paladin history lesson."

Mr. Wicklow chuckles. "You'll get the grand tour."

*A history lesson could really jump start Rave's memory.* Thankfully only Ethan and I know that his Corvus is the Master Corvus. Too much bad blood in the past could create issues with him visiting the sanctuary. "Speaking of history, Mr. Wicklow, you know how you told me about the Master Corvus destroying the sanctuary all those years ago? What happened to his human host after that? Did he remember any of what had happened? Did he leave the Order?" *If we could find him, he might also help jog the Rave's memory.*

"Unfortunately, when the dust settled around the destroyed sanctuary, we found Adder among the rubble," Mr. Wicklow says in a sad tone.

*Adder?* My heart jerks. The last host the Master Corvus' took over was the one that gave Ethan his musical inspiration? I'm surprised Rave let anything happen to his host. He's usually so aware of his surroundings. Shaking off the shock, I say, "What happened to him?"

"Adder wasn't harmed by the destruction at all. Our doctor determined that his body had completely shut down. I suppose it makes sense that when a powerful force like the Master Corvus deserts its host's body that only a husk would be left behind. As upset as we all were that the Master Corvus had killed our leader and destroyed our home, we mourned Adder's death. We didn't get to see his whole personality often, the Master Corvus dominated most of the time, but when he decided to interact and share, he was a strong, talented individual. His music was missed by many."

I swallow several times trying to dislodge the dismay clogging my ability to speak.

"Nara? Are you still there?"

"Yes," I finally croak out. "I'm here. Thank you for sharing a bit more about the history, no matter how sad it is."

Mr. Wicklow sighs in my ear, then his voice enters my head. *Yes, it is sad, but it's also how we learn and grow and adapt. Stronger Paladin/ Corvus relationships are encouraged now. We do everything we can to assure the Corvus stays tethered to his host's humanity.*

I'm so upset by what I learned about Adder, even Mr. Wicklow speaking in my head doesn't feel invasive like it normally would. It actually feels a bit comforting, which I'm sure was his goal since this is the second time he's shared his ability with me. "I didn't realize you could speak mentally across a phone line," I say softly.

"That wasn't always the case." His low chuckle floats across the line. "Apparently 'old dogs *can* learn new tricks.' I do so adore that American saying and never thought I'd get a chance to personally use it."

I can't bring myself to laugh along with him. "I've got to go, Mr. Wicklow. Please let Drystan know to check his text message from me later today."

"I absolutely will, Nara. Your visit will be wonderful for Drystan. Take care and I'll see you in a few days."

Maybe Adder was physically weak and only the Master Corvus held him together. That could be why he didn't survive. It's not like Mr. Wicklow is an expert on human survivorship after the Master Corvus vacates the body. According to him, it was the first time in history that the Master Corvus had decided to live alongside the human race, so he only has one example to go by. There has to be a logical explanation. Michael will clear this up.

The moment I hang up, I call loudly, "Michael! I must talk to you. It's important."

Nothing.

Gripping my steering wheel to keep from yelling like a crazy person, I start to call his name again when Lainey pops her head out the gym's main front door. She frowns and waves me in.

The game doesn't start for a good ten minutes, but I know Lainey wants me in there to warm up, so I open my car door and grab my bag.

I enter the hall and just as I put my hand out to catch the gym door before it swings closed behind someone, it halts mid-swing and all sound stops.

I turn to see Michael standing in the bathroom doorway at the end of the hall. He's wearing a burgundy cashmere sweater and dark gray slacks, and not a single golden blond hair is out of place around his handsome face. I set my jaw and the moment I follow him inside, the bathroom door closes by itself with a clicking lock behind me.

When I don't speak right away, he folds his arms, his tone curt. "I don't have time for guessing games, Nara. What is so important?"

"Maybe the fact that the Master Corvus despises all of humanity for starters," I answer in a flat tone.

Michael quickly lowers his arms, his expression tense. "Has he remembered who he is?"

While I tell him what Ethan learned about the Master Corvus's mind while the spirit talked to me directly, Michael crosses his arms at the base of his spine and begins to pace. "Ethan doesn't think it's a good idea for the Master Corvus to remember," I finally finish. "He's worried what the spirit's reaction will be."

Michael stops pacing and faces me. "What's the alternative? You let Lucifer win? Because that *will* happen if Ethan tries to fight my brother. The *Master Corvus* must be the one to face Lucifer, Nara. Ethan isn't strong enough. And now that the Corvus acknowledges that he has a blank spot in his memories, he won't stop until he uncovers them. You mustn't try to prevent that. Together, you and Ethan are strong enough to help him through whatever he remembers. As his past comes back to him, the Corvus will grow stronger. This is a good thing."

"But Ethan will have to work that much harder to maintain control." I'm shaking at the realization of what that'll mean.

Something flickers in Michael's golden gaze. "Ethan doesn't have a choice. He *will* have to let go of his control."

"What are you saying?" My soccer bag drops from my shoulder to my feet as I wait for him to answer. When he doesn't respond, other than to give me as close to a sympathetic look as an angel can muster, my stomach knots. Mr. Wicklow was right. I feel the blood draining from my face and then it's swiftly replaced with fiery heat. Curling my hands into fists by my sides, I bite out, "So this whole time you were encouraging me to help the Master Corvus remember, you knew...*knew*...that as soon as his memory returned Ethan would cease to exist?"

Michael steps closer to me, his voice lowering. "No matter how much he wants to, Ethan won't be able to hold onto himself, Nara. The Master Corvus fully unleashed is too powerful."

"No!" I say, shaking my head back and forth, refusing to accept the truth. Tears trickle down my cheeks and my chest feels as if someone's trying to pull it open with their bare hands. Boiling fury builds until my whole body feels like it's going to explode.

"I can't change what is."

Michael starts to clasp my shoulders, but I shove at his chest and dislodge his hold, my voice hoarse with devastation. "Ethan doesn't deserve this!"

The archangel's expression hardens with anger and cold prickly fear unlike anything I've ever felt when facing the nastiest demons washes over me, seeping deep into my bones. The realization that Michael could end me with a mere thought flashes through my mind, but I'm beyond caring. I'm fighting for Ethan's life, because someone has to. "You *can't* let this happen!"

I'm shocked when Michael steps forward and wraps his arms around me. Pulling me against his chest, he whispers into my hair, "I wish it could be different, little Nara. But the world can't wait." A sudden calmness washes over me and all the worries I'm feeling melt away. I look up at Michael and frantically shake my head. "Don't take the fear and worry from me. I don't want to forget it."

"You mortals do love your pain." Michael releases me, a heavy sigh escaping as his piercing angelic gaze searches mine. "Use all that pent up passion in whatever way you can to help the Corvus get his memory back. My brother broke though the veil. Lucifer's here. I feel him skulking, looking for the right time to strike. He won't wait long to wreak havoc on your world in the most destructive way possible. The Master Corvus must be ready."

Loud banging on the bathroom door draws my gaze and Miranda bursts into the room. Pushing her sport headband higher up into her spiked bangs, she scowls and sniffs the air. "What were you doing in here that you needed to lock the door?"

I gape, surprised Michael didn't pull his vanishing act like he normally does. Instead, he's eying Miranda with a disapproving frown.

She appears not to see him at all, because she walks right up to me and shoves her chest against mine, her bigger boobs bouncing me back a step. "Hey, I'm talking to you."

Michael tenses beside me, but I put my hand out and tell him, "I've got this."

"Who are you talking to?" she says, but I get right in her face.

"You are a road bump in my world. Once soccer season starts, I'm going to roll right over you and take the captain position on the team. It's about time someone did."

She snickers and jabs two fingers into my chest, her gaze narrowing to menacing slits. "You're welcome to try, wannabe. I rule that team and always will. I'm the best captain they'll ever have."

"You're a bully."

A pleased smile spreads across her face. "It works. We've had the best record since I became the leader."

"What *works* is earning the respect of your teammates. Something you know nothing about."

"Those who seek *respect* are too weak to take total control."

My chest tightens with renewed anger at this dictator in a pixie haircut. "You're forgetting a key ingredient in your goal to stay on top."

"Oh yeah?" She juts her chin out and folds her arms. "What's that?"

"Soccer is a *team* sport. No *one* player can win the game by herself. Leading through fear means you'll always have to watch your back."

Her jaw works back and forth. "No one would dare try to challenge me."

This chick picked the wrong day to mess with me. I hold her gaze, my stare unflinching. "You're looking at her." She's so predicable, her ego so big, I'm prepared for her swing and I quickly deflect her punch. Moving back a step, I goad her, needing an outlet for the injustice raging inside me. "Is that all you've got?"

Miranda screeches her fury and swings wide with another fast moving fist, but I duck and pivot to avoid her attack. Before she can recover, I sweep my foot out and tap the back of her knee to show her I'm not someone she wants to mess with.

She stumbles forward and catches herself on the stall door, her momentum sending the door swinging against the stall wall inside with a horrific metal-on-metal reverberation.

The moment Miranda unhooks her hands from the top of the stall door and whirls to glare at me, a woman in a referee shirt rushes into the bathroom, her whistle still swaying around her neck. With a couple of girls from our team flanking either side of her, the referee's gaze narrows between us. She doesn't skip a beat before pointing to the door and barking, "Both of you, *out*. Go home. You're banned from this scrimmage."

"You showed tremendous restraint back there," Michael says as he strolls beside me in the gym's parking lot.

I'm surprised to see the archangel pop up again so soon. After he disappeared while Lainey alternated between fussing at me for not being able to scrimmage and cheering me on for standing up to Miranda, I figured he'd left me to wallow in my guilt and frustration over Ethan's situation. But as far as I'm concerned, Ethan's future isn't set in stone. There's a way...I *know* there is. I have to believe that.

We stop at my car and I glance at him, hoping he'll get my point. "Fighting isn't the only way to win a battle, Michael." When his eyebrows pull together in obvious disagreement, I snort. "Since you're constantly having to battle to keep evil from breaking through the veil, you would probably disagree with that." The tension in Michael's face disappears with his laughter. The sound is so wonderful, despite my anxiety, I tilt my head to listen.

"Your mind is quite fascinating, Nara. The way you strategize is highly admirable if misguided."

Despite his backhanded compliment, my spirits lift. "There's *always* another way, right?"

Sadness fills his expression. "I know what you're asking...and there is no option. The Master Corvus must fight and defeat Lucifer."

"But you said I'm meant to help and that Ethan can't do it without me."

"That is true. He needs you, now more than ever." Michael glances in my car's window and nods toward something. "I believe that's for you."

"Huh?" I look through the glass and see a cell phone sitting in my driver's seat. "Where'd that come from..." I trail off and when I look up, Michael has disappeared.

Hurriedly unlocking my car, I turn on the phone, but a passcode is needed to access the main screen. I bite my lip and quickly type in TTTWFO. The phone instantly opens to a notes app with an address located downtown.

Just an address and nothing else.

My heart races as I start my car and plug the address in the GPS. *Where is Ethan taking me?*

# Chapter Nineteen

### *Nara*

I stare at my phone to confirm this is the address, then glance around at the people on the downtown mall; ladies with strollers out for an evening walk, older men powerwalking, some kids playing a game of chase around the few trees in the center of the brickyard area. McCormicks, the restaurant/bar where Ethan sometimes fills in for the band Waylaid is just five storefronts down. My gaze returns to the door in front of me.

*What is this place?*

Tucking my phone away, I pull open the door and start up the narrow stairs. I'm surprised when I reach a wide landing, but I step forward and knock on an old-style barn door.

"Ethan?" I say in a low voice.

The door suddenly slides open and Ethan pulls me inside.

Before I get a chance to say a word, he slides the door closed and I'm pressed against its hard surface, his warm body covering mine.

"What is this place?" I ask as strong fingers cup my jaw.

"Later," he murmurs, tilting my chin up to press his lips to mine.

I give into the heat of his kiss for a couple of seconds, then my brain reengages and I pull back, searching his gaze.

Ethan nods slightly. "It's me, Sunshine." Leaning over, he hits the light switch. As the room douses in darkness, I exhale my tension when his hand grips my waistline and his thumb moves in glowing strokes across my exposed skin.

Throwing my arms around his neck, I let out a soft sob and pull him close, welcoming his strong arms wrapping me in a tight hug. I don't want to think about what I just learned from Michael. I will never share it with Ethan, because I refuse to believe it's true. I won't accept that this amazing person will cease to exist once the Corvus takes over. Ethan is too strong. He's gone through so much and is larger than life in his own right. We will find a way.

When he whispers against my temple, "I'm glad to know you've missed me as much as I did you." I finally take in the big open loft-like space behind him and look out the tall windows at the breathtaking view of Central Virginia with the mountain peaks along the horizon.

"What an amazing view. Is one of the Weylaid guys letting you borrow his place?"

Ethan hooks his finger under my chin and pulls my gaze back to his. Pressing his mouth to mine once more, he says in a husky voice, "Right now...you're the only thing I can see."

All thoughts evaporate as his hands clasp my waist and lock me to him. I don't even remember sliding my fingers into his hair, but his teeth raking along my neck encourage me to bolder moves.

When I start to pull his shirt out of his jeans, he steps back and grasps my hand.

"What are you—"

But I'm suddenly upside down across his shoulder and he's walking, a low seductive chuckle rumbling as he clasps my thighs to his chest.

"You'd better have protection, Ethan," I say on a squeal and smack at his butt just before I'm flung down on a massive bed.

*We're covered*, he says in my mind as his hard body instantly flattens me into the soft covers. Ethan's fingers dig into my hair and his mouth devours mine in a kiss so intensely hot, all I can do is mewl and melt against him, encouraging this rougher, almost desperate side of him.

My shirt and bra disappear and it takes us even less time to shed the rest of our clothes. When his warm chest presses to mine and his mouth sears a molten path down my neck to the top of my breast, tears leak out before I can stop them. I love him so much, the thought I could lose him is almost overwhelming.

Ethan glances up and lifts his hand to my face, his thumb capturing the moistness. "No tears, Nara. Forget everything out there. This is just you and me. We're the only ones who matter. Right here, right now…don't let anyone spoil that. I need you to do that for us. Can you?"

The sheer determination in his voice makes my heart jerk. I want to ask him what's wrong, but he seems to need this as much as I do, so I sniff back my tears and slide my hands into his hair. Crushing the soft thickness between my fingers, I wrap my legs around his hips. "I love you so much it's hard not to cry, but I'll try."

His lips twitch and he nips at my jawline. "Then smile while I love you, Sunshine. Show me that all this Corvus stuff hasn't changed our connection…that it's strong no matter what."

Tugging my hand from his hair, Ethan presses his lips to my palm, but when he slowly runs his tongue along the tiny scar there, I arch against him, gasping in shock that the smaller scar seems to have magnified my reaction.

"Hmm, that's what I want to hear," he says on a dark laugh. Releasing my hand, his muscular frame lights me on fire as he slides down my body. Warm breath runs across my sensitive skin as he grips my hips and glances up, a wicked look in his eyes. "Might want to hold on for this one, sweetheart."

I barely get to sink my fingers into his hair and dig my toes into the covers before I'm shaking and panting his name. I try to make him feel as much as I do by sliding a hand to the sword tattoo on the back of his shoulder, but Ethan's grip on me tightens and he growls in my head, *Don't even think about it, Nara.* As if he doesn't trust me, he ups his intensity to where I completely forget I even have hands, let alone a brain.

Euphoric can't begin to describe how he makes me feel. We tumble to the floor in a tangle of bed covers and I snicker at our vigorous passion, rolling onto his hard chest to prove that floors can be just as much fun.

With each new kiss and passionate touch, we chase away our own demons and shut out the world, letting our love for each other reflect in an intense melding of our bodies and hearts.

Ethan's quiet as I rest my chin on his warm chest. My body's in full-satiated mode half-slung across him and my legs tangled with his corded thighs and the thick covers. An hour and a half has passed and we're still on the floor, but neither one of us seems to mind. Hooking one arm behind his head, he slowly trails his hand through my hair, spreading the long strands along his ribs. While I'm afraid to burst this bubble of loving peace we've created, I'm worried about his broody silence. I know something more is bothering him than typical Corvus stuff. Something new.

"Are you going to tell me or am I going to have to drag it out of you?" I ask, waiting for him to meet my gaze.

His deep blue eyes snap to mine and I want to weep; he's such a brutally beautiful even when he's troubled.

Folding both arms behind his head, he stares up at the high, open-rafter style ceiling. "Samson kicked me out today, so there's that."

"What?" I immediately sit up, pulling the covers with me in my outrage. "Why would he do that?"

Ethan's gaze slides briefly to me before returning to the ceiling. "It's for the best, Nara. My family will be safe now. Just like yours is."

"Wait? You're agreeing with this? Tell me what you brother said. All of it."

He shakes his head and swallows a couple of times. "It doesn't matter. I can live here."

I glance around the huge furnished open loft apartment that must span three of the storefronts downstairs. "This…is yours?"

"Actually, it's ours." He sits up and tucks my bedhead hair behind my ear. "I bought it as a safe house. It's off-the-grid, so it's a place you can get away from…life." He shrugs. "Or whatever. I've had a key made for you."

Tears quickly blur my vision. I hate how emotional I've been lately. Teenagers are supposed to laugh and do stupid stuff like sneak out and go to kick-ass parties, and manage to survive despite themselves—not *need* a safe house to hide from demons or a place to stay when family doesn't understand the end-of-the-world crap they're dealing with. This is bullshit.

Anger quickly dries my tears as I shake my head. "Tell me what Samson said, Ethan. Where does he think you are right now?"

Ethan lowers his wrist to his bent knee. "He thinks I've gone home. My father and mother have decided to buy the house they're currently renting and renovate it." He pauses, a slight smile tilting his lips. "Nearly dying changed my father, Nara. He's like a different person. He's patient and forgiving and…well, different."

Lightness fills my heart and I lay my hand on his chest. "That's wonderful! I'll bet that's Samson's way of pushing you to reconnect with your parents then. That's why. He loves you Ethan. He's trying to help you."

Ethan takes my hand and kisses my palm. Rubbing his thumb along the inside of mine, he shakes his head. "He's afraid of me. He remembers hurting our father and is horrified by that. He also remembers me stabbing him with a sword and the look on my face when I did it."

"Did you tell him the truth?"

Ethan's jaw muscle jumps. "The less he knows about the Corvus stuff, the better. All of it, Nara. My brother knowing the truth doesn't change the fact that my presence puts him in danger. Samson was very clear. He knows I'm at the center of this. I'm a constant reminder of his own disgust with himself for beating up our father. He blames me for making him fearful in his own home. He told me that he wanted me gone…so I left."

I can't believe how heartless Samson was. None of this sounds like the brother who gave up so much to save Ethan's life all those years ago. If I didn't see the demon expelled from Samson with my own eyes, I would think it was still squatting in him and screwing with Ethan's head. "Samson doesn't know about this place? You didn't tell him, did you?"

Ethan shakes his head. "He asked me where I got the money to buy my plane ticket to London. To keep the Corvus stuff out of it, I told him that I've been doing odd jobs here and there. That's when he exploded at me. Samson doesn't understand exactly what happened, but he knows enough to be wary. He wants me out of his life and away from his home before his girlfriend returns in a few days. He doesn't want anything to happen to her." Ethan glances away, his voice lowering. "As much as it hurt to feel unwelcome and unwanted in my own home, it's nothing new." Returning his gaze to me, he slides his fingers into my hair. "I would do anything to protect you, so I completely understand Samson's desire to keep Emily safe."

I want to rail about his brother, but instead, I just say, "Samson's an idiot." Leaning forward, I kiss his neck and then his jaw, whispering against his skin, "Now I'll get your awesomeness all to myself."

Ethan snorts and slides his fingers under my hair to curl them around the back of my neck. "You always make me feel better, Sunshine. When I'm with you I feel needed and...necessary."

Pressing my lips softly against his, I whisper, "You're definitely necessary to *my* happiness." Before he can kiss me back, I tilt my head and meet his gaze. "You're needed too, and not just by me either."

The moment his brow furrows in confusion, I lean over and grab my phone from the back of my jeans, then pull up the text I received as I was parking downstairs.

*Lainey: Please ask Ethan for his help. He's been able to calm Matt down before. I hope he can talk some reason into him again and convince him that his tattoo isn't changing!*

The second Ethan's blue eyes jerk to mine, I explain everything Lainey told me about what's going on with Matt.

"Do you think his tattoo really is changing?"

"I have no idea," I say, shrugging. "I'm hoping you can determine that without alerting Lainey—"

My phone starts ringing with the "Death of a Shopaholic" ring tone. I quickly answer. "Hey Lainey, what's up?"

"Please tell me you had a chance to talk to Ethan?" Lainey says, whispering. "I'm in the guest bathroom at Matt's house and he's ranting about his tattoo again. And no, it still looks the same." She pauses and sighs. "Is there anyway you can ask Ethan to come over right now while this is going on? Matt's parents will be getting back in from out of town tonight. He needs to settle or they'll think he's lost his mind, Nara!"

I glance at Ethan. "Yes, I talked to him for you. Do you want him to meet you at Matt's house? I can text him and ask him to."

"Thank you, Nara. Yes, please have him meet me there."

"Okay, I'll let him know. I really hope Matt's going to be okay."

"Me too!" she says on a strong exhale. "Thanks, Nara. I'll talk to you tomorrow at school."

When she clicks off, I do the same and watch Ethan stand and start collecting his clothes. As he steps into his jeans, I glance around his apartment. It's decorated in a modern style with black leather furniture with red and navy throw pillows and soft gray area carpets, but I don't see any of his stuff. "When are you going to bring your guitar and other things?" I say, my heart hurting that I even have to ask the question in the first place. I want to strangle Samson.

"One upside to moving out…I'm a lot closer to McCormicks now," he says as he buttons his jeans. "I'm sure my brother assumes I'll get my stuff over the next couple of days, but since I left my key, I'll just move my things out while he's asleep tonight."

"You left your key too?" He must plan to sneak in and out using his Corvus powers. He'll never see Samson that way…then again maybe that's the point. It's probably too painful to face his brother. Standing, I slip back into my own clothes, my heart breaking for him. How can Samson not see what he's doing to his own brother by kicking him out?

Ethan tugs his shirt on, then a lightweight gray fleece. "It's for the best."

"No, it's not, Ethan. Not at all."

Walking up to me, he cups my face and kisses me on the forehead. "You're all that matters to me, Sunshine. Let it go."

"But—"

He kisses me senseless, cutting me off. Once he lifts his head, my eyes flutter open and my whole body buzzes with wooziness. I narrow my gaze at his dark smile; he knows exactly what he's doing to distract me. "Why don't you concentrate on the surprise I have for you on this London trip instead?"

"Surprise?" I gasp, my fingers hooking onto his jeans' belt loops. "What kind of surprise?"

"I'm not going to give you any hints. You're just going to have to wait." Tapping the tip of my nose, he looks behind me on the floor. "Do you have everything?"

I nod, then grimace. "I wish I could go with you."

Ethan glances toward the phone I'd set on the concrete island earlier. "Take that with you so we can keep in touch without your father freaking out. I'll text you with an update about Matt later."

As I pull open the door, Ethan yanks me to him for one last kiss. "Thank you for loving me, Nara. You have no idea how much your belief in me keeps me sane."

"I will always believe in you, Ethan." Hugging him close, I press my head against his chest, my heart twisting in pain that Michael has outlined a future for him that I can never accept.

# Chapter Twenty

### *Nara*

My stomach is tied in knots and I exhale a nervous breath as I stand on the dark porch and knock on the door.

A light flips on and Samson opens the door only part way. "I know you're here for Ethan, but I've said all I need to say."

I'm surprised by his clipped tone, but I don't let it intimidate me. Grabbing the doorjamb, I quickly stick my foot in the door before he can close it on me. "Then it's a good thing you're done talking because now you're going to listen."

Samson's light blue gaze narrows. "Please remove your shoe. I'm not in the mood."

"I'll move my foot when you invite me in," I say, growing bolder with his resistance.

He bristles, his jaw tightening. "If you don't leave, I'll have to call the police."

"Go ahead. I'll be happy to explain to them that you beat up your father and he's too scared to report you. It's your choice."

Samson visibly pales, then his face hardens before he pulls open the door. "You have five minutes."

I nod and follow him inside. We reach the living room and Samson folds his arms, his face a stone mask. "Have your say and then leave."

"Have a seat," I say, gesturing to his leather couch.

His whole body stiffens. "I prefer to stand. You won't be here long."

"You wouldn't be here at all if it weren't for me, so *sit down*, Samson. You're going to need it."

Holding my gaze, he stiffly lowers himself to the couch. The moment he's seated, I move to the other side of the coffee table and face him. "I don't know what you remember about that night here in your house—" When Samson starts to speak, I hold up my hand. "Never mind. Everything you think you've pieced together from snippets of memory, you haven't got the whole picture. You're going to sit there and *listen*, Samson."

His chest puffs out. "I don't want to hear—"

"You're going to listen because Ethan's life is at stake!" I yell over him.

Samson's face turns white and his entire demeanor changes to full attention. "It's because of me, isn't it?"

"What?" I quickly shake my head. "No...not directly. Your brother needs your support. He needs to know he's loved and that he matters."

Samson digs his fingers into his blond hair, tears glistening in his eyes. "Of course he matters. Do you think I wanted to kick my brother out? That I wanted to hurt him like I did?" Lowering his hands to his knees, palms up, he stares at them like they don't belong to him. "I'm terrified I'll hurt him like I did our father, Nara. I'd rather Ethan hate me than for me to hurt him like that."

I'm so relieved that I didn't have to reveal all the Corvus stuff to get Samson to open up, I walk around the coffee table and sit beside him, my tone softer. "Tell him to come home. That you made a huge mistake. Explain your fears."

Samson's hands curl into tight fists. "I can't take a chance it'll happen again. I could black out...I could—"

"It won't happen again, Samson. I promise," I say, clasping his wrist in the hopes it'll assure him.

"You don't know that," he whispers in a tortured voice as he shakes his head. "There's no guarantee."

"Yes, there is." I sigh. I'm not going to be able to avoid the truth. Samson needs to understand how important he is to his brother. Releasing him, I continue, "I'm going to tell you a story. It's long and involved and I need you to sit here and just listen, no matter how crazy it sounds."

I start seated, but eventually I stand to pace. By the time I get through telling Samson everything, including the fact he has a Corvus symbol on his back to protect him from demons, my voice is hoarse and I'm a bit winded. The only thing I leave out is Michael's assertion that the Corvus will absorb Ethan. I refuse to believe it's true, so why torture Samson with that worry?

Samson hasn't moved or said a single word. He's perched on the edge of the couch, his hands locked tightly on his knees. *Is he in shock?* "I know it's a lot to take in." Moving closer, I offer what I hope is an encouraging smile, but it feels more like a grimace. "Is that because you think your brother has hooked up with someone as equally delusional as he is?"

When he doesn't speak, worry grips me. "Are you okay?" Just as I start to touch his shoulder, he slips off the couch onto his knees, his face completely stricken. "What have I done? Ethan will never forgive me."

I drop to my knees beside him and squeeze his shoulder. "He *will* Samson. He loves you."

Turning his pained blue eyes my way, he quakes all over. "I've tortured myself endlessly over the fact I appeared to find pure joy in pummeling my father. *Thank God* it wasn't truly me, Nara."

"Ethan and I know that," I croak as I tug on his arm to help him up.

As soon as he stands, Samson walks into the kitchen and the sink water runs briefly. Returning with a glass of water, his hand shakes slightly as he offers it to me before sitting once more. While I gulp several swallows, he blows out slow, even breaths as if trying to calm himself down. "I've recalled enough of my memory from last week to know you're not making this up, no matter how fantastical it sounds." Shaking his head, he murmurs, "I remember the doctors saying they couldn't explain why Ethan was still in a coma at the hospital...so you're the one who pulled Ethan out of that dream world he was stuck in? He really wasn't in a coma?"

Now that my throat feels less parched, I take a more reserved sip of my water before answering. "Not the whole time, no. As a host of a Corvus, his body heals very fast—which is probably why it took so much to sedate him—but his dreams are very powerful, reflecting all the negativity he absorbs on a daily basis. There's so much evil out there, Samson. I'm in awe that Ethan managed to overcome what he was seeing in his dream world every night, and that he rose above it." I pause when it hits me that Ethan's dreams were like a huge training ground. Is that what the Corvus was doing the whole time? Was the nightly monstrous torture that Ethan endured the Corvus' way of preparing him mentally before the physical stuff began?

Samson's uneven sigh draws me out of my own thoughts. Leaning forward, he rests his elbows on his knees and lowers his head as if in shame. "I was only trying to protect Ethan, when the poor kid was out there risking his life every day to save others…" He looks up at me, his expression heavy with guilt. "I'm a horrible brother. I can never take back what I said and the hurt I caused. Ethan is so far beyond my reach, yet I can't help but want to wrap him in a bubble and keep him safe like I did when he was younger." His voice breaks as tears slowly track down his face. "I feel powerless and I hate that he's having to live this violent double life with the weight of the world on his shoulders. Why does he have to be the one, Nara? Why can't he reject it?"

My eyes glisten with tears too. I feel his pain. "Ethan is powerful and so worthy, Samson. I've seen him in action too many times to deny he was meant for this. As much as I wish he could walk away from this responsibility—you have *no* idea how much I wish that— if he did, then Lucifer would run free in our world and everyone would suffer."

"When will he have to fight…" Samson swallows back his fear for his brother. "…evil incarnate? God, I can't imagine a being more vile than the one who took over me."

"We don't know. That's why he has to be ready, and going to London is part of that. Ethan never wanted you to know any of this, Samson. He didn't want to put you, your parents, or anyone else you care about in harm's way. It tore him up what that twisted demon made you do to your father, but his relationship with *you* is extremely important to his overall happiness. He needs to know that you love and support him, and that he has a family to fight for and come home to after our trip to London. Ethan may never forgive me for telling you the truth, but I'm fighting for him the only way I know how."

Samson shakes his head. "Never stop fighting, Nara. No matter what my stubborn brother says. Neither of you should have to shoulder the heavy burden for a completely oblivious world, but I'm so grateful Ethan has you in his life." My throat clogs as he folds his hand over mine, the tension in his fingers conveying deep appreciation. "You truly are his 'sunshine' in the darkest world imaginable. Our parents could never handle this kind of truth, so thank you for helping me understand what my brother is dealing with."

I squeeze his hand and smile. "Just let him know you love and support him. He needs to hear that now more than ever."

# Chapter Twenty-One

*Ethan*

As soon as I pull into Matt's driveway, Lainey waves me in from the front porch. Tugging her long cardigan sweater tighter around her against the brisk near-freezing air, she hops on the porch to keep warm in skinny jeans and socks. "Come on," she calls quietly, her gaze panicked.

"What's wrong?" I say, stepping inside behind her.

She tugs me down a hall, her voice shaking. "I can see him wincing every so often and now he's refusing to let me see his back."

We stop outside a closed bedroom door and I don't miss the strain on her face. "Do you want to go home, Lainey? I can stay and talk to him."

She jerks her head back and forth. "I won't abandon my boyfriend just because I don't get what's going on with him. Instead..." Lifting her hands toward me, she finishes with a self-deprecating smirk. "I'm bringing in reinforcements to confirm that I'm not being completely intolerant."

Before I can suggest she wait outside, Lainey opens Matt's door and walks in, her voice a forced, upbeat tone. "Ethan's here, Matt. I asked him to come as an unbiased third party. Will you at least let *him* look at your back?"

The moment I walk in, Matt sits straight up in his gaming chair and lowers the joystick controller to his lap. He nods to me. "Hey,

Ethan. I'm sorry Lainey dragged you into our dispute, but since you're familiar with the symbol I had inked on my back—well, at least the original version—maybe you're the best person to..." He cuts a frustrated look Lainey's way. "To tell me if I'm losing my shit or not."

"Do you feel it changing now?" I ask carefully.

He rolls his shoulders, tension in his face. "Yes, it's pretty much non-stop."

"Why don't you remove that and let me have a look," I say, gesturing to his Gamers Do it Better shirt.

Matt eyes Lainey, who's perched on the end of his bed. Nodding, he sets the controller down and pulls his T-shirt off.

His body radiates warmth as I move close to him, but it's the stiffness in his frame that makes me drop my hand to his shoulder and do what I can to settle him. "Take it down a few notches, Matt."

He glances up at me and blows out a tense breath, then lowers his chin to his chest so I can easily see his back. "Every time I try to look at it in the mirror, I can't see anything, but I feel it, Ethan. The movements are ever so slight...like a slow moving stop-motion movie, but they are happening."

The moment I look at his back, my Corvus senses kick in and I instantly detect the slight ghosting of ink left behind where the birds in the tattoo have bent a wing or turned ever so slightly. As I stare at the dark ink and try to determine what the movement of the birds mean from a Corvus perspective—and why it's happening to Matt's tattoo—he quickly sucks in air and says through gritted teeth, "I feel heat building. Do you see it? Is my skin red? God, feels like it's blistering!"

"What do you think is happening with your tattoo?" I keep my question neutral, knowing that Lainey is watching intently.

He turns his head and eyes me, sweat coating his upper lip. "I think the birds are pulling back into the symbol. It's weird, huh?"

Just as his skin begins to warm to my touch, Lainey briskly walks up and grips Matt's other shoulder. Pulling him forward, she leans over to look. "Well? Do you see anything, Ethan?"

I blink a couple of times, because everything I'd seen and experienced a few seconds before is gone. There's no ghosting whatsoever and his skin feels cool underneath my fingers.

My attention shifts to Lainey. "Could you do me a favor and let go of Matt for a second?"

"Uh, sure." Straightening, she releases his shoulder and meets Matt's gaze while trying to hide the tension on her face.

I stare at Matt's back for another minute and sure enough the ghosting starts to happen once more.

"I'm not crazy, right?"

As Matt's gaze begs me to confirm his question, I look at Lainey. "Could you get Matt some ice water? He feels like he might have a fever."

"Oh my gosh, that's it! You're getting sick." Lainey looks so relieved as she turns to open the door. "I'll get you some fever medicine too."

The second she walks down the hall, I bend next to his ear and keep my voice low. "You're not crazy, but even though I can't explain what's going on with you, Lainey can't handle this. You need to chill around her. I'm going to talk to Mr. Hallstead and see if he'll add you as a special guest for the trip to London. Since you're on Yearbook staff, I'll convince him that you'll do a full spread write up about the trip. As long as there's a plane ticket available at this late notice, will your parents let you go?" When he quickly nods, excitement in his gaze, I grasp his shoulder. "Maybe getting away for a little bit will do you some good."

"Hopefully I'll get a chance to see Drystan. I think he knows something about it."

As far as I know Drystan still hasn't become a Paladin. He's not involved with the Corvus at all, and he knows better than to talk about the Corvus with outsiders. "Why do you think that?"

"Because he got all edgy when I told him about my crazy dreams. He asked me if I'd talked to you about them—I assume because he'd seen your sword tattoo too—and that's when I showed him my tattoo. Right after, he got quiet and then he said he needed to go. It was after we talked that my skin on my back started to feel weird. I felt fluttering and movements."

Before I can ask him more, Lainey walks in smiling, her entire attitude much brighter. "Here you go, my poor sick guy," she says, handing Matt a glass of water. Dropping a couple of pills into his hand, she looks at me. "He'll be better soon. Thanks, *Doctor* Ethan."

While Matt takes the medicine, my gaze shifts from Lainey's hand on his shoulder down to Matt's tattoo. It's back to its original inked form once more and only a twinge of ghosting flickers in and out as I stare at the ink. *Interesting.*

*Does the design on Matt's back ring any bells?*

*Are you talking to me?* the Corvus asks.

*Who else?*

*I have a name.*

I mentally snort my annoyance. *Does that imagery mean anything to you, Rave?*

*The design means nothing to me,* he scoffs. *What is going on with his tattoo? Why does it keep changing and then reverting back?*

Ignoring the Corvus' questions, I meet Lainey's gaze. "Have you talked to Drystan since he moved to London?"

"Only one time when I called him from my mom's phone. He answered and I thought for sure he was going to hang up when he heard my voice, but…" She messes with Matt's hair, finger-combing it after he pulls his shirt back on. "Once I told him how much Matt wanted to talk to him, he said he'd call and we chatted for a little bit about me losing Matt's favorite baseball hat. Drystan gave me a couple ideas where it might be, which it turned out were right. I found it. That's probably the most we've ever talked one-on-one." Rolling her eyes, she sighs. "Of course, he didn't answer any of my worried calls about Matt this past week."

Matt stands to his full height and tugs Lainey against his chest, wrapping his arms around her waist. "I'm sure he's just busy, Lainey. I'll be as good as new soon enough. Don't worry."

When she turns in his arms and hugs him, Matt gives me a lopsided smile over her shoulder. I can tell by his expression he's excited about possibly going to London and seeing Drystan, but he's also hoping that the trip will help him figure out whatever's going on with him too.

# Chapter Twenty-Two

*Nara*

"You are the bravest person I've ever met." Ethan's whisper in my ear pulls me wide awake in the darkness. *Has he talked to Samson? He doesn't sound mad...* Tension gripping me, I start to sit up in my bed, but he slides the covers back and slips under them.

"Actually, *you're* the bravest considering my father is downstairs on the couch snoring away. He 'conveniently' stayed until the roads turned too icy to drive back to my aunt's, but then got Houdini-blocked. Yep, even though I caught my parents sharing a kiss in the kitchen while making dinner, my dog parked his butt on the stairs and wouldn't budge."

Ethan chuckles as he settles beside me. I shiver at the cold fabric of his jeans and fleece brushing against my sleep-warmed skin, but he tucks my body against his and presses warm lips against my throat, a warm-nightlight glow accompanying it. "I'll risk your father's wrath so I can tell you how much I love you."

Pulling back, his glittering dark eyes meet mine in the darkness. "Thank you for being braver than me. I don't think I would've taken the risk you did, but I adore you so much for it. Samson was waiting in my room tonight when I tried to sneak in." He snorts and shakes his head. "Caught me as I walked right through the wall, no less."

Eyebrows raised, I snicker. "If there was ever a way to prove I was telling him the truth, at least you did it in style. What was his reaction?"

Ethan smiles. "He handed me a beer from the six pack he had sitting beside him on my bed and said, 'Let's start with this and my apology, and once I've had a couple of beers, show me the sword and the freaking wings.'"

Stroking my cheekbone with his thumb, he smiles in the darkness. "Thank you for giving me my brother back, Sunshine. Not only did we have a very honest conversation about a lot of things, but I think you've just earned yourself 'superhero' status in his eyes."

"Um, I would think you being responsible for saving the world from Lucifer's ruin would make *you* the superhero."

Cupping the back of my neck, he shakes his head. "I'm just the vessel, Nara. You're the real deal. Being a superhero isn't about physical strength, it's being brave enough to face odds you know aren't in your favor but you do it anyway."

"So you're basically saying I'm more stubborn than you."

"You just aren't going to take a compliment tonight, are you?"

"Nope." I wrap my arms around his neck and settle fully against him. "I didn't do it because I was brave, Ethan. I did it for the simple reason that I love you and it broke my heart to see you so hurt. I hoped you would forgive me."

He rolls over and pulls me on top of him. Folding his hands around my waist, he slides me up his body until we're nose to nose. "One day I'll do something equally unselfish, but right now I just want to hold you until you fall asleep again."

I rub my nose against his jaw and inhale his wonderful smell. "Like I'm going to be able to sleep with this hot body in my bed."

His fingers flex against my skin. "You're going to have to for now, Sunshine. I hope to one day earn your father's respect and getting caught having sex with you would pretty much nullify any chance of that for all of eternity."

"Spoilsport," I pout, making him flash a wide grin in the darkness.

"I've created a monster!" Kissing my nose, he settles back against my pillow, his hands sliding up my shirt to gently massage my back. "I also wanted to tell you what happened with Matt."

I lower my forehead to his shoulder for a second and groan. "I was so worried about you and Samson, I completely forgot about

Matt. Your text said everything was okay."

"He's fine."

Even though he used the right words, the tension in his body tells a different story. "So he's fine, but not quite? Is his tattoo changing?" When his mouth sets in a grim line, my pulse jumps. "Holy cow, it really is? What did Lainey say? Did she freak out?"

"That's...why I wanted to talk to you in person. Lainey would never accept the idea of an evolving tattoo, so I convinced her that Matt was feverish. While she went to get medicine for him, I told Matt that he's not crazy and I'd try to get him an invite on the London trip. I think it'll be best for him if he goes."

"You didn't tell him anything else? Like about the Corvus?"

He shrugs. "What would I tell him? He's not Corvus. Neither Rave, nor I have any idea what his tattoo means or why it appears to be changing and reverting back."

"Changing ink is *not* normal, Ethan. It has to be connected... but it's reverting back? Wait..." I interrupt myself, eyebrow arching. "*Rave?*"

He grunts. "Don't get me started. It's just easier to have a conversation with the spirit if he's less annoyed. But back to Matt... yes, it's reverting *back* as if it's trying to form the Corvus symbol once more. That's the whole reason I suggested that he go to London."

I shake my head, confused. "But if you're not planning on sharing anything about the Corvus, why are you encouraging a trip to London where all kinds of Corvus stuff could come out?"

Ethan sits up. Facing me, he rests his hands on my shoulders, his tone calm and even. "I need to get him away from Lainey."

"Why? Is she freaking him out? I know Lainey can be aggravating and a pain at times, but she really cares and is genuinely worried about him." When his fingers tighten around me, I stop talking and my whole body tenses. "What is it? What aren't you telling me?"

"I haven't said anything to him about the Corvus yet, because I haven't seen what his tattoo is evolving into. Since it keeps resetting back to his original tattoo, it's not progressing and I need that to happen. I'm hoping that by then, Rave will have his memory back and he can help interpret it."

"And you think Lainey freaking out over all this is keeping that from happening?"

He nods slowly. "I saw it in real time, Nara. Lainey freaking out isn't the issue. Lainey is."

I give him a doubtful side-eye. "You're saying that black-and-white, doesn't-believe-in-the-supernatural *Lainey* is preventing his tattoo from transforming? Is denial *her* superpower?" I finish on a sarcastic snort.

When Ethan shakes his head but doesn't smirk, I stop joking. "Are you serious?"

"Every time Lainey touched him, his tattoo went back to the original one he had tattooed. The more upset she was, the faster it happened."

"Are you sure it's not his body reacting to her tension? In other words, it's not Lainey, but all Matt?"

"Yeah, it's Lainey. The second time I saw it happen, she wasn't even talking about his tattoo. She just touched his shoulder in conversation, yet the tattoo instantly stopped morphing the moment she connected with him. It's like…" he pauses as if searching for the right words. "She negates the supernatural from happening."

I blink at him. "Well…the only way to know for sure if your theory is true is to test her on someone else, like say Drystan when he's using his ability to find an object or—"

"I did that, Nara. When I first got there, Matt was upset, so I touched his shoulder to settle him down. Then Lainey walked over and the second she grabbed his shoulder, he riled right back up again. Once I put my hand on his shoulder a second time, he calmed down and stayed that way. By then Lainey had settled too after I suggested Matt was feverish. She immediately jumped to the conclusion that's why he was feeling a bit out of it."

"Oh, that's a bit more conclusive." Biting my lip, I shake my head. "I wonder why Lainey's power-zap didn't work on me in the past? I've used my ability to see my next day to protect her more than once."

"Maybe her ability is recent like Matt's."

"That could explain it, but don't you think it's weird that first Matt and now Lainey have some kind of supernatural thing going on when they didn't seem to before? What are the odds?"

Ethan leans back against my headboard. "I've been thinking about that…and you're not going to like my conclusion. I think Drystan is the reason."

I press my lips together and shake my head. "I know you don't like him, Ethan, but—"

"Let me finish my reasoning, then you can try to poke holes in it, okay?"

"Fine," I say on an annoyed exhale.

"For starters, Drystan is the one common denominator between Lainey and Matt."

"So are we, and if it were Drystan, then why wasn't I affected?" He slides his fingers down my cheek. "But you *were* affected. You can't deny that your powers have grown. You started to control your dream world, and not just your own, but you controlled mine. How did you do that when you never have before?"

I shrug. "I just assumed that my powers were evolving naturally."

"That's always a possibility. Has anything else changed for you?"

"I was surprised…" I pause and furrow my brow. "That I was able to expel a demon from Mr. Dixon and then do the same for Samson."

Lifting my hand, Ethan folds our fingers together. "I don't think that is a power that can be stripped away like Fate did your father's, or boosted like *your* dream ability seems to have been, Nara. I think it's innate and fundamental to your core self."

"How can you know that?"

He shakes his head. "I just do…" Trailing off, he grunts. "Rave is snidely telling me that I know this because he does. He says he tried to tell you about your 'light' the first time you two talked in my dreams."

I nod, remembering that Rave said I was different.

"Okay, instead of the past, let's focus on the present then," he says in an even tone. "Since you've been keeping in touch with Drystan, has anything changed for anyone at the sanctuary? Has he mentioned anything?"

I start to shake my head, then whisper, "Oh no…"

Ethan sits up straighter. "Tell me."

The fact that I received a text from Drystan before I fell asleep saying that he has an overnight school field trip during the couple of days we would've been able to see him burns in the back of my mind. At the time I was very disappointed, but now…I can't help but wonder if he's avoiding seeing us on purpose. Ethan squeezing my fingers brings my thoughts back to the issue at hand.

"Drystan was happy that he'd connected with two of the newer Paladins at the sanctuary. He mentioned that their powers were growing and he thought that was pretty cool and remarked that he didn't realize that was possible. Then he just kind of disappeared and I didn't hear from him for a while. It turns out that one of them had died in a fire. Apparently his ability to super-conduct heat created an out-of-control fire in his room. Drystan's been torn up about the loss of his friend ever since. The other Paladin has been put under strict training to help her control her growing ability. They don't want another incident like that to happen."

"Do you believe me now?" he asks quietly.

*I'm starting to.* I grimace. "His uncle just mentioned an expansion of his powers to me."

"Why are you talking to Wicklow?" Ethan's whole body tenses. "Is he still trying to convince you to become a Paladin?"

"No. I called to let him know we were coming and want to tour the sanctuary."

"*You* want to tour the sanctuary," he corrects. "So what is Wicklow's ability?"

"He can speak in your mind and the way he talks has a calming effect. Using his power over the phone is the new part."

Ethan scowls. "I'm not liking that power."

"Why?" I snicker. "Do you plan on calling him?"

"No. And when we arrive, I think it's best if you only contact him via text."

Snorting, I shake my head. "I wonder if he would even respond. He's pretty old-school." *Maybe I could ask Drystan's uncle to get him out of that school trip? It's too important that I talk to him.*

"Nara—" Ethan cuts off his sudden sharp tone and closes his eyes. Taking a deep breath, he opens them. "Rave is raging in my ear. He absolutely doesn't want you to go to the sanctuary."

"Drystan lives there. If he's somehow enhancing people's special abilities, he needs to know that so he can learn to control it and shut that part of himself down. Just like with his Paladin friend, he's in the best place to get help. I'll bet he doesn't even know that he's doing it."

"Or he's doing it on purpose now that he's discovered he can," he says in a serious tone.

"Drystan wouldn't do that."

"He's got an entire sanctuary full of Paladins with abilities he can push to their limit, Nara. Wielding that kind of power would be hard to resist. Trust me…I know."

I release his hand and fold my arms. "You are *wrong*."

"I hope I am," he says, his tone softening.

I'll have to convince Mr. Wicklow to help make sure we get to see his nephew without alerting his uncle as to why. Ethan and I could be totally wrong and the last thing I want to do is widen the rift between Drystan and his uncle with false assumptions.

"Nari?" My father calls in a low tone outside my door. Just as I jerk my gaze in that direction, he opens it. "Is everything okay? I thought I heard voices," he says, stepping into my room.

"Huh? Oh…I…um." My stomach knots as I try to think of something to say, but a scratching sound outside my window draws my attention. Patch is walking along the windowsill. Exhaling my relief that Ethan's Corvus' abilities allow him to practically vanish at a moment's notice, I gesture toward the window. "I was just talking to the bird who's decided he likes my windowsill."

"I'll take care of that." He starts to walk toward the window, but I put my hand up, waving him back.

"Leave him alone, Dad. He's just being protective." I've missed the raven. Lately Patch has come late and left early before I could get a chance to open my window. My father's determined expression falters, and I realize that he considers protecting me as *his* job. "I'm fine, Dad. Go back to sleep. You're going to have to get up super early to head back to Barboursville for a shower and a change of clothes before school starts."

He glances at the three AM time on my nightstand clock and grumbles, "Don't remind me."

When he turns to leave, I can't help but tease him. "And next time, try the direct approach and ask to stay. Maybe then I can convince Houdini that your intentions are honorable."

Holding my doorknob, he turns back to me. "I can't believe he sat on the bottom of the stairs and growled at me."

"I think it's sweet that Houdini has bonded with Mom."

"*Sweet* is not the word I was thinking. Night, Nari."

"Night, Dad."

He shuts my door and just as I close my eyes to attempt to sleep,

Ethan slides into bed next to me.

"That was close. Where did you go?" I ask, relieved he didn't leave for good.

"Shhhh, no more talking," he says in a low voice. Kissing my forehead, he pulls me into his arms until my head is resting on his chest. "I just want to hold you."

"That's why you came back?" I inhale deeply and I snuggle closer. "Why do you have to make me love you so much?"

He folds his arms around me and whispers into my hair, "Because you are my light, Sunshine. Now go to sleep."

# Chapter Twenty-Three

*Nara*

"I hope you have the best time in London. Make sure Drystan and his uncle take good care of you until you meet up with your classmates," Mom says, brushing my hair out of my face. "And be sure to text me each step of the way, so I can rest easy and not worry about you."

"I will, Mom," I say, watching my father walk to his car at the end of the driveway with my suitcase in tow. He's in an unusually chipper mood. Whereas my mom has already asked me three times if I have my passport, hugging me each time my father had grabbed my bag out of my hand and practically skipped down the driveway to stow it in the back of his car.

I should be offended that he thinks several thousand miles and a few days away would somehow sever what Ethan and I have. Our relationship could be a beat up old clunker car that just rolled over to two-hundred-thousand-miles and we'd still say we'd be together until the wheels fell off.

TTTWFO. It's more than a saying. It means that no matter what, we're there for each other.

I know my father loves me and is doing what he thinks is best to protect me.

*Ethan's got me covered there too, Dad.* I smile as I watch him turn from the trunk to chat with a neighbor out for a late afternoon walk.

When my mom tucks my hair behind my ear, I shift my gaze back to hers, surprised to see a sad look in her eyes. "Before you travel thousands of miles away, I have a confession to make. I snuck into your room yesterday and found the video your father made for you. I've been trying to find my way back to forgiving him so I can let go of the past. I thought that seeing his love for us in that video would help. Why did you destroy such a heartfelt memory before I could enjoy it, Inara?"

With everything going on, I'd completely forgotten about the destroyed CD, and now that Mom's confronting me, I'm frozen. I don't know what to say that won't put some doubt in her mind and douse the sparks of their slowly rekindling romance.

I open my mouth to speak, but nothing comes out. Just as I clear my throat to try again, Gran speaks gruffly from behind my mom. "*I* snipped your safety net."

Mom and I turn and gape at Gran, who's leaning on her cane, her boney hand holding her coat closed around her neck against the cool air. Over the last week, Gran has made great strides from having her cast removed, to standing for longer bouts with the help of a cane, to her ability to string coherent phrases together. Well, as coherent as Gran's funky sayings can be.

"Why would you do that?" Mom sputters in disbelief. Gran gives her the kind of withering look that only a motherly figure can. My mom glances my way. "I know the video was meant for Inara, but I think it could've really helped me."

Gran points her cane toward my father, who looks amused by our neighbor's overuse of his hands as he tells a story. "*He* didn't make that video."

"Of course Jonathan made it." Mom frowns, frustrated. "I just want to see—"

I clasp Mom's arm. "I think Gran's trying to tell you that Dad is a different man from the one who made that video."

"B.I.N.G.O," Gran sing-songs, then narrows a shrewd gaze on my mom. "Stuck in a rut or skip to the gooey stuff? Choose Elizabeth."

Coughing her embarrassment at Gran's word choice, Mom glances Dad's way, her gaze hopeful but wary. "Well, I—"

"Banana splits tonight!" Gran cackles, her eyes sparkling with mischief.

When Mom's eyes bug, I bite my lip to keep from howling in laughter and squeeze my mom's arm. "Dad's making homemade ice cream for dinner."

"Oh!" Cheeks flaming, Mom throws her hands up and shakes her head at Gran. "You're completely incorrigible." Glancing at me, she says, "I'm going to go rescue your father from Mr. Thompson. He'll keep him there all night. Say goodbye and we'll take you to the airport."

As soon as Mom walks way, Gran wraps her hand around my arm, her demeanor turning serious. "Look for me, Inara."

I frown for a second, then realize she's saying she wants me to take pictures to share for her. I lean over and give her a hug. "I will, Gran. "

I'm surprised when Gran drops her cane to wrap both arms around my neck, squeezing me tight. "I'm going to miss you, sweet pea."

"I can't believe I'm going to London!" I hug her frail frame as gently as I can, so thankful she's almost back to her old self. "I'll be back before you know it, Gran."

Gran kisses me on the cheek and when she pulls back, her eyes are glistening with tears. "Don't forget to look for me, okay?"

I get a little misty-eyed myself and sniff back my tears. "I promise."

Gran lifts my hand between hers and points to my ring with the Corvus symbol on it. "Ethan?"

I glance back at Mom and Dad who are smiling and chatting by his car, then whisper to her, "He's going. I won't be alone while visiting Drystan."

Smiling in conspiratorial approval, Gran taps her headphones. She still wears them even though she doesn't use them as much. "He's special, Inara."

I nod and smile back. "He is…and I'm glad you like him."

Gran looks at Mom and Dad and then back to me, her gaze softening. "My happy girls."

Gran's never said anything so heartfelt. I choke up and hug her once more, whispering, "Thank you for always making me feel like your granddaughter, Gran. I'm so glad you came to live with us."

"I'm here for you," she says when I release her, then shoos me on before I get a chance to ask her if she misses her retirement home.

Once I settle in the car with my parents, I wave to Gran. When I get back, I'll offer to take her over to Westminster for a visit if she wants to go.

I receive a text from Lainey as I walk toward my gate.

> Lainey: Tell Ethan thanks for convincing the teacher to invite Matt on the London trip. Even though I'll miss him, he seems less stressed out and just excited now.
>
> Me: I will and I'm glad to hear it.
>
> Lainey: Have a great trip. I can't wait to hear all about it when you get back! #sojealous

As I approach the gate, Ethan waves me over where he's standing next to the gate agent's stand. Smiling, I tug my bag behind me and stroll over to him.

"Are you excited about your first flight to Europe?" I say, pushing up on my toes to kiss his jaw.

Ethan smiles and wraps his arm around my shoulder. "Are you ready for your surprise?"

"Now?" I ask, eyebrows shooting up.

The gate agent laughs and taps on a few keys on her computer. "Can you hand me your ticket and your passport, please?"

Eyeing Ethan sideways, I hand the smiling lady what she asked for. A couple minutes later, she hands me a print out and my passport back. "Here you go."

Completely baffled, I move to take it from her, but she doesn't release it immediately and instead slides a gaze Ethan's way. "You do realize you have a very special guy here, right?"

I can only imagine how big Ethan's head is going to be after all the attention the attractive woman is giving him. Still, I grin widely and nod, because he's all mine. "Yep, I know I'm a lucky girl."

The woman releases my paperwork and smiles. "Have a wonderful time in London you two."

As we walk away, I briefly glance down to make sure she handed me my ticket back along with my passport. My gaze lands on the First Class designation on my ticket and I jerk my attention to Ethan, squealing quietly, "First Class! You got us First Class tickets?"

"Surprise!" he says, laughing at my delight as I turn and throw myself into his arms. Grinning down at me, he drops a kiss on my nose. "I'll need to spend a small fortune more often if this is the kind of reaction I get. The look on your face was worth every penny."

I stop smiling and gulp. "A small fortune? Do I want to know how much a first class ticket costs?"

Ethan tugs me over to a chair and sits down beside me. "As much as I wanted to surprise you, it was also a practical decision. It's an overnight flight. We need to be well rested, so we're awake and aware once we get there."

Nodding my understanding and appreciation, I tap his chest. "How's Rave doing? You seem calm, so he must not be protesting too much."

He folds our fingers together and rests our hands on his thigh. "The spirit is strangely reserved. I'm not sure if he's a bit anxious or just content we're going to be together for several days." Shaking his head, he smiles. "You truly settle him, which is a feat considering how obnoxious and disagreeable he can be."

I lift our clasped hands and kiss his knuckles. "Maybe it's because he feels your peace?"

Ethan rubs his thumb along mine, his deep blue eyes reflecting amused contentment. "I seriously doubt Rave has ever felt true peace. He's restless and constantly assessing everything and everyone around him. Even now, while I'm trying to just have a conversation with you, he's looking for threats. As a result, I'm hyperaware whether I want to be or not."

"How is he feeling about visiting the sanctuary? Even if Drystan can't be there, it truly could be the best place to help him regain his memory."

Ethan releases my hand and turns to fully face me, frowning. "What do you mean, 'Drystan can't be there'?"

"Er, well…the other day Drystan let me know that he now has an overnight school trip. I've asked his uncle if he could help Drystan get out of it and he said he'd try, but I haven't heard back from him yet."

"Why are you just now telling me about this?"

I press my lips together, frustrated that he's getting upset. "While I'm disappointed that Drystan might not be able to see us, his being there or not doesn't change our plans, Ethan. I believe it's important for Rave to see the inside of the sanctuary, especially since Adder isn't around for us to ask questions."

"Adder?" he says, tensing.

"Yes, Adder was Rave's last human host before he lost his

memory. His body didn't survive the destruction of the sanctuary thirty years ago."

Ethan glances away and swallows, emotions flickering across his face. "I had no idea that Adder was the one."

"Mr. Wicklow said he was well liked and respected at the sanctuary and his music was very much appreciated and missed." I know Ethan's thinking about his connection to music…that he got some of that talent from Adder.

Suddenly Ethan closes his eyes, his hand fisting tight on the back of the chair. "Ethan? What's wrong?" When he doesn't respond, I turn and face him. "Ethan?"

"Rave just got a flash of memory," he says through gritted teeth. "He's not sharing, but he's starting to get supernova angry."

"Can I help?" I whisper, worried when I see sweat pop up on his forehead and I feel his chair start to shake.

"Touch me, Nara," Ethan grits out as if he's in excruciating pain.

Just then the PA system crackles and the gate agent starts announcing flight boarding instructions. Panicking, I fold my fingers around his fisted hand, then speak in a low tone. "Calm down, Rave. I'm here."

Ethan suddenly exhales and his eyes fly open. They're as black as night and shining brightly. Trying not to flip out with worry for Ethan, I hold Rave's gaze and keep my tone calm. "Why did learning about Adder upset you?"

He puts Ethan's other hand over mine. "Adder felt so much pain. How did I fail him so miserably?"

"What happened? Do you remember?"

He shakes his head. "He suffered deeply." His gaze glistens and he tilts his head as if surprised. "I've never *felt* before."

I squeeze his hand under mine. "Do you feel now?"

When he looks down at our hands, a couple tears drip onto them. "Yes."

"Does it hurt?"

He looks at me. "It feels…pleasant, calming."

"That's what Ethan's feeling. You're experiencing our emotions. If something from your past upsets you, we'll ground you. You just need to let us help."

He frowns. "I don't like *feeling* pain."

"How would you recognize pleasant if you never felt pain?"

Rave tilts his head, his gaze contemplative. "Do you think of something pleasant when you're hurting?"

His straight-forward logic makes me smile. "If it helps, yes."

"I have no pleasant memories to recall," he says, his brow furrowing.

I tap my fingers against his knuckles. "Well, now you have at least one." When he smiles, I nod toward the gate. "I need you to release Ethan now. They're starting to board our plane."

"I don't want—"

"Rave!" I warn, squeezing his hand, my tone low but sharp.

"Fine," he sighs. Ethan tenses in the chair and then leans back against it, his breathing heavy and erratic.

When bluish-black eyes shift my way, the visual proof that Rave appears to be lingering makes my stomach drop. I want to tell Ethan to blink more so his eyes readjust to his normal color faster, but instead I focus on him. "Are you okay?"

"The Corvus swatted me aside like yesterday's trash, Nara." Lacing his fingers with mine, his voice in my head shakes slightly. *I hope that doesn't happen again. I'm not sure how long I can keep him out when he demands to speak. None of the mental exercises I did to shove him out worked, nor could I see you at all. All I could do was try to hold off all that negativity in his subconscious; it honestly felt like it was eating me alive.*

The fact that Ethan's eyes still haven't returned to their normal blue color while he talks worries me, but I squeeze his hand and smile my confidence. He needs to know that I believe he can hold onto himself. "I think Rave will be okay now that he understands that we're here to help him and how to tap into us for support."

The gate agent announcing general boarding drowns out what Ethan says, and we spend the next fifteen minutes boarding and getting settled in our seats.

Once the plane takes off, a whirring sound opens the partition between our side-by-side facing seats and Ethan holds his hand out. I clasp his hand and snicker as I glance at the closed partitions along the outside part of our seats. "This is very cozy and cocoon-like." Dropping my voice, I give him a secret smile. "But it can't hold a candle to the Corvus Submarine."

Ethan's low laughter as we hold each other's gaze and remember our heavy make-out session warms me all the way to my toes. His chuckle fades and his expression turns serious. "Exactly how is Rave using us for support?"

I drop my gaze to our clasped hands and the low glow that's slowly fading in the darkened cabin now that we've moved on from the intimate memory. "That's how."

He snaps angry eyes to me. "I don't want him tapping into our most personal moments—"

"Calm down," I say, squeezing his hand. "That pain you were feeling was Adder's before Rave shoved you out. When I put my hand on yours to settle you, instead of pain, Rave felt the comfort that you did from my touch and calmed down. That's all. We can help him through this, Ethan. Together we can keep him grounded."

*And as I look at your eyes reflecting doubt, they're also shining just like a raven's. Keeping the powerful spirit settled might be the only way I'll be able to save you, Ethan.*

Ethan's fingers tense against the back of my hand, making me wonder if he somehow heard my thoughts. My gaze locks with his and his voice rasps in my head. *I didn't see the glow of our hands together in that dark space, Nara. Not like I did the last time. The only reason I'm here right now is because he allowed it.*

*Oh God...Ethan's worried!* My heart plummets, but I refuse to repeat what Michael told me would happen to him once the Corvus got his memory back. That would mean acknowledging that I believed that Ethan couldn't handle the Master Corvus, which I don't believe. With our elbows resting on the console between us, I push Ethan's hand upright and hold his gaze as I slowly trace TTTWFO into his palm.

When I'm done, he clasps our palms together, then leans forward to kiss the back of my hand. "I love you, Sunshine."

His husky deep voice never fails to send shivers down my spine and my heart racing. I smile and squeeze his hand. "I love you, too."

Just like I'm connected to Ethan, for whatever reason the powerful Corvus spirit feels connected to me. I'll use that connection and do whatever it takes to keep Ethan safe.

While the Corvus protects the world's back, I'll have Ethan's.

# Chapter Twenty-Four

### Ethan

"Wake up, sleepyhead." I brush a strand of blonde hair away from Nara's face and slide my fingers along her cheek. I hate having to wake her. I slept solid for four hours and then dozed in and out after that, so I know she's only truly slept for a couple hours.

In my in-and-out state before I woke for good, I dreamed the last conversation my brother and I had about the Corvus.

*After I answered all his questions that night in my room, Samson looked at me and said, "If I told you not to go, would you listen?"*

*I shook my head. "Nara's my future. I won't let her go alone...the world needs him to remember, Samson."*

*With a nod, Samson got right in my face, beer bottle clasped tight in his hand. "This is the last we'll talk about this, because it freaks me the hell out." His light blue gaze searched mine. "Bring my brother home, you scary bastard."*

Samson's far more agreeable than you.

*When I grunt in response to Rave's comment, Samson says, "What?"*

*"The Corvus likes you better than me. He says you're more agreeable."*

*Samson barked out a laugh and held up his beer in salute. "And now that I've officially gone over to supernatural land, I'll say welcome back home and goodnight, little brother."*

Nara yawns and stretches, drawing me out of my thought. "Whaaaat'd you say?"

I clasp her hand to help her sit up. "We'll be landing in twenty minutes."

Pushing the blanket off her legs, she glances around and blinks to wake up. "I guess I missed breakfast, huh? Ah well, that just means I'll really enjoy the hotel's infamous scones."

I smile that food is the first thing she's thinking about. "If you want, we can grab something once we're through immigration and customs. Do you have everything?" I ask, glancing around her area.

She quickly sets her chair back to a seated position and then steps into her shoes. "Yeah, I'm good. I put everything away before I fell asleep."

Once we're through security, Nara snags a couple of London maps from a kiosk, including the Underground one for all the tube stations, while I look for the entrance to the tube that'll take us to central London.

As the metro doors slide closed behind us, Nara tucks her hair behind her ear and studies the tube map. "It looks like it'll take us about thirty-five minutes to get to Piccadilly Circus station."

Switching to the zoomed in map, she slides her finger down the London points-of-interest. "Big Ben, Westminster Abby, London Eye, Buckingham Palace." She glances up at me, her eyes bright. "I'm so excited to see them all on the school trip, but I want to visit the Tower of London tomorrow on our own if we get time. I'd like to see the ravens and meet the Ravenmaster."

"Of course you want to see the ravens," I say, smirking. "Do you think Patch will show up to dominate them like he does his American brethren?"

Nara laughs. "He would if he could! I'm going to miss him while we're here. I've gotten used to having him around."

When she returns her attention to the map, I inhale her hair's sweet scent and kiss the top of her head. Wrapping my arm around her waist, I love the freedom of being able to hold her close and let the world know she's mine. With our families far away and safe, every breath I take, even in this crowded, stuffy metro car, feels like a weight has been lifted.

A few seconds later, she glances up and points to her map. "Here's the Library of London. Once we get checked in and grab a bite, we should probably head there."

Smiling at the peace I feel when I'm with her, I turn her to face me. "First, you need to call your parents and let them know you made it here safe and sound, then after we check in at the hotel, look at your messages and see if you've heard back from Mr. Wicklow. I'd feel a lot more comfortable visiting the sanctuary with Drystan there. I want someone who hasn't joined the Paladin ranks touring with us."

"I *know* his uncle," she says, tucking the maps against her chest.

"You know what I mean, Sunshine."

"I do." She nods. "I just hope Drystan *is* able to be there."

"After we're settled, let's walk around some. There's no rush to get to the library right away. It's open all day. But before that, I do want to make sure we get the whole sanctuary thing locked down for tomorrow."

Nodding her agreement, she glances up at the tube map. "It's a good thing I've ridden the metro in DC. Otherwise this would be really confusing to me," she says as she grabs her suitcase handle. "We're switching at the next stop."

The moment the doors open, I let her lead the way. Mainly because she's adorable when she's in map-reading, schedule-tracking, on-a-mission mode, but also, because I like watching her walk. Not only do I love her confident stride, but I definitely find her long blonde hair and the sway of her hips visually pleasing. I'm a guy who appreciates *all* his girlfriend's amazing attributes. And if it's a crime that I admire how well her jeans fit her curves just as much as I adore her brain and her heart, then I'm one-hundred-percent guilty.

Once we arrive at the Envoy, I'm thankful that we booked our hotel in central London. Not only is it one street off the very busy touristy thoroughfare, but it's not too far from the library. Only a twenty-minute walk. I shake my head that I know that without looking at a map.

"Aw, they're having afternoon tea in that garden café down there," Nara says by the window she opened as I answered the door to the light knock.

"Welcome to the Envoy," the young guy says as he rolls a cart with a covered dish and a pot of tea into the room. Lifting the lid off the dish, he continues in a proper British accent, "We heard you didn't get to eat on the plane and we can't have that before you pop out to explore the city. Our signature scones, jam, and clotted cream with a spot of tea should fix you right up."

"Thank you for the welcome," I say, handing him a tip.

Glancing Nara's way, he says, "They're having a hen party down there."

"What's a hen party?" Nara asks, smiling her curiosity.

"I believe you call them bachelorette parties in the US." Moving the tray of food over to the small round table next to the window, he bends at the waist. "Enjoy your meal and your stay."

Once he leaves, Nara clasps her hands together, her green eyes wide with delight. "I've always wanted to try this. I can't wait."

Nara's phone ringing on the nightstand surprises us both. She looks at me and then quickly moves to pick it up. "It's my dad. Should I answer it?"

She already touched base with her parents, so I'm not sure why he's calling, but I nod. "It might be important."

"Hey, Dad." When a panicked look crosses her face, I let my Corvus hearing take over.

"Don't know what you were thinking? How could you assume that I wouldn't find out? I work for the school for God's sake. And I *notice* when students aren't in school."

"Dad—"

"Don't you, *Dad*, me, young lady. You flat out lied to us."

"No, I didn't. I said that I'm coming early to see Drystan and I am going to see Drystan."

"Is that boy staying in the same hotel? You know I can find out. I'll—"

"Inara, it's Mom. I—*Jonathan*, walk away or I swear you can permanently live with your sister!" Her voice moves close to the phone once more. "We'll talk when you get home. In the meantime, be the responsible girl I raised and have a wonderful time in London."

Nara glances my way, her smile returning. "I will, Mom. And thanks for talking Dad off the cliff."

"I'm going to kick that man off it if he keeps dancing on the edge like this," she mutters. "Take care and we'll talk tomorrow."

"I'll call tomorrow."

Nara exhales a huge sigh and hangs up. "I'm not sure where I stand, but I *think* my mom has my back."

"I think you're right. Just so you know…I'm officially booked at a hotel down the street."

She walks over and looks up at me, resting her chin on my chest. "You're brilliant, you know that?"

"Yeah well, I try," I say before kissing her soft lips. "We'd better eat these scones while they're hot." Turning to inhale the pastry's buttery aroma, I stir the thick stuff the guy called clotted cream. "I'm not sure how this is supposed to be eaten, but the scone smells good. Eat up. You'll need the fuel for all the walking we're going to do today."

Nara gestures for me to sit down in the wingback chair next to the table. Putting a scone on each of our plates, she cuts it in half, then adds a generous scoop of jam and a nice sized dollop of crème on top of each pastry half still steaming warm from the oven. Sliding a plate my way, she pours us a cup of tea, then sits down in a matching chair with her plate and a fork. "Dig in, Ethan. Drystan described this dish to me and it sounded like manna from heaven. I have to know if he was right."

I've just taken a bite, but grin widely when Nara practically squeals her happiness. "This is so good!" Holding her fork up, she continues, "Don't tell Aunt Sage, but this beats her pies. I'll definitely have to let Drystan know he was one-hundred-percent *spot-on* with his description of English scones."

"It's pretty good." I nod, but slide mine over after I've taken another bite so Nara can finish it. "I ate on the plane so finish mine for me."

She sets her tea down and quickly grabs my plate to start digging in, I laugh. "It's good to know the daily scones won't go to waste while we're staying here."

"Nuh uh," Nara mumbles around the bite she just took. As I lean forward to swipe the berry jam from the corner of her lip with my thumb, a movement to my right has me jumping up and instantly holding my sword.

When a big raven swoops in and lands on the table next to my cup of tea, I blow out a tense breath and start to lower my sword until I see Nara's slack-jawed look. I instantly lift my sword again. "What's wrong?"

Pointing to the bird pecking at the crumbs on her plate, she whispers, "How is that even possible?"

The raven bobs his head up and down, then turns to look at

me, white feathers around his eye standing out vividly. I blink at the rush of whispering voices that flickers briefly through my mind before it stops. Weird. I frown at Patch. "Did you stow away on the plane or something?"

Making low clicking sounds, Patch ignores us and quickly gobbles up the rest of the crumbs on Nara's plate.

"Well, that's one way to make your presence known," Nara says, snickering.

While she chatters with the bird, clearly happy to see him, I can't help the tension rising inside me. The last thing I need is for Patch's protective presence to draw unwanted attention, especially of the demonic kind.

I'm surprised Rave hasn't made a single sarcastic comment since we arrived. The Corvus' silence is making me antsy. "I'd prefer if Patch stayed out of sight all together, but he definitely shouldn't follow us to the Tower. With those white feathers around his eye, they might decide he'd make a unique addition to the Unkindness already there."

As the raven puffs up his chest and lets out a staccato of *tok, tok, tok* noises…the voices start up again, but Nara's laugh drowns them out. "He's too ornery and would never allow the Tower's Ravenmaster close enough to touch him, let alone clip his wings."

I shake my head and try to ignore the constant inaudible whispers, hundreds of low voices clamoring to be heard, that started the moment Patch flew into the room. "You about ready to go, Nara?"

Sliding her hand down Patch's back, Nara rests her wrist on the table for him to hop on. "Just in case, stay away from the Tower. We'll see you later, okay?" The raven walks up her forearm, dips his head, and then takes off out the window.

After we walk around and pass by Big Ben, Buckingham Palace, and Westminster Abby, we grab a quick lunch at a local brasserie and just as we start to make our way toward the library Nara gets a text from Mr. Wicklow.

> *Mr. Wicklow: Drystan wasn't able to be excused from his school event. I hope you and Ethan will still come for the tour of the sanctuary. ~ Rowan*

"Rowan?" I shake my head. "Of course Wicklow has a pretentious sounding first name. Text Drystan directly."

Sighing, Nara types on her phone and turns it so I can see what she sent.

*Nara: Can you at least meet us for dinner tomorrow night? You choose the place. It's important that I see you.*

*Drystan: What's so important?*

I glance her way. "That's not evasive at all."

She eyes me, then types a response.

*Nara: I want to know that you're okay. You haven't been yourself lately.*

*Drystan: I'm fine, Nara. Just busy with school stuff. I'm sorry I'll miss seeing you.*

Pressing her lips together, she fires off another note.

*Nara: I don't accept your non-acceptance for dinner. We will meet, Drystan. Stop avoiding me!*

I snort. "Who knew you had such a demanding side?"

Nara looks at me, her hands shaking. "I'm worried, Ethan. Not just for Matt and Lainey back home, but this isn't like Drystan at all."

"I told you he was untrustworthy."

"You don't really believe that!" Rolling her eyes, she walks away, continuing to head toward the library.

I slide my hands in my jean pockets and fall in line beside her. "Do I think he's hiding something? Yes. But one thing I know about Drystan, he would do anything to see you, and the fact he's not now makes me want to stay as far away from the sanctuary as possible."

Nara presses her lips together as she lifts her phone and types out another message.

I narrow my gaze. "Who did you just text?"

"Mr. Wicklow. I confirmed that we'll be there tomorrow afternoon as planned." I start to argue, but she holds up her hand. "This isn't about us, Ethan. This is for Rave. He needs to go back there. Seeing it, no matter how painful, might help unlock some of his suppressed memories."

I know she's right, but I don't have to freaking like it. I'm honestly surprised I seem to be the only one arguing. Rave must be sulking. He hasn't said jack since his outburst before we boarded the plane.

We arrive fifteen minutes later, and according to the library's layout diagram it's a four-story building. The main floor features a huge open study/quiet room with a fancy wrought iron banister mezzanine above that reaches up to the second and third floors. Tall wooden bookshelves and sliding ladders take up every wall in mezzanine areas in the two stories above. And the fourth floor houses traditional rows of tall heavy wooden library shelving packed with books.

"Look, Ethan," Nara says as she pulls the skinny car drawer files out, her eyes alight with excitement. "They're still on the old-school card catalogue system for where books are shelved."

Pulling out her notepad from the small backpack she's carrying, Nara double checks the number she's looking for against the card in the catalogue, then glances upstairs. "It's on the third floor."

I shake my head as we walk up the side stairs. The voices in my head sound like general conversations happening all around. At first I thought it was my Corvus-hearing going supersonic on me, but here in the quiet-as-a-tomb library, I realize they're not talking to each other, but just talking. Where is it coming from? With each step we take, the volume turns up a notch, making it harder to tune out and ignore them.

"It should be among these books here." When Nara glances back at me, she pauses sliding her finger across the books' spines and turns to me. "You look a bit edgy. Is Rave giving you a hard time?" Poking my chest, she stares hard at me. "Behave, Rave. You have to give us a chance to help you."

I capture her finger and force a smile. "It's not Rave. He's strangely quiet. Instead I'm hearing hundreds of voices. People talking, not in conversation, but more to themselves. It's like I'm hearing their thoughts."

Nara tilts her head. "What are they saying?"

"I don't know. I've been focusing on not trying to hear so I can stay aware."

"Maybe you should listen, Ethan." Stepping close, she flattens her hand on my chest. "I'll be your eyes for a few minutes. Just… listen."

Nodding, I fold my hand around Nara's and close my eyes to shut out everything else. With my vision cut off, the garbled voices slowly come across in forceful clarity.

*Need to find that demon. I sense him in this building.*

Then a woman's voice. *Why does a demon have to choose my boss to squat in?*

And another man's deep Scottish brogue rumbles in my head, "*I dinna expect such a fight out of ya. Yer a bit on the scrawny side. But mah sword'll take care of ya either way.*"

Over and over, snippets come through. "They're Corvus," I say to Nara, a bit shocked that I can hear them.

"You hear all the Corvus talking?" she asks, excitement in her voice. "Is Rave speaking to them?"

Her question jacks my worry. "He hasn't said anything since we arrived in London."

"Nothing?"

I start to shake my head when I hear a man's voice whisper in my mind. *Is that you?*

Then another, sounding shocked. *Are ya there, Master Corvus? I'm Kellan. Yer close. I feel ya.*

As more and more of the Corvus start to sense me tapping into them, they try to communicate with me individually in a flood of voices.

*Never felt you before.*

*Is this what you feel like?*

*What do you want? You're killing my focus.* Another growls in a gravelly voice.

Suddenly Rave roars, *Get the hell out,* and like a light switch, the voices cease, leaving nothing but his resounding decree.

"Ethan!" Nara whispers as I grit my teeth against the echoing pain in my skull.

*Do* not *do that again,* Rave commands, his fury jolting through me all the way to the soles of my feet.

*I didn't even know what I was hearing, Corvus,* I snap, reverting back to my combative tone. *And once I did I couldn't control it. It's not like you were present to help.*

*I don't want their voices in my head,* he says, his voice settling.

*Why? They are part of you. Did you not hear how awed they were to feel the Master Corvus? With your ego, I would think you'd eat that worshipful crap up!*

*I don't* know *who I am! You're supposed to be helping me regain my memory, not sight-seeing!*

When I set my jaw at his renewed anger, Nara whispers, "Are you talking to Rave?"

I quickly nod as I answer him. *Nara and I are here for the sole purpose to help you. Don't be an asshole, and don't you fucking check out like that again just because London makes you feel more than you want to.*

*I don't feel.*

*Bullshit! You have to stay aware to keep Nara safe. Do your part or I won't help you at all.*

When the Corvus grunts, I know he's finally settled and I fold my arm around Nara's shoulders. Pulling her close, I kiss her forehead. "I'm fine, Nara. Let's see if the book is here."

She looks up at me, her brow creased with worry. "You'll tell me about it later?"

I nod and she turns back to skimming the books. "Here's where the book is supposed to be," she says, pulling a paperback book out about the Tower of London. "This touristy book is what Drystan said he found when I asked him to come here and look for a possible second copy."

I can tell she's disappointed as she flips through the book filled with glossy picture pages and descriptions of the Tower. "This book obviously got put in the wrong place."

"Maybe we should look for the place where this book goes? It's possible they had shelved incorrectly."

"That's a great idea," she says, glancing at the spine. "Hmm, this book has the same ISBN as the *Ravens* book on the inside, but there's no Dewey decimal sticker on the spine. I wonder if it's even listed in their system?" We walk over to an old computer against the wall and Nara types in the title of the book she's holding, but the computer doesn't recognize it as a valid part of the library's collection.

"It's possible someone put it there on purpose," I say in a casual tone.

Nara flips to the back of the book. "Well, there's no check out card option in it, which confirms it doesn't belong to the library." Biting her lip, she furrows her forehead. "But then why does it share the exact same ISBN number as the *Ravens* book?"

"I think that means we should take it with us."

Nara rolls her shoulder and gives me a side-eye glance. "Are you suggesting that we just—?"

"Slide it into your backpack while no one is looking," I finish, glancing around to make sure there aren't any cameras.

"The last thing I need is to get in trouble for stealing in a foreign country," she whispers while tucking the book away and zipping her backpack closed.

I step in front of her as a person passes by. "It's better to take it. That way we can keep someone else from getting it...just in case there's some clue we haven't figured out yet."

An hour later, after we've flipped through the book on the Tower of London while seated at a small table in the Envoy's heated outdoor garden café, Nara drains the last of her coffee and rolls her head from one shoulder to the other, sighing. "It's frustrating not to see anything helpful. It has to be important somehow."

I nod, ignoring the sounds Patch is making up in the tree near the building. He's definitely wanting extra attention. "All I felt from Rave as we paged through it was a growing sense of impatient annoyance. Other than the ravens, nothing in these pictures felt familiar or helpful to him."

Despite having an American sized mug of coffee, Nara yawns and then shrugs as if trying to wake up. "We should probably flip through it once more just to make sure."

I sign the bill, then clasp her hand. "You need a nap. I promise I won't let you sleep too long, but if you want to walk around more later, sleep is in order."

She tries to argue but yawns again, making me chuckle. I pick up the book. "We'll look over it one more time in the room, okay?"

### Nara

I let out a gasp of delight the moment we walk into our room. A huge bouquet of sunflowers has been placed on the center of the double bed that takes up the majority of the small, cozy space. The contrast of bright yellow blooms against the stark white sheets instantly evaporates my tense mood, making my heart soar. I glance up at Ethan, my gaze misting. "They're gorgeous."

His mouth lifts in a half smile as he sets the book on the bed. "I know a lot of girls like roses, but when I thought of us, I could only picture a sunflower. Me, surrounded by you, so that's what I ordered when I called ahead."

"They're perfect," I say, choking up as I reach out to touch the bright petals.

Hooking his finger on my chin, he turns me to face him. "Just like you, Sunshine."

"I love you too." Leaning into his warmth, I push up on my toes to meet his lips with mine. I close my eyes at the sensation of his fingers threading into my hair and welcome his dominance as he tilts my head to deepen our kiss. I grasp his fleece with tight fingers and open myself fully to his passion, loving the fact we finally have more than a few minutes of alone time. With my worry for Ethan reaching epic levels every time Rave decides to make himself known, the need to show Ethan how much he's loved grows stronger with every single touch. I don't want to believe that I'll lose him; I can't accept that fact and feeling his strong, muscular arms pulling me impossibly close helps muffle the very real threat that Rave's presence represents. Not to mention the constant tug of war that wages between my brain and my heart each time Rave reveals more and more of his Master Corvus powers.

While his lips sear a hot path down my neck, Ethan tugs my jacket off, his intensity ratcheting my own. I quickly help him pull my sweater off, which hasn't even hit the floor before he's lifting me into his arms, his big hands sliding down to my jean-covered rear.

As he settles me against his hard body, I wrap my arms around his neck and my legs around his hips.

Just as I lean in to press my mouth to his, Ethan frowns and sets me down.

"What?" I ask, worried by the look of concern on his face when he swiftly turns me around.

"When did this happen, Nara?"

"When did what happen?"

He tugs me over to the bathroom and flips on the light. "Your feather?"

I glance over my shoulder in the mirror and gasp to see my feather is now half black from the top of the feather to the middle of the vane, and then the rest is white all the way down the shaft.

I shrug and try to ignore that the spot is itching and burning slightly, which isn't easy now that Ethan's forcing me to focus on it. It has bothered me ever since we walked into the library.

Clasping my shoulders, Ethan massages them. "What's wrong, Nara?"

"I have no idea when it changed colors or why, but it has been itching ever since we went to the library."

His fingers flex against me. "Do you think it's because of the book?"

"I don't know. The last time it felt like this the feather started to peel off and then I ended up plotting out locations for all the Corvus on that map."

Ethan turns me around and inspects the tattoo. "It doesn't appear to be coming off."

I turn to face him in the small bathroom and start to tug his shirt and fleece up. "I don't want to think about it right now. I want you to finish what you started."

He clasps my face, his hold firm. "Are you sure? We can wait."

I shake my head. "I just want to be with you without having to leave after."

Ethan releases me and tugs his shirt and fleece off. Dropping his clothes on the floor, he scoops me up and carries me to the bed.

I don't let him push me back on the bed. Instead, I kneel on the mattress and impatiently tug his belt open, then unbutton his jeans while holding his intense blue-black gaze.

The second I unzip his pants, he releases a low rumbling groan and quickly clasps my thighs, flipping me onto my back.

The bouquet of flowers bounce to the end of the bed with our movements, but I'm too caught up in his hungry gaze as he prowls over me to pay them any attention. Putting a knee between my legs, Ethan dips his head and slides his tongue from my belly up past my bra, to the upper curve of my breast, his voice full of heat and want. "You're so addictively irresistible, Sunshine."

Arms over my head, I arch my back and smile. "Resistance is unnecessary, Ethan. As a matter of fact, I want your complete surrender."

Elbows on the bed, he aligns his hips to mine, his weight pressing me into the bed as he nuzzles my throat. "What will I be surrendering to?"

Folding my legs around his hips, I lower my arms over his head, then touch the top of his tattoo. "This," I say, sliding my fingers tantalizingly slow along the edge of his ink.

Ethan's eyes flash with heat and he takes a deep breath. "I don't know what will happen, Nara. It's too risky."

I clasp his jaw and hold his gaze. "There's no one I'd rather take a risk with than you. Please let me explore loving all of you. If it gets too intense, I'll stop, okay?"

When he slowly nods, then takes his time sliding off my clothes, I snicker. "Are you worried I won't be able to handle you?" I tease as I help him remove his.

With a dark chuckle, he rolls me over, fisting his hand in my hair. Tugging it out of the way, he nips at my back, then slides his tongue along the feather on my shoulder and whispers in my ear, "Actually, I'm scared shitless of giving you too much power over me."

As I start to laugh at the silly idea, he clasps my hip and sinks his teeth into my shoulder, sending liquid fire flashing from my head to my toes.

*You could completely tear me apart.*

"I'd rather build you up," I say, breathless at hearing his voice in my head in such a passionate moment.

"Be careful what you wish for," he says, then tugs me onto my back.

I pant as he holds my hands over my head and eases inside. "I love you, Ethan." My voice quivers with emotion. I can't help it. He's so irresistibly sexy in his intensity. "Please release my hands, so I can love all of you."

Instead of releasing both hands, Ethan lets go of one. When I pout, he kisses the tip of my nose, his chest starting to rise and fall at a faster pace. "I'm going to need an anchor, Sunshine."

Smiling, I hook my free hand around his neck, pulling him as close as I can. "I'll keep you tethered to me. I won't let you fly apart...well, completely."

When my smile turns cheeky, he grunts and acts like he's going to recapture my hand, but I quickly flatten my palm on his tattoo.

Ethan arches and drops his head to my shoulder, his entire body shaking. "Holy shit, Nara! I don't think I'll be able to—"

I whisper against his neck. "You need this as much as I do. Just move, Ethan. Let yourself fly."

Darkness has descended over our room, creating a cocoon of deeper intimacy as he begins to move like a beautiful panther. I gasp in pleasure of how powerful he feels and dig my fingers into his skin to further encourage him.

Ethan releases a guttural groan against my neck, his fingers tightening around mine. The moment we start to glow, I shake from the passion and babble incoherent words of love and awe as the light grows brighter. As I fly apart, somehow I manage to keep my hand on his back, never letting go.

Exhaling a fierce growl, he slows to a stop and kisses my jaw, touching his hot forehead to mine. "I'm not certain, but I think you just shattered me."

I trail my fingers up his spine and then back down, then smile at the shudder that passes through him. "You feel completely put together to me. Maybe we should try it again just to be *certain*." I start to slide my hand to his tattoo, but he quickly captures it and rolls us to our sides.

Kissing my knuckles, he gives a wry smile. "Let's not go crazy, Sunshine. I might spontaneously combust a second time around and take you with me."

I burst into pleased laughter as he slides off the bed and heads for the bathroom.

My eyes are barely able to stay open when Ethan crawls back into bed. Turning on the light, he immediately tugs me across his warm chest and once I hook my leg over his, he locks me to him, tracing his fingers along my bare back.

"Is your feather still itching?"

His question is calm, but I can sense his worry. I smile as he touches my feather tattoo. I still have no idea exactly where it came from. If I was "marked" by an angel as potential Corvus material, then why did mine raise up but never change? It's supposed to be invisible to everyone but the Corvus. Or is this tattoo something else Corvus-related, but since Rave has forgotten his history, he has no clue if he was the one who inadvertently raised the angel's marking on my shoulder? I know the feather turning black is Ethan's biggest concern. Corvus hosts who've been chosen by the Master Corvus start off with a black feather that eventually morphs into a sword across their backs with the same feather etched along the metal. Ethan doesn't want that life for me. I don't either. Just like I wish his life was different.

The feather is itching more now that he's mentioned it. I reach up to touch it and feel the edge starting to peel away from my skin. I tug and my skin pulls as the feather separates from my body. Ugh, I'll never get used to that.

Twirling the feather, I hand it to Ethan and rest my head on his chest as I point to the shaft. "I wish I knew what that jagged part along the bottom edge is all about. That is definitely different from a regular feather."

Ethan inspects the feather all over. "I agree. It's stronger than a regular feather too. How did you get this to plot out the Corvus locations on that map?"

I shrug. "It just kind of happened on its own. I barely remember holding the feather beyond that sharp edging cutting me. The map was glowing with bright lights and when I touched the feather to it, the lights went out and a red dot was left behind."

Ethan lays the feather on the book he'd set next to him and holds them up together beside me. "Do you feel any kind of urgency to hold the feather now?"

I sense something, but my sleep-deprived body is hitting a wall and my eyes drift closed. "It feels more like curiosity than urgency," I slur.

Ethan sets the book down. "Go to sleep, Sunshine."

The sensation of him sliding the feather across my shoulder makes me smile in my drowsy state. He chuckles when it starts to tug against my skin and releases the feather. As it floats down to my shoulder and I feel it meld into my skin, he murmurs, "If you're not Corvus, what are you, sweetheart?"

I yawn and answer, "I'm your Sunshine."

"That you are." I hear a smile in his comment as he kisses the top of my head. Once he pulls the covers over us, I sigh my contentment at the secure feeling of his chest rising and falling, while his strong arm surrounds my back, making me feel safe and protected. I want to wallow in this peaceful moment, to roll around and coat myself in this pocket of euphoria, but Michael's statement about the Master Corvus absorbing Ethan weighs heavily in the back of my mind.

I close my eyes tight, guilt welling in my chest. I want to tell Ethan what Michael said, but I refuse to say anything that could rattle his confidence, even if that means keeping my worry for him buried. At the same time, I know that Ethan fears what the Master Corvus will do once he regains his memories and the full powers that'll entail. Rubbing my nose in his warmth, I choose to believe in Ethan. I believe he's stronger than any of Rave's past hosts, and together we can help the Corvus handle anything he remembers, no matter how bad.

Ethan folds his arms around me and whispers against my hair. "I've got you, Sunshine. I'll always have you. Now go to sleep."

Releasing my breath, I let my body relax against his and surrender to my exhaustion.

# Chapter Twenty-Five

*Nara*

"Nara?" Ethan touches my shoulder and I turn to him and blink, completely confused.

"You look a bit out of it." He glances down. "Do you remember what happened?"

I'm sitting cross-legged style in the bed, covers tucked under my arms. Both hands are resting on my covered knees and I'm holding the Tower book in one hand and my feather in the other. *Why is it half-black and half-white now?*

"I was asleep?" When I slowly shake my head and start to tremble, he brushes my hair back from my face and pushes it over my shoulder.

"You were asleep when I went to take a shower, but then I found you like this."

Setting the feather down, I open the book and quickly begin to flip through it, looking for red dots. The problem is, the book is a guide and the legend used to point out historical facts is comprised of red, blue, green and yellow circles. Every page has a few colored dots on them. I look at Ethan, frustration mounting. "How will I be able to find what red dot I marked versus what was already there? There's dozens in this book!"

Ethan lowers his hand to the back of my neck and massages it. "Calm down, Nara. We'll figure it out. At least now we know the book means *something*. That's a start. We can go to the Tower tomorrow morning before we head over to the sanctuary."

When I look up at him and exhale to relieve some of the tension inside me, he smiles, making my heart flip. "Get a shower. You'll feel much better."

"I'm supposed to keep you grounded, yet you're the one being my rock."

Ethan's brow furrows and he sits beside me on the bed. "You're not *supposed* to do anything but love me, Nara. You owe me nothing beyond that."

I blink back tears. He has no idea how hard it has been trying to keep it together for him. "But loving you means all of you, and your Corvus is part of that. Keeping you settled means that I get to *keep you*." It's hard not to break down when I say that last part, so I distract myself by reaching for my feather. Twisting, I look behind me. "Where'd my feather go?"

"Back where it belongs." Ethan taps my shoulder and smirks. "As for your worries, I'm not going anywhere, Sunshine. Now get a shower so we can go to dinner. The hotel recommended a great place."

"Why are we going up?" I say when Ethan opens a side door in the hotel lobby, then tugs me behind him up a narrow flight of stairs.

"You said you wanted to get a really good view of London." He opens a door at the top and we step into a rooftop garden. "This is the owner's private garden, but I convinced them to let us come up here for a little bit."

"Aww, Ethan…it's breathtaking!" I say, hooking my backpack onto my shoulders as I walk over to the edge of the building to see all the city lights sparkling.

"There are a few buildings in the way. Otherwise you could see the Tower bridge from here," he says softly behind me.

"I'm sure it's spectacular." I turn to thank him for the sweet surprise and gape that he's pulling off his sweater. "What are you doing?"

"Showing you the view." A cocky smile spreads across his face and his raven wings unfurl in a magnificent spread behind him.

"Ethan!" I whisper, glancing around nervously. As much as I love it when I get to see his wings, I don't want him exposed. "Someone might see you."

Laughing, he flexes his muscular arm as he lifts his hand to trail his fingers along my neck. "It's a bit foggy tonight. We'll be fine."

"We'll—" I yelp when he moves so fast, lifting me into his arms to settle me against his chest. I quickly wrap my arms around his neck and shake my head. "What do you have in mind?"

"I'm going to show you the city the way only a Corvus can." He grins and with a swoop of his wings, we vault straight up in the air. Squeezing my eyes shut, I feel gravity pulling against us with the speed, but I hold back the combined squeal of fear and delight that threatens to escape. I don't want to give anyone a reason to look toward the sky.

When we're easily a hundred feet up, we slow and his massive raven wings move in perfect waves, keeping us aloft. "Open your eyes, Sunshine, and look at the beauty of London."

I stare at the cityscape and smile at the gorgeous sight of Big Ben, the London Eye and the London Bridge off in the distance. *I'm looking for you, Gran. I so wish I could take pictures while in the air to capture this for you!* "I can see why people love London. This is like looking at a moving painting."

When Ethan hmmms his agreement, I glance up at him, wondering why he sounds distracted. "Do you see it, Nara?" His gaze is wide with awe and he's looking around as fast as his eyes can track. "I can see right through the buildings and even through the people inside." He looks upward. "Whoa, check out the stars!"

My stomach tensing a little, I touch his jaw to get his attention. "It's amazing, isn't it? I'm pretty sure you're seeing through your Corvus' vision right now. I'm glad Rave's sharing it with you."

Ethan looks down at me, his dark eyes searching my face. "This is a pleasant memory, yes?"

I stiffen in his arms. "What are you doing, Rave? You can't just pop in and out like that. Every time you do, you shove Ethan into a dark place. It's not safe for him there."

Rave frowns and his wings suddenly bat harder, the movement pulling us higher in the air. "What do you mean? Explain!"

I try to take a breath, but I feel woozy. "I—I can't...breathe," I wheeze, then point down. "Oxygen, Rave. Take me back to the roof."

The cool night air streams through my hair as we descend. The moment he lands on the roof, I squirm in his arms. "Please put me down."

His arms tighten. "But you enjoy being held. It makes your heart beat faster."

"By *Ethan*. Could you please set me down and return him to me."

"It wasn't pleasant?"

When I hear the pout in his tone, I realize that I've hurt him. "Was it your idea to go flying tonight?"

He glances away, his expression frustrated. "That was Ethan's."

I put my hand on his arm, my tone softening. "But your idea was to let Ethan see how you view things. Wasn't it? Thank you for sharing with him. *That* was pleasant."

"But you didn't experience it." His gaze returns to mine, his brow puckered. "How is that pleasant for you?"

I smile at his confused expression. "It made me happy to see Ethan experience such an awesome sight."

"Until you told me what you saw, I had forgotten that I could see differently." He shakes his head. "It's gone now. I can't seem to control it, but I'm glad I could share it briefly tonight."

I start to smile, but his expression turns all business. "Tell me about this dark place? What does he see there?"

"Nothing," I say, since Ethan doesn't technically 'see' anything whenever he's stuck in Rave's subconscious. "Your thoughts aren't his. He prefers being in his own head, not yours."

Rave frowns, unconvinced. "Why doesn't he feel safe there?"

"Um...because he can feel some of your repressed memories. Not the actual memories themselves, just the feelings. And they're not his. He just wants to be back inside himself."

"I have no feelings," he says in a curt tone.

I touch his arm. "But you said that Adder felt pain, so you know what that felt like."

"Have a good dinner," Rave says stiffly. "I'll leave you alone now."

"Rave," I start to say, but he blows out a harsh breath and then quickly pulls me against his chest, wrapping his arms in a fierce hold around me.

"I hate that he yanked me out while you were being held up in the air," Ethan says, his voice sounding raw and hoarse. "I yelled your name over and over all the while cursing him."

I hold on tight, relieved to have him back. Glancing up at him, I offer an encouraging smile. "I think this was his way of sharing with you. Seeing through his eyes is pretty amazing, huh?"

Ethan cups the back of my head, his hold tense. "That wasn't worth the fear I felt when I couldn't get back to you and know you were safe on the ground, Nara."

Nodding, I kiss his jaw. "I know, but I think this helped him too. He really was trying to share, not dominate you."

"It sure didn't feel like that," he grumbles.

I pick up his sweater from the rooftop and hand it to him. "Come on. Let's get out of the cold air and go find this restaurant you wanted to try."

We have to walk a couple streets from the hotel to a main road to flag down a cab. Once a black taxi pulls up, a brunette in her early forties, who's also been trying to wave down a cab, grabs the door handle at the same time we do.

She shakes her head when Ethan tells her she can have the cab. "You can have it, or we can share. Where are you going?"

"Piccadilly Circus," I answer.

She smiles. "That's close to where I'm headed. I don't mind sharing."

"Hop in if yer coming," the gruff cabbie says.

The three of us pile in and before we're even fully seated, the cabbie takes off, calling over his shoulder, "Where to?"

Ethan calls out, "Piccadilly Circus," and the woman nods.

"That's fine for me. My street isn't far from there."

While the man grunts and focuses on driving, she turns soft brown eyes to Ethan and me. "You're American? Is this your first time in London?"

"Yes," we say in unison, making her laugh.

"Are you having a grand time?"

Ethan clasps my hand and we exchange a look. Despite our reason for being here, we are. "Absolutely," he says quietly, giving me a smile that makes my heart thump.

"Damn traffic," our cab driver mutters, then quickly takes a small side road to avoid the stopped cars ahead.

We all jerk forward when he suddenly brakes. A huge moving truck is parked diagonally across the road. Just as our driver honks his horn and gripes about ignorant people, a rumbling starts underneath our vehicle.

As the vehicle fills with smoke, we look at each other. My eyes burn from the thick, toxic fumes. The moment the driver slumps over, Ethan turns to me, "Don't breathe in," then grips his door handle. The lady tries to open her door, but both the handles are stuck. Growling in frustration, Ethan gestures for me to cover my eyes, then slams the side of his fist against the glass. It cracks but doesn't shatter, so he turns in the seat and kicks the door with his boots.

My heart jumps as the metal creaks. *Please let it be open!* I'm having a hard time seeing, but I try to stay calm so I'm not tempted to breathe through my nose. I know Ethan will get us out of here.

When the woman next to me passes out, Ethan's eyes flash black and he says in a calm tone, "Cover your ears, Nara." Once I lift my hands to my ears, he hits the door with one foot. The pressure of his powerful kick slams against my chest. As the door flies off the vehicle, every single window shatters. Quickly jumping out among plumes of thick smoke, Ethan turns and puts his hand out for mine.

Lungs screaming for air and eyes tearing from all the noxious fumes, I clutch my backpack in one hand and stretch my other toward his. Just as our fingers touch, Ethan grunts and falls to his knees.

"Ethan!" I flutter my stinging eyes to try to see beyond the smoke, but Ethan just shakes his head and grasps my hand. Tugging me forward, he orders in a harsh tone, "Run, Nara!"

Stumbling out of the taxi, I take deep breaths, but before I can even try to help him up my vision quickly fades and I fall forward as everything goes black.

# Chapter Twenty-Six

*Ethan*

Something sharp is hammering at my head like an ice pick. Wincing, I swing my arm to make it stop. Just as my brain registers the cold, rough surface behind my back, a loud *raaaaaaack* right in my ear completely jars me to full consciousness.

Leaning against a brick building, I blink at Patch standing on my outstretched thigh. He bobs his head and makes staccato *raaaaackkk* sounds over and over. The sight of broken glass in the empty street before me sends me scrambling to my feet as everything comes back. *Nara!*

No taxi. No door. Nothing is left behind but broken glass to prove what had just happened to us. We were ambushed! *Who did it?*

"Nara!" I yell, my heart thumping with worry for her as I shove my hands in my hair and turn left, then right, looking for a clue.

Patch had flapped to the ground when I stood, but he now flies right at me with his clawed feet extended. I start to fend him off, but he just grabs at my sweater before coming away with something clutched in his talons.

Dropping it at my feet, he lands on the ground and pecks at a folded piece of paper, bobbing his head up and down.

I bend down and retrieve the paper.

*You want her back? We want what was hidden in the
spine of the raven book. We'll call your hotel room with a
meet location at midnight.*

Crumpling the paper, I pull my phone out and dial Nara's cell.
My heart jerks at the sound of a faint ring. I search until I find it
tossed among some trash. The demon fuckers dumped it so I
couldn't track them. I turn and narrow my gaze on Patch. "Where
did they take her?"

He squawks, then taps his beak on the ground three times before
looking back at me.

"What the hell does that mean?" I scowl at the bird, furious that
I can't read him.

*He's trying to tell you something. Stop ranting so I can focus.*

Patch hammers on the ground once more, which only makes
me growl in frustration. Pacing, I take several deep breaths, but my
heart won't stop jerking. I can't lose her. I won't. *Don't you have some
magic Corvus powers you can pull on to help me find her?* I rant at Rave.

*Not that will help in this situation,* he says. *What is Patch trying to
tell us?*

I pause to see the raven literally jumping up and down and
flapping his wings as if he's having a hissy fit. I gesture to the bird
and command, "Go call on your raven buddies to help you locate
her."

Patch stops jumping and I swear if it were possible for a raven
to glare at me, he just did before he hammers the ground harder this
time.

*He's telling you that he can't find her because—*

"They took her underground," I finish, my stomach sinking. I
don't have what the demons want. I could come up with something
to try to fake them out, but if I fail, they could hurt Nara before I
could get to her. How will I find her in time?

*I'll fly.* I pull my sweater off and fist it in my hand. *And we'll use
that freaky x-ray vision of yours to scour the underground.*

*I can't control it,* Rave says. *It shifts in and out. Nara could be
anywhere. They could've taken her underground but didn't stay there.
They could still be down there or somewhere else. We don't know.*

*What good are you to me then?* I growl at the spirit. *Nara is the one
person you should always keep safe. Not* after *me, before* me. *She might've*

*been able to run away if she'd gotten out of the car first. She—*

*Enough*, Rave barks, his authority sending a shudder from my head to my toes. *She would've been the one hit on the head instead of you. We'll find her. Do less talking and more thinking.*

Patch makes a snorting sound and bobs his head. I consider punting the bird across the street, but instead I clamp my jaw shut and take several deep breaths to get my head on straight.

I can't stand here in the street all night. I need to think. Unfurling my wings, I look at Patch. "If you want to help find her, you need to keep up." He takes flight at the same time I shoot to the sky and disappear into the fog.

As soon as I land on the hotel's roof, I glance down at the useless phone in my hand. Wait…Nara's phone can still be helpful.

When Drystan doesn't answer after I dial his number from her phone three times, I growl my fury and barely stop myself from slamming the phone down on the rooftop. "Why the hell isn't he answering? Of all people, I would think he would never ignore a call from the girl he would steal from me in a heartbeat if he could."

*Something is wrong.*

Rave's even tone tells me how worried he is. Not only had he stayed quiet on the flight over to the roof, but his vision had switched briefly to the Corvus' vast one a couple of times. Unfortunately, the switch wasn't long enough for me to focus and try to find Nara among the millions of living beings in London.

I start to dial Drystan's number once more, but Patch lets out a low croaking sound as he paces on the bench.

I look at him and hear more ravens repeating his call. He fluffs his neck feathers, his actions showing that he's boasting. "Do you think you can find Drystan?" I ask as I quickly scroll through Nara's photos until I find one of Drystan, Matt, Lainey, and Nara sitting in a booth at what appears to be a coffee shop. Zooming in on the photo of Drystan, I point to his face. "Can you ask the other ravens to help you scour the city for him?"

Patch lets out a loud *raaaackkk*, then flies away, and suddenly the sound of all the birds repeating his call echoes over and over. The cacophony bounces off rooftops, buildings, and other structures, boosting its strength. The domino effect would be interesting to listen to and appreciate if I weren't so worried for Nara.

It feels like I wait forever for him, but when Patch does finally return thirty minutes later, I'm anxious for him to show me the way.

I thought he would lead me out of the city, where a student fieldtrip at a historical country manor might be taking place. The last place I expect Patch and his crew of ravens to bring me is an abandoned, graffiti-riddled building. The anti-establishment symbols coating every brick, empty liquor bottles lined up against the building, and the smell of pot in the air instantly puts me on full alert.

Firelight glows inside from old metal drums in the corners of the huge open building. Through the smeared window, young guys and girls are jumping and screaming in the darkness to the band playing a thrash metal music. They're blaring so loud I can barely hear Rave over the din when the sound of glass crashing against brick reaches my ears.

Tugging on my sweater, I immediately duck inside to the sight of two guys chucking beer bottles at the wall in some kind of accuracy/strength contest. The shorter one with stringy straw-colored hair notices me watching them. He waves me over and sweeps his hand toward the shattered glass that didn't make it into another barrel and slurs, "Which one of us won?"

"Neither of you morons," I snap, glancing around the crowd in the darkness. "Where is Drystan?"

"What do you want with Drystan?" The guy with a horrible buzz cut asks, his expression turning bullish. At the same time several of their friends walk up, their stances tense, suspicious.

"Where *is* he?" I roar, stepping forward with my fists clenched. I have no patience or time for bullshit and will swat every one of these guys like flies if necessary.

The guy stumbles back from my Corvus ferocity and raises a shaky hand, pointing to the far corner of the room where a group of guys and girls are lounging on sofas, drinking, smoking, and laughing. I don't hesitate to stalk over to the group.

Drystan's hand is fisted around a vodka bottle as he nuzzles a blonde girl wearing a mini-skirt and combat boots. Sliding her fingers into his hair to keep him at her neck as I approach, she bats heavily-lined eyes at me and puckers her red-stained lips in a silent kiss. "Hello, gorgeous. You don't look like you belong here." Patting the empty space beside her on the sofa, she gives a wicked smile. "Come join us, Buttoned-Up. Let me corrupt the both of you."

Drystan's completely oblivious to my presence, which only infuriates me more.

"Lover-boy has other plans." Grabbing Drystan by his jacket, I yank him to his feet, and hold him up on his toes. "This is the *fieldtrip* you ditched Nara for?"

Bottle hanging by his side, Drystan stares at me, bleary-eyed. Blinking a couple of times, he shakes his head as if confused. "Wh— what are you doing here?"

Furious with him on so many levels, I yank the bottle out of his hand and slam it against the wall, then drag Drystan over to a table with a big metal beer-bin and dunk his head into the icy water. "Sober the hell up!" I say after I pull him out, then slam his head back into the frigid depths once more.

"Stop! Fecking hell! Enough, Ethan!" Drystan's shaking but coherent as he shoves away from my hold. Then as if everything is finally registering, he pushes his wet hair away from his forehead and looks around, worry on his face. "Is Nara here?"

"I *wish* she could see what a disappointing shit you are right now," I snarl. "The least you could've done is answer her call!"

Exhaling a relieved breath, Drystan glances away. "I was protecting her. I've screwed up so many lives—"

I grab the front of his coat and yank him toward me, letting him see the fury in my eyes. "I don't give a damn about your bullshit reasons—"

"Hey Dryst…you want us to toss this wanker?" One of the guys from earlier says. The blonde girl is standing beside him, looking frightened and a slew of other guys are behind him. The music has stopped and hundreds of angry eyes are on me.

I slide my gaze from Drystan as his group of friends moves a bit closer, some with wary gazes…and others with combative stares. Leaning close, I say in a deadly tone meant just for him. "Call off your *friends* or I'll take them all out, Drystan. I swear it!"

Raising a hand, Drystan's says in an elevated, steady voice, "It's all good." He smiles and pats my fisted hand around his damp jacket. "This is how my American friend greets me." Gesturing to the band, he nods. "Play on!"

When the crowd just stares at us, I release Drystan's jacket and smack him on the back *hard*, forcing a smile. "It's always good to see you, Drystan," I say for their benefit.

The moment the crowd shakes their heads and turn back to the band starting their music once more, I bite out, "Let's go!"

"What's going on?" Drystan frowns. "Where is Nara?"

I set my jaw. "Why do you think I'm here? Demons took her. And she's somewhere even the ravens can't determine. You're the only one who can find her."

"Why didn't you start with that?" Drystan snaps, scowling.

As soon as we're alone outside the building where the music is down to a screaming minimum, he turns to me. "I need something Nara has held recently."

When I grab his arm, he immediately pulls away, shaking his head. "No, I don't want to affect you. I'm poison. I won't be responsible for destroying you."

"My Corvus is spirit." Gripping his hand, I fold it around my forearm. "His power is constant. And since you don't care about me, we're good."

Drystan's eyes widen, but he doesn't try to pull free again. "You know what I can do?"

"I made an educated guess based on the changes in Matt and Lainey."

"Lainey too?"

The pained look on his face tells me that Nara was right about him—that it was most likely unintentional. Before his hand can fall away, I flatten my other hand on his and lock him in place. "Focus, Drystan! Nara's life depends on us finding her."

His green gaze holds mine. "She will never forgive me if I destroy you."

"Then don't. Instead, help *Nara!*"

Drystan closes his eyes and grips my arm tight. He starts to shake and he says through gritted teeth, "You might just destroy me...wouldn't that be poetic?"

*Dial back your intensity, Rave. We need him.* "Just be quiet and find her, Drystan."

*Does that mean I can zap him into oblivion when we're done with him?*

*Why don't you work on that vision issue of yours? That could really come in handy the closer I get to them.*

Blowing out a breath, Drystan's fingers flex against my skin. "I feel her."

"Is she okay? She's not hurt, is she?"

He shakes his head, his brow puckering. "I'm trying to reach out to her, but either something is blocking me from getting through or she's…asleep?"

"They gassed us." My tone is sharp, but I'm glad to know that she's not being tortured. "Can you see where they're holding her?"

Drystan turns his head left and then right, as if listening. "I hear water…a boat horn? She's near the Thames."

I shake my head. "That's too broad. I have less than two hours."

I start to walk away and Drystan calls after me, "We need to do this together. I can help." When I open my mouth, ready to reject him, he gives me a determined look and pulls keys out of his pocket. "I also heard bells, but the water is messing with my ability to see outside the location like I normally could. If I were closer, I might be able to pinpoint better."

I take the keys from him. "You're in no condition to get behind the wheel."

"You ever driven on the opposite side of the road before?" Drystan asks, frowning.

"I'll manage. You focus on zeroing in on Nara's exact location."

Before I get into the car, I tell Rave, *We don't know how many demons have her, but Nara's safety takes precedence over your memory issues right now. I'm opening a channel to all Corvus who can get here quickly.*

*Agreed. Call them.*

# Chapter Twenty-Seven

### *Nara*

"Sweetie, are you okay?" Someone gently pats my face, then whispers next to my ear, "You need to wake up if we hope to get out of here." My eyes quickly open and whatever I'm on squeaks as the woman from the taxi leans over me, concern on her face. "I'm so glad you're okay. I was getting worried when you didn't wake up right away."

"Where?" I glance around the small room with nothing but twin beds, one on either side of the room, an old-style radiator for heat next to the bed, and a small window with bars over it near the ceiling. "Are we in a prison?" Woozy, I sit up and shake my head to try to clear it as I stare at the shut door.

"I have no idea. Maybe a detention center? I'm just glad I'm not here alone," the woman says in a shaky voice. "There are a couple of men outside. I woke up first and they told me this room is soundproof so we shouldn't even bother trying to scream for help. Why did they take us? What do they want?"

I start to speak when the door suddenly opens and a tall, barrel-chested guy with a thick beard and short salt-and-pepper hair walks into the room, carrying my backpack. "Get back to your side of the room," he bellows at the woman. She blanches at his intimidating presence, then hurries over to sit on the other bed. I face him, my gaze unflinching. Between this massive man and the other guy with limp brown hair standing guard at the door, escaping isn't an option at the moment. All I can do is hold onto the hope that Ethan is out there looking for us…and try to determine exactly what these men want. "That's mine. Can I have it back please?"

As I stretch for my backpack, he holds it aloft, then reaches inside the bag. Pulling the Tower book out, he says, "Is this what you want?"

"Yes, please give it to me."

He lowers the book and just as my fingers brush the edge, he rips it away. "Unlike the other book on ravens, this book appears to be quite useless."

He turns the Tower book around, then holds part of the pages and lets it flop open. Normally I would cringe at someone treating a book so disrespectfully, but his comment about the raven book shocks me. Ethan and I had looked all over his house for the *Ravens* book after he sent that demon possessing his brother to Under, but we never found it. We assumed that wherever he hid it, the book was safe from demons.

"What ravens book?" I keep my expression carefully schooled. "I don't know what you're talking about."

The man curls his lip and the sheer evil in his sneer makes his demonic persona more obvious now. "Nice try, Nara. You didn't count on the fact my demon brother in the States had a backup plan. He knew you and Ethan were coming to London, so he sent the raven book to me just in case you got rid of him."

"Got rid of?" The woman gasps. "What's he talking about? Did you hurt someone? Am I here because of something you did?" she shrieks, looking at me with horrified eyes.

"Silence!" the demon snarls. "Or I'll end you permanently."

She locks her lips together, eyes watering as she quickly nods. I feel awful that she got caught up in our battle with the demons, so I draw his attention back to me. "She has nothing to do with this. Just let her go."

"So you're a hero, are you?" Beard demon says in a conversational tone as he slides his gaze from the woman back to me. "It's an admirable quality, this…wanting to protect others. Maybe then you can appreciate that I have a similar goal. Lucifer is here and I want to give him the best ammunition possible so he can remain here permanently." He gestures to the other guy who unfolds his arms and pulls the blue *Ravens* book with gold edged pages from under his thick bicep.

I stare at the book, wanting to rip it from his hands. Instead, I shrug. "It's just a book."

The demon in front of me moves fast, grabbing me by the throat. All I can do is claw at his hand as he lifts me up onto my toes. Brown eyes turning even darker, he gets in my face and growls, "You will help me, whether you want to or not." I feel sudden pressure as if something is under the top layer of my skin, and I know he's trying to take possession.

I hammer at his wrist to try to break his hold and am surprised when he shoves me back and spits on the floor near my shoe. "You reek of Corvus. It's on you somewhere." Dropping the Tower book on the floor, he steps forward and pulls my shirt and sweater away from my neck to look at my throat. "Where is it?" he roars his frustration. When I shake my head, he releases me. "Strip!"

"No!" I fold my arms to keep from trembling.

"I'll find that fucking symbol if I have to rip every piece of clothing off myself." Grabbing my sweater at the neck, he yanks hard and it tears open with his sharp tug.

I scream at the violation, but he just knocks my hands away when I try to keep him from reaching for my button-down shirt underneath. He ignores the woman yelling for him to stop and smiles as he curls his fingers in a fist around my shirt.

A phone rings just as the material begins to fray. I glare at the demon and lift my chin high, tears of defiance welling.

"Edgar, they want an update," the demon in the doorway says, holding the phone out.

Grunting his annoyance at the interruption, Edgar pats the top of my head with his meaty paw. "Don't go anywhere. This isn't over, *pet*."

The second both men walk out and lock the door behind them, the woman runs over and quickly picks the Tower book up. Putting it in my trembling hands, she wraps her arm around my shoulders and sits down with me on the bed. "Are you okay?"

I clutch the book tight and slowly nod, my whole body trembling.

Pushing my hair back from my face, she says quietly, "Please give them what they want. I know these chaps sound like nutters talking about Lucifer, but maybe then they'll let us go." When I look at her, she puts her hand on her chest. "I'm Emily. And you're Nara? Is that right?"

I nod. "It's a bit more complicated than that, Emily. I can't give them what was in the spine of that book because I don't have it."

"Oh." Emily's expectant expression falls. "Then tell them where to go get it. Maybe then they'll let us go."

I shake my head. "They aren't going to let us go."

Her bottom lip starts to quiver and her eyes tear up. "I don't want to die. At least tell them where to find it and then while they're off to look for it we can escape."

"I'll think of something," I say with far more confidence than I feel. "For now I'd just like to lay down if you don't mind. I'm suddenly not feeling so well."

"Of course," Emily says before she walks over and sits on the other bed.

I put the book close to my chest and then roll over in the bed that sags in the middle so my back is to her. Holding my hand out toward the radiator, I rest the edge of my ring against it and quietly ask, "Did you see where they brought us? Do you know what side of town we're on?"

"No, I didn't see anything, but I heard water rushing and what sounded like a boat captain talking."

"So we're not far from the water," I say quietly.

"Yes."

"Did you hear anything else?" I carefully turn the heated ring until the Corvus symbol is between my two fingers, then press it against the inside of my pinkie finger. As the hot metal sears the symbol into my skin, I bite my lip to keep from crying out. *God, that hurts like a mofo!* That demon can strip everything off my body, including this ring, but he will never get my soul. Holding the ring in place, I squeeze my eyes shut and I keep talking to try to distract myself from the pain. "Are you sure it's just two guys?"

"I only heard those two talking. Why?"

I start to say something when I hear a click. I immediately roll over and meet Emily's gaze. "Did you hear that? It almost sounded like the lock…"

Holding onto the book, I get up and quietly walk over to the door. I start to turn the handle, but Emily's right by my side, whispering in my ear, "I don't know if that's a good idea, Nara.

These men seem the type to hit first and then hit again."

"If there's a chance the door's unlocked, we have to at least try to escape."

Emily presses her lips together, then nods as I slowly turn the knob. I exhale an uneasy breath when the door unlatches, then bite my lip and gently pull the door open, hoping there's no one standing outside.

Thankfully the hallway is empty, except for an old-style desk/chair combo sitting a few feet down the hall from our room. Maybe Emily is right about this being a detention center.

Opening the door wider, I press my finger to my lips and keep my voice to a whisper. "We need to move quickly."

I lead the way and Emily follows, but she's so nervous, that every couple of steps she looks back as if she's afraid the men will round the corner at any moment.

When Emily's foot catches on the desk's chair leg as she turns back around, I wince and we both freeze at the loud scraping sound.

The moment we hear a guy yell, "Bloody hell, they've gotten out!" we bolt down the hall and just as we turn another corner, Edgar is standing in our path, muscular arms folded and a furious scowl on his face.

He grabs Emily and me by the back of our necks and drags us down the hall like a couple of rag dolls, then tosses us into the room.

"Stay!" he growls and for good measure, swipes his massive hand toward my head. I duck and put an arm up to deflect his blow, but he snags my hand instead, bending my fingers back painfully. "Do you really think that you can beat me, little gir—" He jerks his hand back, looks at his burning fingers, then grabs my hand once more and yanks the Corvus ring off my finger.

Tossing the ring past the other demon now standing guard in the doorway in a ready-to-attack stance, Edgar grabs my shoulder, a pleased smile on his face. "No more obstacles."

I have no idea if the Corvus brand will keep me protected, so I kick him in the knee as hard as I can and try to knock his hand off me.

Emily begs him to let me go, but he ignores her. Keeping his gaze focused on me, he smiles as if pleased. "Go ahead, struggling makes it hurt more."

I instantly freeze as my body shakes with the invasive pressure around me and my arms briefly go limp, dropping the Tower book at my feet. From the top of my head, it feels like gravity is growing stronger, pulling me toward the floor, but that's as far as the feeling goes. I'm so thankful the symbol's protection is holding. The demon releases my shoulder and gives a disgusted sneer as he grabs my hand once more. Once he finally discovers the brand on my finger, I hold my chin up. "You won't corrupt me."

The last thing I expect is for him to laugh. "Well, well…aren't you quite the resourceful twat. Good thing I'm resourceful too." Glancing briefly at his buddy, his laughter turns into sheer delight as he grabs hold of my pinkie finger and retrieves something from his pocket. He flicks his hand, opening a switchblade. Emily rushes forward and hits him in the arm, screaming for him to let me go.

After he bats her away, barely missing slicing her arm in the process, true fear drives me to pull painfully hard in order to free myself from his hold. "Hu—hurting me won't get you what you want," I stammer through the pain.

The demon twists my finger, sadistic glee reflected in his gaze when I cry out at the sharp jolt of pain. "Oh, I'll find out the truth from you eventually. What makes you think that torturing you isn't *exactly* what I want?"

As the other demon's laughter draws Edgar's attention, I lift my foot and nail him in the groin as hard as I can.

Edgar grunts and doubles over, but doesn't let go. Instead, he jerks me closer, his gaze slitted in retribution. Emily rushes up once more and hits his forearm with her fists. "Let her go!"

I'm shocked when he quickly releases me and straightens, punching her hard in the stomach. Emily lands on the floor gasping for breath. Edgar snarls and kicks her thigh with his steel-toed boot. "That should keep you quiet." Pausing, he tilts his head, observing her whimpering. "Or maybe you need a few more."

"Stop it!" I scream when he lifts his boot to kick her in the head. He grabs my hair as I try to move between them and yanks. "Hmmm, isn't this interesting…" Pulling me close, his foul breath bathes my ear, he says, "If you don't want me to use this sack of waste as a punching bag, start talking. I want what was hidden in that book's spine."

My hands are shaking. I want to help Emily, but if I tell them I don't remember what was on that scroll before it evaporated in my hands, they won't believe me and will most likely kill us anyway.

"Hey Edgar. There's nothing to say we can't have some fun while getting her to talk. Did you bring your tools?"

Edgar gives a sinister smile, then shoves me away from him. He starts to follow the other guy out, then turns with his hand on the door handle. "It won't take me too long to collect my tools. Inflicting maximum damage is my specialty."

The second he closes and locks the door behind him, I shake all over and fall to my knees on the cold floor. Picking up the Tower book with trembling hands, I crawl over and brush Emily's tousled hair away from her face, whispering, "I'm so sorry, Emily. I didn't expect him to take his anger out on you."

Emily whimpers in painful sobs. Leaning up on her shoulder, she turns mascara-streaked cheeks to me. "I won't survive being tortured, Nara. I have a very low threshold for pain." Blubbering, she continues. "Ple...please tell them what they want to know."

"I truly can't. I'm not lying." There is no point trying to explain that I can't remember the image on that scroll, since it's gone. "The moment I removed that scroll from the book, it disintegrated in my hands."

She sniffles, blinking at me with disbelieving eyes. "So you don't even know what it said?"

"I'm truly sorry, Emily." I shake my head and sit back on my legs, tucking the book against my chest. As the cold seeps through my jeans making me shiver, I swallow the hard knot of guilt. "I'll come up with something to buy us some time."

"I honestly think you care more about that stupid Tower of London book than helping me get out of here." Sliding her gaze from the book in my hands, she presses her lips together and pushes herself to a seated position, turning a hateful glare my way. "I can't believe I had to take that fucking beating for *nothing*."

At the same moment it hits me that I've just been played by *three* demons instead of two, the door lock clicks once more.

When Emily's eyes widen and she tenses as if preparing to attack, I lift up on my knees and swing the book as hard as I can, catching her in the jaw. While she slams to the floor, I rush for the door, my heart racing.

I scream when she grabs my arm and yanks me back, tossing me onto the floor. I hit the floor and slide, the impact on my elbow sending the book flying underneath the bed. I moan in pain, but force myself to roll over and reach under the bedframe for the book.

My fingers land on some kind of metal pole. It must be part of the bed frame. Just as I grasp it, Emily grabs my ankles in a painful grip. I'm yanked away from the bed, but I grasp the pole and bring it with me.

"Come here, you little bitch," she says as I try to roll over. Yanking on my hair, she spins me around. "I'm going to give you a taste of what I had to endure to get you to talk!"

When she yanks me upright, I try to swing the pole toward her face, but she easily captures the metal piece with an amused chuckle. "That's all you've got? What a disappointment—"

She crumples as I swing my foot out and hook the back of her knee. As she hits the floor with a loud *oomph,* I yank the pole from her loosened grip and slam the metal against her belly.

Wheezing for breath, she continues to fight, trying to grasp my ankle, but I jump away from her hand and whack the pole hard against her shins.

While she howls in pain and rolls over, I dive for the book. Retrieving it, I bolt for the door while she curses and tries to stand. Quickly pulling the door closed behind me, I set the book on the desk, my stomach knotting as I try to figure out how I'm going to lock the demon in without a key. An idea hits as I glance down at the pole in my hands. I step to the door and wedge the pole between the doorjamb and up under the doorknob. Once it's locked into place, a blast of cold air encircles me. My skin prickles just before the locking mechanism on the door latches into place.

As I blink at the door, the sudden charge of electricity in the air raises the top layer of my hair, making it very clear who just helped me. "I may regret saying this, but, 'thanks,'" I mutter to Fate at the same time the handle rattles. The heavy thump hitting the thick wood on the other side makes me back away quickly. Relieved that the door seems to be holding and thankful for the soundproof room, I grab the Tower book I'd set on the desk, and quietly run down the hall.

Just as I round the corner, I slam into someone. Jerking back, I immediately lift the book, intending to use it as a weapon once more.

"Nara!" Drystan says in a low voice, holding his hands up to deflect my blow.

I'm so thankful he wasn't another demon bent on torturing me that I lower the book and inhale and exhale in fast breaths.

"I've got you." He pulls me into a tight hug, his voice hoarse. "I'm so sorry, Nara. I'm here with Ethan—"

We both jump at the sound of someone slamming against the wall at the end of the hall.

I turn to see the demon who guarded our door scrambling to get his feet under him as Ethan steps into view.

Sword drawn, he gazes solely on the demon as he grabs the guy by the shirt and slams him so hard into the floor that the big floor tiles crack all around him.

Gurgling his fury through blood-soaked spit, the demon tries to pull Ethan off him, but Ethan doesn't even hesitate. He jams his sword into his chest. With a pained, yet evil laugh that reverberates down the hall, the demon puts his foot on the wall and twists his body at the last second, effectively turning Ethan's sword in his body.

When the guy explodes, leaving nothing behind but a cloud of dust, Drystan murmurs in my ear, "Holy shite! Remind me *never* to piss him off. I thought Corvus weren't supposed to hurt humans."

"The demon did that, not Ethan," I quickly whisper back, shocked by the demon's action. The fact that an Inferi demon purposefully chose to send himself back to Under in a truly painful way in order to create a Furia demon worries me. *Why did he do that?*

Swinging his sword in a circle, Ethan bends down and picks up the raven book the demon had been carrying. The moment his gaze shifts in our direction and narrows on Drystan's arms around me, Drystan instantly pulls me behind him. "Did you get them all?"

"There was only the one," Ethan says, pointing his sword where the demon used to be. "Are you okay, Nara?"

I step out from behind Drystan. "There were two others, a man and a woman. The lady from the cab was also a demon. She's trapped in the room you passed with a pole jammed under the door handle."

Ethan shakes his head as he approaches us. "The door was open. She's gone."

"When have you ever known demons to *not* stay and fight until the bitter end?" I gnaw my bottom lip as I stare at the raven book in Ethan's hand, then jerk my gaze back to his, eyes wide. "They're going to the Tower!"

Drystan frowns. "Why would the Tower interest them?"

"Because the woman saw me trying to protect this book," I say, holding up the tourist book on the Tower of London.

"Isn't that the book I found in the library?" Drystan asks. "I thought you wanted the book about ravens that Ethan's holding?"

Ethan nods to the book in my hand. "Did you find where you marked in the book?"

I start to shake my head, then glance at Drystan. "But maybe Drystan can find what I'm looking for."

His light brown eyebrows shoot up. "Which is?"

I open the book and point to the red dot in the legend, then to several dots on the page pointing out different parts of the Tower. "These red dots are part of the legend. I um, might have created other red ones in the book that look the same."

"What were you marking?"

"That's the problem." I shake my head and hand him the book. "I can't remember. I was kind of in a trance."

"A trance? What the 'ell, Nara." He jerks an accusing gaze to Ethan, but I quickly pull his chin back to me.

"This is about me, not Ethan. I have a feather...it's hard to explain, but in this trance-like state I used the feather to mark a place or places in the book that might be important."

His gaze narrows. "Important for what?"

"What the demons were hoping to find in the raven book," Ethan supplies. "A way to defeat the Master Corvus."

Drystan drops his gaze to the book in his hand and begins to flip through it. "To defeat the Master Corvus? How is that even possible?"

"It's not," Ethan snorts. "They're just chasing a fairy tale."

"But I want to be certain," I say. "Do you think you can find what I couldn't in there? If so, what will you need to hold onto to get a sense of it?"

Drystan glances up at me. "I don't need anything. I've already found where you marked it."

"You have? But how—"

He quickly turns the book toward me and points to a map of the buildings, then slides his finger down to the gift shop in the basement of the White Tower. "It's here."

"In the gift shop? How did you find that so quickly? You didn't seem to need any way to connect."

Drystan presses his mouth in a thin line. "I didn't use my ability to find it. It had a vibration that stood out."

"What do you mean, vibration?" Ethan steps closer, his gaze suspicious.

"Ever since that demon possessed me, every so often I've seen a kind of vibrational signature, which has actually helped me avoid areas demons might be."

"Nara is *not* a demon," Ethan says in a deadly tone.

"That's not what I meant," Drystan says. "But whatever she used to mark that book with isn't from our world."

*Anything* Corvus is *part of the mortal world,* Ethan says in my head as he hands me the raven book. *Show Drystan your feather.*

"What do you see, Drystan?" I ask, turning to show him the feather tattoo on my shoulder.

"Are you fecking kidding me?" Drystan takes a step forward to touch my tattoo, but then stops short and drops his hand. " What is that, Nara?"

"This is what I used to mark the book," I say, glancing at him over my shoulder.

"You can remove it?" When I nod, Drystan blinks as he stares at it. "It's weird. The whole tattoo is coated with a thin vibrational layer I can see, but the feather itself isn't."

"Huh?" I cover up my tattoo and turn to face him.

"Think of it like…the iridescent colors on a raven's feather. You know, how the purples and blues only stand out when the sunlight hits it a certain way. That's how I see your tattoo. It has an otherworldly layer over it, but the feather underneath doesn't."

Ethan snorts. "Which explains nothing."

"I just call it like I see it," Drystan says, holding his hands up in innocence.

"Well, at least you've identified the location I marked," I say, tilting the page he pointed to in the book to get a better look at it. "I have no idea if the demons saw it, but they know I didn't want to lose the book." I glance at Ethan. "We need to get over to the Tower."

Drystan glances at his phone. "If we're going to try to sneak in, it's probably best to wait until after the Ceremony of the Keys happens in forty minutes or so."

"What's that?" I ask.

"It's the official gate locking ceremony that has happened every night for seven-hundred years where The Chief Yeoman Warder of the Tower is escorted by armed guard to lock up the gates. We'll want to wait until there aren't soldiers about. The guard might be wearing ceremonial garb, but every single one, even the Yeomen Warders who live on the Tower grounds, are all ex-military. They can and will defend it."

Nodding, Ethan closes his eyes and takes a deep breath. A few seconds later, he looks at me. "Six Corvus are in London now. I've told them to meet us at the Tower."

Drystan's gaze darts between Ethan and me. "Since when do Corvus work together or communicate mentally?"

"They don't," Ethan says in a curt tone before walking ahead of us down the hall.

Drystan's expression shifts from confusion to frustration, and I sigh that Ethan purposefully left him hanging like that. "They don't normally, Drystan, but Ethan's not—ugh, it's hard to explain," I say, before following Ethan.

"What were you marking in that Tower book, Nara?" Drystan falls into step beside me once we're outside. We follow Ethan toward a car parked not far from the building.

"I honestly don't know what we'll be looking for once we get to the Tower, but it'll have something to do with Corvus, because the last time my feather took on a mind of its own, it was Corvus-related then too."

When Ethan opens the driver's side door, I raise my eyebrows. "Isn't this your car, Drystan? Why aren't you driving?"

Ethan and Drystan exchange a look before Ethan says, "I told him I wanted to practice driving on the wrong side of the road."

"That's the *correct* side of the road, Dark One." Drystan flashes a brilliant smile as he opens the front passenger door for me before he climbs into the back. Gesturing to the front seat, he gives me a cocky smile. "In ya go, Nara. We can talk about your poor taste in boyfriends on the way there."

Even though I know Drystan's just trying to rile Ethan, it's the first time I've seen him genuinely smile since he was possessed. Snickering, I slip into the car. Ethan grunts, his tone surprisingly mild as he starts the engine. "Keep your thoughts to yourself, Welsh boy."

My gaze pings between the guys. I never thought that Ethan and Drystan would form a semi-truce. I don't know what transpired to make that happen, but I'm thankful. And I'm glad to see my friend getting back to his confident, entertaining self.

As we pull away, Ethan glances at Drystan in the rearview mirror. "Why don't we talk about this power of yours that you failed to mention? How *many* people have you brought out their hidden talents or enhanced their existing abilities?"

When Drystan drills the back of Ethan's head with a hard stare, I sigh.

*Ugh, so much for a cease-fire between them.*

# Chapter Twenty-Eight

*Nara*

"Do you really believe that crap you're trying to sell?" Ethan cuts the engine after parking down the street from the Tower and swivels to stare at Drystan in the backseat.

"I do, because it's the *fecking* truth!" Drystan leans back and crosses his arms, his mouth set in a straight line.

"Calm down, you two." Exhausted from refereeing their sparring, I straighten the books on my knees and turn to Drystan. "So you're saying that this ability didn't show up until you got here, and you believe that's why your two Paladin friends were affected?"

"Correct," he says, nodding.

"What about your friends in the US?" Ethan demands, his gaze skeptical.

After I quickly explain what's been going on with both Lainey and Matt, Drystan sighs and rubs his forehead. "I don't know about Lainey." He furrows his brow and glances out the window, then looks at me. "Maybe it happened once we talked about Matt over the phone? That's the first time she and I have spent time talking at length." As he talks, he nods. "Yeah that was after my Paladin friends' powers had already changed and I was in denial that I could be the cause."

"And Matt?" I ask quietly so Ethan won't have to. "That's been going on much longer, Drystan."

He's quiet for second. "I can't explain Matt. I assumed this ability started here."

Ethan stares intently at Drystan. "That's why you tried to avoid talking to Matt and Lainey, isn't it? And the same reason you refused to set up a time to meet with us?"

Drystan swallows and meets my gaze. "You know I'd never miss a chance to see you, Nara. I was trying to protect you from..." He pauses and glances down at his hands. "This power...I don't even know *how* I'm doing it. It's like just being around me—"

"Turns on or amplifies others' abilities," Ethan cuts in.

Drystan rests the back of his head on the seat and stares at the ceiling. "I wish I could control it, but I don't know how."

"It hasn't been all bad, Drystan." When he sits up and meets my gaze, I give Ethan a side look. "If you're right that my recent ability to control dream worlds came from Drystan, then you have him to thank for me being able to pull you out of that nightmare maze you were locked in while in a coma."

"Is that true, Nara? You can control what happens in dreams now?"

"Well, so far just mine and Ethan's—"

"Something's happening," Ethan cuts in. "I feel the Corvus, but they are all suddenly very alert." He rolls down the window and inhales, then grates out, "Demons. At least twenty-five or so."

I look around but don't see anything out of the ordinary. People are walking along the lamp lit night streets without a care in a world. "Where are they? I don't see anything."

Ethan's jaw sets and his whole body stiffens. "They're around the other side of the Tower. Just outside the gate. The Corvus are going after the demons they sense; their instincts are pushing them to do what they do best, protect and defend the Tower." He opens the door and turns to me. "I'm going to help them. I don't want any demons getting in."

"Ethan..." I'm torn. I understand his need to fight, but we are on a mission *for* him inside the Tower. "You need to be with me. Rave may recognize something familiar."

"He does." Nodding toward the Underground sign a half a block away, he continues, "You and Drystan take that Underground entrance, but instead of following it to the Tube, turn right. You'll run into a yellow door marked Danger/High-voltage. That door will lead to another tunnel that'll take you inside the Tower. I'll come as soon as I can."

My heart racing with concern, I say, "But won't the door be locked? How will we get in?"

He digs into his jean pocket and pulls out my ring. "I found this in the hallway. I thought you might want it back."

"My ring!" I say, sticking my hand out for him to put it back on. "Just hold the handle with your ring on and the Corvus symbol should open the door," he says, sliding the ring on my finger. Pushing it completely up my finger, he stops and runs his thumb over the brand on my pinky. Jaw muscle jumping, he folds his fingers around mine. "You did that to yourself?" he asks, concerned pride reflected in his gaze.

"I wasn't letting any demon in," I say, squeezing his hand.

"That's badass, Nara" Drystan murmurs, then nods to Ethan. "Go on. We'll get inside. You meet us once you've taken out the demons."

Lifting my hand to his lips, Ethan kisses my knuckles, a spark of anticipatory excitement in his dark eyes that wasn't there a second ago. "See you soon, Sunshine."

Rave is itching to join in the Corvus/demon confrontation. Before I can beg Ethan to stay, he takes off, the flash of his sword catching beams of lamppost light in the darkness.

"Let's go, Nara. After you get us past the Corvus entrance, based on where we are, it could take us a good ten minutes to get to the Tower underground."

I move to open the door and the books start to fall off my lap. I catch them before they tumble, but the blue *Ravens* book was crushed underneath the demon, damaging its spine and misaligning the pages. I start to straighten the book, but my gaze lands on the gold-edged pages. Excitement thrums through me as I lift the book closer so the streetlight shines on the image that has been cleverly and meticulously painted along the very edges of the pages in such a way that it's only visible if the pages are fanned. The sight of the three ravens: one on the ground, one in the air, and one flying below ground jogs my memory. *It's the same image that was on the scroll I found in the spine.*

"You coming, Nara?" Drystan says, jarring me into action. I quickly hide the books under the seat and follow him out of the car.

The last thing I want is to have them with me in case we run into demons.

Once we reach the Underground and the secret door closes behind us, leaving us in total darkness, Drystan pulls out his phone and turns on its flashlight.

As we follow the narrow path of Drystan's light along the tunnel, I ignore the squeaks of rats and the trickle of dripping water on the cool stone walls. To distract myself from thinking of things crawling across my feet, I tell Drystan about Fate, Michael, Ethan's Corvus, the disintegrating scroll that I found in the spine of Freddie's book, and the matching image I just discovered painted on the edge of the pages.

Drystan stops walking and stares at me. "And here I thought you shared everything with me."

"I'm sorry, Dryst, but would you have believed me if I'd layered Fate and archangels on top of the Corvus revelation?"

"Good point," he says, his mouth twisting as he begins to walk once more. "So we're heading for the Tower to help the Master Corvus."

I nod. "My feather pointed us here and the demons are trying to find a way to defeat the Master Corvus. They don't know he's been living as a general Corvus because he's forgotten who he is. No one knows that. But the safety of our world depends on us helping Rave remember."

"I can't believe Ethan's the Master Corvus," he says, shaking his head.

"Believe it. Now we just need to help Rave regain his memory. It's a good sign bits of his memory are returning since Ethan knew about this tunnel. I'm hoping we'll be able to find something else here to help trigger more of Rave's memories."

"My uncle would flip to know the Master Corvus is here living among us once more."

I stop walking and grab his arm. "You can't tell your uncle, Drystan. No one can know." My fingers tighten. "I'm only telling you because I trust you, but you have to keep this between us. Okay?"

"I understand, Nara. I won't say anything." He folds his hand over mine. "I'm not that close to my uncle. I haven't really let him in, but I do think he has some regrets about that time in his life."

When we reach a heavy metal door with a raven head carved on the thick wrought iron door handle, Drystan gestures to it. "Have at it."

Unsure who or what might be waiting for us on the other side, I turn the knob as quietly as possible and hold my breath. Exhaling slowly at the silence and stale air that greets us, I step into a narrow hall lined with brick instead of stone. Drystan flicks a switch and a lone light glows above a solid floor-to-ceiling door several feet ahead of us.

We approach the door and stare at the blank piece of wood, and then glance at each other. His eyebrow hikes. "No knob? Now what?"

Shrugging, I put my hands on the door and start to push, then jerk back when the whole panel slowly swings open toward us.

"Now that's a true hidden door," Drystan murmurs after we step into a far corner area of the gift shop. The door closes on its own, the wall melding back into itself until all we see is a wall full of hanging wire baskets with kitschy knickknacks from erasers, to pencils, to key chains with the Tower raven logo emblazoned on them.

"You'd never know that's not a solid wall," I whisper as I try to visually see the seams but can't.

Drystan nods his agreement, then gestures to the shop. "Where do you think we should start?"

"I don't think what we're looking for is on this floor, but below it."

"What makes you say that?" he says, giving me the side-eye. "We're already in the basement of this building. There isn't anything below us."

I quickly explain what I just discovered on the edge of the *Ravens'* book pages. "I know Corvus are from this world and that they can fly, so that accounts for the raven on the ground and the flying raven, but the image showing a raven below ground is new to me. That's why I believe it's below us."

"I think we should scour this raven section first. That seems the most logical place to start."

Nodding my agreement, we spend a few minutes looking through the raven books, postcards, and the knickknack areas. "Nara, over here," Drystan calls as he stands next to a podium that appears to hold a guest book for signing in, except there's a light highlighting the book and a glass box with a keyhole lock holding it closed.

"Come look at this," he says, pointing to the book through the glass. "Check out the title beside each of the signatures."

"Yeoman Warder," I say when I join him.

"The signatures are of the different Beefeaters—that's another term for the Warders. Even on the front page, I can see that the signatures go back at least three years. There's no reason given for these signatures. What are they signing this for?"

"Good point," I say and try to see if I can lift the casing off.

Drystan shakes his head and points to the lock on the side. "Not without a key."

I raise my eyebrows. "You can't get past a measly lock?"

"Are you asking me to pick it?" Drystan teases as he pulls two raven-headed paperclips from his pocket.

"Did you take those from the baskets?" I say, frowning slightly.

"You're worried about paying for paperclips, yet you want me to break into this case for you?" When I frown and tell him they are different scenarios, he laughs. "Don't worry, I left some coins next to the till."

It takes Drystan less than a minute to unlock the case and just as we start to flip the top open, a man calls out in a gruff voice, "Release the case and step away from the book."

Drystan and I both freeze at the sight of an older man with curly salt-and-pepper hair. Shifting forward into the light in his pajamas and slippers, he raises a shotgun toward us.

"You're not supposed to have guns," Drystan says, eyeing the man warily.

The man grunts and holds the weapon tighter, his gaze hardening. "Laws don't apply when *demons* are involved."

"We're not demons." Drystan carefully lowers the glass cover back over the book.

"Are you responsible for caring for the ravens?" I ask, hoping to gain his trust.

"I'm the Chief Warder and Ravenmaster. How did you get in here without setting off our internal alarms?" he demands, raising the gun higher as he inches closer.

"We came in through the tunnel." I keep my voice calm. The last thing I want to do is spook the guy. "I'm going to lift my hand and show you something, okay?"

The man scowls, his stance stiff. "No sudden moves or I'll blow you to bits."

Trusting he'll do exactly as he claims, I carefully lift my hand and show him my ring. "Do you see the Corvus symbol? I wouldn't be able to wear it if I were a demon." I take Drystan's hand and fold my ring hand over the back of his. "He couldn't stand this if he was a demon."

The guard squints as I release Drystan's hand, but doesn't relax. "So you're not demons, yet if you were Corvus, you'd be out there fighting off the demon vermin currently outside the gates. Who told you about the tunnel?" His tone grows harsher, his gaze darting suspiciously between us. "Was the demon attack just a distraction to get you two in here?"

"Show him your shoulder, Nara," Drystan says, his voice on edge.

"We're not out there, no, but…" I turn and pull the shoulder of my shirt and torn sweater down to let him see my feather tattoo. "I do have this."

The man stares at my shoulder in confusion and lowers his weapon. "Are you a different kind of Corvus?"

Shaking my head, I turn to face him, but then I glance down in surprise when my feather suddenly appears between my curled fingers. I hold the feather up and give him a wry smile. "I guess you could say *this* is my weapon."

The man straightens to attention, disbelief in his gaze. "Can I please see your shoulder again?"

I turn slightly so he can see that my shoulder is ink free. Holding my feather, I lift an eyebrow. "I have a feeling you know what I'm supposed to do with this."

"No, we were just told that one day someone would show us a raven's feather unlike any we'd ever seen and we were to offer our assistance in any way necessary." Lowering his gun, he holds his free hand out. "James, at your service, miss."

I shake his hand. "I'm Nara and this is Drystan."

"You wanted to see the book." James gestures to the glass case. "Lift that again, young man."

Once Drystan opens the case, James nods toward the book. "Go ahead."

I quickly flip forward a few pages, then return to the most current page. "How far do these signatures go back?"

"Hundreds of years." James' thick eyebrows elevate expectantly. "Well, go ahead, sign the book."

"But I'm not a Beefeater. All these signatures are Yeoman Warders, right?"

"That's correct. They are all Beefeaters, sworn to protect the Tower and the ravens. Sign the book, Nara."

Feeling honored, I ask, "Do you have a pen?"

"I don't think you'll need it," Drystan whispers in my ear.

The awe in Drystan's comment draws my attention back to the book where my pen is hovering over a blank line, a drop of blood dangling from the tip.

I grimace at the realization that the toothy edge on the feather must exist to provide *ink* whenever necessary. "Signing in blood feels so morbidly archaic," I mutter and set the pen tip to the page, signing my name.

*Nara Collins.*

As the ink dries and my name starts to disappear, I murmur, "Well, that was a bit anticlimactic."

"Look up, Nara," James says, chuckling.

I follow his line of sight. Where there was once a wall directly behind the podium, a narrow door is now open with stone stairs leading downward.

"There's your lower floor," Drystan says in a dry tone.

When a crash of glass somewhere in the building shatters the silence, James lifts his gun, instantly on alert. "Go! The door will close after you." He nods to the staircase. "Whatever you're here for, the answer is there. If the demons are after you, they won't be getting past me."

I anxiously glance back at James while Drystan tugs me toward the entrance. "Have you seen any Corvus? I'm waiting for one to meet me."

A thundering boom vibrates the ceiling above our heads, reverberating throughout the floor at our feet and rattling display cases around us. The Chief Warder looks up as plaster dust falls on his head, then back to me. "I haven't seen anyone else. You'll be safe hidden in there." He follows us over to the doorway. "Once you're in, only you can release yourselves."

"Why can't a Beefeater let us out?"

A serious expression settles on his face. "This passage opens for one reason. You're the only exception I've seen in my entire time here. Whatever your purpose for accessing this place of honor, it must be important to bring a demon attack on the Tower. That has never happened."

I feel horrible that I brought the demons to their door, but I don't like moving forward without Ethan, especially if I'm the only one who can open the door so he can follow us. "I want to wait for Ethan; he's the Corvus I'm asking about."

"If there's a way for Ethan to get through, these thick walls won't stop him," Drystan reminds me as he tugs me onto the narrow staircase.

The only reason I let him pull me in and don't try to stop the heavy stone door from starting to close, is because he's right; Ethan can walk through walls

"Godspeed," James says, then turns away at another loud boom.

The stone door shuts with a heavy thump, shrouding us in darkness and total silence. At the bottom of the stone staircase, Drystan flips on a light and we both stare in awe at the room full of crypts that seems to go on forever.

Drystan and I walk in silence down the main center aisle between rows and rows of crypts and read the ornate engraved area spotlighted on a far wall at the end of the aisle.

*We honor your sacrifice to protect us from the true evil that constantly seeks to destroy our world. Your families buried you, but here is where your body resides in a place of true honor worthy of a Corvus.*

I look at Drystan, then back at the crypts with engraved nameplates and dates, my voice barely a whisper. "All these years, the ravens walking the Tower grounds were just symbols for the actual job of the Warders."

Drystan nods, his gaze scanning the vast space with awe. "It was about protecting so much more than the crown. They honor the ravens who protect the entire world. Every single fallen Corvus."

I approach one of the crypts and touch the cool stone, then run my fingers over the name plate. *Joseph Reinhardt, III.*

"Is this why I'm here?" I look at Drystan, feeling humbled and insignificant. "Is this what Rave needs to see to help him remember?"

"No," Ethan says from the top of the aisle. Walking toward us with purposeful strides, he holds his hand out. "We don't have a lot of time, Nara. Come help me look for it. Some demons have breached the Tower and I don't know if more are coming."

Instead of taking Ethan's hand, I run into his arms and press my face to his bare chest. He'd ditched his sweater and scratches, bruises, and smeared blood now mar his skin, but he seems unfazed. "I'm so glad you're okay." I quickly scan past the blood spatter on his face, my stomach churning at the thought of what's going on outside. "I was worried that you wouldn't be able to find us."

When Ethan clasps my shoulders and steps back, his black eyes shining, my heart sinks. He's more Rave then Ethan. I'm losing him already. I want to scream and yell and hit the Master Corvus, but Ethan is as much a part of him as he is Ethan, so I swallow my fear and nod. "What do you need me to help you find?"

"Something is hidden down here." His brows pull together in concentration as he scans past the rows of crypts and into the vast space. "Rave's vision briefly led me to you, but there's something about this space. It's like the moment I stepped into it…it's a black void. I haven't been able to sense anything."

"What are we looking for?"

He shakes his head, his fingers flexing on my shoulders. "I don't know, Nara. Just something vital. This space is familiar to Rave. Whatever it is, it's calling to him. He's truly tense, demanding that we find it."

"Find what?" I insist, glancing at Drystan with worry.

Ethan closes his eyes and shakes his head, then meets my gaze. "He doesn't know. He just says to look for an image."

Drystan spreads his arms. "Look around. There are images everywhere," he says, pointing out the detailed carvings of warriors fighting battles on each of the crypts, then on to the images carved around the inscription on the dais.

Cupping my face, Ethan stares at me. "You *know*, Nara. Rave thinks it was on the scroll that was in the book's spine. You just need to remember."

"We know what it looks like!" I say, nodding. "It's an image of three ravens: one on the ground, one flying above toward the sky, and one below, flying downward. Drystan can help us look."

"You know? When did you remember—" He cuts himself off

and looks at Drystan. "Take that side and start looking. We'll do the same on this side."

After we've scanned our thirtieth crypt, I'm rounding the corner to move on to the next one when I look up at the spotlights that are shining down the walls every ten feet or so. I push on Ethan's chest to stop him from moving forward and point to the massive scene carved into the stone walls. "We need to look here too. I think we'll have to stand back to see the whole thing."

With a curt nod, he says to Drystan, "Check the scene on the wall as well."

"Got it," Drystan calls.

We meet in the middle aisle once more, but the spotlights are spread so far it's hard to piece together what we're seeing with ten feet of darkness in between each light.

"Can you put your phones together?" I say, squinting to see.

When Ethan and Drystan turn on their phones' lights, Drystan murmurs, "Holy mother."

"That's it!" I say excitedly as the guys slowly slide their lights together. From the wall to our left, to the back wall and then to the wall on our right, the triple raven image spans the entire length of the room.

Glancing at Ethan, I realize that he hasn't spoken. "Does Rave recognize it?"

He flexes his jaw, then clasps my hand. "Come."

When we reach the spot where the raven is flying underground, Ethan releases my hand. "In all the research you did on raven lore, do you remember the story of Brân the Blessed?"

"It's from Welsh mythology," Drystan supplies. "The name Brân translates to raven in Welsh."

"I remember now," I say. "Brân was the son of the god Llyr, right?"

Drystan nods. "During a battle he was mortally wounded and his head was cut off and brought to the Tower of London. Legend says that as long as the head of Brân remains there to guard, Britain would be safe from foreign invasion."

"It's interesting how closely that lore parallels London's current tradition of keeping the ravens at the Tower to protect the crown," I say, looking at Drystan.

"It's always been about defending." Ethan looks at me and

points to the raven's claws holding something behind him as he flies. "What do you see?"

"Is that a rock?" I squint, then gasp. "It's a man's head, isn't it?"

"Look closer," Ethan says, rubbing his fingers along the carved lines meant to represent hair on the man's head. "Does that shape look familiar?"

I blink at the small round hole with a narrow rectangular tab on the top and bottom of the circle. "What is that—?"

Drystan nudges his shoulder between us to shine his phone on the hole. "Is that some kind of strange keyhole?"

I glance down when my feather appears in my hand. A shiver trickles down my spine as I lift the two-toned quill and stare at the ragged edge near the tip. "This could fit in one side of the slot, but the shaft appears to only be half as wide as it should be."

"The stone down here is impenetrable. I can't walk through it." Ethan's raven wings whooshing out in a half-spread send Drystan flying.

Landing on his butt, Drystan stares in shock at the massive black wings. "Holy shite!"

Snorting at Drystan's comment, Ethan reaches back and pulls a black feather from his wing. He winces and I see blood dripping from the end that's as uneven as my feather's tip. I shake my head. "What *are* you doing?"

"Drystan's right. It's a two-sided keyhole." Taking my feather, he lays his black feather against mine and lines the jagged edges opposite of each other, then he slides them into the hole.

When he turns the "key" and part of the stone wall begins to swing inward, I start to shake. "Wh—what's in there?"

Ethan turns to me, relief in his pitch-black eyes. "This is where Brân's head was buried. I must've thought it was the perfect place for my memories."

"*Your memories?*" My lips tremble as he hands me my feather back.

Ethan shakes his head. "I'm still here, Nara." He cups my jaw, his gaze sad. "But Rave is so strong now I'm barely keeping myself in the forefront." He glances into the darkness beyond the stone door. "I don't know what will happen after I walk in there."

"You won't do it alone." I slide my fingers between his and fold them around his palm. "I'm going with you."

My heart shreds when he untangles our hands and shakes his head. "This is Rave's journey, not ours, Nara."

Tears stream down my cheeks. I start to crush the feather between my fingers, but it's no longer there. Lifting my hand, I grip his wrist tight. "Hold on, Ethan. I love you. Please hold on!"

His eyes mist, but he forces a smile as he cups my face and thumbs my tears away. "I love you too, Sunshine." Glancing at Drystan, he gives him a curt nod. "Make sure she stays."

Drystan grabs my hand before I can follow Ethan through the doorway. "No, Nara," he says, his voice gruff with emotion and wonder.

Once the stone door closes behind Ethan with a scraping thump of finality and Drystan says, "Don't worry. He's tough, Nara," I release the deep sob I've been holding back and let him fold me into his arms.

# Chapter Twenty-Nine

*Nara*

The rumbling of the stone floor beneath our feet instantly jerks my head up from Drystan's shoulder. I have no idea how much time has passed. It could've been five minutes or a half hour.

"What's happening?" Drystan says, grasping my arms as he glances around the room.

We both freeze at the surreal sight of Ethan leaning halfway through the stone door. With an intense expression, he grips my hand and commands, "You're needed."

Drystan yells when I'm tugged free of his grip. Before he can grab my other hand, Rave yanks me into the stone.

When I finally emerge out the other side and Rave releases me, I feel woozy and only partially put back together. I take the cell phone he shoves into my hand and turn on the flashlight. Quickly glancing down to make sure all my limbs are still intact, I look up, ready to rail at the Master Corvus, but he's literally shaking along with the ground underneath us.

"Did you know that ravens' feathers used to be white?" he grits out. "All this darkness I've fought for eons: demons influencing mortals, mortals' own hatred and their vile acts upon each other… takes its toll. I thought if I could live as a mortal for a while, I might understand how they could be so broken. Adder was the host I chose."

Turning, he begins to pace. "I lived his life...and knew what it meant to love. Then mortals showed their true colors. Wanting to control, to have all the power...traitors to their own kind!"

Raven wings sprout from his back and he pauses in front of me. "Because of their betrayal to Adder, I broke every rule, betrayed everything that I stood for. I finally hated every last mortal and I killed without remorse. I became the very thing I fought against, Nara!"

The stone room is no more than eight feet by eight feet. It's cold and so small his wings scrape the low ceiling, but the closeness also creates an intimacy that I hope I can use to help him.

I instinctively clasp his hand, then suddenly feel like my entire body is going to fly apart. "Calm down or you'll kill me!"

Closing his eyes, the Master Corvus takes several breaths. The room temperature rises and my body's vibration shifts to a manageable hum so I can at least talk without my teeth chattering.

When his gaze snaps open, I fold my other hand around his. "Do you hate me, Rave?"

The floor rumbles louder as he shakes his head, his gaze imploring. "I can't stop the pain, Nara. Adder suffered because of greed for power and their desire to get to *me*. I feel like I'm going to explode. Too many memories and so much darkness."

He shuts his eyes once more, and I feel his energy tugging against mine. It's draining, but I tighten my hands on his. "Would a pleasant memory help, Rave?"

Shining black eyes seek mine. "Share it now!"

I nod. "I will, but you have to promise me something."

"What!" he snarls, anger rippling off him in waves.

His energy tugs against me so hard my spine feels like it's breaking apart a piece at a time. Shaking all over, I set my jaw and strengthen my hold. "Promise you'll keep Ethan safe. That when this is all said and done, Lucifer...everything...that Ethan will survive. Promise me, Rave!"

"I promise," he roars, then yanks me close until we're nose to nose. "Now share, lightweight!"

"You must let Ethan in," I insist. "I can't do this without him."

Gnashing his teeth, he blinks and then Ethan suddenly glances around us in confusion. "The ground is shaking. Where are we?"

I squeeze his hands hard. "No time, Ethan! Close your eyes and remember that time at the pond when you pulled me into the cold water."

His eyes shine with anger and he shakes his head. "He can't have that, Nara. It's ours!"

"I prefer you over a memory." A few stones above our heads fall and I call over the loud shaking, "He's losing it, Ethan. The memories are too much. Let Rave feel your emotions so you *can* take me Corvus submarining again one day!"

Ethan closes his eyes and I do the same. As I begin to recount what it felt like experiencing that time in the water with him surrounded by his powerful raven wings, the room stops shaking and everything goes quiet.

When I open my eyes, the small space is so bright I have to quickly close them once more. "Ethan?" I say a couple seconds later, peeking through one eye.

He releases my hands and smiles. I start to smile back when I realize that the glow is gone and Ethan's lips are tilted in that wiser-than-the-world smirk I've only seen Rave use.

"Thank you, Nara," Rave says, folding his wings away. "The fact that moment included Ethan's Corvus side is very special. Now I truly have my own pleasant memory to recall."

"Are…you good now? Are all your memories intact?"

His mouth sets in a firm line. "They are, with some additional details that living as Ethan has provided." When I look at him in confusion, he nods briskly. "We must go. I need to sweep up the demon spawn trying to destroy this sacred place."

"But what if they've already found the answer to defeating you? What if I missed it somehow?"

Rave laughs. "Ah, it's refreshing for someone to care about my wellbeing, but…" He sobers, his eyes shining so black I shiver. "All this was about my memory loss. It was the only advantage Lucifer could have had over me." Clasping my arm, he starts to urge me forward, but I dig my heels into the floor.

"You are *not* pulling me like human taffy through that door again! That felt…" I pause and shiver, unable to put into words how strange that made me feel.

"The door no longer opens, Nara," he says, then sighs. Unfurling his wings once more, he lifts me up into his arms in one fluid movement. Once his wings close around us and he starts to move,

I hold onto his neck and whisper, "I do care…and thanks, Rave."

"You're such a lightweight," he murmurs against my temple, a pleased smile evident in his comment.

The moment we pass back through the stone door, Drystan is holding a heavy stone slab in the air. "Let her go, you crazy bird!"

Rave sighs and while he sets me down, he plucks the slab out of Drystan's hands like a piece of Styrofoam. "I do not have time for your childish attempts to protect."

"She's done everything she can to help you. Don't risk her life like that. It might be insignificant to you, but it's not to me!"

"I'm glad to hear you'll guard her life with your own." The stone shatters to bits when Rave tosses it behind Drystan. "Because you're going to keep her safe until this is over."

"What?" I quickly shake my head. "I go where you do!"

Rave ignores my protest and keeps his gaze on Drystan. "In return, I will show you the truth. You deserve that."

Drystan frowns. "What truth—" He stops and stares into space when Rave clasps his shoulder.

"What are you doing to him?" I say, waving my hand in front of Drystan's blank expression.

When he releases Drystan, Rave gives him a stern look. "Are we in agreement?"

Drystan looks upset and a little dazed, but he nods. "Even if you hadn't shared, I would protect Nara with my life."

"Hello, you two." I point to myself. "Non-helpless girl right here, hearing every word."

Rave hooks a hand on the back of Drystan's neck at the same time he grips my upper arm. "Let's go."

"Wha—"

"—aaaaah!" I let out a half-yelp when I look around. We're standing in an office building not far from the Tower. *Why am I not surprised distance doesn't matter with a spirit who can see through every molecule?* "Ugh, Rave! A warning would be nice."

"That's not what I imagined teleportation would feel like."

While Drystan pats his chest and looks down to make sure he's still in one piece, I move in the dark to the window and frown at the crush of people clashing in front of the Tower. "That doesn't look good."

"Keep the lights off," Rave says as he pulls open the office coat closet and snags someone's black v-neck sweater. Grabbing some paper towels, he wipes the blood off his face, then opens the window and calls with authority, "Come." When Patch instantly appears and lands on the sill outside our window." Rave says to the bird, "Stay here. This shouldn't take long."

I blink at Patch and wonder where he came from. He couldn't have followed since the last time he could've seen us was when we went into the tunnel. As I ponder how he knew where we'd be, it suddenly hits me that he listened to Rave. "Why does Patch understand and respond to you when Ethan hasn't been able to connect with him?"

"Why do you think?"

I huff that he just vanished, but Drystan stares, eye-wide. "Did you know Ethan could teleport?"

I start to shake my head, then pause, thinking back. "He might've done it a couple of times. I'm pretty sure that was his Corvus instincts kicking in to save me, not a conscious action on his part."

"But Rave can do this at will?" Drystan joins me at the window, his gaze locked on the group of demons and Corvus clashing outside the Tower.

"Apparently." My hand shakes a little as I run my fingers over the feathers on Patch's back. I hope the demons haven't done too much damage to the Tower grounds. Glancing his way, I need a distraction from the fight below. "Tell me what truth Rave shared with you, Drystan?"

He slides his hands into his pockets. His green eyes might be shrouded in the darkness, but I can see them glittering with moisture. "Everything I thought I knew about my father…wasn't true. Now I know why he never married my mother. It wasn't because he didn't think we were good enough; he was trying to protect us. He didn't want his brother to know he had a child and passed his abilities on to him. He didn't want me to be recruited to the sanctuary."

"Your uncle knows about your abilities?" I ask, shocked. "So you did inherit them from your dad?"

Drystan swallows and looks out toward the Tower bridge. "The Master Corvus shared his life as Adder with me. Through his eyes, I saw my father at the sanctuary. He worked alongside my uncle, believing he was making a difference just being there in a supportive role. My father didn't know about his ability; he was blissfully unaware of his influence on those with special skills."

His lips twisting in frustration, Drystan continues, "I think this will make more sense if I go back a bit. When Adder stumbled upon Olivia, she was a drugged out junkie who'd been taken over by a demon. He had every reason to leave her behind after he expelled the demon, but he couldn't. There was something about her. Instead he took her to the sanctuary and asked them if he could stay and help her learn to be a Paladin."

"But she didn't have any unique talents," I say. "I mean, isn't that a prerequisite for being assigned to support a Corvus?"

Drystan smirks. "She'd already snagged a Corvus' attention. One who was willing to stay at the sanctuary to help her. A first for the sanctuary. Corvus have never stayed there. It's a place purely to help train and be a support system for the Paladins as the Paladins in turn support the Corvus on a one-on-one basis. A Corvus championing her made her special in her own right, so the sanctuary took her in.

"Olivia got better, but she didn't necessarily trust Adder." Drystan pauses and smiles. "Actually, she hated him at first while she was detoxing. She even gave him the name Adder; his real name was Addison. She called him "Mad Adder" to be exact, because he was tough and came up with crazy ways to challenge her. Corvus aren't the warm and fuzzy type, but considering he was the Master Corvus, he was especially stoic. Rave didn't let Adder get close to Olivia. He wouldn't allow it, but he did want her to get better so he let Adder help her in his own way. Through music Adder and Olivia formed a bond. Turns out she had an amazing voice and with his guitar skills, they performed together for those at the sanctuary.

"A few months later, Olivia told Adder that she'd fallen in love with him and that she knew he wasn't capable of returning her love, so she was glad they at least made beautiful music together. She didn't know that Adder kept parts of his thoughts hidden from the Master Corvus. He had fallen hard for Olivia, but he never voiced his thoughts so the Master Corvus wouldn't know."

"So he never told her how he felt? Aww, that's so sad," I say, my heart aching for the star-crossed couple.

A bitter expression forms on Drystan's face. "One day, Adder was called to meet with the leader of the sanctuary. As second in command, my uncle brought Olivia to the meeting and my father joined them."

"But your uncle told me that he didn't hear what the meeting was about."

Drystan cuts angry eyes my way. "He lied. About many things apparently."

"What happened?"

"The leader told Adder that he knew he was the Master Corvus and he demanded that he share the location of every single Corvus."

"Why would he do that?"

Drystan shakes his head. "I can only tell you what Adder thought was the man's motivation. He thought the demand was a power play. That the leader wanted a way to keep tabs on the Corvus and by doing so, he would feel like he had some sort of control over them instead of playing a glorified support role. Of course, Adder denied the leader's belief that he was the Master Corvus. His role there wasn't to be discovered, but to observe and understand."

He glances outside. "Olivia was just as shocked to learn Adder might be the Master Corvus, but before she could say anything, the leader grabbed her and plunged a needle in her throat."

"What were your uncle and father doing during all this?"

Drystan shakes his head. "Adder's memories show my uncle appears to be frozen in place, while my father jumped into action the moment the leader attacked Olivia. My dad tried to convince the leader to let her go, but the man became so angry that Adder didn't react, he pushed the heavy dose of drugs into Olivia's neck to prove how far he would go."

Drystan looks at me, his expression sad. "Adder was screaming inside, but the Master Corvus wouldn't let him move or speak. So all Olivia saw was the man she loved not defending her."

I sniff back tears and shake my head. "Is that when the Master Corvus lost it?"

Drystan folds his arms and hunches his shoulders against the cool wind blowing into the window. "The drugs were too much for Olivia. Adder heard her heart stop and that's when the Master Corvus unleashed holy hell on the place."

As tears fall, my heart twists. Now I understand the pain Rave felt. So much unrequited love lost in an instant. So much betrayal and hurt. No demons were involved and yet, Rave snapped after all the built-up rage he'd endured. It was the final bell toll for our mortal world. But there was still good in him even when he felt consumed by all the darkness. It could've been so much worse. He could've destroyed everything. "That's why Rave got rid of his memories," I whisper. "He couldn't bear that he'd killed a mortal and he didn't know how to continue to fight for a world he'd given up on."

"I understand the need to run away after taking a life."

I jerk my head up, back ramrod straight. "What?"

Drystan closes his eyes, his jaw tight. "I killed Harper."

For a split-second, I blink, then shake my head. "The demon did that, not you!"

"It doesn't change the fact a life is gone and my hands took it. I'll have to live with the guilt forever. Something like that haunts you."

"You can't change a past you didn't consciously cause, Dryst." I clasp his forearm and squeeze. "Instead, find a way to turn it into something positive. Pay it forward and help others make the most of their amazing skills so they can protect themselves and others from demons."

He snorts. "You mean by using the powers I can't control? I'll pass. The sooner I get away from those with abilities, the better off everyone will be."

"Even me?" I ask, my heart heavy.

With a serious look, he hooks his arm around my neck and pulls me to his side. "Never you, Nara. Never you."

# Chapter Thirty

### *Ethan*

Rave reappears near a corner of the Tower where a crowd of people has started to form. They're enthralled as they watch the skirmish between the six Corvus and the few remaining demons. At least the Corvus are being stealthy in their sword use. Some of the people who've already been freed from their demons have run away, but some stayed to watch the demons and Corvus fight with wide eyes and gaping mouths.

*This would be entertaining if I didn't have somewhere to be.*

Normally Rave's droll tone would annoy me, but now I'm just anxious to get back to Nara. I want her to know that I'm not gone. I hate that Rave back-seated me, but I wouldn't know how to teleport and he definitely got Nara out of there in the safest way possible. Now that he has his memories, at least I'm not locked away in that dark cesspool. For now, I'll let him lead. *Why are we here, Rave? Those Corvus can take care of the rest of the demons. And where do you need to be?*

*You'll* let *me lead? A* mental snort. *Get used to the view from back there. I'm here for the duration.*

*What's that supposed to mean? Duration of what?* I grit out, angry that he's not sharing his plans.

The entire time Rave and I argue, he's scanning the crowd. Once his gaze lands on a man's dark head weaving and bobbing as he shoulders his way through with a determined stride, I zero in on him. *Damn it. Get him out of here now!*

Rave expels a sigh of impatience. *What's he doing here?*

Her father looks tired but on a mission. He had to have taken the first flight he could get after he got off the phone with us. *I have no idea. Just…get him out of harm's way before Nara sees him.*

With a cold smile, Rave mutters, *I might actually enjoy this,* and steps directly in front of Nara's father as the man finally wrestles his way through the throng of people.

"Ethan!" he snaps, his gaze sharp with dislike. "I should've known you'd be in the middle of whatever's going on here." When he finally notices the telltale signs of blood on my face and chest, he raises his voice above the din of onlookers encouraging the fight. "Where's my daughter? I swear if anything has happened to her…" He tries to look around me, but Rave moves to block his line of sight, which only makes Jonathan Collins angrier. "I want to see Inara right now. Take me to her!"

"Enough!" Rave grabs the man by the upper arm.

"Let go of me." He tries to jerk free, but Rave doesn't even blink as he cinches fingers tighter around his biceps like a vise.

"It's time to go, Mr. Collins," Rave says with a slight smirk and just like that we're gone.

When we reappear beside Mr. Collin's car in what appears to be a private airport according to the Virginia Skyline Air's sign, the stunned man goes completely white as he looks around. I instantly rail at Rave. *I meant get him away from the crowd to somewhere IN LONDON! Her father won't be able to process this!*

"What the hell? Am I…back in Central Virginia?"

"You're lucky I didn't take you to Iceland," Rave snaps. *I don't have the patience to babysit family members. Nor do I wish Nara to lose her father once more. This was the most efficient choice.*

Nara's father warily reaches out to touch his car, then yanks his hand back to jerk his attention to Rave. "Whatever you are, you're more unhinged than Fate!"

I can feel Rave's building irritation and sense he's about to skip out, so I roar in his ear, *Don't you dare leave him like this!*

"This is beyond—" Nara's father stops talking and grabs Rave's shoulders, squeezing hard. "Where in God's name is my daughter? What have you done to her?"

*Explain, Rave. NOW!*

He exhales an exhausted sigh.

"You're fucking sighing? Do you think this is a joke?" Her father hauls back and hurls a fast-flying fist.

Rave catches his hand mid-air and lets out an ominous snarl that rumbles the ground beneath his feet. "Iceland is still an option."

*Rave!* I warn to calm the spirit down.

Rolling his head from one shoulder to the other, he sniffs disdainfully. *Fine, but it'll be my way. Efficient.*

Flicking her father's fist away like an annoying gnat, he quickly grabs his shoulders. "I'm not Ethan. Pay attention and keep up!"

When her father sways and his expressions morph through various emotions—from pain, to sorrow, to regret, then anger and worry before shifting to pride, and finally fear—I realize that Rave is sharing *everything* that Nara held back from her father. The entire truth in one huge visual upload based on her father's eye movements.

If it's like a movie…oh, shit! *For the love of my survival, DO NOT SHARE ANY INTIMATE SCENES BETWEEN NARA AND ME!* I yell at Rave, but he remains silent and my only feedback is her father's constantly shifting expressions. Is it possible to have a heart attack in my head? Yes, it's possible! I feel like I'm going to explode, but I don't even have a chest to pound and make this panicky feeling stop. *Fucking hell, I'm going to kill you, Rave!*

Releasing her father, Rave folds his arms. *Stop angsting. You never shared any of the fun stuff with me. Much to my annoyance.* Snorting, he continues in an amused tone, *Though I did enjoy sharing parts of the Corvus submarine scene with him. I even added my own commentary, since I was there in* spirit.

*Thanks a lot,* I grumble as he chuckles at his own pun and wonder which of those expressions on Mr. Collin's face related to *that* particular scene.

The fact that Nara's father hasn't moved since Rave released him begins to worry me, but then it's like he suddenly comes out of a trance. Squaring his shoulders, he points to the ground next to him and his voice shakes a little but then builds up in parental steam. "Bring Inara home right now. Just like you did me."

"No."

*I want her safe, Rave. Nara has done her part and helped you regain your memory.*

"No?" Mr. Collins repeats in disbelief. A muscle thrums along his temple and his face turns redder as he pokes Rave in the chest. "Ethan, if you have any sway over this heartless entity squatting in your body, you'll tell him to bring her home!"

*Bringing her home is best for her,* I argue with Rave.

*But is that what's best for you?* Rave asks, cryptically.

*What do you mean by that?*

"This is all your fault, Ethan!" her father cuts into our discussion, his voice even more forceful. "If she hadn't met you, none of this would have ever happen—"

"And your world could already be decimated!" Rave roars, leaning over her father. His tone deadly, he continues, "Do *not* speak to Ethan like that. He has heart and a strong mind, unlike any I've seen. As for your daughter…she is special in so many ways you can't begin to fathom. She is *needed.*"

When Rave straightens to his full height and Mr. Collins just gapes at him, I'm so stunned by the ornery spirit's comments, I can't think of a single thing to say.

"Inara *is* special." Her father's sharp tone tempers slightly. "I know that. But I want what's best for my—"

"Stop blathering." Rave narrows his gaze. "Ethan and Nara deserve praise and respect, not a lecture or censure. They are beyond their years and are trying to save ALL of you. But instead of protecting your world from Lucifer and his demons bent on destroying it, I'm wasting time explaining this to you."

When he immediately blinks out, I know Rave won't acknowledge my thanks, so I give a response he would expect. *I'm pretty sure that was the Master Corvus equivalent of dropping the mic.*

Before everything fades to black, Rave grunts. *You're going to be insufferable now. I preferred you stuffed in a corner and unable to speak.*

*I'm glad you heard me,* I say when we're suddenly standing in Matt's bedroom instead of back in London.

*You didn't have to tell me,* Rave says. *I felt your thoughts.*

*You felt them?*

*Focus!* he snaps at me as he leans over and taps a sleeping Matt on the shoulder.

Matt rolls over and rubs his eyes. "Ethan? What are you doing—" he pauses to glance at his clock. "It's four a.m., dude. How'd you get in here—wait, aren't you supposed to be in London?" He suddenly stiffens. "They haven't cancelled the trip have they?"

"No. You still leave tomorrow. Have you stayed away from Lainey for at least twenty-four hours?" Rave asks.

Sitting up, Matt quickly pulls his T-shirt off. "Yeah, the tattoo on my back has stopped shifting, but I haven't looked since yesterday." He tries to glance over his shoulder, then points behind him. "What do you see?"

Rave steps around and stares at the newly morphed ink. *Interesting full circle outcome,* Rave muses.

I stare at the Corvus symbol that's completely whole now. It's as if the artist never inked it any other way. *The symbol is intact, but I can see the pulsing movement like it's a living breathing being. I sense them all. Past and present Corvus. Touch it,* I say to him.

*I already know every single one. They are a piece of me. There's no point in this exercise.*

It's hard not to roll my eyes at the spirit's linear thought process. *Just touch it!*

With a sigh, Rave flattens his hand on Matt's back. "It's warm," he says to Matt. "Do you still feel a burning sensation?"

"It's muted now. Much more manageable," Matt says, nodding. "But I think that's because of the dream I had."

"Explain this dream," Rave demands.

Matt gives Rave a side-eye look, then says, "Are you okay, Ethan? You're acting a bit strange."

"You're the one with a constantly morphing tattoo on your back."

Matt snorts at Rave's comeback. "Point taken. Okay, about my dream. I saw a dungeon? I don't know…it was somewhere below ground, very old stonework. There were stone coffins too."

"Crypts?"

Matt nods. "Yeah, that's what they're called. Men pushed the stone tops off the crypts and then more men came with torches. They burned the skeletons inside. Every single one." He drops his head in his hands and shakes it. "I yelled at them to stop. I was so upset, but I'm not sure why." Glancing up at Rave, he continues, "Other than grave desecration, I had no connection to them. I've never been to a place like this in my life. Why did my dream feel so real?"

"You'll see this place one day," Rave says. Shutting me out, he clasps Matt's shoulder and whispers something in his ear.

When Rave straightens and releases Matt, I can finally hear again. "I *knew* I was meant to do something," Matt says smiling. The spark in his eyes dims slightly. "Is Ethan okay in there? Let him know I said thanks for supporting me."

"He can hear you. Take your trip to London. Soak it all in. You've got a lot to learn if you choose this path."

*What does his tattoo mean? What did you say to him?* I barely get the words out before we're standing in the sealed room below the Towers once more. *Why are we here, Rave? I know his dream is about this place, but—*

*Matt's tattoo is a living tapestry. It moves and morphs based on the Corvus as a whole. After I got my memories back, all the broken parts depicted in the ink on his back pulled together in his tattoo. His tattoo's changes, combined with his dream, make me believe that the burning Matt's feeling is a prophesy.*

*Are you saying that the men he saw in his dream were demons?*

*Who else would desecrate a sacred Corvus burial place? With Matt's vision, we've been given a glimpse into a possible future.*

I stare out across the rows of crypts. Generations of past Corvus laid to rest. *We have to destroy them, don't we?*

*For the safety of the living Corvus, yes.*

Rave lifts his hands and I feel vast energy gathering inside him. He pushes his hands forward and every single crypt's stone top slides open at once. A sudden heaviness weighs on me. *If we burn them, won't we be creating the very ash that demons could use against us?*

*There is another tunnel that connects to this secret place where a rushing river runs,* Rave says as he walks over to the altar below the inscription about the Corvus. A lone candle, worn down from repeated use sits in the center. *Once the bodies are turned to ash, they'll be scattered into the river and eventually carried out to the Thames.*

*The Warders' entire existence is about to change,* I say, frustrated that Corvus ashes can help demons thwart our ability to detect them residing in a person.

Rave lights a match and stares at the flame. *The crypts will survive. The Warders' tradition of honoring and protecting the Corvus' memory will continue.* He tosses the match and halts its descent with nothing but an energy boost from his hands. As the flame hangs midair, he continues, *The Warders' duties will change in how they prepare each new crypt, including a ritual to destroy the body fully, leaving no trace left behind. The Corvus' essence will remain here, as they should, but their physical bodies will not. It's too dangerous to our existence.*

While Rave talks, the tiny flame grows larger and begins to spin into a ball of white-hot fire. I can feel the heat radiating from it.

*And Matt?* I need to know what Rave's plans are for our friend.

*Matt's tattoo and dreams tell the Corvus' current or potential future status. The mortal world hasn't had someone with his abilities.*

He's not Corvus. I would've felt that.

*As a Corvus keeper, his role is important, just like Nara and Drystan.*

*I don't think Drystan's going to be involved with the Corvus or the sanctuary after this, Rave. His uncle has kept too much from him.*

*Drystan can't fight who he is. He just needs to control it. He'll have questions for his uncle after what I shared with him, but I want to talk to Wicklow alone first.* The flame Rave's controlling grows even hotter. *There's only one reason Adder's body isn't down here; the Warders couldn't locate it all those years ago. Wicklow needs to tell me where he had Adder buried. Then the Warders can make sure his body is moved here and taken care of under the new protocol.*

*So the Warders move the Corvus bodies without anyone's knowledge? I take it the sanctuary doesn't know about this place?*

*No one knows the Tower's true significance or the Warders' role in bringing the Corvus home and honoring them. You, Nara, and Drystan are the only three, beyond the Warders, who know about this place.*

*Matt has seen it in his dreams*, I remind him.

*And he will again one day, if he chooses to embrace his role.*

When he doesn't say anything more, I prod him. *Which is?*

Rave's only response is to shove his hands forward, sending the massive ball of fire toward the crypts in a sweeping wave of white-hot heat.

# Chapter Thirty-One

### *Nara*

I jump when Ethan suddenly appears beside me. Putting my hand over my racing heart, I exhale my relief. "We saw the Corvus defeat the last of the demons, then they left. That was almost an hour ago. Where did you go?"

"I had to take care of something."

*Rave.* I don't like that he's being evasive. Ethan would tell me. I try to look in his eyes, but it's too dark in the office space to see if his eyes are all black now. Has Michael's prediction come true? The thought makes it hard to breathe and my stomach feels like it's full of lead. I start to ask to talk to Ethan, but Rave speaks before I can. "I'm going to the sanctuary. I want you two to stay here."

"Not without me you're not." Drystan's tone is sharp and angry as he steps closer. "My uncle has a fecking lot to answer for, the first of which will be why the 'ell you're the one who confirmed my ability to boost others' powers and not him."

"I want to know why he told me he didn't know what was said between the Master Corvus and the leader," I say, lifting my chin. "We're both going."

"I prefer to talk with Wicklow alone."

Drystan folds his arms. "You can pop us into the sanctuary no problem, but if you refuse, I'll just drive us there."

"Not without your keys." Rave gives Drystan a cold smile.

Drystan snorts. "It's amusing that you think I need a key."

As Rave's gaze sharpens on Drystan, I sigh. Apparently sparring with Drystan is one thing Rave and Ethan have in common. I step between them, facing Rave. "Just take us. We're going to follow you anyway."

"I don't want you there at all, Nara."

"Too bad. I'm here for a reason." I tilt my chin up and stand a little taller. "You may as well get used to that."

Rave sighs and pulls the keys out of his pocket. "I'll drive."

When he doesn't hand the keys over, Drystan scowls. "I'm fine to drive."

"My reflexes are faster."

Just as Drystan opens his mouth to argue, Rave grabs both of us and we're suddenly standing outside Drystan's car.

While I shudder and remind Rave about warning us, Drystan shakes his head to clear his disorientation and grumbles, "Showoff," before he climbs into the backseat.

As we drive to Westminster, Drystan tells me about life at the sanctuary. "I haven't connected with many of the Paladins, but Maggie, the head chef in the kitchen, is wrapped around my little finger. She makes my favorite hot meal whenever I ask, which is lovely because it can be quite drafty back in our living area. Did I tell you the sanctuary used to be an old boarding school? Other than my Paladin friend, Chloe, there's one other person I think you'd like, Nara. Warren's closer to our ages, maybe eight or ten years older, but he's so confident being just a regular bloke among so many with unusual abilities that my uncle assigned him to help Chloe control her growing abilities."

"Is Warren a doctor?" I finally get in a word. *Why is he being so talkative?*

Drystan shakes his head, his brow furrowing. "Actually, he's not. He doesn't have any powers that I'm aware of. He's just a great listener who seems to get what you're going through. He's so calm that when he speaks, it's with such confidence and authority, people listen. He even blocked Uncle Rowan from his sessions with my friend, telling my uncle he was making Chloe tense." Drystan glances out the window and says in a lower tone, "I can't believe Uncle Rowan didn't tell me about my father's ability. I'm just glad my mum is back in Wales visiting family right now. She doesn't need to overhear the very loud conversation I plan to have with him."

Ah, now I see. He's tense about confronting his uncle. Drystan suddenly stops talking and glances around. "Why are we slowing down? The sanctuary is just around the corner."

Rave pulls over to the side of the road and parks the car. Shutting off the lights, he holds his hand up to silence Drystan and turns his head as if listening. "Something's not right."

"What is it?" Drystan says.

Rave's gaze narrows. "It's too quiet."

"Can you see inside?"

"No, apparently the expansive vision is a spirit thing. It's not something a mortal host is supposed to be able to experience or their Corvus for that matter. The fact you and Ethan were able to, and for it to flicker in and out for me while in a host, is unprecedented. But now that I've integrated with Ethan's body—"

"Ethan's gone?" I stare at him with wide, teary eyes, my heart suspended. He spoke about Ethan in the third person.

"He's not." Rave clasps my hand on the car seat, his gaze holding mine.

The moment he touches me, Ethan's voice rushes in my head. *I'm here, Nara. I can hear you, but he's not letting me talk—*"

Rave releases my hand, his tone gruff. "He's safe, but my spirit sight is too intermittent." As he turns slightly in the seat to include Drystan in his comments, I want to demand that he let me talk to Ethan, but I know Rave's in Corvus defender mode and my concerns are irrelevant. "You two stay here. I'll be back." He glances my way with a fierce scowl, then focuses on Drystan. "Make sure she stays."

I'm frustrated that the only way I can hear Ethan is if I'm physically connected to his body, but before I can push the issue that we should stick together, the driver's seat is suddenly empty.

"I will *never* get used to that," Drystan muses as he leans forward in his seat. "So what do you think riled him?"

I press my lips together, then shake my head. "I don't like him going out there alone."

"He's the *Master* Corvus, Nara. He can take care of himself."

"Maybe. Why didn't he at least call the other Corvus to back him up?"

"Because they're inferior," he says in a "duh" tone.

I'd laugh at how American that sounded if I weren't so tense. Actually a lot of his comments sound American now. I guess he really did pick up a lot in his short time in the US. As I continue to gnaw my lip, Drystan moves closer, his gaze drilling into my profile.

"What aren't you sharing, Nara?"

I turn, putting my arm on the back of the seat. "Do you believe in destiny, Drystan? That you were meant to do something?"

"I believe we were meant to meet if that's what you mean," he says, resting his chin on my arm.

I smile, despite my worries. "I definitely believe that people are put into your life for a reason. Including *your* Welsh arse." Sobering, I continue, "Michael told me that Rave will need my help. I can't help feeling like I'm still needed."

"But the way you explained it to me, what the archangel told you was in relation to helping the Master Corvus remember who he is. You've done that, brilliantly." Lifting his head, Drystan clasps my hand. "The Master Corvus has fought demons and Lucifer himself on his own for millennia, Nara. And while it's uncommon for him to interact with us or even the other Corvus, don't take this the wrong way, but why do you think that a supernatural being in full possession of his memories and abilities would need your help?"

"When you put it that way, I feel pretty ridiculous." Giving him a wry smile, I sigh. "I've just been in this mode for so long, it's hard not to think I should be doing something." Clasping his hand tighter, I continue, "Rave touched my hand before he left. For my peace of mind, could you please use your ability to find Ethan? That'll at least tell us where the Master Corvus went."

Drystan nods and folds his hand around mine, closing his eyes. He shakes his head a minute later. "What?"

"I can't find him. Close your eyes too and concentrate."

My heart starting to thump harder, I close my eyes and focus my thoughts on finding Ethan.

Drystan exhales deeply a minute later and I open my eyes, worry making my heart race. "What?"

"I can tell that he went into the sanctuary, but I can't find him in there."

My other hand is already on the door handle when Drystan tightens his hold. "Where are you going? Rave was pretty adamant that we stay. You, ah, did hear the implied threat in his tone that I keep you safe, remember?"

"I'm going to at least take a look. We're blind around this corner," I say, pulling my hand free and opening the door. "You can come with me or not."

"If we're going to do this, let's do it, right," Drystan says as he grabs my hand and tugs me across the street.

"Where are we going?" I whisper while he leads me through a narrow alleyway. Turning the corner at the back side of a building, he punches in a door code.

Once we're inside, Drystan takes a side door and holds it for me to follow. "This goes to the roof. We'll be able to get a better view up there."

When Drystan pulls the lid off a rubber box next to the roof's edge and retrieves a pair of binoculars, I raise my eyebrows. He shrugs and puts them up to his face. "There's an older man who comes up here every day. He feeds the pigeons and observes people."

I forgo asking him how he knows the code and gesture to the sanctuary. "Since this building is much taller, what can you see in the sanctuary's courtyard?"

"Nothing. Which isn't surprising. It's almost midnight." He lowers his line of sight. "Though the line of cars parking outside is a bit unusual."

"Can I see?" I ask, holding my hand out for the binoculars.

The moment I put the binoculars up to my face, I gasp, then shove them toward his chest. "We need to go, right now."

"What did you see?" Drystan pulls me to a stop as I head toward the roof door.

"The demons who kidnapped me, Edgar and Emily, just casually walked inside the main gate with men following behind them."

"Nara, you can't go running toward a group of demons. That's suicide!"

I take a deep breath and hold my hand out. Concentrating on the Corvus, I call on my feather. When it appears in my palm, I take Drystan's hand and place it over the feather in mine. "Try to reach out to the other Corvus like you do me."

"You mean mentally?" he asks, folding our hands together around the feather.

"Yes, use our connection to call them. I'm praying the feather will help you."

Drystan closes his eyes and inhales deeply, then exhales on a rush. "I feel them, Nara." He frowns and begins to shake, then falls to his knees. "Feck, their collective power is strong! Rave must really hold back in our presence." He shakes his head and exhales, then his breathing ramps. "They're not happy. I'm not supposed to connect with them like this."

His comment about Rave holding back worries me, but I drop to my knees in front of him and tighten my hand around his. "Hold on, Drystan. Tell them this message is from me. Let them know the sanctuary is crawling with demons and we can't reach the Master Corvus, but he may need their assistance once more."

When Drystan nods, and then a few seconds later he releases me to fall onto his back and take deep breaths, I lean over him to press my hand to his chest. "Are you okay? Did they speak to you?"

Breathing through his nose, he nods. "Holy shite that was intense. I felt the power of their anger at my intrusion until they heard my message. They never spoke to me; it's more that I sensed their collective agreement to assist."

I clasp his hand and help him to his feet. "Can you walk now? I'm hoping you know a back way to get inside the sanctuary so we can see what's happening."

"Yeah, I'm good and I do know a secret entrance." As he steps into place beside me, he pulls out his phone.

"Who are you calling?"

"My uncle."

Before he can dial, I grab his arm. "You can't call him. We don't know who in there might have been taken over by a demon."

"I will not have another death on my hands, Nara. There are fifty people living in the sanctuary." Drystan frowns as he pulls from my grasp. "They deserve to know that demons have invaded our home and my uncle will know the fastest way to sound the alarm."

"Yes, of course," I say, then shove my hands in my jacket to keep from stopping him. While I don't think his uncle is evil, the man not sharing vital information with Drystan makes me leery.

Drystan's phone doesn't work while in the building. Just as we walk outside and he lifts the phone to dial, Patch swoops down and tears it from his grasp.

"Hey, you thieving bird!" he calls, shaking his fist after the big raven.

"Shhh, Drystan!" But I'm too late. A couple of men step outside the sanctuary's gated area.

When they narrow their gazes on us and take a step in our direction, Drystan pushes me behind him. "Run, Nara!"

I take off running along the side of the building we just left. I only have to run a few more feet to get to the corner. I call to Drystan for the door code and realize that he isn't right behind me.

Slowing, I glance back and see Edgar coming up on me fast. I burst into a run once more, but the demon yanks on my arm just as I reach the corner, hauling me against the wall. He laughs at my gasp of pain. "Didn't I tell you that I'm the best at inflicting pain?"

With my shoulder hurting like hell, I'm too disoriented to fight him. Even Patch can't help; the alleyway is too narrow for his wide wingspan. He lets out a frustrated *raaaackkk* of anger, then flies high, his loud calls signaling alarm. The demon quickly drags me back down the alley. He hauls me into the street and ravens, crows and magpies instantly swarm down, attacking him. Flailing his arm to ward off the birds, he battles against the onslaught before shoving me inside the sanctuary.

The moment I stumble through the main gate and into the covered part of the courtyard, Drystan calls my name. Holding his hand over his right eye, he tries to pull free of the other demon's hold, but the bald guy just grunts and yanks him to his side, saying in a low deadly tone, "Be still or I'll pop your other eye too."

While we're quickly tugged across through the main door and then down the hall right off the entryway, I whisper to Drystan, "Where is everyone?"

"Most people are in bed this late, but there's usually a few people around. This is eerily quiet," he replies in a low tone.

Edgar laughs. "No one is rescuing you two tonight. Everyone's asleep thanks to the gas we pumped through the ventilation system."

Another man opens one of the heavy double doors at the end of the hall and the guards escort us into an atrium with a vaulted three-story ceiling. My gaze is instantly drawn to Ethan struggling to stand in the middle of a huge wrought iron cage with a curved domed top. "Ethan!" I call and take in the heavy-duty construction grade chain strung from a steel beam-reinforced ceiling and attached to the top of the cage.

As Ethan groggily shakes his head to clear it, I try to determine if he's wounded, but it's hard to see him clearly through the metal screen covering the entire outside of the cage. When Rave reaches over his shoulder and pulls something out of his back, I recognize the colorful fluted end of a big game tranquilizer dart and my stomach roils.

The dart, the cage, gas in the ventilation system. At the same moment it occurs to me that this was a carefully planned and executed trap, Mr. Wicklow, flanked by two men, registers in my peripheral view.

Ethan moves his mouth and points to Drystan who has just turned to address his uncle. I can tell Ethan's talking, but I shake my head in frustration that I can't hear anything. "Let Ethan go!" I call to Edgar, then quickly sweep my angry gaze among the dozen men in the room in case one of them is in charge.

"I'm sorry, Uncle Rowan," Drystan says. "I tried to call and warn you but I wasn't fast enough."

His uncle looks subdued behind his goatee. "It's okay, Drystan." Taking a step closer, he smiles. "Welcome, the both of you. We've been waiting to start the grand finale."

Drystan slowly lowers his hand from his swelling eye, his entire body tensing. "You're a part of this? Why would you betray everything you've worked so hard for to sell out to *demons?*" Narrowing his gaze, he shrugs from of the demon's hold and steps right up to his uncle. "What did they promise you?"

The two men on either side of Mr. Wicklow stiffen, ready to pounce on Drystan, but his uncle raises his hand, silently telling them to stand down. "Poor misguided Drystan...it's what I promised *him.*"

When Drystan gives him a confused look, Mr. Wicklow buttons his suit jacket and steps back to spread his arms wide in a grand gesture.

"Isn't this just wonderful? We've come full circle, where all the players are together once more." Pointing to himself, he says, "The duplicitous uncle." Then to Drystan, "the oblivious yet complicit relative." He turns and holds his hands out toward Ethan. "The heroic boy and—" he barely gives me a glance as he waves toward me dismissively— "the girl in need of rescue."

"But..." Mr. Wicklow claps his hands and spins in a full circle, grinning widely. "Last but not least, the two most important." Pointing to Ethan once more, he says, "You and me, Corvus. How's that for history repeating itself?"

Rave grabs hold of the wrought iron bars and shakes the cage, clearly yelling his fury, but only silence and rattling metal greets us. "Oh, I forgot." Mr. Wicklow pulls a remote from his vest pocket. Once he clicks a button, Rave's voice booms throughout the huge room.

"You weren't present the last time, *Lucifer*." The bars creak with his tightened hands and the room grows cold with his deadly tone. "Things would've turned out differently if you had been."

Mr. Wicklow clicks the button once more to cut off Rave's voice and *tsks*. "There he goes spoiling my surprise." Spreading his hands wide, he announces gleefully, "Surprise, the *devil's* in the house!"

Drystan and I exchange worried glances, but then determination flickers in his gaze as he demands, "What did you mean by 'oblivious but complicit relative'? The Corvus showed me what happened. Uncle Rowan is the one who stood by and did nothing to save Olivia from a crazed, power hungry leader. My father tried to *save* her. How does that make him complicit?"

Lucifer shakes his head and clicks his tongue. "Your uncle didn't just *stand by* that day, Drystan." The devil lets out a pleased laugh. "Rowan was the mastermind behind the whole thing. The sanctuary 'leader' was nothing more than a puppet. Your uncle pulled all the strings."

"Uncle Rowan can't make people do things against their will," Drystan says, frowning. "All he can do is speak in people's minds."

"Persuasively?" Lucifer twirls his hand as if waiting, then sighs. "Come on, Drystan. Eventually that puny brain of yours will finally catch up."

"He can't persuade!" Drystan shouts, folding his arms against his chest. "He's not that effect—ive…"

When Drystan trails off, his face draining of color, I look at him. "What's wrong?"

"I think he's saying that my father unknowingly boosted my uncle's twisted manipulation of the leader by being present in the room." Drystan shakes his head, his tone going flat. "Uncle Rowan is the one who wanted to control the Corvus the entire time."

Lucifer leans close and taps the end of Drystan's nose. "I knew you'd eventually work it out. After Olivia died, your father put two-and-two together and finally acknowledged the ability he'd been denying existed for years. Evan Wicklow left the sanctuary not long after that. But once your uncle located him after years of searching and discovered he had a son, well...Rowan certainly couldn't pass up the opportunity that you might've inherited your father's skills, now could he?"

"My father never would've allowed him in our lives!" Drystan's shaking with fury, his back ramrod straight.

Lucifer straightens and runs his thumb and forefinger down either side of his goatee. "Of course not, so what do you think your uncle did? After all, you were young and malleable. If only your father wasn't in the picture..."

"Murdering bastard!" Drystan yells as he lunges for his uncle, grabbing him by the throat.

Lucifer just stands there and allows Drystan to attempt to choke the life out of his uncle. He even shoos the other demons away, while I try to tug Drystan off him. "Drystan stop! Don't let him get into your head." But I can't pull him away. He's just too angry, too full of rage.

Craning his neck as if Drystan's hands around his throat are nothing more than a snug tie, Lucifer adopts a sympathetic tone. "It feels terrible...being betrayed by family, doesn't it? I feel your pain, Drystan. Go on, squeeze harder. It feels *good* to hurt your uncle, right? You must remember what it felt like to do this to poor Harper. Is this more satisfying now that it's your choice?" After Drystan grits his teeth and leans in harder, Lucifer exhales a bored sigh and peels Drystan off, tossing him across the room like a wet leaf. "That's enough of that."

I try to go after a groaning Drystan, but Lucifer locks his fingers around my arm. "Ah, ah...no running off, Nara. I want you to see this part." The cage's sudden rattling and the shaking rafters overhead draws my attention back to Ethan as the cage starts to rise. Two demons are pulling on the end of the chain that's linked through a pulley in the rafters. Once they raise the cage a good fifteen feet off the floor, Rave grabs ahold of the bars and belts a roar. Even though silence fills the room, I can tell by his expression how loud it must be. The cage sways with his fury and just as he bares his teeth at Lucifer, he suddenly holds his hands over his ears as if the sound is deafening. *What's happening to him? Why hasn't he ripped through that cage's metal like a sardine can by now?*

"It's rather poetic, don't you think?" Lucifer cuts into my thoughts as he sweeps a hand toward the raised cage. "I've really got to give old Rowan credit. This Faraday cage is not only pure genius, but I'm really enjoying the visual of the Master Corvus locked up in a birdcage like the vermin he is."

"Faraday cage?"

"A metal structure built to keep out electrostatic or electromagnetic forces. It's used to protect electronics from being fried," Drystan says as he drags himself to his feet.

"Or to keep the same forces in. And since the Corvus is spirit, it's pure energy. I've been quite entertained that this particular device also reflects those forces back on the occupant." Lucifer grins as he addresses Drystan. "Young Warren using a Faraday caged room to help your Paladin friends learn to control their growing powers gave your uncle this idea." Gesturing to Ethan in the cage, he continues. "I certainly can't have that damn bird phasing in and out to rescue Paladins or..." He leans close to my ear. "Snatching Nara from me. But since he's looking a bit restless and more cognizant..." Lucifer snaps his fingers and one of the men hands him an inch-wide silver band of metal. "Some insurance to keep the Corvus in line while my demons take over the sleeping Paladins."

As his men subdue us to keep Drystan from interfering and me from moving, Lucifer snaps the metal closed around my neck, then attaches a much smaller chain to the collar. Lifting the chain, he directs my line of sight to where it's connected. My small chain grows into bigger and bigger links, eventually connecting back to the massive chain holding the cage up. "If that cage so much as moves an inch, you'll enjoy the shock of your life, my dear." To prove his point, he nods to one of his men who uses a long pole to make the cage sway. The moment it moves, a sharp jolt of electricity shoots through my body, dropping me to my knees. I gasp in pain until the demon stops the movement. Lucifer chuckles and lowers the chain to the floor next to me. "I've always found an example of swift punishment to be much more effective than words."

*Nara, can you hear me?*

I blink back tears at the reassuring sound of Ethan's voice in my mind. I nod, but keep my gaze averted from the cage.

*The chain must be conducting our mental connection. When Rave met with Wicklow, he couldn't see Lucifer in the man's body. You know what that means.*

Oh God, if Lucifer now knows about using Corvus ashes that means the Corvus' job of finding demons squatting in people just got a lot harder. While I nod to let Ethan know that I understand the ramifications, my breath begins to billow in a cool frost directly in front of me.

"I don't care if you're the devil or my uncle. I'll take you both out," Drystan growls as he leans down to help me back to my feet.

Lucifer snorts at Drystan. "Despite what my *Father* thinks, I don't hate mortals. After your uncle witnessed the Master Corvus annihilate the sanctuary and then the chaos that ensued with the Corvus ever since, he came to believe that keeping the Master Corvus here in the mortal realm was the very best option."

"What? Like some kind of pet?" Drystan snaps.

Lucifer flashes a pleased smile. "When Rowan met Ethan for the first time and saw how all the ravens followed his command to find Nara and even extended their protection to her, he knew he was talking to the Master once more. Upon my arrival, I was ever so happy to offer my services. I told your uncle that I would help him bring the Master Corvus to heel so he could maintain control. Wicklow believes that if he can control the Master, he will be able to manage all the Corvus. He wants to maintain the balance between Corvus and demons, so I told him I would be his muscle to contain the Master Corvus. I just didn't tell him *who* he made a pact with. Oh, FYI…if you ever sign a contract with *the devil himself,* always check the fine print." Chuckling at his own deviousness, Lucifer turns and begins to bark orders at his men when Emily and Edgar rush into the room.

"Several Corvus have breached the main gate," Edgar says, anticipatory brightness in his gaze.

"But the Master Corvus hasn't been able to communicate outside the cage. How did they know we were here—" Lucifer cuts himself off and narrows his gaze on Drystan and me. Growling his fury, he waves to the men in the room. "All of you, go! Get out there and help fight off the Corvus. Keep them away from this room!"

When I exhale and Drystan sees the frosty air in front of me, he gives me a strange look. I shake my head, telling him not to call attention to it. I realize that it's Fate trying to help, but I'm not sure yet what his plan is. As the temperature grows bitterly cold directly in front of me, I resist the urge to shiver. "What do you want me to do?" I whisper, hoping Fate will give me a sign.

Drystan frowns at the chain as Ethan speaks in my mind. *I can see from here that the chain has iced over. You can break it like glass now. Do it, Nara.*

"Ethan says it's cold enough to break the chain. Yank it off," I tell Drystan in a low voice and grab hold of the collar.

The moment Drystan tugs hard and the chain shatters, Lucifer turns to us, fury stamped on his face. "You will not ruin this for me!" Roaring, he steps toward us and shoves Drystan.

I scream when Drystan lands across the room with a heavy thump, but then jump at the ear-deafening boom as the metal bottom of the cage hits the floor. Dust floats around Rave as he straightens to his full height and curls his hands into tight fists, his tone lethal. "Don't even *think* about touching her! This is between you and me, Lucifer, and it always has been."

"Yes, but it's incredibly satisfying." He sneers.

I never even saw Lucifer's arm coming. Pain explodes across my chest and the air whistles around me as I soar across the room.

Rave catches me before I hit and quickly sets me down, barking in my ear, "Grab Drystan and get the hell out of here!" right before Ethan quickly says in my head, *Something is blocking his ability to teleport. Get out now, Nara!*

"Oh...Drystan. Have a seat!" Lucifer calls as he sends a couch flying toward my friend.

While Rave intervenes at the last second, deflecting the heavy piece of furniture before it crushes Drystan, I run for the door and try to open it, but Lucifer has bent the heavy lock installed on the door, trapping us in.

Letting out a battle cry, Lucifer arcs in the air toward Rave. The two powerful forces collide with the force of a sonic *boom*. Once they hit the floor, the entire building rattles and shakes, sending the rest of the cage slamming down to the ground.

Another quake rocks the room, and I tense at the snarls of anger and fists connecting with bone. Grabbing Drystan's arm the second he moves to my side, I call into his ear, "We have to figure out how to open these heavy doors another way. Lucifer has broken the lock, blocking us in here."

While I anxiously watch Lucifer swinging the cage's thick chain toward Ethan, Drystan glances around and then runs over to the desk and grabs a bottle of oil from his uncle's dinner tray. Rushing back, he pours some of the oil over the pin in the hinge and then mumbles, "I need something thin and strong to push the pin out."

I shudder at the metallic sound of the cage scraping the floor as it slides with Lucifer's yank on the chain, then jerk a worried gaze Ethan's way when the whole cage topples over with a reverberating crash. Relieved that he avoided being hit, I start toward the desk, but am suddenly yanked out of the way just as the cage rolls past.

Once the cage slams into a wall, Rave drops me back to my feet and zooms toward Lucifer. As they tumble across the room exchanging powerful punches, I'm reeling from the near miss, my heart jumping to my throat. Worry for Rave nearly paralyzes me, but I force myself to stay focused and look at the desk for something to help with the door. We have to get out so Rave can focus only on the battle and not have to worry about protecting us.

When my foot kicks a pencil on the floor, I quickly scoop it up and run back to Drystan. "Try this!" I yell over Rave and Lucifer's horrific battle snarls.

Drystan shoves the pencil into the bottom of the hinge, hitting it with the heel of his hand. "It's working!" he says as the pin begins to move up a little.

"Keep working at it." I move to his other side and try to pull the pin, helping him jimmy it out of the hinge.

Just as I pull the pin free of the door and Drystan moves to work on the second hinge, Lucifer speaks directly behind us. "Now, now…don't you know it's rude to leave early?"

We were so focused on opening the door, I didn't even notice the room had gone quiet. My stomach plummets as I turn to see Ethan lying across the bars of the overturned cage. His clothes are torn, his face bloodied and his breathing is so shallow, his chest is barely moving with each breath. Oh God! He looks broken and beaten… and near dead.

"No!" I start to run toward him, but Lucifer hooks his arm across my chest to keep me from moving past him. I try to go around him, but he moves to block me again.

"Ah, ah. You're staying right here. I have to say, it was far easier to defeat him than I expected. Almost too easy and a bit disappointing."

Stepping back a little, he stares down at me, curiosity on Mr. Wicklow's bruised face. "I don't really see what all the fuss is about. There's nothing special about you that I can see. At least Drystan has skills that will come in handy."

"I'll never help you." Drystan moves closer to me, his stance protective.

Lucifer doesn't even acknowledge Drystan's presence by my side. "But you, Nara? Before I finish the Master Corvus off, I have to know why you're worth keeping around."

"Screw you!" I yell, tears streaking down my face.

Lucifer rubs his blood-streaked beard and shakes his head, amusement in his wicked chuckle. "You know…I might be the cause of the old adage about women being the root of all evil, but in your case, little Nara, the saying could actually come true. You've made the Master Corvus weak. Once again, a female will be your mortal world's downfall. It's amusing how often history does indeed repeat itself." Smirking, he runs a finger down my cheek, leaving a streak of blood behind. "So is that your superpower? Destroying your world?"

"Don't listen to him, Nara," Drystan's voice fades out as my gaze strays to Ethan. Guilt wells up, knotting my chest and throat. Rave was weaker because he let me convince him not to fully overtake Ethan. I can't change the damage I've caused already, but to save Ethan and give Rave the time he needs to recover, I can help even the playing field.

Returning my gaze to Lucifer, I rub the blood off my cheek with the back of my hand. "No, my superpower is saving it."

When the devil throws his head back and barks out booming laughter, I quickly put my hand on his chest and focus every bit of power in my body, every ounce of positive energy and shove it down my arm and through my fingertips.

"Wha—what are you doing?" Lucifer says, his eyes widening. He tries to yank my hand off him, but it's fused to his chest like a supercharged magnet.

My ears buzz and I feel light-headed, but I push even harder. "I'm showing you what light feels like, Lucifer. In your dark world, I doubt you've experienced that in a very long time."

Stumbling slightly, he shakes his head to clear it and grips my shoulders in a brutal hold. "I hate everything about this. I don't want it."

He tries to loosen my energized hold on him by growling and emitting such a horrific stench that my eyes water and my stomach knots in pain. I swallow to keep from throwing up, but I can't stop the shudder of revulsion that rolls through me.

Lucifer snarls and jerks his head back and forth, as if he's phasing in and out between our world and Under. Then he stops and looks at me with such evil and hate as a thick black tar begins to pour from his nose and down his chin. As it insidiously rolls along his clothes and spreads over my fingers, hand and down my arm... the foul smelling tar turns into thousands of black bugs with sharp stingers jabbing into my skin.

The pain is excruciating and I turn when Drystan's hold on my hand starts to shake. He's completely covered with the insects too. They're moving in and out of his ears, nose, and mouth, leaving oozing blood trails behind from hundreds of bites. I scream and try to let go of his hand to stop the evil from spreading over him, but he shakes his head and tightens his grip, his voice in my head. *I'm not letting you go!*

The infestation crawls toward my nose and mouth and I twist my head away, knowing that they'll smother me. I shake my head as they move up my chin and along my jaw, and for a brief second, Mr. Wicklow's face goes back to the bruised, bloodied one I saw earlier. No bugs or tar at all. Gritting my teeth as the stinging insects try to gain access to my mouth, I tell myself over and over...*It's not real. It's just an illusion. Keep fighting the insects. Ignore the pain. They can't smother you. You can breathe through them.*

Anger fuels my resolve and the blackness covering my eyes begins to fade, the pain subsiding. "I'm giving you *all* the power you crave," I grit out. My heart is racing out of control, my pulse thrumming so fast I can't even feel it. Michael was wrong. Ethan will live, because I have the ability to help him. As the bugs completely disappear from Drystan and me, I can feel Lucifer's dark power fading in the face of light. He's trembling and having a hard time staying in Mr. Wicklow's body. As I take a deep breath to push for more, out of the corner of my eye, I see Ethan starting to stir. *Come on, Rave. Get up!*

Lucifer shudders then straightens his spine, roaring, "Let go!"

A sudden heavy banging on the double doors behind us makes my heart jerk.

"You can't do this forever." Lucifer's laugh sounds strained. "My demons are coming!"

"Nara, it's working. He's weakening, but you're so pale. You have to stop." Drystan grasps my other hand locked to his uncle's chest and tries to tug me away. "Don't worry about the door. I think it'll hold. You've got to let go. This is going to kill you!"

The banging outside briefly stops to be replaced by a loud boom of something much bigger. God, they're trying to knock the door down.

"Wake up, little Nara. I'm here to stay!" Lucifer snarls and my head snaps sideways, my vision blurring from his vicious slap.

"Hit her again and I'll use you as a punching bag, you sack of shite," Drystan says right as he lands a swift punch to his uncle's eye with his free hand.

Drystan's defense distracts me from the pain and dizziness and helps me refocus on Lucifer. "Thank you, Drystan," I whisper and squeeze his hand. Concentrating on turning my body into a conduit, I try to draw on Drystan's amplifying ability as I direct everything I've got left at the demon.

When Lucifer shoots away from my hand like he's been hit by a truck, I crumple and Drystan catches me. Folding me in his arms, he lowers us to the floor.

"Is Fate back?" I mutter, shivering. "It's suddenly cold in here."

Drystan shakes his head. Pulling his jacket off, he drapes it over my chest, then presses his fingers to my throat. "You've barely got a pulse." He gathers me close to his warmth, his voice breaking. "Don't you dare leave us, Nara. I'll never forgive you."

As Drystan's tears drip onto my temple, I can hear his rapid heart beat in my ear while my own heart slowly thumps. Its rhythm is so lethargic that everything seems to be moving at a snail's pace. I try to speak, but the words remain stuck in my head like fruit suspended in Jello.

"Nice try." Lucifer's comment sounds slurred, but then his voice grows stronger. "It'll take more power than you've got to end my time here."

"Rave's getting up, Nara! Stay here, stay for Ethan. He loves you. He's coming. Hold on!"

My heart speeds up for a second, but then it drops right back to a sluggish thump. I think I hear fighting in the background, but everything is so distorted, I can't tell. I choose to believe that Ethan and Rave are kicking Lucifer's ass. The thought gives me comfort as my vision moves in and out. I try to stay awake, to strain for sounds of victory, but I feel myself fading. The last time death came for me I fought it with every bit of my energy, but this time I feel hollow. Like there's no reserves left to pull from. The room starts to dim and I muster my last bit of energy. Forcing my lips to move, I hope that Drystan will hear. "I'm sorry, Dryst. Tell Ethan that I never stopped believing in him."

"You can tell him yourself when you—Nara? Nara!" Drystan shakes me, but I barely feel it. I'm more aware of the darkness quickly closing in. It's like a warm blanket.

*Nara!* A deep voice calls my name, the booming authority vibrating the floor is so clear but also weary-wise. *Hold on, lightweight!*

*Rave.*

An ear is pressed against my chest and Drystan's cologne washes over me as the darkness spirals inward. *Tired.* I'm so very tired.

*I love you, Ethan.*

# Chapter Thirty-Two

*Ethan*

R ave moans and rolls off the cage. He forces my body to move,
stumbling while trying to clear his groggy head. As he grabs
hold of the cage to steady himself, my breathing rattles and sticky
blood coats several wounds. My body is completely broken; bones
that shouldn't be used are somehow still moving, torn muscles
barely holding them together. Lucifer's hits were harder than facing
a legion of demons; I'm not healing like I have in the past. But as
near-death as I am, the fear that strikes me hardest isn't for myself.
It's the one that always hits me when Nara's in danger.

When Rave looks up and I see Nara shove Wicklow's body
across the room with nothing but a powerful rush of energy from
her hand, panic grips me. For her to do that…God…the energy it
took?

*She doesn't have that kind of power, Rave! Make sure she's all right!*

*Lucifer is still a threat.* Rave stalks straight for Wicklow as the
bastard pushes himself to his feet. *I'm no good to Nara while he remains
in this world. I won't let her efforts to weaken him be for nothing. I have to
defeat him while we're on level ground.*

*Why did he beat you in the first place? I thought you were his equal?
You're the only one who can defeat him!* When he doesn't respond
even though I sense his wrath over Nara, despite his cold, logical
response, my fury jacks even higher. *I know you care, you freaking*

*bird. Don't you let her die!*

*Either help or shut the hell up!* he growls as he fists his hand around Lucifer's jacket lapels and hurls him toward the metal cage.

*Help? You've destroyed my body. I'm a walking fucking zombie! When you're done, I won't survive.*

*Bullshit! Despite yourself, you're a survivor!* he rants at me as he goes after Lucifer once more. *Focus, I need your mind in this!* he says as he lowers his head and rams it into Lucifer's gut.

When the demon uses the opportunity to slam his fists on my spine, and I hear it crack along with the *oomph* that escapes Rave's lips, I bellow at him, *Use your damn sword and end this!*

*Are you mad enough yet?* Rave asks as he raises his head and slams his fist into Lucifer's face.

Lucifer bounces off the cage and comes back at me with a flying punch into my eye.

*You fucking didn't even try to move. You let him hit me,* I yell as Rave stumbles back from the impact and blinks through the dizziness.

*I need your focus.*

*My* focus *is getting back to Nara,* I growl and for a brief time, I'm not sure how, but I'm in control. Rushing forward, I pummel the shit out of Lucifer with a half dozen rapid power hits to his chest and face.

While Lucifer sways on his feet, Rave yanks me out of the driver's seat and grabs Wicklow's jacket once more. "This is for Nara," he grates as he jams his sword right through the man's heart.

Lucifer makes a guttural sound of pain, then he glances down at the sword and begins to laugh. "Consuming Adder's ashes came in handy after all. You're going to have to work a lot harder to send me back to Under, Corvus! Actually, to send my demons back too now that we've discovered how to hide from your kind."

"You won't remember any of this once you pass through the veil. My Corvus will decimate the rest."

Wicklow's eyes narrow. "Do you think I don't have a way to make sure my demons will re-discover this valuable information when they come back?"

"Thanks to Nara's ideas, my Corvus will have a better way to detect when demons break through the veil. Your demons will never get that far." Rave gives a cold, arrogant smile. "My sword in your heart was just to get your attention."

*Ethan, think about the first time the glow happened between you and Nara.*

*Why?*

*Do it now!*

While I recall every detail of that intimate moment in Nara's tiny bathroom, Rave says in a deadly tone, "For every soul you stole while I wasn't myself, for every person you corrupted and Furia demon that resulted, you're going to pay." Flattening his free hand against Lucifer's chest, he continues, "Experience the brightest light shining all over your darkness."

When Wicklow's body begins to pull apart in long taffy-like strands, Lucifer bellows in agony. Thrashing his head back and forth, he pants through the pain as he tries but fails to pull Rave's hold off him with quickly disintegrating hands. "You've never been able to do this."

*I can't feel Nara! I fucking can't feel her, Rave!*

*Keep that moment in your head, Ethan,* Rave commands sharply.

My heart is torn. It doesn't want to stay in the past when the present is crumbling to pieces.

*Don't lose it now, Ethan,* Rave says before he addresses Lucifer. "While you believe that mortals are beneath you and unworthy of your father's love, I've learned a thing or two from them."

"They are pathetic, anemic shells!" Lucifer spits, blood trickling down his chin.

"They're stronger than us in their own way. There's a reason they are special."

"You mean their *mortality*?" Lucifer jeers in disgust, then shudders through the pain as the back of his head elongates and pieces of him begin to float into the air. Glancing at the bits of Wicklow's body suspended all around him, Lucifer snarls, "It makes them weak!"

"No, it makes them fight for what matters *because* their lives are fleeting!" Rave barks. "Mortals are worth the effort. They have a lot to teach us. They're worth fighting for."

"I will never accept them as equals!" Lucifer roars, his voice cracking.

"And I will always be here to protect them." Leaning into what's left of Lucifer's face, Rave snarls, "Bring it!" right before he twists his sword in his chest. The moment Lucifer explodes out of

Wicklow, the man's scattered body quickly draws back into itself before he slithers to the ground in an unconscious heap.

The pounding on the door intensifies and the heavy wood finally bursts open, breaking on its one hinge. Four men rush into the room, their Corvus swords at the ready.

Rave acknowledges the Corvus, then glances down at Wicklow with a snarl. Barely resisting the urge to spit on his unmoving form, he stalks over to Drystan and without a word takes Nara from him, lifting her in his arms.

"She's not breathing. I can't hear her heart or feel a pulse," Drystan says in a hoarse voice, his teary gaze pleading for a miracle. "Can you help her using your Master Corvus abilities?"

As Rave shakes his head, I yell as loud as I can, *No!* My mind feels like it's cracking. I can barely think the despair is so painful. *Give me my body back. I've saved her before. Let me try to bring her back!*

*She's gone, Ethan. I wish there was something I could do, but I can't sense even a sliver of life. Her body has completely shut down. There's nothing that can be done for her now.* I've never heard Rave sound defeated. The realization wrenches every bit of hope from my soul. I try to reason with him, but he just ignores my rant and folds her against his chest.

Drystan quickly stands and wipes away his tears. Holding his arms out, his voice shakes with emotion. "If you can't help her, then please leave her with me. I'll contact her family and make arrangements for her."

"No," Rave simply says, curling his hands tighter around Nara.

Drystan tries to argue, but Rave gives him a withering look that instantly silences him. While his raven wings slide right through his clothes, unfurling in furious splendor, Rave silently nods to the four men awaiting his command, then he addresses Drystan. "My Corvus have taken care of all the demons. They will stay and secure the sanctuary."

He slides a furious glance to Wicklow. "I left your uncle intact so he can be punished for his crimes against your family, the Corvus, and all those in the sanctuary. With your cousin's support, make sure that he does."

Drystan jerks his head up, eyes wide. "What cousin?"

Rave nods toward the dark-haired man who just ran into the room holding a sword he must've swiped from the suit of armor in the hallway. "Before you and Nara arrived, Wicklow grumbled that he hated how so many here respected his bastard more than him."

"Warren is Rowan's son?" Drystan gapes at his cousin who isn't close enough to hear the revelation as he steps around the Corvus and heads in his cousin's direction. "So many little things make a lot of sense now…" Drystan trails off, then presses his lips together in renewed anger, his gaze snapping back to Rave. "My uncle will pay for everything he's done."

With a curt nod, the Master Corvus blasts skyward, shooting right through the ceiling and high into the dark sky.

Landing on the roof of our hotel, Rave sits on the cement bench and cradles Nara in his lap. I feel his pain as he holds her limp body and the sensation only amplifies my own devastation. I ache when I stare into her slack features. She's so pale and still.

*Why didn't you get up sooner? Why didn't you fight Lucifer harder the first time? You could've beaten him if you had just tried harder.*

As he gently pushes her hair back from her face, it occurs to me that he sensed more than he let on while lying across that cage. *You knew what Nara was doing, yet you didn't stop her!*

He doesn't react to my anger. He's not reacting at all.

*Fuck you, Rave! Fuck you for destroying a beautiful heart and soul and the most important part of my life. You could've saved Nara!*

*I honored her!* he snaps, his pained roar so heartfelt that I actually feel his anger all over as if I still had a body.

*By letting her die? How is that respecting the one person who gave up so much to help you? I told you that Nara's safety came first. Always.*

*Do you think I wanted this?* His hand shakes as he straightens her shirt's collar around her neck. *I made a promise to Nara and I will honor my word.*

*What promise could you possibly have made that involved her dying?* I yell, my voice sounding like gravel.

*That you would live! I never fully integrated to protect you from my spirit's power. That meant I wasn't as strong as I would normally have been. After the first battle with Lucifer, you needed to heal. Even a few minutes would make a difference. If I had gotten up and continued to fight Lucifer, as powerful as he is, your body wouldn't recover once I left you. You would most assuredly die. By using her inner light to drain Lucifer, Nara gave us…you a fighting chance. No other mortal who has hosted me has ever lived, Ethan. Somehow Nara knew that.*

My brain is on overload. I'm so devastated, my voice lowers to a hoarse rasp. *Do you think I'll want to live without her?*

*You* will *live,* Rave commands. *You will not dishonor Nara by doing anything less.*

I look down at the beautiful girl I love, my heart imploding. *Everywhere I look I'll be reminded of you. Of us. I won't know how to live without your light in my life. Why did you make Rave promise, Sunshine?*

*Let me hold her,* I demand, my heart shredding.

Rave shakes his head. *Not yet.*

Fury eclipses my anguish. *Give me my body back! I need to feel her in my arms. You're done. Lucifer has been defeated. Fly into the sunset or whatever the hell Corvus spirit does until the next time that demon bastard tries to take over our world!*

*I will remain until your body has healed enough for you to survive. If I leave you now, you will die.*

*Then leave! Take off so I can at least spend the last few minutes of my life holding Nara.*

*No.*

*Don't you dare take that choice away from me. It's not yours to make!*

*It was* Nara's. Rave says in a terse tone. *Do you want to take that away from her?*

His harsh question silences me. I can't look at Nara without aching to touch her and gather her close, so I shutter my eyes and tune out, closing myself completely off.

# Chapter Thirty-Three

### *Rave*

After Ethan shuts me out, I inhale deeply to help his broken body heal even though I know he doesn't want me to. Each breath I take is painful and sharp as Ethan draws further into himself, his inner light dimming. I remove the offending metal collar from Nara's neck and when I gather her close, her shirt slips down her slack shoulder. I start to pull it back up but notice that the feather on her back is completely black. Angered by all the darkness she absorbed in her battle with Lucifer, I tamp down my fury and gently tug her shirt into place, tucking her head under my chin.

She feels so frail now that she's not poking at my chest and frowning at me while demanding that I become who I was meant to be. I know she was right to protect Ethan—he will survive no matter how much he doesn't want to—but this slip of a girl, with her boundless belief and inner strength, has forever changed me. "No one deserved to live more than you did, lightweight," I rasp as I look at her pale face. "I promise to always look for the light. Maybe one day…I'll find it again." When my vision blurs, I blink and shake my head in confusion, then touch my wet jaw. *Tears?*

A man with light hair suddenly appears in front of me, and I instantly grip Nara tight, my sword burning down my arm. As soon as my gaze zips over his impeccable suit to lock with golden eyes, I know he's from the Celestial realm. I mentally halt the sword's progression, but remain on guard. "I thought we couldn't communicate with each other? Which one are you?"

"You're speaking to your equal, Corvus. I'm Michael."

"We are *not* equals," I snap, offended he would dare to make such a bold statement.

"We are both warriors." Michael shrugs. "Since you didn't allow your full powers to manifest in Ethan, I'm able to communicate with you despite my Father's dictate that I remain impartial in the Mortal world." He slides his hands into his dress pants' pockets, his gaze dropping to Nara. "But I have bent several rules for her."

I narrow my gaze. "Like the glow Drystan saw on her feather? That's the only reason I didn't tell Nara that her tattoo is an original Corvus feather. I couldn't explain what the boy was seeing."

Michael's face reflects affectionate pride as he looks at Nara. "I chose her for her ability to see beyond the surface, but she was so young I wanted to protect her as best as I could. She grew into a brave, stubborn young woman who wasn't afraid to challenge me at every turn..." Trailing off, he exhales deeply as he stares into the night sky.

"She's special to you. I can sense it. Why didn't you save her?" I demand, the rooftop shuddering under my feet.

His gaze snaps to me, full of righteous, angelic conviction. "She died to *save* you and in turn her world. I will mourn her loss, but her death was necessary."

"It isn't right. She was innocent!" I release my tight hold on Nara so he can't help but look at her face. "This nearly destroyed me the last time with Adder."

Sorrow reflects in his gaze. "Nara's sacrifice helped you come back to yourself. She reminded you why mortals deserve a warrior to protect them, didn't she?"

"You couldn't have predicted that outcome," I snap, scowling.

"I believed in her. I told Nara that Ethan would have to die in order for you to defeat Lucifer. That is how it has always been." Michael slowly shakes his head, a bemused yet respectful look in his gaze as he stares at her. "She was adamant there had to be another way."

Infuriated by the angel's impassiveness despite his obvious fondness of Nara, I narrow my gaze and challenge him from one spirit to another. *When a young mortal out-strategizes the military leader of the Celestial realm, how could you not think hers was a life worth saving?*

# Chapter Thirty-Four

*Nara*

My eyes flutter open to a brilliant blue sky and the smell of fresh cut grass tickling my cheek. Birds are chirping happily and the warm sun shines bright, inviting me to bask in its glow. I stretch and inhale deeply, catching the faint scent of gardenias and lavender.

*Where am I?*

I roll over and take in the immaculately trimmed hedges lining on either side of the manicured lawn that seems to stretch forever, but my gaze is drawn to the half dozen dandelions standing proud in the crisp green grass. I stare at the weeds that managed to thrust up on this well-tended lawn, wondering where they came from and why they hadn't been pulled.

*Shouldn't I be doing something? Don't I have somewhere to be?*

As the thoughts flit lazily through my mind, the faint sound of a woman humming reaches my ears. I turn my head in the direction of the upbeat song and strain to catch the tune, but it's too far away.

Pushing myself to my bare feet, I wiggle my toes in the soft grass and glance down at my white spaghetti-strapped dress, surprised there isn't a single dirt or grass stain.

The woman's hum is catchy and sounds so happy and content. I lean over and pluck the six yellow buds, then follow the sound. I wind my way around the hedge maze for a while before I come to an all glass greenhouse full of gorgeous flowers and greenery.

A petite woman wearing a big floppy hat and a light green summer dress bends over the potting table. Moving dirt around the lone sunflower, she appears to be around twenty-five and is obviously a cheery person as she bounces on her bare toes to the beat of the music in her head.

For some reason I can't explain, the sunflower pulls at my heart. I glance down at the tiny faces of the yellow dandelions in my hand. They pale in comparison to the contrast of the bold dark center of the sunflower fringed by bright yellow petals.

"Hello?" I say, not wanting to startle the woman. "Can you tell me where I am?"

She looks up at me and smiles. "Inara, you found me!" she says, dropping the trowel onto the potting table.

As she approaches with a welcoming look on her face, her green eyes sparkling with happiness, I squeeze the flowers and try to place her. She appears to know me and seems a bit familiar, but I don't recognize her.

I stiffen a little when she pulls me into an affectionate hug like we've known each other forever. Releasing me, she touches my hair, her gaze searching my face. *Why does she look familiar?* "Are you okay, dear?"

"Your humming led me here," I say awkwardly, then lift the wilting dandelions. "I pulled these weeds. They seemed out of place on your beautiful lawn."

The woman looks at the flowers, her brow puckering. "I have no idea how they keep popping up, but every so often they do." Sighing, she takes the weeds from me and tosses them into a compost pile, then removes her hat to let her long dark brown hair tumble around her shoulders. Hooking her arm in mine, she steers me out of the greenhouse. "So tell me about London."

*London?*

I stop walking, my heart starting to race. Something happened in London. Frowning, I try to remember.

The woman blinks at me and touches my jaw. "You don't know who I am, do you?"

I shake my head. "I'm sorry, but I don't."

"Come with me, I have to show you something." Her eyes begin to sparkle and she does a little hop of excitement as she re-hooks her arm with mine and turns me to the right, taking a different path into the maze.

As we walk along the perfect carpet-like grass, the woman hums another tune that sounds vaguely familiar. I start to ask her about it, but she releases me to run ahead and snatch up the lone puffy seedhead of a mature dandelion.

Spinning in a circle, she calls excitedly, "Make a thousand wishes, Inara!"

I laugh and shake my head. *Doesn't she know she just released hundreds of dandelion seeds onto her perfect lawn?* "I can't think of anything to wish for," I say, smiling despite the feeling of tension building in my chest.

She drops the weed and waves to me as the seedlings float all around her. "Hurry up, slow poke."

When we reach the end of the row of hedges and there's nowhere for us to go but back the way we came, she releases me and cuffs her hands over her ears. "Does this remind you of anything?" she asks, her voice slightly louder.

I snicker, unable to stop myself. "No. Should it?"

She gives me an exasperated look, muttering, "Surely I don't look *that* different," before she waves her hand in front of the hedge.

As the foliage begins to thin, the light that shines through the leaves is so bright my eyes water. Just when I lift my hand to shield my eyes, a woman with strawberry blonde hair, blue eyes, and a kind smile steps through the hedge. I gape at the impossibility of seeing her in the flesh instead of old pictures. My heart fills with happiness and I throw myself into her arms and call her a name I never got to use without a second thought. "Nana!"

Peace instantly envelops me with her hug, temporarily washing away my earlier tension. "Hello, little one. Look at how big you are!" she says, stepping back to take me in. "Thank you for keeping an eye on Inara," she says in appreciation to the woman beside me, then returns her gaze to my face, smiling broadly. "She grew into a beautiful young woman."

"Of course she did. I took watching over her seriously, Margaret," the woman says with a tinge of indignation.

As my grandmother's brow puckers slightly, it suddenly hits me who's standing beside me. I should've known by her questionable gardening skills and playful streak. "Gran?" I whisper, releasing my grandmother to turn to her. "Am I dreaming? Is that why Nana's the age I remember from pictures and you're decades younger?"

"Have you not told her yet, Corda?"

"Told me what?" My gaze pings from my grandmother to my grand aunt, my brain still trying to reconcile their decades-apart ages.

"We can choose whatever age we wish," my grandmother explains. Glancing at her sister, she purses her lips. "Corda decided that she wants to be young forever."

"Don't give me that judgy look, Margaret. You didn't have to watch your skin turn into paper-thin leather." Gran rubs her arm and grins. "Soft and firm."

"But if this isn't a dream, that means that you're—" I gasp and throw my arms around Gran, tears streaming down my cheeks. "You can't leave me. You were getting better!"

She returns my hug, then leans back to lift my chin so I have to meet her gaze. "I told you I was there for you. Remember? You're the only reason I returned."

"I don't understand." My sobbing slows and I brush my tears away. "If you returned, why couldn't you stay?"

Cupping my cheek, love and sadness reflect in Gran's gaze. "Because I needed to be here, waiting for you."

"Waiting for me?" My hands begin to shake. *Am I dead?* "What happened in London?"

My grandmother steps forward. "Close your eyes, Inara. And remember." The moment her fingers feather along my temple, a floodgate of imagery opens in my mind and I fall to my knees as all the fear, pain, sorrow, anger and sadness of my last day at the sanctuary comes rushing back.

I'm dead. The realization that I'll never see Ethan or feel his arms around me again, leaves me feeling empty inside. I finally open tear-swollen eyes. Gran tucks a strand of my hair behind my ear and murmurs that she likes my new style. Lowering her face to mine, she says, "They beat Lucifer, Inara. They wouldn't have done it without you, sweetie."

I quickly clasp her hand, squeezing it tight. "Ethan survived, right?"

She shakes her head, pressing her lips together in frustration. "I'm not allowed to share all the details." Helping me to my feet, she continues, "I'm sorry you had to experience that all over again, dear.

I convinced my sister it was better for you not to wake here with the full extent of your memories intact."

I'm shaking with worry that she didn't answer my question. I turn to drill my grandmother for the truth about Ethan, but I only see the hedge's greenery. I turn left and right, frowning. "Where did Nana go?"

Gran waves toward the hedge she'd come through. "She exists on a different plane, but couldn't resist coming here to speak to you."

I want to demand an answer about Ethan, but I know she'll keep her word. The only way I calm the screaming in my head is with the logic that he'd be here with me if he'd died. Right?

"I don't understand. We're not in the Celestial realm?"

"Not yet. I asked Margaret to let me wait here for you."

*Is Ethan there?* "Why?"

Gran spreads her hands. "Because I wanted to make sure you were ready."

"Ready for what?"

"To go or stay, of course."

"Are you saying that I have a choice?" I ask, my heart rate picking up.

"Take it from someone who has died twice." Gran flattens her hand on her chest and mimes a death spiral expression, tongue-lolling and all. "I know what death feels like. Time might work differently here, but you most definitely have a choice."

"But you won't tell me if Ethan survived," I say, frowning.

"Your choice mustn't have outside influences. It should be your decision and yours alone, but if you decide to return it will come with a price."

My eyebrows hike. "Which you can't tell me either?"

Shaking her head, the sympathy in Gran's gaze doesn't help my decision.

If I choose to return and Ethan didn't make it, I'll be beyond devastated. I bite my lip, hating that I'm not being told everything. Ethan means everything to me, but if he—I close my eyes, not wanting to even finish the thought. With my heart twisting, I meet Gran's gaze and nod. If the worst happened, I will honor Ethan's sacrifice. I'll become a Paladin. The sanctuary needs those who truly believe in its purpose more than ever now. "I choose to live, Gran."

Gran smiles and hugs me close. "I thought you might." Clasping my hand, she tugs me back through the maze, taking a different branch.

"Where are we going?" Hope for Ethan swells in my chest, making me giggle at how fast Gran can move. She sure is going to miss this young body.

When she suddenly stops at a T in the hedges, I stop too, trying to catch my breath. Sheesh, being in this place has really improved Gran's stamina. She gestures to the left branch. "Follow that path. This is where I'll say goodbye."

As she starts to release my hand, I capture hers between mine and shake my head. "You're coming too."

"I'm afraid this was always my last ride." Gran smiles sadly and shakes her head. "You were my assignment. I didn't have all the details and had to figure some things out on my own—don't get me started on having to relearn to walk and talk!—but after arriving here, I finally got filled in. You were amazing at the sanctuary; I was so proud! Your parents may never know just how brave their daughter is, but we do." Brushing away the tears sliding down my cheeks, she sniffs back her own. "Don't cry, dear. It was my time."

Gran tilts her head toward the maze on the right, indicating her path. "I'm not sure what I'll be doing now that you've made your decision, but rest assured I'm going to shake this place up." Grinning mischievously, she shrugs. "For now I have some catching up to do with my sister and Clara. I can't wait to see what age my friend chose. Does it make me a little bit bad that I hope I'm younger than her?"

I shake my head at Gran as I fold her into another tight hug. "I don't want to let you go."

She kisses my cheek and taps her fingers over my heart. "I'll always be in here. Some of those badass genes you have came from me, you know."

I don't bother to point out that her sister is my actual grandmother. I love the idea of being just like her one day: fun and full of sass.

Gran releases me and wriggles out of my fierce hold. "Now go!"

When I force myself to walk away, she calls after me, "And make sure your mother and father take that cruise! I've left specific instructions that I don't want a funeral. They're depressing as hel—

" She ducks and glances around as if waiting for lightning to strike, then flashes a relieved smile. "*No* funeral. Got it, sweetie?"

Even though Gran seems happily content here, I can't imagine my life without her. It's hard, but I give her an understanding nod.

"Go!" Gran mouths and shoos me on.

I follow along the path she told me to take until I don't have a choice but to go left. As I take the turn, all I see in the wide-open space is a massive patch of dandelions.

Not the bright yellow variety, but the puffy ones just waiting for a strong wind to blow their seeds all over the place. Go figure that in a garden full of beautiful flowers and plants, I'm being sent home through a bed of weeds.

With a bittersweet sob for Gran's unique sense of humor and tears for her loss streaking down my cheeks, I take off running down the hill toward the huge white patch. Leaping into the air as high as I can, I twist my body to face the sky and spread my arms wide. When I land in the cottony seedpod patch and bounce high in the air, an image of Gran spinning in sheer joy with that one stem in her hand flits through my mind and a slice of happiness joins the sorrow in my soul. As my body settles among the dandelions and millions of fluffy seeds float all around me, turning the blue sky into a summertime blizzard, I close my eyes against the warm, fuzzy flakes and whisper, "I'm making my wish, Gran."

# Chapter Thirty-Five

*Nara*

My eyes fly open at the same time someone's fingers slide away from my forehead. I feel whole, the life that drained out of me fully restored.

"Welcome back, Inara," Michael says with a sage nod, but instead of responding, I quickly yank my attention to the person holding me, my heart jerking with hope.

Ethan smiles down at me, his gaze twinkling in the darkness. "I thought I'd never see you again, lightweight."

*Rave.* Oh God. Not Gran and Ethan! *I will never survive this.* My heart crushes and the emotional floodgates open. Sobbing on a hard wail, I push at Rave's chest. "No, no, no! You promised that you'd protect him!"

Rave looks at Michael, then down at me. "I honored my promise, but I couldn't make him stay. He's—"

"Bring Ethan back like you did me," I plead with Michael.

The archangel shakes his head. "It doesn't work like that."

"Nara…" Rave tugs my chin so I have to look at him. His gaze is intense and regretful and he smells and feels just like Ethan, making my heart ache. "It's up to—"

My sob cuts him off; my heart shredding.

He takes a sudden deep breath and mist gathers in his eyes as I'm tugged into a bear hug. Pressing his lips to my forehead, he whispers harshly, "Never, ever do that again! I couldn't bear the thought of life without you, Sunshine."

*Ethan!* As relief floods through me and I fold my arms tight around his neck, hugging him close, a new round of sobs begin to flow.

"It's okay, Nara. I'm here," he murmurs against my temple. "After I lost you…I'd buried myself so deep, Rave had to yank me back." He exhales a shaky breath, his brow furrowed. "I…don't feel him any more."

I cry harder, my emotions swinging wildly between sadness that I didn't get to say goodbye to Rave, elation that Ethan was spared and grief that Gran wasn't. "She's gone, Ethan."

He leans back, his brow furrowed with sudden concern. "Who's gone?"

"Gran," I say, burying my face against his chest once more. Sniffling, I hug him even tighter. "She helped me come back. The only reason she survived her heart attack…was to help me."

"I'm so sorry, Nara. Your Gran was an amazing person. I will miss her too." Clasping my waist, he settles me on the bench beside him and touches my hair, his mouth twisted with a grim look. "It looks like you didn't come out completely unscathed."

"What?" I ask as he slides his fingers all the way to the ends of my hair, then lifts the tips for me to see that an inch-wide hank of my blonde hair framing my face has turned completely black. My eyes widen as I clasp my hair and stare at it. *Is this what Gran was referring to by my new look?* "Is it like this all the way up?"

"You just have the one streak, but yes, it's all the way to your roots." He kisses my forehead at my hairline, his lips lifting in a half-smile. "Actually, you rock it."

"Your return to the mortal realm comes with responsibility, Nara," Michael says, pulling my attention back to him. "Did your Gran tell you that?"

"What responsibility?" Ethan turns a sharp gaze on the angel, his fingers sliding between mine in a tight hold.

When I nod, Michael folds his hands behind his back and looks at Ethan. "I know that you no longer sense the Master Corvus, but you will always have the sword and Corvus abilities. In return for your life, the Master Corvus requests that you be his vessel if he ever needs to communicate with the Corvus or those who support them."

"He cost me Nara once." Ethan stiffens. "I won't be taken over *ever* again."

"He's asking that you host his voice, not his spirit, and only when absolutely necessary."

Ethan narrows his gaze and appears to debate if there's some loophole he's not considering. "What responsibility will Nara have to take on? She will *not* be Corvus." His fingers tighten around mine. "She has given more than she should have ever had to."

"You didn't agree," Michael challenges, his expression hardening.

"And I won't until you answer me about Nara."

"Stubborn mortals are the *most* exhausting beings." The archangel sighs heavily and turns to me. "Finish what you started, Nara. Teach the sanctuary how you tracked natural disasters and determined places where the veil could be thinnest and vulnerable to demon breakthroughs. Yes, your ability to see the veil tearing is rare, but you can still get the sanctuary started in learning to identify areas where demons could enter this realm.

"Becoming a source of such important information will help the Paladins develop a partner-like bond with their Corvus. If Lucifer wasn't bluffing during their battle and what he told the Master Corvus is true—that he found a way to retain the knowledge of using Corvus ashes to hide his demons from Corvus' detection—then helping the Corvus' discover the demons' entrance into this world much faster will help level the playing field between demons and Corvus once more."

"That's it?" Ethan asks. "She does this and she's done?"

"When will I ever be done trying to protect the world?" I turn to face Ethan on the bench. "Through my dreams, I was already doing so, but on a much smaller scale."

He searches my gaze, frustration in his. "You should be able to live the life you've been given, free of demons and Corvus, Nara."

"And what about you?" I gesture to him. "You're technically not Corvus any longer, but you have their abilities and sword. Do you just plan to walk away now that it's your choice?"

Ethan's mouth sets in a determined line. "The Master Corvus might be gone, but the spirit of his mission remains. I will honor his request to support the Corvus. This was always my destiny."

Michael steps forward and takes my hand, pulling me to my feet. "The Master Corvus challenged me for your life, Nara. He believes in you as much as I do." When he slides my ring off, I'm surprised that the Corvus symbol I burned into my pinky is gone. "Things have returned to the way they were: Fate will no longer be able to see anything Corvus related. He's too self-serving to be an objective participant. However, the feather on your back will remain. Like your dreams, it's a part of you now."

Happy that the feather is permanent, I nod my understanding and quickly turn my hand over once he puts my ring back on to see if the old scar Ethan's sword left behind is gone as well. Relieved it's still there, I glance up to see Michael staring at the raised skin. Flicking his gaze to Ethan, he returns his attention to me as I rub the newly healed skin on my finger.

"You never needed the Corvus symbol to protect you."

"I don't understand," I say, shaking my head. "The symbol kept those demons from taking over my body."

"You're not Corvus, but you are...*other*. As such, they cannot possess you." Michael clasps my hand between both of his and dips his head in a respectful nod. "I've decided to waive the requirement of your return."

I shake my head, thrown by his deference. "Why?"

Admiration reflects in his gaze as his angelic power vibrates through me. "Even though you're no longer honor-bound to help the Corvus, I have a feeling you'll do it anyway. Warriors never quit."

"Is that why Nara was able to expel demons and weaken Lucifer?" Ethan asks as he moves to my side. "What *other* is she?"

"She knows." Michael releases me and slides his hands in his pants pockets, his body already starting to fade. "In her soul...she knows."

"Do you, Sunshine?" Ethan folds warm fingers across the back of my neck once Michael completely disappears.

*One scar healed. One left behind.* I quickly reach for the old scar on my forehead. As my fingers connect with smooth skin, I shift my attention back to the scar on my palm. "When Michael brought me back, I was healed everywhere. Not a single scrape, bruise or ache remained. Even old scars are gone. This is the only one left behind."

Ethan clasps my hand, his brows pulling together in a deep

frown. "Are you saying that Michael couldn't heal it?"

"I can't explain how I know, but I think that whatever makes me *other* is coming from Michael. That connection is tethering us together on a spiritual level. If the archangel ever wondered if angels were also vulnerable to a Corvus sword, after seeing my scar, now he knows."

Ethan holds my gaze, the ramifications setting in. "Angels have fallen before, and if balance between good and evil is the ultimate goal for our world, then Corvus are the only true equalizers."

"No one can ever know about this, Ethan. We have to believe that Rave and his Corvus will fight for the right side no matter what."

"Protecting mortals is the Corvus' only priority, not catering to those from Under or the Celestial realms." Ethan wraps his arms around me. "If any of the Corvus needs to be reminded, we'll help set them straight."

Resting my head on his shoulder, I tense at the sudden whoop from Drystan echoing in my head. *I felt you just as I put my coat on. God, I was devastated to lose you, Nara! I don't know how Rave did it, but you're alive and that's all that matters. Call me and fill me in later. My cousin and I are heading into a meeting to discuss how we want the sanctuary to run in the future.*

"Where'd you go?" Ethan asks, his arms tightening around me slightly. "Are you okay?"

"Drystan just learned that I'm alive. He said they're discussing how they want to structure the sanctuary now," I mumble against him as I bask in the strength of his arms holding me close. I feel so very blessed to be here with him after everything we've been through.

Ethan grunts. "Good. That saved a phone call."

"Apparently some of Rave's matter-of-factness has rubbed off on you." I snicker and push my nose into his sweater, inhaling his scent and enjoying the feel of his steady heart beat against my chest. "Together 'til the wheels fall off," I whisper, loving that I can say that to him once more.

Ethan's arms tighten around me and he kisses my forehead, murmuring, "No matter the realm."

# Chapter Thirty-Six

*Two weeks later*

### Nara

"Have a wonderful time," I say as my mom hugs me tight. Houdini steps into the open doorway of our house and leans his heavy bulk against my thigh, his body vibrating with anxious tension as he watches my father load their luggage in the car. "You and Dad deserve this trip."

Mom clasps my face, her eyes misty. "I feel better knowing that Sage will be staying with you some while we're gone. I know you'd be fine here alone, but *I* don't like leaving you for this long. A month seems…excessive."

"It's not. Gran's note insisted that you go and reconnect with Dad. Now's the best time." I hug her once more when actual tears fill her eyes this time. "She wouldn't want you to be sad, Mom."

Nodding, my mom takes a deep breath to calm her emotions. "I still can't believe she found the cruise tickets your dad bought and tucked her note in the envelope on the island so I couldn't miss it. It's like she knew she wasn't going to wake up." She sighs and continues. "Her passing makes me even more thankful that she came to live with us. That time was so special." Mom steps back and dashes her tears away. "Okay, I'm going to wait in the car now so I don't insist that you go with us and derail your father's romantic plans."

Snickering, I wave after her and smile as my father approaches. "Are you all ready to go, Dad?"

"I don't think I've ever seen your mom so out of sorts." He briefly glances back to the car just as Mom closes the passenger door. "I hope that while we're away, she'll decide what to do with Corda's ashes."

"*We* were Gran's home, Dad."

"With her urn just hanging out on the shelf in the living room…" He shakes his head. "Not burying or spreading her ashes feels unfinished to me."

"You miss her too, don't you?" I say quietly.

"Of course," he says gruffly and slides his hands in his pockets. "I left a note on how to contact us through the cruise line on the desk if you need to get in touch for anything."

"I'll be fine."

"When is Ethan coming by?"

I still haven't gotten used to my father's change of heart about Ethan. I don't know if Mom ripped into him for freaking out and calling me in London, but no matter what changed his mind, I'm just thrilled that he approves of Ethan now. He was tense but quiet when I got back home from my school trip. Then everything seemed to change last weekend after he took Ethan to a football game while Mom and I went shopping. I was a nervous wreck until they pulled up in the driveway and I saw my father clap Ethan on the shoulder as they made their way to the house. "Ethan's stopping by later. He had to help his brother with some chores after work."

"Okay, good. There's some extra cash in the kitchen desk drawer for meals, bowling, movies or whatever you two want to do… preferably *out*." I don't miss his meaning and mentally snort that he's still the protective father no matter how much he likes Ethan, but I let him continue on without comment. "While we're gone, I'd like you to gather all the information for this summer. I know Drystan will be there, but I'll need the company name and complete contact information, along with the full description of duties and applicable work experience you'll have during your internship before I'll fund your trip back to London."

"I know. I'll get it all together." Stepping close, I fold my arms around his neck and whisper in his ear, "Now go help Mom fall deeply in love with you all over again."

My father gives me a bear hug, then steps back and clasps my shoulders. "In case I haven't said it, I'm proud of who you've become, Nari." His fingers flex, tightening a little on me. "You are my daughter in so many ways, but these shoulders are only so strong. Make sure you continue to surround yourself with those who not only love you but will always have your back."

*Where is this coming from?* I smile to ease the tension that seems to have gripped him. It must be trip jitters. "My circle of friends always look out for each other. Did I tell you that Lainey and Matt are coming to London for a visit this summer? So I'll have tons of peeps watching my back. Don't worry, Dad."

His mouth twists as he releases me, dark brows lifting around serious green eyes. "Even when I'm old and gray and you have a family of your own, I'll always worry about you." Houdini whimpers and my father pats his head before backing away. "Okay, your mom and I are off."

I wave goodbye, watching until their car leaves our street before I shut the door.

When Houdini runs into my bedroom ahead of me and sniffs the crystal ball game laying in the middle of my floor, I pick up the fun gift my aunt gave me a few years ago and glance at the shelf behind my desk where it usually sits. *How did you get over here?*

Flipping the grapefruit-sized ball over, I turn on the digital display and shake it, waiting for a typical comment like: *Try Again Next Time* or *You'll Win Big Today* to scroll across the screen.

*Finally! I've waited forever for you to turn me on!*

"That's one I haven't seen before." I blink at the digital readout and shake it once more, muttering, "Since Ethan doesn't always share my dreams, do you have any good advice, oh mystical one?"

*Stop speaking to this ball like it's really going to answer you, Inara!* Scrolls across the screen.

I immediately drop the ball and take a couple steps back, my heart hammering. *Is my toy possessed by a demon? Why isn't Houdini reacting to it?*

Leaning as far away as possible, I nudge the ball over with the toe of my shoe until I can see the display once more. "Who are you? What do you want?"

*My sister is making me pay for my vanity by sending me here without a body.*

I furrow my brow and pick up the toy once more. "Who are you?"

*I'm here because I chose to be. I want to continue to look out for you.*

My hands start to shake around the ball. "Gran?"

*In the flesh...well, sort of. We'll have to communicate like this until I'm no longer considered "Willfully Defiant."* When I snort, another message scrolls across the readout.

*Yeah, it might be a while. :)*

"Oh, Gran..." I sniff to hold back tears of happiness and sit down on my bed, cradling the crystal ball. "I'll take you any way I can get you. I miss you."

*I miss you too, dear. I'll pop in to see how you're doing whenever I'm not assigned other duties. I'm happy to see that your father and mother took my advice.*

"Yeah, they're off on their cruise."

*I'm glad Sage will be coming to stay with you some. I really like her— Oh great, after a week of silent treatment, NOW I'm being summoned. I'll be back when I can...*

Houdini whimpers and nudges my knee with his nose. "Hold on, buddy." I absently rub the top of his head as I stare at the crystal ball for a few more minutes, but it remains quiet. Setting the toy on the floor next to my bed, I walk over to the window.

Every night since I returned home, Houdini whines until I open the window. He sits in front of it, his ears popping up, then swiveling left and right as he listens to the outside sounds. I know he's waiting for Patch to arrive, but sadly I haven't seen the raven since London. It's like he disappeared right along with Rave.

I move to stand beside Houdini and pat his head, my hand pausing at the small chunk of skin missing from the tip of his ear where Patch had snapped at him to get him to focus on guarding me. Houdini had avoided the bird after that, yet now that Patch hasn't shown up for his nightly guard duty, my dog hasn't stopped looking for him.

I shiver at the cold evening air seeping into the room and pat Houdini's head once more. "I'm sorry, boy, but I think Patch has moved on—"

Houdini ducks when the big raven swoops into my room to land on my bed. Turning his big body, my dog yips and jumps with excitement, his wagging tail slapping at my leg.

Patch spreads his wings and lets out a barking *raaaaaack* and my dog quickly settles. Resting his chin on the edge of my bed, Houdini looks from Patch to me, eager anticipation shining in his big brown eyes.

"Hello, stranger," I say as I slowly sit down on the bed beside the bird. "I've been worried about you. Did you love London that much?"

Patch doesn't even hesitate. He immediately steps up on my thigh and runs his head and beak along my cheek. Awww, this is the most affectionate he's ever been. As I start to run my hand down his back, he shifts his beak over to my hair and flicks the strands. Once it hits me that he's playing with the part of my hair that is now jet black, I reach up and clasp the ends of my hair and smirk. "Yeah, this is new."

Patch bobs his head and steps back down onto the bed. Turning sideways, he pokes his beak at his right wing, and I gasp at the sight of a single white feather folded among the black ones.

"Where did you get that?"

Patch makes low guttural sounds and just as I rub my fingers across the feather, Ethan speaks from my doorway.

"He says that it's an original raven feather, like the one on your shoulder."

I turn to see him leaning against the doorjamb, an amused smile on his face. "I thought you couldn't communicate with Patch."

Ethan steps into the room. "Patch was always Rave…or at least a piece of his subconscious. Maybe putting a bit of himself in Patch was a way to keep an eye on things?" He shrugs. "All I know is that since I had Rave's conscious mind crowding my own, I think that's why I never could read Patch like other animals. Rave's two separate minds couldn't speak to each other."

I glance down at the bird in shock. "This is Rave?"

"For now." Ethan folds his arms and narrows his gaze as the bird moves back to my lap and presses his head into my hand. "He's telling me to let you know that a part of him will always watch over you through Patch."

I gulp back my emotion and smile at the bird staring at me with wise, soulful eyes. "I'd like that. I consider Patch and *you* family. Thank you, Rave."

Patch fluffs his feathers arrogantly, then squawks harshly at Ethan before taking off through the window once more.

"So you're able to communicate with him mentally now because he's no longer sharing your mind?" I ask as I stand next to Ethan.

When he nods, I gesture toward the open window. "What did he say to you? Even in raven babble, it um…sounded terse."

Ethan trails his fingers over the black streak in my hair. "Did you know there are other colors in this strip of black? I see purples and blues when the light hits it in certain ways."

"Really?" Reaching up to touch my hair, I adopt a mischievous grin. "Since the feather on my back is white once more thanks to Michael, this will be like having my very own Corvus feather. Badass in the front, Good-For-Now in the back."

"I should be worried about your Good-For-Now comment." Ethan laughs and pulls me into his arms. "But damn if it doesn't make you sexier."

"What did Rave say before he left?" I ask as I lightly poke his chest.

Sobering, he grunts. "He told me that too much time with the band and not enough time training is showing."

"Why? Because you look happy?"

"He's saying that I'm going soft. Of course, I don't agree with him, but I am happy. Shifting my mind to 'alert and prepared' mode versus actively hunting for demons has taken some getting used to, but when we go to London this summer, I'll get more than my share of training and hunting time with the Corvus there. Rave insists I continue to build on the trust I initiated between the Corvus in the regional area while I'm in the UK. Hopefully they'll go on and do the same with other Corvus they cross paths with."

"I think that's a wonderful idea. And for what it's worth…" I kiss his jaw and snuggle closer. "I feel just as safe in your arms today as I always have."

As we exchange a smile, Houdini nudges the crystal ball with this nose and it rolls into my ankle. Picking up the toy, I hand it to Ethan. "Oh, I have something to tell you."

Ethan eyes the mystical looking globe, his eyebrow raised. "You're not going into the fortune telling business, are you? Let's not invite Fate back into our lives."

Snickering, I shake my head, then tell him about Gran.

Ethan turns the ball over and chuckles as he stares at the blank digital display. "If anyone could find a way to live on indefinitely, it would be your feisty grand aunt."

When he sets the ball down on the carpet and gives it a good nudge with his shoe, rolling it out into the hall, I lift my eyebrows. "What are you doing?"

Once Houdini follows the ball into the hall, Ethan shuts the door behind him and moves back to my side, quickly lifting me into his arms. "The last thing I want is for your Gran to return for a visit at an inappropriate moment."

"Ah, I see." I wrap my arms around his neck and giggle when he presses a lingering kiss along my neck. "What did you have in mind?"

"Dinner and a movie," he rumbles huskily, his breath warm against my skin.

"What?" I quickly lean back and try not to show my disappointment. We've barely seen each other this past week since we've both been catching up on missed schoolwork from the London trip. "*That's* what you want to do?"

Ethan nods. "Absolutely."

"Okay, then." I sigh and start to push my legs out of his hold, but Ethan's arms tighten around me, locking me to his chest.

"I definitely plan to do those things later, but right now I just want to spend some quality time with you, Sunshine."

The adoring look in his eyes makes my heart swell with love. Tightening my hold around his neck, I move my lips close to his and whisper, "I think we deserve some *just us* time."

**I hope you loved this final book in the BRIGHTEST KIND OF DARKNESS series!**

If you found **AWAKEN** an entertaining and enjoyable read, I hope you'll consider taking the time to leave a review and share your thoughts in the online bookstore where you purchased it. Your review could be the one to help another reader decide to read AWAKEN and the other books in the BRIGHTEST KIND OF DARKNESS series!

To keep up-to-date when another P.T. Michelle book releases, join my free newsletter http://bit.ly/11tqAQN . An email will come to your inbox on the day a new book releases.

Did you love Ethan and Nara's story and want more books with an EPIC storyline?

If you haven't read my IN THE SHADOWS series, the first three books in my *New York Times* bestselling contemporary romance series: **MISTER BLACK, SCARLETT RED** and **BLACKEST RED** tells Sebastian and Talia's love story. Please note, this is a series meant for readers 18+, so if you're under 18, please wait until you're of age to read it. The IN THE SHADOWS series has it all: mystery, romance, and an intense love story all rolled into one. If you're interested, here's the series trailer for Talia and Sebastian's story. https://www.youtube.com/watch?v=9ERYQ3HU2mw

If you want to read other contemporary romances by me, check out my **BAD IN BOOTS** series written under Patrice Michelle. This is a series meant for readers 18+.

If you want to read other paranormal romances by me, check out my **KENDRIAN VAMPIRES** series written under Patrice Michelle. This is a series meant for readers 18+. Links are on the following page.

Other Books by
# P.T. MICHELLE

**In the Shadows Series (Contemporary Romance, 18+)**
*Mister Black* (Part 1 - Talia and Sebastian)
*Scarlett Red* (Part 2 - Talia and Sebastian)
*Blackest Red* (Part 3 - Talia and Sebastian)
*Gold Shimmer* (Book 4 - Cass and Calder)
*Steel Rush* (Book 5 - Cass and Calder)
*Black Platinum* (Book 6 - Talia and Sebastian) Coming 2017


**Brightest Kind of Darkness Series**
**(YA/New Adult Paranormal Romance, 16+)**
*Ethan* (Prequel) This is written in Ethan's point-of-view and is best
read after BRIGHTEST KIND OF DARKNESS
*Brightest Kind of Darkness* (book 1)
*Lucid* (book 2)
*Destiny* (book 3)
*Desire* (book 4)
*Awaken* (book 5)

# Other works by
# P.T. MICHELLE
## writing as
# PATRICE MICHELLE

**Bad in Boots series (Contemporary Romance, 18+)**
*Harm's Hunger*
*Ty's Temptation*
*Colt's Choice*
*Josh's Justice*

**Kendrian Vampires series
(Paranormal Romance, 18+)**
*A Taste for Passion*
*A Taste for Revenge*
*A Taste for Control*

**Scions series (Paranormal Romance, 18+)**
*Scions: Resurrection*
*Scions: Insurrection*
*Scions: Perception*
*Scions: Revelation*

# Acknowledgements

To my exceptional beta readers: Joey Berube, Amy Bensette, and Magen Chambers, thank you for your eagle eyes and wonderful feedback for the BKoD series as a whole. Joey and Magen, I appreciate you reading *Awaken* so quickly and for your valuable input. Amy, thank you for your moral support with *Awaken*. Each of you helped make Ethan and Nara's story a fabulous journey.

To my wonderful critique partner, Trisha Wolfe, you're the best! Thank you for reading *Awaken*, for your spot-on critiques and for being a fantastic cheerleader! I couldn't ask for a better crit partner!

To my family, thank you for understanding the time and effort each book takes. I love you all and truly appreciate your unending support.

To my amazing fans, thank you for your patience in waiting for this final book in the BRIGHTEST KIND OF DARKNESS series to finally release. I hope you felt it was worth the wait! I appreciate each and every one of you for spreading the word by posting reviews and telling all your reader friends about the series whenever you get a chance. And who knows…maybe one day there will be other stories to tell. After all, the BRIGHTEST KIND OF DARKNESS world has other great characters whose stories are just beginning. :) Thank you for all the fantastic support you continually give!

# About the Author

P.T. Michelle is the *NEW YORK TIMES*, *USA TODAY*, and International Bestselling author of the contemporary romance series IN THE SHADOWS, the YA/New Adult crossover series BRIGHTEST KIND OF DARKNESS, and the romance series: BAD IN BOOTS, KENDRIAN VAMPIRES and SCIONS (listed under Patrice Michelle). She keeps a spiral notepad with her at all times, even on her nightstand. When P.T. isn't writing, she can usually be found reading or taking pictures of landscapes, sunsets and anything beautiful or odd in nature.

To keep up with information on the next P.T. Michelle release, be sure to sign up for P.T.'s NEWSLETTER: http://bit.ly/17paDiG. It'll come straight to your inbox.

**To contact P.T. Michelle and stay up-to-date on her latest releases:**

Facebook: https://www.facebook.com/PTMichelleAuthor
Instagram: https://www.instagram.com/p.t.michelle/
Twitter: https://twitter.com/pt_michelle
Website: http://www.ptmichelle.com/
Goodreads: http://www.goodreads.com/author/show/4862274.P_T_Michelle
Pinterest: https://www.pinterest.com/ptmichelle/
Facebook Readers Group: https://www.facebook.com/groups/PTMichelleReadersGroup/

73058997R00199

Made in the USA
Columbia, SC
03 July 2017